PENGU

A Queen This I

Stacia Stark is a fantasy romance author who loves writing about found families, self-reliant heroines and brooding, grumpy heroes. Originally from New Zealand, Stacia spent over a decade traveling and living in various countries around the world as a freelance copywriter, and attributes both her wanderlust and creativity to those adventures. When not traveling or writing, Stacia is usually lost in the pages of a good book.

Come say hi on Facebook: facebook.com/groups/starksociety
Or learn more at Staciastark.com

A QUEEN
This
FIERCE
and
DEADLY

STACIA STARK

PENGUIN·BOOKS

PENGUIN BOOKS

UK | USA | Canada | Ireland | Australia
India | New Zealand | South Africa

Penguin Books is part of the Penguin Random House group of companies
whose addresses can be found at global.penguinrandomhouse.com

Penguin
Random House
UK

First published in the United States of America by Bingeable Books LLC 2024
First published in Great Britain by Penguin Books 2024
001

Copyright © Bingeable Books LLC, 2024

The moral right of the author has been asserted

Map by Sarah Waites of The Illustrated Page Design
Interior Design by Imagine Ink Designs

Printed and bound in Great Britain by Clays Ltd, Elcograf S.p.A.

The authorized representative in the EEA is Penguin Random House Ireland,
Morrison Chambers, 32 Nassau Street, Dublin D02 YH68

A CIP catalogue record for this book is available from the British Library

ISBN: 978–1–405–96765–5

www.greenpenguin.co.uk

For Cristina Weiner.
I would sneak into a tyrant king's dungeon for you.

Life is mostly froth and bubble,

Two things stand like stone,

Kindness in another's trouble,

Courage in your own.

—Adam Lindsay Gordon

Prologue

PRISCA

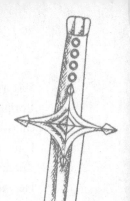

Regner ducked, and together, Regner, Zathrian, and Eadric lifted an object they'd kept carefully hidden.

A mirror.

When the waves are coerced...

And reflection deceives...

Conreth's power hit the glass. But instead of freezing and exploding, that mirror reflected his power.

Dread exploded through my gut. I hauled my power to me.

It didn't work.

Time didn't stop.

I wasn't out. I still had power left. In the ship next to Regner, my cousin smiled at me.

He'd *neutralized* me.

That's why he was here. He'd saved his power just for this.

A trick. Regner had sacrificed some of his most important people, making sure his wards appeared useless, ensuring Conreth couldn't help but use his power...

That power was heading back toward our lines. But instead of Conreth, it was aimed at us.

I launched myself at Lorian

Just as his brother's power hit him in the chest.

Lorian looked at me, and realization flashed across his beautiful face.

I saw him forming the words.

"In another life."

He was turning to ice, eyes blank. Gone.

For a single moment, I felt him next to me, his soul caressing mine.

I love you.

The ice exploded into thousands of pieces.

Conreth screamed his brother's name.

Everyone was shouting, ducking for cover.

But the sound dimmed.

No.

No, Lorian wasn't gone.

He'd promised.

"I want you to feel how much I love you. I'll always be with you, Prisca. It's you and me."

My hand snapped to the hourglass. Behind me, Telean was screaming.

"No, Nelayra, don't! It will *kill* you!"

I stopped time with a mere thought. I could feel Zathrian attempting to neutralize me, and I ignored him. He'd used all of his power to neutralize me once.

And one day, he would pay and pay and pay...

It was rage that drove me now, thundering through my body. Through my soul.

I'd frozen time, but it wasn't enough.

No, if time restarted now, Lorian would still be gone.

Telean's voice seemed to echo through my mind.

"The world must be balanced."

I didn't care about the world.

The warnings I'd received pounded over and over in my ears.

Ysara, sympathy flickering through her eyes. *"Enjoy your time with your fae prince. But know this—you cannot keep him."*

The queen's seer, her voice matter-of-fact. *"The Bloodthirsty Prince will die."*

The gods might have demanded his death. They'd gotten what they wanted. But I would bring him back.

I didn't care that it was impossible. That, at the very least, it was forbidden. That if I succeeded, the gods might just smite me for my audacity.

Throwing back my head, I screamed, pulling every drop of power to me. I had so little left, and yet I took it from every part of my soul. And when there was nothing left, I took more.

Agony raged through me. And for the barest moment, Lorian's presence was next to me once more.

"Let go," he whispered. And there was so much love in those two words that it suddenly felt as if my chest were being crushed.

I didn't let go. I dug deeper. I pulled harder.

I pictured Lorian's soul reentering his body. Pictured the tiny, shattered pieces of him reforming.

The hourglass heated, as if even the ancient artifact were screaming at me to stop. Pain burst through my head, dropping me to my knees. Gritting my teeth, I held on. He didn't get to leave me. He didn't—

Blood poured from my nose, leaked from my ears. It wasn't working.

Still, I held on.

"In every life, wildcat. No matter what happens, you hold on to that. It's you and me in every life."

I bared my teeth and shoved everything I had into defying the laws of nature and the gods.

In every life, Lorian.

1

PRISCA

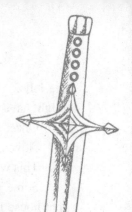

Pieces of Lorian hung in the air, the glacial statue of his body like a shattered vase frozen at the moment of impact.

I'd lost so much. Over and over. But I couldn't lose him. Couldn't endure this. It would break me into pieces just as small as the icy shards I stared at now. So I clutched my hourglass until my hand ached and continued to claw at my power with everything I had.

The edges of my soul began incinerating, tiny pieces turning to ash and drifting away. Blinking away the blood dripping from my eyes, I focused on my mate.

Finally, one single second slipped backward. And then another. The edges of my vision dimmed. I couldn't breathe. Couldn't think. But I used my magic like a rope tying me to him.

And I held on.

I couldn't fail him. I *refused*.

But a strange, dizzying rush swept through my body. And two women were suddenly standing just footspans away, on the ship, their features eerily similar to mine.

A sob rattled my chest. The woman on

the left... If not for the faint lines around her eyes, we might have been twins.

Once, I'd hated Ysara for not showing me her face.

Now, I knew I saw it each day in the mirror.

This was my mother. My real mother.

Some part of me had hoped she'd made it out of that house the night I'd disappeared. That she was alive somewhere. I hadn't realized until now how foolishly I'd clung to that hope.

Letting go of it hurt.

The woman standing next to her also looked at me with eyes the exact same color as mine. But those eyes were old and wicked, the smile playing around her mouth suggesting she knew the secrets of the world—and was unimpressed by them. This was the woman who had used her power to age her enemies. The one who had lashed out in her last moments, turning Eprotha's capital into the Cursed City.

My grandmother.

My mother reached out her hand, as if to stroke my cheek. But no warmth radiated from her skin. I would never know her touch.

"Let go, Nelayra. This is forbidden for a reason." Her voice was soft. Gentle.

"I can't."

Her eyes filled with such grief, my chest clenched.

"I love him. I'm—I'm sorry."

My grandmother's mouth curved. "Let the child choose her own fate. Just as we did."

Both of them were dead. Was that a warning? I continued to pull my power to me, and my grandmother laughed, glancing at my mother. "Such reckless disregard for the laws. It's like looking at my younger self."

My chest hollowed. My grandmother's rage had leveled an entire city. Was such destruction my fate?

"Please, Nelayra," my mother begged. "If you do this…"

My grandmother gave her a hard look and then returned her gaze to me. "In the unlikely event that you don't join us in the afterlife, there will be consequences. Grave consequences."

I'd known that the moment I'd used the hourglass to begin turning time backward. And nothing would stop me. Nothing.

She shook her head at me, and pity gleamed in her eyes. "You think you know what it is to suffer. You will live with the repercussions of this choice for the rest of your life."

"I can't save our kingdom without him." I couldn't *live* without him.

Her gaze hardened. "Do not attempt to justify your actions in such a way to me, girl. You are my blood. And I expect better from my granddaughter than a queen who hands her power over to *anyone*."

Shame curled in my gut, and I lowered my head. My mother stepped closer, and this time, I could almost feel the heat of her hand as she cupped my face.

"I loved your father the same way. I wouldn't have listened either." She hesitated, and then her lips firmed. She held out her hand, and an amber ball of light appeared, the exact color of all our eyes. With a flick of her wrist, she pressed it to my chest, and I watched as that light disappeared within me.

When she glanced at my grandmother, the older woman rolled her eyes.

"Oh, very well."

Her own amber fire burned even brighter. "Change the world, granddaughter. And heal our kingdom."

LORIAN

I had the vaguest sense that something had gone terribly wrong. A feeling of...disquiet that curdled through my chest.

Boom!

I whirled. A rush of exhilaration swept through me as the barrier fell, and some of the humans in the skiffs began to glow, striking out at Regner's fleet with their returned power.

I let out a triumphant laugh.

Prisca's scent hit me before she did. I'd expected to see elation, but her face was deathly pale. She fought like the wildcat I'd named her, lashing out, her foot moving behind mine in an attempt to trip me.

Something was wrong.

I allowed her to push me back several steps farther down the deck, even as I reached out to cup her face.

The ship beneath us exploded.

I had a single moment to reach for her, to grab her...

Her eyes were wild, and she leaped toward me, only

to be thrown through the air.

I twisted my body in an attempt to catch one of her limbs. But she flew sideways, hitting the icy water somewhere on the opposite side of the ship.

Screams fractured the air around me, immediately replaced by the muted roar of water in my ears.

But I was already swimming toward her, saltwater suffocating my senses.

Where was she, where was she, where was she?

"Prisca!" I roared.

Parts of the ship lay burning on top of the water, black smoke further impeding my vision. I ducked, diving deep, squinting into the churning water. My heartbeat, loud and erratic in my ears, seemed to synchronize with someone else's.

Prisca.

My head spun with relief. My lungs burned like they were aflame, but I let my instincts guide me. Each shadow, each floating silhouette, brought a surge of hope, followed by the crushing weight of disappointment.

Desperate, I clung to the bond between us.

The bond that was fading. I drew deep for my power in an attempt to push debris aside with my wind.

Don't you dare leave me, wildcat.

In the distance, I caught a flash of white-blond hair, standing out like a beacon in the ocean. The sight allowed me to use the last of my power to drive myself through the water. Prisca was sinking, as if the waves were hungry for her. Her face was as white as a corpse, eyes closed. No bubbles floated from her mouth.

She wasn't breathing.

Catching her in my arms, I pressed my mouth to hers, giving her the little air remaining in my lungs.

Fight, Prisca. Please.

Kicking my legs to power us up through the water, I kept my mouth fused to hers in an effort to make her *breathe.*

Finally, finally, I burst through the surface of the water, the cool, life-giving air hitting my face. I sucked in one desperate breath and fixed my mouth to Prisca's once more.

"Lorian!"

I spared a single glance in the direction of the frantic voice. Madinia stood carefully balanced in a skiff full of hybrids. Likely, Galon had used his power to send her skiff toward us. I treaded water long enough to push Prisca over the edge and into the small boat, immediately hauling myself over after her.

The boat rocked dangerously. Madinia crouched, and several hybrids let out screams.

Madinia pushed Prisca's hair off her face. "You have to restart her heart. I saw Regner's healer do it once."

I shoved my hands against Prisca's chest, pumping again and again. Her body lay limp on the bottom of the boat. No response.

My entire body went numb. It was as if I were watching someone else's hands attempt to save my mate. As if it were someone else who leaned down to blow air into her lungs.

The skiff was eerily silent. No one even moved.

I pumped harder, faster, my movements increasingly desperate.

One of her ribs cracked. I felt it like a blow to my own.

"I don't know what you did," I ground out. "But you don't get to leave me here without you. You will fucking come back to me, or I will follow you and drag you back myself."

"She's gone," someone said.

I snarled. Above our heads, lightning split the sky. Where was that power earlier when I needed it?

"That's the Bloodthirsty Prince attempting to save his mate," someone else whispered. "I suggest you be very, very quiet."

Madinia leaned close, checking Prisca's pulse. Her eyes met mine, and she shook her head.

I ignored her, slamming my hands into Prisca's chest. Another rib cracked. Oh gods.

"Please," I begged. "Please, wildcat."

The bond between us was fading. I could feel it, barely lingering. I clutched it to me.

This was not how we ended. I would never accept this. Could not be expected to endure it.

Movement.

For one terrible moment, I thought I'd imagined it.

And then water poured from Prisca's mouth, and Madinia was pushing at my hands, attempting to shift Prisca to her side. I rolled her gently, conscious of the damage my hands had done to her fragile bones.

The water choking from her lungs seemed endless. Finally, she stopped coughing. Her chest lifted and fell.

She was breathing.

But she wasn't opening her eyes.

MADINIA

The distant cry of gulls was a constant refrain. The sound warred with the pirates yelling back and forth to one another as they performed minor repairs on the ship with the cheerful banter of people who were well aware they were lucky to be alive.

The taste of salt lingered on my lips, while my hair had become unmanageable. Still, I lifted my face to the sun, basking in its warmth like a cat.

It had been three days since we'd brought down the barrier.

And Prisca still hadn't woken.

The fact that she was breathing was a miracle itself, given the way she'd lain so pale and unmoving in that skiff. My stomach swam, and I took a long, slow breath of the salty air to clear my head.

Daharak had given Lorian and Prisca a cabin near her own. Lorian refused to leave Prisca's side. Anyone wanting to check on her was forced to also interact with her crazed mate. Even the fae king had attempted to talk to Lorian multiple times, only to be turned away. I'd peered into her room once when Lorian had fallen asleep with his head angled on the bed next to her, and her face at least had regained some of the color it had lost.

The barrier was down. The moment it fell, Regner had somehow managed to sink Prisca and Lorian's ship.

Most of the pirates on that ship had died. Telean had only managed to survive because one of them had kept hold of her, refusing to allow her to drown.

But Prisca's aunt was currently walking around with a strange look on her face. As if something had gone terribly wrong and she couldn't quite determine what it was.

The rest of us were celebrating. Eryndan was dead, and Regner had been forced to retreat as the humans were filled with a surge of power from the barrier. Rumors from the city reported that humans across Eprotha were suddenly able to do more with their magic than they'd ever dreamed.

Daharak strolled across the deck toward me. She walked with her usual swagger, but her mouth was tight. "I thought I'd find you here. Lorian wants to see you."

"Is Prisca awake?"

"No."

Panic bit at me. "She shouldn't still be unconscious. What do the healers say?"

"There's no physical reason for her to not wake up. Her ribs are healed, and her lungs have no damage. One of my people scanned her for magic. Ceri just checked her again, and she says Prisca's power is depleted or suppressed to such an extent, it is as if it is no longer there."

I turned my gaze to the ocean. The kind of power the woman she called Ceri had wielded was rare. Rare enough that if not for her life as a pirate, she might have been called to work as one of Regner's assessors. And yet she used her gift to heal.

"Prisca drained her power during the battle," I said. "Just as we all did. But this kind of response doesn't make sense."

Daharak sighed. "Who knows what is normal with her kind of power? I've certainly never seen anything like it." When I directed my gaze back to her, she'd turned to look at the sea, toward the horizon where the barrier no longer kept us trapped on this continent.

"You're already planning your next move," I murmured.

"Regner was forced to flee. His alliance with Gromalia is currently no more—at least until Rekja decides who to trust. And with the barrier down, I can make my own plans."

"Is this about the weapon you've been careful not to mention since the day Prisca rescued your ships?"

The pirate queen had been remarkably closed-mouthed about the weapon she'd chased for years. Now that she finally had it, I couldn't help but wonder *who* she was planning to decimate with it.

She slid me an amused look. "I have enemies of my own. And with the barrier down, I'm no longer trapped here."

"Just as long as you don't forget to take me with you when you leave this continent."

Daharak Rostamir seemed like a woman of her word. But still…I wouldn't risk losing my chance to get off this continent.

She studied my face. Her eyes were shrewd, and I kept my expression blank. "You haven't changed your mind."

"No. And I won't."

"I can respect that. I won't forget to take you."

I nodded to her, even as my gut untwisted. I would have to trust the pirate queen. Trust had never come easily to me, but if the fae were willing to trust her, I could likely do the same. "I need to see what Lorian wants."

The cacophony of the deck began to fade as I left Daharak gazing dreamily into the distance and headed toward Prisca and Lorian's cabin. With every step, the noise was replaced by an unsettling silence that thickened the air. The ambient sounds of the ship became muted, as if the world itself was wary of what lay beyond that cabin door.

I made eye contact with Marth, who nodded to me as he stepped out of his own cabin. Like many of us, he'd turned grim. But it was especially jarring from a man who had once encompassed the opposite of the word. "Good luck," he told me.

I frowned at him, but the air seemed to grow heavier and even more oppressive as I approached Lorian's cabin. Apprehension coiled in my stomach, and I shook it off, throwing open the door.

He turned his head, and I had one second of eye contact with blazing green eyes before I dropped my gaze.

This wasn't Lorian.

This was the Bloodthirsty Prince.

The most powerful fae on this continent was watching his mate fade by the day. And the strain of it was obvious in the white knuckles of his fists, the wild, unhinged gleam I'd seen in the single glimpse I'd had of his eyes, the sharp metallic tang in the air—as if lightning was about to spear into the cabin.

"Do you need a moment to pull yourself together?" I asked.

"Careful." The word was a low croon. Clearly, my attempt at levity had failed.

"Prisca would—"

"There are many things Prisca would do if she were awake. She is not."

And I was finished cowering. Straightening my spine, I lifted my head, relief flowing through me as I found him watching Prisca once more.

"What is it you want?"

That gaze slid to mine again. It was *burning*. My stomach churned. With Prisca unconscious, we at least needed Lorian to keep his sanity.

"What is wrong with you?" I demanded.

A shadow stole over his face. "Nothing. I need to release some power. That is all." His eyes returned to Prisca, as if it had physically pained him to look away for even this long. "Vicer has not replied to Galon's message. He was due to return by now. We need to know the current status of the hybrids—both at that camp, and those who will travel toward the Asric Pass."

And he wanted me to go.

I thought about it. I traveled quickly, I was powerful, and if Vicer was in trouble, I felt confident that I could help him. Besides, as much as I would prefer to stay close to the ship that would take me to my new life, such thoughts were useless if we risked losing this war and any chance of a future.

"I'll go."

Lorian nodded. This was the cold mercenary Prisca had likely first met. How she'd fallen in love with him, I would never understand. But my own gaze drifted back to Prisca. She was so fucking pale.

"She's going to be fine," I said. This was not how it ended. Not for Prisca, and not for us. I knew that, deep in my bones.

Because if I was wrong…

"I know." Lorian spoke the words with full confidence, as if he would accept nothing less. But that sharp, metallic scent had filled the air once more.

Swallowing back the useless words on the tip of my tongue, I walked out.

2

THE QUEEN

I clawed at the hand covering my mouth. Another hand pinched the skin beneath my ribs, and I bucked.

"Shh."

That voice was familiar.

I let out a grunt, and the hand tightened. "You made a mistake coming here, Your Majesty. I suggest you pray to whichever gods you favor that we will live through this."

Pelysian allowed me to turn my head just enough to meet his gaze. His eyes were hard, and something in my chest relaxed as they left my own, lingering instead on the thousands of monsters chained within the mine. For the first time since I'd known him, his face drained of color, terror tightening his features.

"We are leaving," he whispered. "Now."

Slowly, as if he couldn't trust me not to scream and get both of us killed, he removed his hand from my mouth. I gave him the look his actions deserved.

He ignored me, jerking his head and gesturing for me to follow. But I still wanted that amulet. When I hesitated, he bared his teeth in a way that made it clear he would carry me out if he felt he needed to.

Once, I'd thought him a loyal subject. Now, Pelysian knew neither of us could afford for the other to be caught. And he was treating me accordingly.

I didn't like it.

But I followed him back down the passageways, gratefully inhaling the fresher air as we left the monsters behind us. Still, the sight of them straining at their chains would be forever imprinted into my mind.

We turned left, and I searched for a hidden spot we could use to have a quick conversation. I wasn't going anywhere until I had that amulet.

Pelysian froze. Every muscle in my body stiffened in response. His power allowed him to hear even the quietest whispers.

My heart jumped in my chest as he whirled toward me, eyes darting. Grabbing my hand, he pulled me into the tiniest crevice. I shook my head. It was too small.

His expression turned thunderous, and he roughly shoved me between his body and the stone wall, pressing me against it. Thankfully, the minimal lighting at least worked in our favor, but the chances of discovery…

Pelysian's heart pounded against my ear. I was wedged between him and hard granite, both of us trembling.

Finally, I heard it too. Booted footsteps walking toward us.

Low voices sounded, and a rush of adrenaline hit me.

What was I *doing*?

I'd had the opportunity to run. I could be *anywhere*, and I was in this hell Sabium had built, just footspans from the creatures he would turn on his enemies and the guards who would arrest me without a thought.

Was I so used to living with terror that I was unable to choose a life without it? Was I truly going to last this many years under Sabium's control and throw it all away with one stupid choice?

"The creatures are restless today," a feminine voice said.

"Probably need to be fed. The king likes to keep them half starved so they'll stay vicious. You're new, right?"

"Yes."

A low chuckle sounded from the male. "What did you do to be demoted to this position?"

The woman hissed but didn't reply. They were so close now, and their voices seemed to echo through my bones. Pelysian's hand moved near my hip. He'd unsheathed his dagger.

I was more than happy for the guards to die, but if they were discovered before we left this place, our own chances of survival greatly decreased.

I strained, and my power jumped within my grasp. Perhaps it would help just enough for us to live through the next few moments.

"How did he get...so many of them?" the woman asked.

"Some fae woman has been handing over creatures from her territory for years. Calls herself a warden or something." He laughed, and the sound was so close to us, I flinched. Pelysian's hand tightened warningly on my arm. "Those fae bastards have no idea what's coming for them." His voice faded as he continued walking past us. The creatures began to screech, likely sensing their approach.

Sweat dripped in a steady line down my back.

Pelysian kept us hidden for several long minutes after they had passed. Finally, he pulled me out of the shallow alcove. His hand remained around my arm as he practically dragged me down the passageway.

I allowed it. He would be alerted to anyone else coming our way long before they heard us.

We approached the entrance of the mine. I clamped down on the urge to sprint into the wide expanse and fresh air outside. Instead, I studied Pelysian. He was covered in dust, and he had the wary look of someone who had been traveling for days.

"How did you know I was here?" I asked.

"My mother. Will your power work on both of us?"

"It's unlikely. It's weak." Admitting such a thing burned, but Pelysian had always known the reality of my magic. Although...perhaps it *had* just helped us avoid detection. "We can't leave yet. The amulet is here somewhere." And everything would change once I took that little artifact from Sabium. Finally, *I* would be the one with the power.

Pelysian's hands gripped my upper arms, fingers digging into my skin as he glared at me. "The amulet is hidden in a cavern somewhere *below* us. There is no way for us to get to it tonight."

I looked into his eyes. They were filled with rage, but I couldn't discern any hint of a lie. Besides, if he could get to the amulet, he would likely attempt to take it for himself this very moment.

But… "You know how to get to it."

"Yes. But believe me, we would need a group of powerful fae or hybrids."

Frustration bit at me with sharp teeth. All of this was for nothing. The time I'd lost, the *risk* I'd taken… worthless.

Pelysian released me, shaking his head. "The barrier has fallen, Your Majesty."

My breath caught. "Jamic?"

"Safe."

My chest lightened, until it felt as if I might float away. The hybrid heir had somehow managed to keep my son safe, while also dealing Sabium a blow he would not forget.

Perhaps she was even more of a threat than I had first anticipated.

"According to reports, Jamic helped bring the barrier down himself," Pelysian said.

Pride roared through me. My son was powerful. It didn't matter that Sabium had forced that stolen power into him. That power was now *his*. And clearly, he knew how to wield it. While he had made the wise choice to ally with the hybrid heir to prevent Sabium from receiving that power, it was a temporary alliance.

The moment I came for him, we would work together.

"And what of the amulet?" I demanded.

"If you are truly determined to risk your life, we need the book you saw the king take from the castle that day. *That* will turn the tide in this war."

My heart raced. I'd known that book was important simply by the way Sabium kept it so close. "How will it turn the tide?"

"The book is a grimoire filled with ancient knowledge and dark magic. It is this grimoire that has allowed Sabium to lie and manipulate with such ease."

I fought to keep my expression blank. This whole time, I had imagined Pelysian as *my* tool. The tool *I* was dispatching to complete various tasks that would help me achieve my revenge.

Instead, he was keeping things from me. He likely knew exactly what that book did and why it was so important. And he hadn't told me.

I silently seethed as he pressed closer to the wall, peering out at the guards. Perhaps Pelysian's usefulness had come to an end. I could use him as a distraction, ensure he was killed, and make my escape.

But if they *didn't* kill him and chose to torture him instead, I wouldn't be able to return to the castle to find that book.

Could I even return, after the way I'd escaped? Perhaps if I convinced the guards I'd lost consciousness in that market. Maybe a kindly merchant had healed me? I would only need to be in the castle for a short amount of time while I searched for this grimoire.

I froze. Was I truly contemplating such a thing?

Yes.

Jamic was free, but Sabium would still kill him if he could. He'd said as much.

And if you find the grimoire, you'll be as powerful as Sabium. This continent will bow to you.

It was a heady thought. Everything Sabium had achieved, the power he had amassed, the creatures he had leashed...

All of it could be mine.

Together, Jamic and I could rule this continent. And one day, we could turn our sights to other kingdoms in distant lands.

I would make the territory Sabium had ruled seem paltry in comparison. *I* would be the one who was ageless. And he would just be dead. My lips curled at the thought, and the expression felt strange. It had been so, so long since I'd genuinely smiled.

"Nelia is here," Pelysian whispered.

My muscles locked up. I'd ordered Nelia to leave.

Craning my neck around Pelysian's huge shoulder, I caught sight of a bush rustling within the forest above our heads.

"She's going to become a distraction so you can escape," Pelysian said.

"No. I'll use my power."

"She knows the limitations of your power."

The one person who had always been loyal without anything in return. The closest person I'd ever had to a... friend.

Loyalty should always be rewarded. It was the one thing my father had taught me that I still believed.

"She's throwing her life away," I snapped. "Stop her."

"It's too late." Pelysian's voice was mournful. "She knows I am here, and she knows we are trapped. Prepare to run."

A stone rolled down the bank, coming close to one of the guards. He froze.

"Show yourself," he demanded.

The branch of a tree snapped. The guard launched himself up the bank, moving faster than I could have imagined. Several other guards immediately deserted their posts, giving chase.

Pelysian was already pulling me away from the mine. I sprinted, cursing Nelia as her screams pierced the night. I'd told her to leave.

But she'd known. She'd known I'd need a distraction, and she'd sacrificed herself.

A smart sacrifice. My life was, after all, worth more than hers. Still, I would have preferred to think of her living the remainder of her life as a wealthy woman somewhere safe. A fitting reward for her loyalty.

I stumbled, and Pelysian pulled me to him, practically carrying me up the bank in the opposite direction of the guards. They would search this forest in an attempt to find anyone who might be with Nelia.

A thud sounded, and as if compelled by some strange power, I turned. Nelia's body rolled down the bank, coming to rest near the entrance to the mine. Her head sat oddly on her neck, her eyes staring blankly—almost accusingly—at me.

Pelysian shoved me down into the underbrush. My hands shook, an endless rage slithering through every inch of my body.

Nelia was *mine*. And Sabium's men had taken her from me.

I met Pelysian's eyes. They were darker than usual, filled with grief. I hadn't known he was close to Nelia.

It seemed there was much I didn't know.

"These are called consequences, Your Majesty," he said bitterly. "I told you not to come here. You refused to listen. Now, stay here while I find our horses."

MADINIA

Kaelin Stillcrest was a tall woman who walked with the swaggering self-assurance of a fae male. Usually, I would have admired her for that alone.

Unfortunately, there was little else about her to admire. I watched her for several long moments as she snarled into the face of a pale man who did nothing but nod, his knuckles turning white where they clutched his crossbow.

When she turned, she swept her gaze from my head to my feet, sizing me up. I gave her a bored expression as she stalked toward me.

"Who are you?"

"Madinia Farrow."

"And what do you want?"

I gave her a dismissive look. "I'm here to see Vicer."

One of her men moved as if to go find him, and Stillcrest lifted her hand, stopping him in his tracks.

"And who exactly are you to come here and demand to see my people?"

I kept my expression bored. I could already tell it would infuriate her.

"We both know Vicer isn't one of your people. Now,

are you going to find him, or do I need to do it myself?"

I let my hand light up with a ball of fire, carefully studying her reaction.

She stepped back, positioning one of her men in front of her. That, more than anything, solidified exactly who and what she was.

Prisca would have shoved her body between a threat and any one of her people. It was how she was made. I might not agree with her blind loyalty and self-sacrificing nature, but they were some of the traits that would make her an excellent queen.

I let my gaze flick between the guard and Stillcrest, making it clear I'd noted her actions. Her cheeks flushed, her eyes fired, and she opened her mouth.

"Madinia." Vicer neatly stepped between us. "What are you doing here?"

I turned my attention to him. His eyes were filled with warning.

I pulled my power back into me. It took longer than usual, a stubborn spark lingering in my palm, as if it, too, was disappointed that we wouldn't be setting anything ablaze.

"I was sent. Because you didn't reply to our messages."

Vicer went still. His gaze slid to Stillcrest, and he was quiet for a long moment. When he spoke, his voice was deadly. "You prevented me from receiving messages from our queen?"

Stillcrest's face paled and then immediately flushed. "I prevented you from giving detailed information about my people. And she's not my queen until she's sitting on her throne with a crown on her head. Even then, she will have to prove herself worthy to rule us. My people are tired of their lives being dictated by royals."

That was a reasonable point. And I would have believed her, if I hadn't already watched her walk around this camp as if she wore a crown.

Vicer gave her a look of such disgust, Stillcrest dropped her eyes. She immediately snapped her gaze back to his, her cheeks heating. I was small enough to enjoy her discomfort.

Vicer's eyes met mine. "Come with me."

I followed him into the camp, weaving through tents in neat rows, all of them in various shades of earth-toned canvas. The camp blended seamlessly with the surroundings of the forest, and the hybrids who lived here wore various shades of greens and browns to evade prying eyes. Even with the directions Vicer had passed to us, it had been difficult to find. But Regner's soldiers could simply use the process of elimination as they searched every inch of his kingdom. Eventually, they would find this camp, and all the camouflage in the world wouldn't help them.

Several pairs of curious eyes turned toward us, but Vicer quickly led me to a tent situated on its own, near what looked like their armory. Paths weaved through the camp, while the air was thick with the mingled scents of campfire smoke, roasting meat, and pine.

"I know you brought the barrier down," he said as we stepped inside the tent. It was sparse, with a small cot and one chair. He gestured for me to take it, and I shook my head.

"There are humans here who suddenly received an influx of power," Vicer said. "Even Kaelin was forced to admit how incredible an achievement it was."

I just shrugged. "Lorian and Prisca want to know the status here," I said. "From what I can see, there hasn't been any movement toward the Asric Pass."

Kaelin likely had spies in this place, and I wouldn't risk her learning that the hybrid heir was currently still unconscious.

Vicer pinched the bridge of his nose, his gray eyes glinting. "The hybrids we managed to get out of the city... most of them stopped here for food and rest, and then left in small groups, continuing their journey. My people set up hidden camps with food and water in various locations on the way to the pass. They'll wait there for the signal to cross—once the soldiers Regner is hiding in the pass have been dispatched."

That part of his plan made sense. It was brilliant, even. But...

"What about the people remaining in this camp?"

"I'm trying." He opened his mouth, closed it. Frustration slid through his eyes.

"What is it?"

"Regner's scouts have been drawing closer. Kaelin insists her people will kill any who discover the camp. But if the scouts don't return to their commanders, more will be sent. These people are running out of time. But this is their home. They refuse to leave."

Several children ran past the outside of our tent, laughing in the unrestrained way such children did. If Regner's iron guards found this place, that laughter would end. Forever.

I met Vicer's eyes. "Here's what we're going to do."

PRISCA

I was so very, very comfortable.

The world spun around me in a sickening whirl. But here, with my cheek pressed against the hard ground, I was safe.

Nothing could touch me here.

There was no pain. No grief. No responsibility.

Coward, a voice whispered. *He's waiting for you.*

I felt myself frown, but the movement was distant, as if it didn't belong to me. Still, the spinning slowed, and a gruff voice called to me from a great distance.

"Prisca."

Something about that voice made my heart ache. Made me want to lift my head, even if it meant losing myself to the awful, dizzying mess around me.

"Wildcat. Please."

That voice pierced the dark chaos above me, stabbing deep into my gut. I never wanted to hear that powerful, male voice beg. Ever.

Lifting my head, I pressed my hands into the firm ground below me and *pushed*.

The world came into focus.

Lorian's eyes met mine, dulled with exhaustion. Why was he so tired? It wasn't like him to sleep poorly.

His hands cupped my face. The world continued its slow spin. But he'd joined me here in the eye of the hurricane.

"You're awake." His kiss was desperate, tasting of grief and hopelessness. Dragging his lips away, he pressed his mouth to my forehead.

I wasn't lying on the hard ground at all. No, the pillow beneath my head was soft.

"Healer!" Lorian roared. A door was flung open, and a woman was suddenly bustling toward us. She pressed her fingers to my pulse, frowning as my heart began to pound faster and faster.

The room listed slightly, and this time, I knew it wasn't just me. Ship. We were on a ship...

Blind terror slammed into me, and I clawed at Lorian, dragging him close.

"You're alive." I leaned into him, saturating my lungs in his scent.

Confusion creased his brow. "You were the one who nearly died."

I'd done it. He was talking and breathing and *alive*. I'd defied the gods for him. And I would do it a thousand times if I had to.

But my memory still served up the image of him, shattering into a million pieces. Anguish stabbed into my chest, and my entire body shuddered.

"We need a moment," he said to the woman, who fled the room, not even bothering to close the door behind her. Despite myself, I felt my lips curve.

"Have you been completely unreasonable again, prince?"

He ignored that. "Prisca. What is it?" His voice was low, soothing, but a muscle ticked in his jaw, and his eyes were dark with concern.

"When…when Conreth attacked Regner, the human king used a mirror to reflect Conreth's attack back at us. I think it must be the mirror given to the humans by Faric—one of the meddling gods who started all this," I said bitterly. "Conreth's power…it hit you." My mouth turned watery as that sickening terror lurched through me once more. "You died, Lorian."

My voice cracked, and I blinked back the tears that flooded my eyes. "You turned to ice. And I watched you sh-shatter."

His face lost color. "And you brought me back. That's why you almost died."

Someone sucked in a sharp breath. Conreth stood, one arm braced against the doorway as he stared at us, his expression devastated. His gaze met Lorian's, and my chest burned.

I'd vowed that one day I would make Conreth pay for everything he'd done to Lorian. But now…now, I didn't need to.

He'd just learned what he'd done—that he'd killed his brother.

And his eyes…

Something had broken in the fae king. Within a single moment, he'd become a shell of a man.

And even knowing he deserved it, pity stirred within me.

Without a word, Conreth backed away, shutting the door behind him. Lorian immediately turned his attention back to me, his gaze searching my face.

I cleared my throat. "I want to sit up."

He shoved several pillows beneath my head while I surveyed the cabin. My stomach rumbled, and he stepped away, opening the door and speaking to someone.

"The healer will return in a few minutes," he said. "Tell me. All of it."

So, I did. Tears streamed down my cheeks as I told him of my desperate, stumbling gait as I'd attempted to cross the ship to get to him. I told him how he'd *left* me, and the way I'd felt his presence for a single moment right next to me. I told him of the way Telean had screamed at me, warning me not to do what I'd done next. And I told him about my mother, my grandmother, the consequences they'd warned of, and the fact that I could no longer feel a single spark of my power, even with the hourglass around my neck.

By the time I finished, my voice was dead. No more tears flooded down my cheeks. Lorian looked like I'd punched him in the gut, and when he caught my chin, his hand shook.

"You... I don't need to tell you how dangerous that was. You already know it. Any consequences, we'll face them together. But I need you to promise me, Prisca. Promise you will never do such a thing again."

"I don't think I'd even be able to," I said. I didn't tell him how I'd been feeling tiny slivers of my soul burning to ash. That I'd felt the gods take everything I had to give and demand more. And that if my mother and grandmother hadn't been there to give me the tiniest pieces of whatever was left of their being...

I likely wouldn't be here either.

Part of me wondered if I had hallucinated my mother and grandmother. If coming so close to death had simply allowed my imagination to provide me with the people I had wanted to see most.

But I remembered my mother's gentle smile. And my grandmother's wicked eyes.

"Change the world, granddaughter. And heal our kingdom."

Heal our kingdom.

"What happened?" I asked. "I felt the barrier come down."

Lorian nodded. Getting up, he opened the door, gesturing for the healer to enter. She was a small woman, with dark hair almost as curly as mine. Her eyes glimmered with curiosity, but they shifted immediately into the appraising look I'd seen on Tibris's face a thousand times over the years.

"I'm Ceri," she said. "How do you feel?"

"Fine. Weak," I admitted when Lorian narrowed his eyes at me. "And...I can't feel my power."

After a few minutes of taking my pulse, checking my breathing, and examining what felt like every inch of me with her magic, she pronounced me in need of rest. I wasn't surprised. My body had begun to tremble from fatigue.

"And my power?"

"I don't have much understanding of power like yours," she admitted. "But I'm assuming it is simply a burnout. It is unlike anything I have seen before, but I expect your power will return."

"Thank you," I told her, attempting to silence the voice that asked me what I would do if it didn't return.

She just nodded, opening the door and waving through a young girl who carried two bowls on a tray. She took the tray and nodded to the girl.

"Thank *you*," Ceri said to me. "My grandmother's mother had family in Myrthos. The continent to our east," she clarified when I frowned. "I've dreamed of visiting them my entire life. Now, with the barrier down, I'll be able to." She bowed her head at both of us, placed the tray on the bedside table, and bustled away.

"So, I died," Lorian mused. "I knew something had happened, because I saw a single glimpse of Cavis. But I'd never imagined that could be it. Because our ship exploded, and you were drowning. I couldn't get to you." His eyes turned haunted. "It felt like several eternities before you began breathing again."

Cavis. My eyes stung at the thought. I'd hoped he was truly at peace.

I frowned, my mind lingering on Lorian's other words. The ship had exploded? Of course it had, because Conreth's power must have missed Lorian. But that meant...

"Telean?" I gasped, sitting up.

Lorian gently pushed me back down. "She's fine. One of Daharak's people kept her safe."

I collapsed back against the pillows, exhausted from my sudden movement. I attempted to ignore the panic that fluttered inside my chest. I wouldn't be like this for long. I'd regain my strength. And my power.

A knock sounded on the door, and Lorian gave me a

rueful smile. "Clearly, people are learning you're awake. Enter," he said, and the door swung open, revealing Rythos, Galon, Marth, and Telean.

All of them were alive and healthy. My cheeks ached from my grin.

They crowded into the small cabin, Rythos sitting on the end of my bed. "You scared us, darlin'."

"I know. I'm sorry."

Lorian nudged me until I began to eat, while everyone seemed to talk at once.

"Regner fled," Rythos smirked. "With Eryndan dead and the barrier down, he obviously decided the gods weren't on his side that day."

"Biding his time," Marth muttered.

Galon raised his eyebrow at him but nodded. "He'll be regrouping."

I glanced at Telean. She hadn't said a word but was watching me silently. Her gaze dropped to the hourglass lying against my chest, and she studied it for a long moment before her eyes finally met mine. A chill rippled through me.

"Since the moment I was pulled out of that water, I've had a feeling of *wrongness*," she said. "As if the world has shifted. As if I've forgotten something of utmost import."

"Ask me," I said, my heart sinking.

"I can see from the look on your face that I don't need to. You used your power in the *one* way that is forbidden. For your own gain. You risked all of us. You spat in the face of the gods. And you almost died."

My aunt shook her head, and I hunched my shoulders. Telean was the closest thing I had to a mother. I'd known she'd be disappointed, but seeing her disgust... It hurt more than I could have imagined.

But everyone in this room deserved to know what would happen. Because any consequences I faced would likely affect them too.

"Yes. Lorian died, and I turned back time."

No one spoke. Galon's jaw was tight. Marth's skin was draining of color. Rythos was staring at Lorian with horror in his eyes.

Telean flicked Lorian a single blistering glance, as if he had been the one to do this. "Then that was the will of the gods."

Fury rattled my bones. "Fuck the gods," I snapped.

Telean's eyes went wide, and I kept speaking, unable to stop. "What have the gods done for our people? How have they helped us? All they've given us is suffering. I won't apologize for saving my mate."

She took a step back from my bed, and her gaze cut through my chest. It was as if she could no longer recognize me. "I expected better of you. Your mother and grandmother would be ashamed."

I opened my mouth to tell her I'd spoken to them, but Lorian was already getting to his feet, expression flat.

"Leave," he said.

I wanted to argue, but Galon shook his head at me, flicking his eyes toward Lorian. Tiny sparks were darting across his skin.

Turning my attention back to Telean, I stared at her with no idea what to say. Her eyes softened, but she clenched her jaw, making her way out of the room.

"She's right to be ashamed," I said into the silence.

"And disgusted. She warned me over and over that I could never use my power that way. I did it anyway." I met Lorian's eyes. He watched me carefully, as if bracing for a blow. "And I'd do it again."

"Of course you would," Galon said. Lorian continued watching me, and his eyes had turned tender.

"Your aunt will forgive you."

I hoped so. But even knowing the gods would likely make me suffer for this, I didn't have it in me to regret it.

Lorian ordered the others out of the cabin when I began to yawn. When I woke a few hours later, I insisted on speaking to Natan—since Galon had mentioned he was currently staying on this ship.

Once, Natan had been just another boy from our village. A friend with an easy sense of humor but a caged look in his eyes, who drank to numb the pain of the Gifting and Taking ceremonies.

I'd thought he was dead. And yet I'd never forget the way he'd joined us in that barely seaworthy merchant ship, as many humans as he'd been able to gather on board, working to bring down the barrier.

I wished Tibris could have seen it. He wouldn't have recognized his childhood friend.

"Prisca..." Lorian's voice had turned cajoling, and his eyes flickered with frustration. I understood. It hurt him to see me this weak.

"Galon's right. Regner will be making new plans. We need to begin preparing."

"Fine," he conceded, holding up a hand as I attempted to swing my legs over the side of the bed. "But he can come here. I'll send word."

While we waited, one of Daharak's pirates brought warm water. I freshened up, then sat on the edge of my bed, forced to admit I couldn't have made it up to the main deck anyway. I would need to shake this off quickly. We didn't have time for me to be lying around.

Lorian watched me the entire time, his eyes dark. When Natan knocked, Lorian opened the door. "Five minutes," he said.

I didn't bother arguing. I was too busy studying the man who'd once been a friend. The day Lina had lost her grandparents and been taken to the city, he'd attempted to pretend not to be affected. But I'd seen the terror in his eyes.

There was no sign of that boy now. Natan's expression seemed carved in stone. Dark circles had hollowed his eyes, but he stood tall, with an easy confidence that had replaced the swagger and bluster he'd once worn like a favorite tunic.

"Prisca."

I nodded. "Natan."

"No one will tell me where Tibris is."

I sighed. I wasn't surprised that everyone was being closed-mouthed. "He's attempting to convince a group of rebels to ally with us," I said, leaving out the fact that he was technically a hostage. Vicer may have arranged for Natan to meet us, but that didn't mean I would immediately disclose all of our plans.

Natan's eyes gleamed with curiosity, but he turned his gaze on Lorian. "They said you're mated to the Bloodthirsty Prince," he mused, meeting my eyes once more. "I didn't believe them until I saw you standing next to him on that ship."

"Don't call him that."

Lorian shot me a look caught somewhere between tenderness and exasperation. Natan just narrowed his eyes at me as if he no longer recognized me. I sighed. "Things are complicated."

"I understand that much."

"I thought you'd…" Died. I thought he'd died along with the rest of our village.

He swallowed. "I was away, selling my father's wolfskins at Mistrun. By the time I returned, it was too late. Everyone was gone. There were only a few of us left."

My chest tightened. "I'm sorry." The words were inadequate, but Natan nodded all the same.

"Vicer told me what happened to Thol."

I nodded, picturing him all alone in that dark cave. It took me three tries to speak around the lump in my throat. "We'd hoped to bring him home, but Regner's soldiers are crawling over the area. We'll give him a proper burial when all this is over. I promise."

"He was hunting you." Suspicion slid through Natan's eyes, and Lorian angled his head. He didn't make a single movement, but Natan stiffened.

I'd forgotten just how intimidating Lorian was to those who weren't in his inner circle. I gave him a warning look, and his lips twitched.

"He was," I said. "But he joined us in the search for this." I held up the hourglass. "I didn't kill him, Natan. You know me better than that."

He frowned. "Never said you did."

But he'd wondered.

I let it go for now. "How many people do you have?"

"If you mean humans who have turned against Regner? Thousands. Caddaril the Cleaver and his criminals are creating chaos for Regner throughout Eprotha. If you mean me personally? A few hundred. More and more villagers have been fleeing from conscription. One of the villages to the east of ours turned on the assessor during a Taking ceremony. The guards killed half the village, but they were eventually killed themselves, and anyone left alive decided to join with us."

It was hard to imagine. Regner's guards, priestesses, and assessors had ensured the villagers I'd known would turn on one another at the mere suggestion that one of them was a hybrid. The day Lina's grandparents had died, the priestess had announced a reward for anyone who would inform them of the presence of one of the "corrupt." One hundred gold coins. For a villager with little to spare, it was enough to ensure their children's children wouldn't go hungry.

Natan must have been following my thoughts because he shook his head. "It's different now, Prisca. I know it's difficult to believe. Of course there are some who will always believe the king's lies, but more and more people are waking up." He grinned suddenly. "And now that the barrier has fallen, and many people will find themselves with more power…it's just further proof that their power wasn't gifted to the gods."

Pride warmed my chest. We'd done that.

"And those who don't manage to flee?" I asked softly.

Natan's grin dropped. "You know what happens to them. And it's getting more dangerous every day."

"Perhaps we don't need all of them to join us," Lorian said. "At least not right now."

"What do you mean?"

Lorian pushed himself off the wall. "It's going to get worse for those who flee. But those who stay will be perfectly positioned and armed with fae iron."

My heart kicked in my chest, and I pictured the chaos we could cause. "They could turn on Regner's armies when they least expect it."

Natan picked at a loose thread on his shirt. "It's dangerous."

"All of it is dangerous."

He raised his head, and his eyes gleamed. "I'll talk to the others."

"Thank you, Natan. For...everything."

"Don't thank me. One day, you'll return to your kingdom with your people. We humans will be left with whatever remains of Eprotha. We have no choice but to make sure there *is* something left."

3

LORIAN

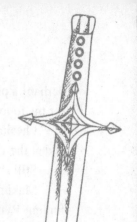

Twice now, I'd watched Prisca drown. Watched her lie still, her chest frozen, face slack. I wished I could somehow keep her away from all water for the rest of our lives.

Her eyes drifted closed, and my chest squeezed, my hand almost trembling as I pushed one of her long curls away from her face.

Sleeping. That's all it was. A normal response to the healing. Still, I leaned closer, watching her chest rise and fall.

Even knowing we were both alive, dread rolled through my veins, thick and bitter. I didn't doubt Telean was right—and that there would be repercussions. But I couldn't bear the thought of Prisca being the one to face those repercussions.

And I kept having the strangest feeling that I was being watched.

Behind me, the door opened, and I hissed out a breath, turning.

Conreth stood in the doorway. His eyes lingered on Prisca for a long moment. Long enough that I showed him my teeth. Usually, that would have at least resulted in an eye roll, perhaps a pithy comment. Today, he just gestured silently for me to join him.

I hesitated, glancing at Prisca. But she was sleeping, and at the very least, I needed to bathe and eat.

Still…

Making my way to the door, I stepped past Conreth, finding Rythos craning his neck, attempting to look into the room. I might have mocked him for his fretting, except that I also couldn't restrain myself from checking she was still breathing.

"Stay with her."

He nodded, slipping into the room. My eyes met Conreth's. "What is it?"

It wasn't often that my brother looked uncomfortable. Almost…awkward. "Can we talk somewhere more private?"

Despite my dark mood, curiosity burned through me. My brother was acting strangely, indeed.

Nodding, I followed him to the cabin Daharak had given him. This part of the ship was quiet, most people likely above us on the main deck, enjoying the fresh air.

Conreth's cabin was the same size as mine and spotlessly clean. Likely, he'd warded the cabin to prevent any accumulation of dust.

My brother remained standing. I studied his face, watching the way his eyes darkened, his lips thinned, and then…trembled.

"What is it?"

He seemed to steel himself, meeting my eyes once more. "I heard what your mate said. I killed you. And Prisca brought you back."

Not for the first time, I was at a loss with my brother. His jaw tightened at my silence. And I truly looked at him. That was…devastation in his eyes. He watched me as if I were still dead, with the knowledge that he was the one responsible.

"Conreth—"

"If not for her and her time magic, you'd be dead. By my hand."

"You heard what Prisca said. Regner used his mirror."

"The effect would be the same."

Fury suddenly burned through my chest. "What would you like me to say, Conreth? We didn't talk before or during the battle. I worked with the others to strategize, while you refused to communicate, attacking whomever and whatever you wanted. You knew of Regner's ward. If you'd thought logically, you would have known your attack wouldn't be successful, and you would have known he'd allowed the wards to falter in an attempt to trap you when you killed his generals. But you weren't thinking logically," I snarled. "You were functioning out of arrogance and ego, hoping you could kill Regner where he stood and everything could go back to the way it has always been."

The blood had drained from Conreth's face, and I let out a humorless laugh. "Did you imagine Regner's death would make me reconsider choosing Prisca? Do you truly think that is why I chose her? Because of my need to be at her side during war?"

Conreth's eyes had lightened—the only sign my words had an effect. "You're right. It was my arrogance that did this. My inability to accept your choice. I'm sorry, Lorian."

For a moment, all I could do was stare at him. Never had I heard a true apology from my brother.

My throat unlocked. "Apologize to Prisca."

He nodded. "I will."

It was difficult to trust this man impersonating my brother. For an absurd moment, I wondered if Regner had infiltrated him somehow. But no, the misery in Conreth's eyes couldn't be feigned.

When I didn't speak, his shoulders slumped. "I want to truly ally with you and...Prisca. I want us to work together to win this war. I will return to our kingdom and attempt to sway the wardens. You can have full access to Hevdrin and all my generals. You were right—you know this continent better than I do."

Any other time, I would have felt sheer triumph at his words. But I knew the price of those words, and it left a bitter taste in my mouth. Prisca had nearly died to bring me back. She couldn't use her power. And who knew what the true consequences would be for defying the gods?

"Do you need anything else?" Conreth asked into the silence.

"Yes. We need you to take Jamic with you. He has so much power, it rivals some of our wardens. Teach him how to wield it in battle against Rekja."

"Done."

I couldn't find it in me to thank my brother. All I could do was nod and stalk toward the door, attempting to ignore the regret in his eyes.

PRISCA

"Enough fussing," I begged. We stood on the deck, where I was finally enjoying some fresh air. Lorian hovered, one hand clamped around my arm in case I felt dizzy.

He just sent me a look caught somewhere between amusement and pure male stubbornness.

"You need to rest."

"Lorian." I'd had two days of resting, and this morning, I'd woken up starving. It was as if my body wanted to replace everything I hadn't eaten since the battle. Lorian kept watching me eat with a pleased, smug expression on his face.

"Fine," he growled.

His brows lowered as he stared at the horizon. "What is it?" I asked.

Green eyes met mine, and I could see him debating whether I was *well* enough to be told whatever it was he had learned.

"Lorian."

He sighed. "Marth received a message earlier from one of our spies. There are rumors Rothnic is working on something new."

Dread punched into me. As one of Regner's patriarchs, Rothnic had been responsible for the horseless carriages in the capital. He'd also been the mind behind the magical cannons that had sunk so many of our ships while we'd worked to bring down the barrier.

There was no question that he was one of Regner's most important tools. Anything he was working on for this war would no doubt bode poorly for us.

I lifted my face to the sun. Apparently, we were anchored in fae waters, south of Quorith. Nearby, a gull screamed. And yet, even in this peaceful moment, all I could see was that mirror. And the man who had countered my power.

"Tymriel sent us a message while you were... recovering," Lorian said, his eyes hard.

I snorted. "Are the elders offering to assist us yet? What happened to the hybrids I asked Tymriel to send to help our people get through the pass?"

"The other elders wouldn't agree. They said it's too dangerous. Regner has stationed his soldiers along the pass."

I let out a low curse.

Lorian took my hand. "Last time we spoke, Tymriel said he was hoping to convince someone to go against the elder's wishes. His letter mentioned a man named Orivan. One of Zathrian's generals. Tymriel is going to find a way to get a message to him."

I knew what this meant. "I'm going to have to kill my cousin," I said.

Lorian's brows lifted.

"I know you're thinking it. We don't have time to tiptoe around the issue. He has twenty thousand hybrids. My people."

He took my hand. "Our people."

His words stole the air from my lungs.

At Conreth's summit, I'd declared that Lorian would

be the hybrid king. And clearly, he was ready to step into that role.

Pushing up onto my toes, I buried my hand in his hair and directed his head down to me, pressing my lips to his. Being able to touch him, feel his mouth against mine, hear his low, rough growl…it was everything.

He deepened our kiss, tongue stroking as he wrapped his arms around my body, pulling me close.

There was a desperation to this kiss. I'd watched him shatter apart, and he'd watched my heart stop beating.

Someone cleared their throat, and I pushed against Lorian's chest. He let out a displeased growl, and I laughed against his mouth.

"Ahem." Galon grinned at me. "Glad to see you're feeling better. I have someone you need to meet. Rekja's people were tearing Gromalia apart looking for his lover, so I asked Daharak to step in. She had some of her pirates keeping her safe during the battle. But I had a feeling you would want to speak to her."

My stomach curdled. I didn't regret my order to let Eryndan learn his son was seeing one of the guards. But I hadn't enjoyed risking a stranger's life for our needs either.

Galon was waiting for me to respond. Forcing my expression into a mask of calm welcome, I nodded. He turned, and I followed his gaze as he gestured to Daharak and the woman standing next to her.

Both of them walked toward us.

Rekja's lover moved with the grace of a panther, her sleeveless tunic showcasing strong, toned arms. Her long legs were encased in the leather leggings Madinia also favored, while her black braid fell to the small of her back. Her dark eyebrows and hair contrasted sharply with her pale skin, her bright-blue eyes a shock of color as they narrowed on my face.

"Your Majesty." She nodded with the ingrained habit of someone who'd been taught to bow to the crown—any crown.

"Please, call me Prisca."

She hesitated but cleared her throat. "My name is Thora."

We stared at each other for a long, awkward moment. But we didn't have time for awkwardness. Perhaps we could skip that part.

"I would like to apologize," I said. "I'm the reason you're here. I wish I could tell you I had a noble reason for stealing you from your life. But the truth is, I used you as a pawn. I needed Rekja to distrust his father, and I knew he would suspect Eryndan of either hiding or killing you."

Thora's mouth thinned, but something flickered in her eyes. "I've never heard royalty apologize before."

I raised an eyebrow. "Not even Rekja?"

She smiled, but it was sad. "No, not even Rekja. The truth is, the rumors of our relationship had already begun to make their way through the palace. Someone close to the prince had been blackmailing me. They learned Rekja was in love with me and then made it clear if I didn't cooperate, I would be killed. When you had me kidnapped, I assumed my life was ending."

I winced. "You must have been terrified. I'm sorry."

Her smile turned genuine. "You should likely

apologize to the fae you sent. I almost killed two of them."

I couldn't help but grin. I liked this woman.

"I need to speak to Rekja," I said. Already, I was using Thora again. But I had no other choice. "We have to work together if both of our kingdoms are going to survive."

It was Thora's turn to wince. "When he learns you were the one responsible for taking me…you'll be lucky if he doesn't attempt to kill you, Your Majesty. There's no way you will be allowed within a thousand footspans of the castle."

She frowned at Lorian.

A predatory gleam had slid into his eyes at her mention of my potential death, and I squeezed his arm.

"Call me Prisca," I corrected absently. I could see her point. If someone took Lorian from me and then wanted to have a *conversation*…

"I may be able to help," Daharak said from where she leaned against a mast nearby. She lifted her hand, and a familiar silver coin appeared in her palm.

The coin represented a favor owed to her by the Gromalian king. "I thought you used that when you helped Lorian and me get through the city."

She smirked. "Since you were so sneaky and we used the cove to get you into Gromalia, I didn't need to use it."

"But Eryndan is dead."

Thora shook her head, a smile playing around her mouth. "The coins—and the favors owed—pass from father to son. Rekja wouldn't risk his honor being questioned, especially so soon after his father's death. If you use the coin, he will see you. But he won't be in

Thobirea. He hates that city. Loathes the castle."

I thought of his father's castle and the way Rekja had been forced to be a puppet for Eryndan. I couldn't blame him for hating the place. "Where will he be?"

"Sorlithia."

Lorian sighed. "A coastal city on the border between Eprotha and Gromalia," he told me. "So far, we've done everything we can to avoid it."

"He'll be there," Thora insisted. "I'll attempt to convince him you helped us, but that coin will only get you in front of him. It won't make him cooperate."

We had no choice. We needed Rekja, and it wasn't as if he was going to meet us anywhere else.

"Then that's where we need to go."

MADINIA

I had never been particularly good at persuading people to do what I wanted them to do.

Personally, I excelled at blackmail, manipulation, and sly coercion.

Unfortunately, those skills weren't going to make these people leave Stillcrest's camp and move toward safety. So, along with Vicer, I had begun my campaign to convince each and every man, woman, and child to leave this place before it was too late.

So far, I was having mixed results.

Most of her people seemed wary of the thought of a

hybrid queen. Vicer had once told me these people were secessionists who loathed the concept of being ruled by anyone. But the truth was, they *were* being ruled by someone.

Kaelin Stillcrest.

She'd strengthened their isolationist ideals, and yet she was the one who dictated everything in their lives. She controlled the food rationing, the security, the little education available for the children. Her refusal to prioritize healers meant she even governed life and death.

And yet Stillcrest had convinced these hybrids that Prisca was the threat. It was utterly infuriating.

So, I was slowly attempting to convince them otherwise—making no attempt to hide my desire for them to leave. I sat with mothers as they watched their children play, and I told them of how Prisca had saved so many children from Lesdryn not long ago—with Vicer's help.

I trained with the sentries and told them about the army Prisca was amassing, ready to defend our kingdom.

I talked to young women and men, who likely dreamed of a life outside this camp—although none of them would admit to such a thing. I told them what Prisca had told me, about the hybrid kingdom known as Lyrinore, and what it had looked like when Ysara showed Prisca all it had to offer. I told them of the markets and the libraries, the people and the magical creatures that roamed the land. And I told them that the hybrid queen was determined to ensure the hybrids on this continent could return home to that life.

A few of them seemed open to at least listening to what I had to say. A tall, thin woman named Tralia had a cool head, and unlike most who merely echoed Stillcrest's insistence that this camp was too well hidden to be found, she actually asked questions about our armies. About Prisca herself, about the fae, and about Regner.

Meanwhile, Vicer spoke of the threat. He told everyone who would listen how Regner's scouts had been drawing closer. He warned them about other camps that had been decimated, and he detailed all he had learned about the devastation of the village he, Prisca, and Tibris had once called home.

We'd rescued almost two hundred hybrids from the city the night we freed Jamic. And most of those hybrids had already moved south. They'd lived beneath the oppressive cloud of Regner's tyranny, and they knew exactly how much they had to lose. According to Vicer, they'd managed to convince a hundred or so people from this camp to leave with them.

Around a third of that number would travel down to the fae lands to join our army. The remainder would make their way to the meeting point near the Asric Pass, where they'd wait for our signal to cross.

Three days after we arrived, I broke my fast with Vicer. I'd spent the early hours of the morning walking through the forest surrounding the camp and searching for signs anyone had been lurking. It was quiet. Peaceful. And yet, it made the hair on the back of my neck stand to attention.

"Galon told me he sent a few of his fae friends to keep an eye on the camp," I said. "But I haven't seen any sign of them."

Vicer looked a little sick.

My fists clenched. "She sent them away, didn't she?"

He gave a sharp nod.

I sneered at him. "How long are you going to tolerate this?"

"We can't force these hybrids to move unless we send in an army. And if we do that, we're no better than Regner."

"Unlike Regner, we would be saving their lives, not killing them."

Vicer dropped his gaze to his porridge. I snorted. Unlike most of the tender-hearts I was continually surrounded by, I had no problems with removing others' rights if necessary. I played with my spoon, but I was no longer hungry.

"Once you cross the line into a certain level of idiocy, you lose the right to self-determination. And that is especially true for those responsible for protecting children."

Vicer said nothing, simply pushed his porridge away. I clenched my teeth.

Not long ago, I'd told him to use his power on Kaelin Stillcrest to make her cooperate. His reaction had made it clear he would never do such a thing. All of us could be moving toward safer ground this very second. Vicer's power was wasted on him.

"The fae Galon sent wouldn't have left the area," I said, changing tactics. "They'll be making themselves scarce. I'm going to go find them. Perhaps they can help convince some people of the danger here."

He nodded. "Those who listened and moved south have been safely making their way to the planned location.

My people have been refreshing the caches of supplies hidden at each point."

"Good."

He angled his head, meeting my gaze once more. And his eyes were haunted. "You feel it too."

"Yes." We were running out of time. This camp may be well hidden, in a strategic location, but it couldn't stay hidden forever. Eventually, Regner's iron guards would find it.

"I would like a word." A sharp voice came from over my shoulder.

I rolled my eyes at Vicer. His mouth twitched, but I turned on the hard wooden chair to find Stillcrest staring furiously at us.

"I know what you're doing."

"And what would that be?"

"Using the hybrid heir's propaganda to convince my people their lives are at risk. We have a good life here. It's a difficult life, but an honest one. And you're determined to ruin that for your own selfish needs." Her voice shook with fury. Clearly, that "propaganda" was having more of an impact than she would like.

I gave her a dismissive look. "Our own selfish needs? We're attempting to save lives."

She sneered at me. "Women like you always enjoy bending over for a crown. But my people aren't desperate for your *queen's* approval."

Slowly, I got to my feet. "I lived beneath the shadow of a power-obsessed dictator. Tell yourself whatever you need to feel good. But I see the truth. You would rather everyone died here than found safety somewhere else, because it would prove just how unimportant you are."

Her eyes flashed, and she took a step closer.

"You will leave," she breathed. "You are not and have never been welcome here." She turned to Vicer. "And your invitation is also rescinded."

And that was it. I was tired of tiptoeing around this woman. Giving her my coldest court smile, I opened my mouth. "You—"

The camp bells began to ring, and the color slowly drained from Stillcrest's face. A young boy ran toward us. I'd spoken to his mother yesterday. His name was... Balin. And he had the power of enhanced hearing.

Stillcrest whirled to face him.

"Hooves." He pointed at his ears. "I can hear them. Hundreds of them. Coming from the southeast."

4
MADINIA

I whirled, grabbing Stillcrest by her arms. "What's your plan?"

Her skin was so pale, it was as if she was a corpse. Useless. I shook her until her head bobbled loosely on her neck.

"Madinia," Vicer snapped.

"She has to have an escape plan. How do we protect these people?"

"Bells," Stillcrest croaked. "When the bells ring, our men surround the village."

"How many men, Stillcrest?"

"Two hundred."

Vicer and I stared at her silently. I'd known she was unprepared, but two hundred men?

"And then what?" I asked.

Her mouth trembled. "There's a pass through the Normathe Mountains. But it's two days away on foot."

And none of these people were prepared to cross through a mountain pass with no warning and no supplies.

I thrust her away, disgusted. "You've signed our death warrants."

Vicer stared at me, and I saw the moment he understood just how many lives were going to be lost. His gray eyes turned bleak.

"The children," he said. "You've got to get the children out, Madinia."

"I have an attack power. They need me on the front where I can do the most damage."

"No, listen to me," he ground out when I opened my mouth. "You need to round up as many mothers and children as you can. You're clever and powerful, and you're their best chance. Any person who can swing a sword will buy them time—Stillcrest, me...anyone. Do you know where the first caches are?"

I nodded. There were several within a roughly equal distance of the camp. It meant if people were fleeing in groups, they could take different routes, and if one group was attacked, there was still a chance some of them would survive. Bile clawed up my throat.

"Regner's soldiers won't be content with slaughtering everyone here," he said. "They're going to come after anyone who runs."

"I know."

Screams sounded. The carefully placed tents became traps of rope and fabric as hybrids rounded up their children, calling to friends. Children cried out for their parents in terrified, high-pitched voices.

The crackling of fire accompanied a series of shouts. This, at least, I could do something about. Narrowing my eyes, I spotted the log, kicked from the fire and setting a series of tents alight. Sucking the flames into me, I smothered the fire with a glance.

Men and women tripped over hastily abandoned belongings. Vicer stood on the table and began directing anyone within yelling distance to bring women and children to us.

Stillcrest stared at the chaos. "This isn't happening."

I barely refrained from taking the sword on my hip and burying it in her gut.

"It's happening. So *do something* before I kill you myself."

Her eyes met mine, and she seemed to break out of her lethargic shock. "We have evacuation points in place. But some of them are on the southern and eastern sides of the camp."

The directions the soldiers were approaching from. Anyone who headed that way would be the first to be cut down.

"We need to create a distraction on the eastern side of the camp to draw their attention while we get everyone away from those meeting points," Vicer said. "I'll make that happen. Madinia, you gather as many people as you can and get them out."

"I'll spread the word and tell everyone to head west," Stillcrest said.

Without another word, we sprinted in opposite directions. The orderly lines of tents were now being trampled as the realization sank into those who had assumed they were safe.

Shouts and screams cut through the air, the terror rising above the clatter of hastily gathered belongings. "Leave them," I snapped at a woman attempting to pack cooking supplies. I recognized her child from yesterday and thrust the wailing girl into her arms. "Run for your life. Now."

The blood drained from her face, and she swayed.

"You were right."

Fury and grief battled for supremacy. "Go."

She nodded, clutching her little girl to her chest, her hand buried in dark curls.

More children clung to the skirts of their mothers, their wide eyes dazed as their fathers kissed them one final time. A woman I'd trained with gave her baby to his father, kissed a child who couldn't have seen six winters, and pointed for them to go west, her sword already clutched in her hand, eyes dark with horror and grief.

Horses were panicking as people attempted to load them with supplies. One bolted, reins dangling as it galloped toward safety.

Panic clutched at my throat, until I could barely breathe. Darting toward a group of hybrids heading east, I grabbed one man's shirt, ducking as he swung at me, eyes wild. "To the west!" I roared, and people began to turn.

"To the northwest clearing!" I screamed again and again, until those around me took up the chant. Several elderly women stopped, only for the same man to grab each of their elbows and haul them with him as he turned and ran.

"You." I pointed at Tralia. "Get to the clearing behind camp and take as many people south as possible." I closed my eyes briefly, attempting to visualize Vicer's various routes. "When you get to the lake, head west along the trail until you reach a tree with a blue shirt wrapped around it." I opened my eyes to find her watching me, clearly memorizing what I was saying. "Listen to me. Take the shirt off the tree so there are no markings for those following you. That's where you'll leave the trail.

Turn left and keep moving for at least six hours until you find a small clearing with seven rocks in a line. Buried beneath the rocks, you'll find a warded chest with food, medical supplies, weapons, and blankets. You'll also find more instructions for the next stop. Repeat that back to me."

She repeated it, the woman next to her listening and nodding along.

"Take as many as you can. Go."

She was gone a moment later.

I had enough time to find two other people who would serve as leaders. They began calling names, directing hybrids toward them. And I gave them their own instructions. To our east, more screams began to sound, followed by the clash of swords. My limbs went numb.

Regner's guards were here.

I scanned the camp. People were moving too slowly. It wasn't their fault. Their instinct was to take whatever they could with them to make the journey easier. A man and woman were crouched, attempting to haul several dresses with them.

I set the dresses on fire.

"Run," I hissed as they dropped the dresses with a shriek.

Blank eyes met mine, right as the screams became louder.

They turned and ran.

Near the edge of camp, three children clutched at one another, trembling with fear. Sprinting toward them, I grabbed the hand of the eldest. She immediately latched on to me.

"Parents?"

"Father went to fight." Her lower lip trembled, and she shuddered, pale with shock. "I don't know where Mother is."

Already, several people had been crushed, unconscious and bleeding from the chaos. There was a chance her mother was one of them. "Take your sisters and follow that woman." I pointed. "Go."

The children were moving too slowly. "Faster," I hissed. "Sprint!" I felt like a monster as they glanced back at me, wide-eyed, but they picked up the pace.

There were still too many people here.

An old woman stood in the middle of the camp, her hand raised.

"What are you doing?" I called, grabbing several people and directing them west. They sprinted, lifting whoever they could carry.

"I have an attack power, child."

"You need to run."

Her lips trembled, her white hair parting with the wind. "This is the natural order of things. The old die first, protecting the young. Now, go."

My heart clenched, but I left the main clearing, sprinting into the tree line. The hybrids had been pushed back within a hundred footspans of the enemy. A group of guards were advancing on some of the hybrids who'd gone in the wrong direction, backing them against a thicket of trees. My power thrummed through me, and I snarled, aiming it at the guards close enough for me to reach. Some of them were too well warded for my fire to break through. But several burst into flames, the commotion providing distraction for our people to escape.

The hybrids were still losing. A young hybrid, no older than sixteen winters, lay crumpled against a tree, his hand still gripping his sword. His eyes, wide open, seemed to be seeking help from the gods. Nearby, an older woman screamed for someone over and over, eyes frantic. When she spotted the boy, she dropped to her knees and shook him, wailing.

A lump formed in my throat, but I couldn't let myself feel it. Forcing myself to go cold, I reached for the woman and hauled her to her feet, ignoring her weak slaps.

"Run," I hissed. "Or die with him."

She hiccupped, eyes wild. So I physically turned her with my hands until she was facing west, pushing her back until she stumbled away.

"Help!"

I darted back toward the guards. Hybrids with attack powers were using them, but it wasn't just Regner's usual guards here. I spotted several iron guards through the trees, their armor glinting in the dappled light. Gifted with an abundant supply of stolen power, they'd also been trained in death from the time they were old enough to pick up a sword.

I picked off as many as I could while making my way toward the meeting point in the clearing behind camp, in case there was anyone left. Stillcrest met me, her hands trembling, mouth a thin line. "Thank the gods," she said, clutching at me. "There are a group of hybrids trapped."

I tripped twice on tree roots and undergrowth, cursing viciously. Smoke curled toward us, thick, choking my lungs. Hybrids were screaming, gathered in groups as they backed away from the approaching iron guards less than a hundred footspans away, while flames roared toward them from the other direction.

Lifting my hands, I sucked the fire into me, starving it of the oxygen it needed. The hybrids didn't hesitate, sprinting toward the main clearing as soon as the flames were banked. "Kill the corrupt!" someone roared, and three iron guards barreled toward us, their black iron armor making them appear even larger than they were.

That iron was a good protection against my fire. But I aimed sparks at the spaces where their eyes were unprotected. They clawed at their faces, and Stillcrest stepped up next to me. She waved her hand.

Vicer hadn't told me what her power was, but several tree branches lifted from the ground, sweeping beneath the guards' feet and sending them crashing to the ground.

"Go," she said. "Get my people to safety."

"Where's Vicer?"

Something that might have been regret flickered across her face. "I don't know."

We stared at each other for one moment. If he was dead, it was this woman's fault. She knew it, I knew it, and there was nothing else to be said.

My gut twisted as I turned, running after the hybrids. A small boy was toddling hand in hand with an older girl, and I lifted him, holding him beneath one arm as I barked at her to run.

The old woman was still in the center of camp as the first iron guards broke through. I could drag her with me, force her to come...

But her expression had turned almost peaceful, the

look in her eyes unrelenting.

She looked at me. "Go."

"May the gods reward your sacrifice."

She merely nodded, lifting her hand.

I reached the tree line as the screams sounded, and I twisted my head just in time to see several of the iron guards clutching at their chests as the woman smiled. They dropped to their knees, then slumped to the ground.

An attack power indeed.

"Where is my father?" The girl sobbed, falling behind me. I grabbed her hand, hauling her faster.

"I don't know. Did you see where your mother went?"

"She died already," she choked out. "Last winter."

In my arms, the boy was still. I glanced down as we reached the meeting spot. Pupils blown. Shock. My chest ached, and I held him closer, giving what little comfort I could.

More hybrids were piling into the western meeting spot. By now, most of them would have joined other groups and left. But around twenty or so remained within the clearing.

"With me," I ordered. My breaths came in fast pants, my lungs and throat burning. Nearby, a heavily pregnant woman sobbed, holding a small child to her chest.

Burns covered one side of his body. He shuddered in her arms, eyes blank. Shifting the boy I held to my hip, I held out my other arm.

"What's your name?"

"Whirna."

"My name is Madinia. You can't run with him. Give

him to me, and I'll keep him safe."

She didn't argue, but tears streamed down her face as she handed him to me. If I lived through this, I would have to thank Demos for forcing me to carry heavy sandbags constantly while we were training.

By the time we were on the trail I'd scouted—the one Vicer had told me to take if I needed to get out—the sounds of screaming were closer than ever.

Several men stalked out of the forest toward us, weapons in their hands.

Screams ripped through the hybrids around me. My hand lit with fire, until I noticed their ears. Pointed.

"Who sent you?" I asked, just in case.

"Galon," the closest fae said. He had a strong, narrow face, and his hand gripped a broadsword so large, I doubted I would even be able to lift it. "Your camp leader sent us away. But we heard the screams."

Thank the gods for fae senses. The fae to the right ran his gaze over us, his eyes lingering on the burned boy in my arms. He'd begun moaning softly, his body trembling.

"Are any of you healers?" I asked hoarsely.

The fae's expression tightened with pity. "No. But I can send him to sleep to spare him the pain."

I glanced at the boy's mother, who nodded, mouth trembling.

"Run," one of the other fae said when it was done. "We'll buy you as much time as we can."

They would die here today. I knew it, and by the grim look in their eyes, they knew it too.

"Thank you."

The fae with the broadsword smiled at a young girl

who was whispering to one of the other children and pointing at his ears. "Get them to safety."

"I will."

They prowled toward the screams, and I gestured for my group to follow me.

Hybrids were dying, and I was fleeing. It left a bitter taste in my mouth. But I would keep these people alive. No matter what it took.

When we reached a clearing large enough for us to gather together, I placed both children on the ground and held up one hand to snag everyone's attention. Already, my arms ached. The pregnant woman leaned down and checked both children. Her son was still fast asleep. The smaller boy cried quietly, and one of the other women lifted him into her arms, giving me a nod.

"From now, I need silence," I said. "If the iron guards hear us, they'll kill us. I'll keep you alive as long as I can, but there's only one of me. Who else has an attack power?"

Several other women held up their hands, along with a couple of older boys. I'd hoped for more, but I wouldn't let them catch a single glimpse of my disappointment.

"We'll do whatever it takes to protect our children," one of the women snarled, her eyes hard. "Just lead us to safety."

"Okay. Keep them quiet. You," I snapped at a boy of around ten summers. "Sheath that knife while you're running. That goes for all of you. I don't want any accidents." Picking up the sleeping boy, I balanced him on my hip. "Let's go."

ASINIA

I'd known the moment the barrier went down. Some part of me had been convinced that Regner was dead and the war was over. And then Demos had reminded me of the human king's wards.

At least a third of the rebels in this camp were humans. When around half of those humans had begun screaming, I'd sprinted toward the main campfire, assuming we were under attack.

But they were happy screams. Those humans could suddenly access more of their power.

Now, days later, Tibris was healing everyone he could. Demos was back on his feet, and we would finally meet with Herne today. His response would determine our next move. In the meantime, Demos had been desperately sending message after message to any of his old contacts, attempting to discover if a man named Torinth was still alive.

Not long before Prisca and the others had left Aranthon, Madinia had sent us a message. Regner's wards were impenetrable—tied to the mirror gifted to humans by Faric. We needed to find a way to steal and destroy that mirror, but according to Jamic, Regner would keep it with him at every point.

Torinth was the one person who might be able to help us. His power? Diminishing personal wards.

If he wasn't alive...

I had absolutely no idea how we would kill Regner.

The sun was warm on my skin, a slight breeze playing with my hair as I walked toward the healer's tent. Tibris glanced up as I approached. He looked calm, relaxed even. But I'd never forget the restrained panic in his eyes when he'd seen the condition Demos was in after the attack.

"How is Demos?" he asked, clearly following my thoughts.

"The usual. He's training. Pretending he was never injured in the first place."

Tibris rolled his eyes, returning his attention to the concoction he'd been mixing.

"Will you come with us to talk to Herne?" I asked.

He measured out some kind of fragrant weed, raising one eyebrow. "You're hoping my presence will help?"

"I know it will."

"You may be surprised. Believe it or not, but Herne is usually more reasonable than you've seen since you arrived. It helps that Prisca and the others managed to bring the barrier down."

I pondered that. The truth was, we could no longer justify staying here. Now that Demos was able to travel, we had to leave. It was up to Herne to make sure his people were not defenseless.

Because if we left and this camp was wiped out... I wouldn't be able to live with myself.

"Asinia?"

I glanced up. A shadow had slipped across Tibris's face. He knew the stakes. He knew we had to leave—no matter how much we had come to care for the rebels.

And so, I changed the subject. "Speaking of power… you used to only be able to heal small wounds. But you managed to save Demos's life. Before the barrier came down."

Tibris gave me a faint smile. "It helped that Demos's power was working to heal him as well. But…some part of me wonders if perhaps I wasn't using my power to its full potential after my father died."

I winced at the reminder. Tibris had almost lost his own life while attempting to save his father. "You think you imposed some kind of limit on yourself?"

He shrugged. "Not necessarily a limit. More like a… subconscious protective constraint. But since I left our village, I've been forced to push my power as much as I possibly could—again and again. Now that the barrier is down?" His mouth twisted. "What I thought were the depths of my power were only the bare surface. I could have saved my father, Asinia. If Regner hadn't stolen this magic from me, I could have saved hundreds of lives over the years." His voice was bitter.

Rage battered my insides. So many lives lost.

I hoped Regner's most loyal people had enjoyed their horseless carriages.

Stuffing down my bitterness, I locked my shoulder muscles. "We'll make him pay, Tibris."

"I know. Some days, I think that thought is the only thing getting all of us through the horrors of this war." He wiped off his hands. "Well, let's go see what Herne says." He winked at me.

Together, we stepped out of the healer's tent, the light outside momentarily blinding after the restful dimness within.

The camp was a hive of activity, the air thick with the scent of the stew cooking over the fire and the sound of blades clashing in the distance as rebels trained for the looming battle.

A pigeon swooped above our heads, dropping from the sky and landing on Tibris's shoulder. He gently stroked it with one finger and freed the tiny piece of parchment it carried.

His face paled. "Conreth killed Lorian during the battle," he said. "Prisca used her power to turn back time and save him," he said hurriedly, grabbing my arm when I swayed on my feet.

"What—"

"Regner used his mirror to direct Conreth's power toward their ship. The ship exploded. Prisca almost died, and Telean is only alive because one of Daharak's pirates managed to save her." He crumpled the letter in his fist, then smoothed it out. "Eryndan is dead. Now, they need to bargain with Rekja if we are to have any hope of an alliance with the Gromalians."

Tibris was already turning, pulling me with him toward Herne and Demos. They stood at the edge of the camp, already deep in conversation. Herne's blond hair fluttered in the wind, the sharp planes of his face catching the light. Demos was a tall, dark shadow beside him, showing no signs he'd been wounded, his eyes scanning the forest as if looking for threats. Herne's own gaze was on his people. On the children running around the campfire, the mother who lifted one of them into her arms and tickled him, and the sentries who trudged out of the forest, coming off their shifts.

Tibris and I joined them, and Herne acknowledged us with a nod. Demos scanned both of us, his gaze lingering on me. Awareness prickled across my skin, and it felt as if the rest of the world disappeared.

"You're going to tell me that you need to leave," Herne said, breaking the spell.

Tibris handed Demos the message.

Demos read it, and his expression turned cold. "I have lingered here as long as I can. But I belong at the front, leading our people." He glanced at me, and now he was the hybrid general. "Asinia comes with me." Another glance at Tibris and his expression turned vaguely sympathetic. "You make your own choices."

I narrowed my eyes at Demos. I wanted to go to the front. Wanted to see Prisca and the others. But if he thought I was another soldier he could command...

I sighed. I longed to be treated like a soldier. Like someone who could contribute. And that meant taking orders. I couldn't have it both ways.

Herne was studying Tibris. He wasn't the kind of man who wore his feelings on his face. But his eyes glinted.

"I need to see my sister," Tibris said. "And...I need to tell her about you. About us."

Herne's mouth tightened, but he nodded.

Herne was...allowing it? I clamped down on my lower lip with my teeth, barely preventing my mouth from falling open. Herne's eyes met mine, and he angled his head.

"I can be reasonable. You are, after all, correct. Those beasts will return to kill all of us if they can."

"Will you evacuate?" Demos asked.

Herne sighed, and pity stirred in my gut. I knew what it was to cling to something, even if it was no longer truly an option.

"Yes," he said finally. "If you can guarantee a safe route for those who can't fight. I doubted you when you said the hybrid heir could bring down the barrier. But you've seen many of the people here celebrating that they can access more power." He gave me a rueful grin. "Not me. Perhaps my power is being stored elsewhere."

I fought the urge to ask what he could do. Next to Herne, Tibris practically glowed with pride. Something told me he was at least partially responsible for Herne's new ability to reason. My chest clenched at the thought of them being parted. This war was unrelenting.

"And will you fight by our side?" Demos asked Herne.

"Yes. But we will reinforce our traps first. This place is our home, and many would like to return."

One of Herne's most trusted people approached, a man named Frenik. His stern face lightened as he nodded at us, but he immediately held up a piece of parchment for Herne, who sighed. "Excuse me."

Tibris watched him go, and his hands fisted at his sides.

"You'll see him soon," I said softly. We're going to make sure of it.

"I hope so."

He said the words as if the likelihood was low. I frowned at him. "Prisca will be able to overlook the fact that you were shot here if you tell her how much you want to be with Herne."

His expression closed off. "I need to get back to the healer's tent."

"What was that about?" I muttered. It wasn't like Tibris to shut down like that.

Demos made a noncommittal sound. I turned to find him studying my face. Strangely, my cheeks heated under his attention.

"What is it?"

"Would you like to take a walk with me?"

It was already after the midday meal, which meant we'd leave tomorrow morning. We had enough time for this.

"Of course."

The forest seemed even more alive somehow— from the earthy scent that teased my nostrils to the tiniest insects I spotted crawling through the overgrowth. I caught a single glimpse of Vynthar as he wound between two trees, and then he was gone.

The Drakoryx came and went as he pleased. His favorite game was to frighten any sentries who seemed close to falling asleep on their shift. But I'd seen the fond looks most of the rebels gave him when he did deign to appear, more than willing to be fed and stroked. It made all of us feel safer knowing he was stalking through these woods, searching for any scents that might not fit.

This wasn't my first walk alone with Demos. In fact, we had a route we usually took. A route that allowed him to keep an eye on the sentries and make sure everyone was alert and in the correct place. After the way we'd managed to sneak up on this camp, he'd practically taken over security matters—something even Herne hadn't been stubborn enough to refuse.

"Have you heard anything about Torinth?" I asked.

Pure devastation flickered across Demos's face, almost too quickly for me to see it. I was so busy looking at him, my heel wobbled as I stepped onto a broken branch, and he caught my arm, instantly steadying me.

He stroked his thumb over the back of my wrist before letting his hand drift away. "I'm attempting to contact anyone who might know where he is. But... there's a chance he won't come, Asinia."

"Even knowing his power might be the only chance we have to take down Regner?"

Demos studied a group of yellow wild flowers growing near the base of a huge oak. "I would like to believe he is the man I remember. But *I'm* not the man I remember." Demos let out a bitter laugh.

It was difficult to imagine, given what I'd seen from everyone I loved so deeply. All of them had put aside their own dreams and goals, their own wants and needs. All of them had sacrificed everything they could. And would sacrifice more.

"We'll tell him everything," I said. "We'll let him know he is our only chance."

"Even knowing I'll do whatever it takes to make him work with us, I don't want him to join us out of guilt. I want him to join us because he has hope."

It was intimate, seeing this side of Demos. He would indeed do whatever it took to get what we needed. He could be logical to the point of ruthlessness. But this side of him... I imagined it was the person he used to be, before he was arrested. Before everyone he loved was put to death.

I reached for his hand. Demos tensed but linked his fingers with mine. His hand was so large and warm, it was likely a mistake allowing myself to feel it clasping my own.

"Tell me about Torinth," I said, pushing the thought away.

"We called him Tor," he said, his voice rough. "Back then, he was almost like a brother to me. He lived close to us in Crawyth. The night it was destroyed, the night Prisca was taken and my parents died, his sister was also killed. She was all he'd had. His parents perished during the invasion. Tor was never bitter, though. He was the kind of boy who would laugh at your worst jokes and then give you his last bite of food. He drew people to him."

My eyes stung. I could almost see the two boys running wild as children.

"We grew up together as neighbors. And after Crawyth, we were raised together in the same house with other hybrid orphans. When...when I told him who I really was, he shrugged." Demos laughed. "He said my name would be good for only one thing in those days—convincing hybrids to trust me long enough to get them out of Eprotha. And so, we did. Until that night, when we were betrayed. Torinth was always late. That night was no different, and it saved his life. I saw him as I was being dragged out. He was running toward us—I don't know what he thought he was going to do, but he would've died. Our friend Greon roared at him to run. And he did. To this day, I don't know if Tor was caught and killed—or if he managed to stay free. All I know is I didn't hear of him in Regner's dungeon."

"What makes you think he won't come?"

"I got everyone we loved killed, Sin. I was the one who'd chosen that meeting place. And they were there because they believed in me."

It was no use attempting to argue with him now. He had that stubborn look in his eyes.

"I…I can't understand how you lasted so long in that place," I said. "I think I would have curled up and given in to death. Welcomed it, even."

He slowly shook his head. "No, you wouldn't have. Even when you were hours from death, your body was fighting it. But me? I begged for death to claim me every day. And always, the dark gods ignored my pleas."

My heart galloped in my chest. The thought of Demos dying alone in that place, the thought that he wouldn't have been there when I arrived…

"I'm glad the gods ignored you."

He let out a humorless laugh. "At first, I prayed for death because I thought I might see the others again. And then I realized they were unlikely to want to see me, even in the afterlife. So, I prayed to be taken to Hubur, where at least I might forget."

It hurt, knowing how broken he had been. Knowing that some part of him was still broken. "Of course they would want to see you, Demos."

His hand released mine, and he shoved it through his hair. "They…screamed for me," he said hoarsely. "As they were dragged past my cell. They trusted me to keep them alive. Many of them believed—up until their final moments—that I had some kind of plan in place. That I was going to get them out. And all I could do was sit in that cell and watch as they were led to their deaths. They were my friends. My family."

My breath hitched. Demos had lost them all. And then he'd remained in that cell for almost an entire year after they'd died. He'd said little to me when I'd first arrived. A few growled instructions to eat, but mostly, he'd ignored me.

Because why would he want to get to know another person who would die?

But then he'd met Prisca. And he'd learned who she was. I'd watched, day by day, as the rage in him had burned so deep, I'd wondered how it hadn't melted through the fae iron surrounding us.

He'd made me talk, even when I'd wanted nothing more than to give in to grief and depression. He'd encouraged me to tell him about my mother, about our village. I'd told him about Prisca...

"You saved my life," I said.

He shook his head.

"You did. You want to know why the gods ignored you when you begged them for death? Because you had more work to do. You've already saved so many lives, and you're going to save more. You're going to help Prisca take our people home."

He gave me a faint smile, taking my hand once more. We walked in silence for a while, until we'd looped back around toward the camp.

"I know you think I'm overprotective and domineering," he said, making it clear he'd noticed my reaction to his declaration I would be leaving with him. "I'm...I'm going to do better, Sin. I promise."

I didn't know what to say to that, so I lifted his hand, pressing a kiss to the back of it. His eyes darkened.

I understood Demos more than I ever had before. He had been forced to watch the people he was supposed to protect die. They'd offered him their trust, their allegiance, their friendship. And he blamed himself every day for their deaths.

Now, if we were lucky and Tor was still alive—and willing to help us—Demos would be forced to face that past once more.

I just hoped it wouldn't tear him apart.

5

THE QUEEN

"Are you sure about this, Your Majesty?"

I pulled the hood of my cloak lower over my head as the sea breeze delved beneath my clothes. Just footspans away, a dockhand argued with a fisherman, while several whores called to a group of soldiers from the window of a brothel. Pelysian had managed to get us back to Lesdryn far more quickly than the route I'd originally taken. But most of our trip had been consumed by him arguing against my returning to the castle.

Pelysian frowned. "You know I will not be able to help if something goes wrong."

I nodded. The twin to the mirror in my bedroom—while warded to only accept the blood of either of our lines—was too far for Pelysian to get to. The hovel his mother lived in was over a day's ride away, so he wouldn't be able to get to her mirror and into my chambers that way.

Any attempt to sneak him into the castle would simply draw too much attention.

"I will be in the castle for hours at most," I said. "By now, the guards would have told Sabium of the fire at the market. You said you have found a merchant who has agreed to our alternative series of events."

And still, my heart thundered at the thought of all that could go wrong. When I'd boarded that ship with Nelia, I had never imagined I would return to Sabium's castle.

He sighed. "Yes. In return for a better life. But I don't need to tell you this is a huge risk. If you would wait a few days, I could speak with my mother and ask what she sees."

I shook my head. The risk was great, yes. But the grimoire... The grimoire would change everything.

"A few days will be too long. Questions would be asked about my injuries and why the castle wasn't notified. My understanding is that removing this so-called grimoire from Sabium's possession could be the blow needed to end this war. Unless you misspoke?"

"No." Silence stretched between us, and his frown deepened. Did he suspect I wanted the grimoire for myself? If so, he would do whatever it took to make sure that didn't happen.

I let my gaze drop to the ground. "It's not just a case of revenge. It's...it's for Nelia. She gave her life for me. For us. She would want the bloodshed to end. If we'd known such a grimoire existed, both of us would have worked to find it long before now."

I kept my voice free of blame. But when I lifted my eyes, I caught the guilt and grief in Pelysian's eyes.

Yes. Feel that guilt. Perhaps if we had known just how valuable Sabium's little book was, neither of us would have gone to that mine. We would have focused our attention on finding that book, and Nelia would still be alive.

I let Pelysian drown in his guilt for a long moment, enjoying the way his eyes darkened.

"These are called consequences, Your Majesty." That was what he'd said when Nelia died.

Now, he could suffer the *consequences* of keeping important information from me. Hopefully, he would learn from such a difficult lesson.

According to our spies, Sabium would have guests for dinner. Important guests. Our spies hadn't been able to tell us exactly who those guests were, but the servants were busy arranging for a formal dinner. Which would buy me time.

Even Sabium wouldn't slice my throat between courses. Not in public.

Things were different now. No longer did I need to play nice with Sabium to stay alive. He'd taken my dignity, my freedom, my *son*. And now, I would take that grimoire from him and wield its dark power myself.

If everything went according to plan, I wouldn't need help to escape the castle. Sabium would be the one screaming as he bled his life away.

"In that case, may the gods be with you." Pelysian nodded at me. His movements were stiff. Since the moment Nelia had died, he'd spoken only when necessary, barely meeting my gaze—unless he was arguing about my choice to return to the castle.

As if her death were my fault, when I'd *told* her to leave.

I didn't bother with goodbyes, simply turned and

stalked toward the closest guard. From there, everything went as planned.

The guard was ecstatic to be the one who found Sabium's missing queen. Of course, my husband didn't bother visiting my rooms himself when I returned to the castle, but that was to be expected. And it was most definitely preferred.

I spent several long minutes walking those rooms. The rooms I'd been so sure I wouldn't see again.

Pelysian had described the grimoire in detail. And I remembered seeing it that day Sabium took the mirror. He wouldn't be stupid enough to hide it in his private library or in the hidden chamber beneath his rooms—the one he likely thought remained a secret. He wouldn't keep it in his rooms either.

The hybrid heir had used Madinia to destroy the castle sanctuary, and it was currently being rebuilt. So it wouldn't be hidden there.

No, there were three places it was likely to be. In the royal treasury, within the royal crypt, or on Sabium's person.

If it was the last option…

No. He would be foolish to keep it with him throughout the day when anyone could see it and become curious. If he really did refuse to allow it out of his sight…

I would have to accept the inevitable. But I had to try. I could almost feel the immense power and knowledge of the grimoire calling to me.

After a long bath, I allowed one of the maids to help me dress, noting the cool, silky feel of the silk, the plush sensation of velvet. Just one day in the clothes of the poor and I suddenly had a new appreciation for my own clothes. I waved her away, stomach churning as I considered my first move.

The crypt would be the easiest to visit. So I started there.

Unlike the graveyard Sabium had continually threatened me with, the royal crypt was well visited by those who mourned the kings who'd come before him. Not for the first time, I wondered which unlucky stand-in had been killed and disguised as each of Sabium's ancestors over the centuries.

Tucked away in a secluded copse on the outskirts of the royal gardens, the crypt was a place of reverence. The entrance was marked by an ivy-covered archway, chiseled from stone older than the castle itself. Weathered by time, the arch bore intricate carvings of the royal lineage. Did Sabium find such things amusing? Knowing him as well as I did, I found it likely that he would smile each time he visited this place, enjoying his lies.

The air was cooler inside the crypt, its vaulted ceilings a tapestry of stone. Beneath that ceiling, stone-covered slabs lay in a row, adorned with effigies of kings sculpted with such precision that it felt as if they might sit up and draw breath at any moment. Light orbs flickered over the gold and gems inlaid in the stone.

I stepped closer to the "resting places," my gaze lingering on Regner, Crotopos, Aybrias, Hiarnus, and finally, the place reserved for Sabium.

My pulse raced as I swept my hands over stone, searching for any kind of hidden cache, a lock to be opened, or a ward hiding the grimoire.

Nothing.

I continued to search, until I was covered in a thin layer of dirt and dust from crawling across the stone floor, unwilling to risk missing even the tiniest clue. Frustration inched along my spine. Perhaps searching the crypt first was a mistake. My spies would have reported back to me if Sabium had been seen visiting it often.

Dusting myself off as best I could, I exited the crypt. It had been early enough when I'd arrived that few people were in the gardens. Now, I was continually greeted, curious gazes meeting my own as courtiers asked about my health, hoping for the smallest shred of gossip.

I repeated my story again and again, hoping I'd removed most of the dust and cobwebs from my gown. My story remained consistent, never straying from the same details. By the time I swept past the fourth group to greet me, I was grinding my teeth.

The grimoire had to be in the treasury. If it wasn't…

No. It made sense for Sabium to keep it there. After all, it had only been recently that I'd learned of its existence. I would have noticed him carrying a book with him everywhere throughout the blisteringly long years of this false marriage.

Unlike the crypt, the treasury was guarded. The guards lounged against the stone walls, straightening when I approached.

"Your Majesty."

I nodded at them, and the guard to the right took a key, unlocking the heavy gold door. He hesitated, glancing over his shoulder at me. "Can I help you find something, Your Majesty?"

"No." I forced a smile. "I merely wish to select a suitable ruby to replace one that became loose from my bracelet."

It was a weak excuse, but he nodded, his gaze lingering on the heavy gold necklace I wore. "Of course."

Sweeping into the vast room, I waited until the door clicked shut behind me. Textures and colors engulfed me, pressing on my senses. The treasury had no windows, and the air was heavy, musty, tinged with the faint scent of old gold and ancient scrolls, intermingling with the subtle fragrance of cedar wood lining the walls.

I ignored the chests overflowing with jewels, the ancient armor from battles long won and lost, and the gold bars stacked taller than my body and sprawling across a space larger than Sabium's ballroom.

Instead, I moved straight for the shelves of ancient books and scrolls.

These were the books that wouldn't be found in any library. The books that contained histories of this world that scholars would kill one another to get their hands on.

I searched every bookcase, peering behind stacks of scrolls and running my hands along the wood of each shelf, searching for any concealed hiding places.

My chest grew tight, my jaw ached from the clenching of my teeth, and I began my third search of the books.

The door opened, and I whirled.

"Tymedes."

He gave me a slow smile. "And what are you doing down here, Your Majesty?"

Icy fingers slid around my throat. We wanted each

other dead. That had never been in question. And from the malice in his eyes, he was hoping he could make my death happen.

I forced myself to sniff dismissively. "Why should I not visit the treasury? I am, after all, queen."

His smile widened. "His Majesty will be looking for you," he said, and a trickle of sweat slid down my spine. "There will be guests for dinner."

"Fine." I was finished here anyway. With a last glance at the treasury, I strode down the hall, ignoring Tymedes's steps behind me.

Perhaps Nelia would know something about this dinner.

I froze.

"Something wrong, Your Majesty?" Tymedes's tone was even more of a taunt than usual.

Ignoring him, I continued walking. Nelia would know nothing. Her face flashed through my memory, eyes blank, staring accusingly at me. Gritting my teeth, I thrust the image away. I'd told her to flee.

I found Lisveth waiting outside my rooms, and her mouth dropped open as her gaze clung to my face like a child clinging to its mother's skirts. "Your Majesty! We were so worried."

There was something strangely comforting about her face—still seemingly incapable of hiding her thoughts. I waved her into my rooms, and she rang the bell that would call the others.

I allowed it. This might, after all, be the last time I saw them.

If I told them to run, they would question me. And

if they knew I was leaving, Sabium's truth-seekers would learn such information the moment I left. No, their ignorance would keep them safe.

Safer than Nelia.

And still...

"I was injured at the market. My guards left me to put out the fire. Thankfully, one of the merchants helped, but I was unconscious until he could find a good healer."

I rattled off the story, nodding at a maid, who turned to find me a clean gown. When she returned with two options, I gestured to the one in her left hand. A deep, unrelenting red.

My ladies returned as the maid was lacing the back of the gown.

Lisveth happily repeated my story, and I ignored the crease of Pelopia's brow, the questions in Caraceli's eyes.

"I believe the king has missed you, Your Majesty," Alcandre said as the maid finished my hair. "Each night, he spends several hours reading and writing in his diary. I'm sure he scrawls his love for you."

My eyes met hers.

Something had made Alcandre emboldened. While Lisveth had allowed the terror of this place to drain the life from her face and the fat from her body, Alcandre seemed to have used it to harden herself. She was brasher. Fiercer. For the first time, I wondered what she might have been like as a true ally.

Everyone in this room knew Sabium held no love for me. I surveyed her, standing in a new gown, a jeweled bracelet dangling from her wrist. A *new* bracelet.

I almost smiled. Alcandre was fucking my husband.

And she was taunting me with it.

But she'd unwittingly helped me.

I allowed a hint of color to rise to my cheeks, even as I glanced away dismissively and then back at her, as if I couldn't help myself.

"He writes about me?" I asked tentatively.

"I would assume so, Your Majesty. It really is adorable. The only place he's without it is his bath!"

Lisveth sighed. "That is so romantic."

No one else spoke. Pelopia stared at Alcandre as if she had never seen her before. Everyone except idiotic Lisveth knew what Alcandre was doing by demonstrating such an intimate knowledge of Sabium's nighttime habits.

I gave her a nod, allowing her to see her point had been made. Victory and fury warred in her eyes.

Alcandre's new attitude proved I hadn't been paying enough attention to my ladies. She had spotted an opportunity to claw at some power and had taken it—I couldn't blame her for that. In fact, some part of me was proud.

But while she thought she was humiliating me by climbing into Sabium's bed, the reality was quite different.

I would need to wait until Sabium was bathing. That would be my only opportunity to take the grimoire.

Lisveth's smile had fallen. It was clear she now knew exactly how Alcandre was taunting me. Her face flushed, and she gazed at the floor.

I rolled my eyes. "I must go dine with my husband." Alcandre tensed at that, and I was small enough to enjoy it. "It's a private dinner," I purred. "So I will see all of you tomorrow."

I arrived to the dining room exactly on time, and yet I was the last to walk in. Two men sat across from Sabium. Both of them had attempted to dress as royalty, but the first man's cloak, though a vibrant shade of crimson, was made of a fabric that lacked the depth and sheen of true velvet, and it hung a little too loosely on his shoulders.

His doublet, while intricately embroidered, featured patterns that were a tad too garish, with the gold threads overly bright. His circlet, though golden, was too thick to suit him, and sat awkwardly on his head.

The second man's robe of emerald silk was too shiny, suggesting a poor quality of silk. The silver embroidery was overdone, and his vest was buttoned unevenly, giving him a disheveled look. The ceremonial dagger at his belt was overly ornate, bordering on theatrical.

Idiots.

Slowly, I walked to the empty chair as a servant pulled it out for me.

"My queen, Kaliera." Sabium's eyes met mine. I searched his face but saw nothing more than the same amused disinterest I'd seen for years. "And this is Zathrian." He waved his hand toward the man in the crimson cloak sitting across from him.

I knew that name. How did I know that name?

"The true ruler of the hybrid kingdom," Sabium continued, and I went still.

Zathrian's resemblance to Prisca was evident around his mouth and chin. But his eyes were cold.

I had spent most of my life anticipating Sabium's decisions. And yet, I couldn't have anticipated this.

He hated the fae. But he *loathed* the hybrids. He

still ranted about his once-spectacular capital city and the bitch queen who had spent her last moments ensuring it would be forever cursed.

Deep down, his loathing was hiding fear. Which made him all the more dangerous.

I took my seat. Zathrian raised his cup in my direction. "Majesty."

His casual demeanor irritated me, and I kept my expression blank as I nodded at him, turning my attention to the man at his side in the poor-quality silk.

He was a well-groomed, attractive man with eyes so dead, it was as if I were looking at a corpse.

"And this," Sabium said, his voice lowering dangerously, "is Eadric. The man responsible for my spider's death and the hybrid heir's escape."

Zathrian's mouth twisted and then straightened. It was a movement so quick I almost missed it. He didn't like Prisca being referred to as the hybrid heir. Sabium's cold smile told me he'd caught it too.

"Apologies have been given and accepted," Zathrian said, his expression neutral.

Sabium nodded at Eadric. "I still want him punished."

Amusement glinted in Eadric's eyes, and he sipped his wine.

Why did he not seem at all fearful of Sabium?

"He has already been punished," Zathrian said. "Need I remind you that you were unaware Eadric was mine? I was kind enough to share that information with you."

My heart stopped. Sabium prided himself on his ability to slip his own people into foreign courts and to turn the most loyal in those courts to his side. But Zathrian had done the reverse to him, sneaking Eadric in among his people.

Soon, both men would be very, very dead. But clearly, Sabium could see some benefit to working with Prisca's cousin in the short term.

Even I had to admit it was a good plan.

"And yet, there is something much more important to discuss," Sabium said. "Your failure to kill the Bloodthirsty Prince."

"*Our* failure," Zathrian said mildly, although fury burned in his eyes. "You told me your little mirror would work."

"It did work. You were supposed to prevent that bitch from freezing time and saving her lover. Instead, the barrier fell, the power returned to the people, and my son is currently a captive, with no hope of release."

My breath almost caught in my throat. My blood had turned to ice, my face turning numb. But I forced myself to keep my expression neutral.

Zathrian angled his head, watching me closely, and I raised one eyebrow, forcing myself to take a bite.

"I want him back," I said. Let them think I was nothing more than a concerned mother.

Eadric's eyes met mine. He'd seen me tremble. I wanted to bare my teeth at him. Instead, I gave him a mild look and turned my attention back to Sabium.

"I think we both know your son is no captive, Your Majesty," Zathrian said.

Sabium's face slowly whitened with rage. I didn't move. I barely breathed.

"Regardless," Sabium bit out. "I would like to know exactly how they are still alive."

Zathrian winked at Sabium. "Because my dear cousin broke the rules. She didn't just stop time. She turned it backward. And she used enough power to prevent me from stopping her." The mocking expression drained from his face, and his words were coated with bitterness. "She shouldn't have survived. Such magic is forbidden for a reason."

Eadric's eyes had darkened, his hand clenching around his fork. My own hands began to sweat. That amount of power...honed until it was blade-sharp...

No wonder Sabium was furious. The populace would rally behind that kind of power.

Sabium leaned back in his seat. "One of my spies caught a glimpse of her on one of Rostamir's ships. She did survive. Could she use this kind of power again?"

Zathrian instantly shook his head. "It is a defiance of the gods for her to have used it even once. They will be paying attention to her now. Likely, it required a piece of her soul to achieve it the first time." Zathrian held up a piece of parchment, raising one eyebrow. Not long ago, Prisca had given me that exact cool, dismissive look. The similarity was eerie. "Now, let us talk about this."

Sabium scanned it, his eyes cold. "My armies are handling it. There is no threat."

Zathrian stroked his chin. "If you don't understand how the rumblings of rebellion can destabilize a kingdom at war—and destroy morale in an army—then we have a problem."

The room went silent.

"My soldiers have made my position clear. Any who abandon the ranks will have their families killed soon after." Sabium hadn't looked at me since we'd sat down, but he glanced at me now. "And what do you think, my queen?"

My heart beat in my throat. I raised my hand to cover the pulse point in my neck, pretending to toy with my hair. "I think our armies can easily handle any such rumblings."

Sabium flashed his teeth in an expression that could never be called a smile. "Precisely."

He was giving me his full attention now. And that same terror I'd felt standing next to Pelysian came flooding back.

He knew I'd disappeared from the market. He hadn't bothered asking where I'd been. It was unlikely anyone at the mine would have recognized Nelia, but he might know she hadn't returned to her duties here.

I had to find the grimoire and leave tonight. And if I couldn't find it, I would still need to flee for my life.

I should never have come back here.

LORIAN

The back of my neck itched, and I glanced around, feeling as if someone was watching me yet again. My fae senses roared at me, and yet each time this happened, I was forced to admit that no one was there.

Occasionally, I heard the hiss of a low, taunting voice. Other times, the voice was familiar.

Prisca watched me closely as we returned to the larger cabin Daharak had made available for meetings. We'd taken a brief stroll on the deck, and my wildcat had a pleasing flush to her cheeks.

A flush that gave me all kinds of ideas.

But the moment the door closed, Prisca faced me fully.

"What is it, Lorian?"

"What do you mean?"

"You've been acting a little strangely over the past few days. As if you're on edge."

As much as my instincts urged me to protect her from any further stress, any potential worry, she deserved better than that. "Can you...feel someone or something watching you?"

She glanced around, wide-eyed.

And just like that, the feeling of being watched disappeared.

"Not at this moment," I said. "Just...in general. Since the barrier."

We stepped into the cabin. I swept my gaze around it. No one lurking behind the desk in the corner. No one hiding beneath the small table in the middle of the room.

And yet unease still tightened my muscles.

"No," Prisca said. I turned to find her chewing on her lower lip, and I instantly regretted speaking. "Do you think it's one of the gods? Watching you?"

Some part of me wondered if that was exactly what

it was. One of the gods taking too much of an interest in me now that I had cheated death. In that case, I hoped I kept their attention. Anything to keep them from focusing on Prisca.

"Are you ready for this meeting, wildcat?"

She narrowed her eyes but allowed the change of subject. "Yes."

While Demos was making as many decisions as possible regarding our soldiers, he was still in the rebel camp, which meant delays as pigeons traveled back and forth.

Since Demos wasn't the type to hoard power or information, he'd ensured several ranked hybrids were able to take over some of that decision-making.

And while Prisca was recovering, I'd arranged for one of them to travel to us.

Prisca opened her mouth, but a knock sounded on the door. Leaning over, I opened it, stepping back so the two men could enter. Outside, Marth gave me a nod.

Prisca had met with Blynth briefly in the hybrid camp—a quick introduction as he'd arrived, around the time she'd been secretly preparing to travel to Lyrinore. But I didn't recognize the shorter man at his side.

The hybrid general seemed to be made of unyielding sternness, his presence commanding attention in any room he entered. His face was etched with deep lines, his eyes a piercing gray that seemed almost impatient with the formalities of rank.

I could relate to that impatience.

His hair was peppered with silver, neatly combed back, as he stood ramrod straight, hands clasped behind his back. His mouth was set in a firm line. His body language projected both strength and reliability.

Exactly what we needed.

"Your Majesties." He bowed his head to both of us.

Prisca nodded back at him. For once, she didn't ask him to call her Prisca. For her generals, she needed to be Nelayra, queen of the hybrids. "Thank you for traveling to meet us."

"A pleasure. I was sorry to hear you were unwell." He said the words as if they were rote, his gaze drifting over her as if determining whether she was now healthy enough to go to war.

She kept her own gaze steady on his face. "Thank you."

"This is Jorvik, my aide."

His aide... "What happened to Thorge?" I asked.

Grief flashed across Blynth's face as he glanced at me, almost too fast to see, as his expression settled back into those unyielding lines. But the groove between his eyes was deeper now.

"He was killed in a battle with Regner's iron guards almost as soon as we left the fae lands."

"I'm sorry," Prisca said.

He nodded, clearly uncomfortable with the subject. Next to him, Jorvik bowed his head, a stark contrast to the imposing general. Jorvik had a youthful face, his hair a vibrant chestnut falling over bright, keen eyes, and a charming smile.

I didn't like him. At all. And I could sense Prisca's unease. I took a step closer to her, and Blynth glanced between us. "Is there a problem, Your Majesty?" He addressed her.

Goose bumps broke out on her arms. I opened my mouth, but Prisca's eyes had turned intent.

"Yes," she said, "there is a problem." She stepped closer to Jorvik, and I barely refrained from dragging her back toward me. "Who are you?"

Blynth frowned, turning his attention to Jorvik.

Slowly, Jorvik raised his arms. "That was fast, Your Majesty. Your cousin made it seem like you were somewhat...challenged when it came to intelligence."

Prisca smiled at him. His face lost some of its color, and he suddenly seemed much younger than his years.

I lunged, wrapping my hand around Jorvik's throat... just as the tip of Blynth's dagger found Jorvik's pulse point. "Tell me this treachery isn't the reason Thorge is dead," he demanded.

"I can't do that."

Prisca stepped up close to me. A fine trembling began to take over her body. It wasn't terror.

Zathrian had twenty thousand hybrids ready to march on us. And now this?

"What does he want?"

"For me to give you a message." Jorvik swallowed, and a bead of blood appeared at the end of Blynth's dagger.

"Speak," I said, and he began to shake. As if it had only just occurred to him exactly how much danger he was in. He had assumed that Prisca was weak, half dead, and presented no true threat.

He took a deep, shuddering breath and looked Prisca in the eye.

"Tell the elders you cede the crown to Zathrian—or die."

6

PRISCA

"How did this happen?" I asked Blynth, my throat tight.

Marth had dragged Jorvik away, stashing him out of my sight while we discussed our next move. Zathrian had once again proven that he could easily get close to me whenever he wanted.

Lightning flickered in Lorian's eyes, and even Blynth looked disconcerted by the sparks rising from his skin.

"It's a power play, meant to frighten you," Blynth said. "But it tells us one thing. Your cousin doesn't truly believe he can take the crown by force. And clearly, the hybrid elders are no longer enchanted by the idea of his ruling."

They may not be enchanted with my cousin, but if they ever learned I'd turned back time, any support they might have given us would be gone. I glanced at Lorian, and he met my eyes steadily. No, we wouldn't tell them. And neither would any of our people.

But which of the elders had switched sides? The last I'd heard, I'd only had Ysara and Tymriel.

We were all sitting around the small

table, cups of wine in our hands. Jorvik's betrayal had accomplished one thing—all formality had disappeared between us.

Lorian's expression was hard. "If he'd gotten her alone, he could have assassinated her."

"You have my sincere apologies. This never should have happened. If I may...Nelayra." Blynth folded his hands on the table. I'd convinced him to drop the formal address while we were in private, but I was no longer fighting my birth name. Nelayra was the hybrid heir. It was Nelayra whom the hybrids would go to war for. "This is a taunt," he said. "Your cousin doesn't think you'll hand over the crown, no matter what he does. But he did it to show you he can get close. To throw you off your stride. To make you feel unsafe."

Zathrian had achieved all of those things.

Blynth studied my face, and I wondered what he could see.

Beneath the table, Lorian reached for my hand and squeezed. "How much does Jorvik know of our plans?"

Blynth carefully considered this, as he seemed to carefully consider everything. "He was only given the position as my aide because we were already on the move and Thorge was dead. He has the appropriate rank, but before this, he didn't have access to any war plans or knowledge of our troops."

"I'll give him to Marth," Lorian said. "He will be able to learn exactly what Jorvik has shared. In the meantime, let's discuss what will happen next."

It was my turn to squeeze his hand in a silent thank-you. I hadn't realized how shaken I was until this very moment. But Lorian knew. And he was giving me a moment to recover.

Blynth didn't argue, simply reached into one of the large satchels he had traveled with and pulled out a map, which he spread out on the table between us.

"Regner's ships were as far south as they could anchor while still remaining in Eprothan waters," he said, gesturing to the area. "They've now disappeared."

"Disappeared?"

He nodded. "Regner must have ordered them north. I just can't understand why. Meanwhile, his regiments are positioned throughout Eprotha, moving closer to the Gromalian border."

"Now that Eryndan is dead, he's going to try to take Gromalia," Lorian said. "Then he'll work his way down to the fae lands, which are fractured—with only some of the wardens cooperating with us. He'll wield the last amulet, taking down our wards with stolen power and brute force."

"With Rekja's army fighting on their own borders and in their seas, they won't be able to spare anyone to fight with us," I said. "Regner doesn't even truly need to conquer Gromalia—he just needs to ensure the kingdom is incapacitated, the Gromalian armies busy protecting their own people. And then we'll be forced to fight in the fae lands. Alone." Icy rage swept through me. How many people would die before he was done?

"Meanwhile, Zathrian will attempt to take the hybrid kingdom. He has taken your army and will use it to attack any who prevent him from becoming king. Including you and any hybrid who allies with you," Lorian said grimly.

"As soon as Regner feels he has adequately conquered Gromalia and weakened the fae, he will target our people—turning on Zathrian."

A heavy silence claimed the room. As much as all of us wanted Zathrian to pay, it was the hybrids fighting under his flag who would suffer.

"One of the hybrid elders has agreed to contact Orivan. One of Zathrian's generals," I said.

Blynth's brows shot up. "I know Orivan. He's a good man—and a loyalist. Before this, I never would have imagined he would follow your cousin. I will attempt to send him a message as well. Hopefully he can be persuaded to listen."

Would I try to steal Zathrian's army—*my* army—out from beneath him?

Without hesitation.

"Thank you, Blynth."

"We need Demos," Blynth said. "Not to imply that you're not necessary, Your Majesty," he said quickly. "But—"

I shook my head. "I understand. Demos has a deep knowledge of our people, our army, and the tactics most likely to work. And sending messages back and forth to him is simply taking too long."

If Demos, Tibris, and Asinia hadn't managed to convince the rebels to join with us by now—after the attack they'd experienced—they likely were not going to be able to. And we were running out of time. The reality was, they couldn't stay wth the rebels indefinitely. My mind went quiet, and the churning in my gut eased. The thought of having all of them back with me, even just for a little while… "I'll ask Demos to meet us after our visit to Sorlithia."

Blynth nodded. "Thank you."

The absence of Regner's fleet made heat simmer through my veins. Where was he? What was he planning?

We'd heard nothing from Kaliera either. Had Regner learned of her betrayal? Was she dead? Truthfully, I doubted there was much she could tell us now. At this point, she would only become a threat. Still, I didn't want to have to tell Jamic his mother was dead before he got to see her again.

"We need Rekja's armies," I said.

Lorian squeezed my hand. "I have some good news, at least. Conreth gave me full access to his generals."

"What?" Lorian had said they'd talked, but his eyes had been so cold, I hadn't asked him about the contents of that conversation.

Now, he nodded, his expression grim. "When we meet with the others after convincing Rekja to help, both fae and hybrid generals will be present."

Blynth nodded at the unspoken command. "I will ensure everyone we need is there." He hesitated. "And the hybrids in the fae lands?"

Some of the tension melted from the back of my neck at the reminder of who we were fighting for. "The moment the time is right, when we've dealt with any of Regner's soldiers hiding in the pass and when our armies are in position, the hybrids are going home."

Blynth's eyes met mine. "Some of them won't go. They won't trust it. They'll have too many memories of last time."

And he was one of them. I could tell by the way his jaw ticked. "I won't force anyone to go," I said gently. "But this is the best way to keep them safe. The pass is clear of snow. Unlike last time when our people were forced to flee, they will be properly clothed, carrying food and other supplies with them. And they will be guarded."

My chest ached at the expression on his face. It was something I'd seen time and time again from the hybrids. The tiniest glimpse of hope, ruthlessly suppressed.

"If you believe it can be done…"

"It can. I will make sure of it."

"I didn't want to serve you," Blynth said suddenly. Next to me, Lorian tensed, and it was my turn to squeeze his hand. "When I learned you were alive," the general continued. "I asked myself what you could possibly have to offer—a village girl who knew nothing of our history."

I wasn't surprised. I wouldn't have wanted to take orders from me either. And still, his words made me tired.

But he was still talking. "If you can achieve this…if you can truly bring our people home…I'll happily kneel to you for the rest of my life."

I attempted a smile, but it was likely more of a grimace. "We need to begin moving our people out of the fae lands and into Gromalia."

Blynth studied the map. "You're hoping Rekja will join you and his army will become ours."

"I'm hoping we will march together, yes."

"And what of the amulets?"

Lorian leaned back in his chair. "We have two of them. My brother has people searching in northern Eprotha for the third. We suspect Regner has hidden it in one of his mines. I am waiting to hear from Conreth, but we may send a group of our own."

Blynth nodded. Slowly, he got to his feet. "In that case, I will take my leave. I hope we can speak again soon, Nelayra."

I smiled at him. "Yes, of course."

The moment the door shut behind him, Lorian silently cupped my cheek. "I'm sorry he got so close. That I allowed him this close."

"Stop, Lorian. You didn't allow Zathrian to do anything."

My cousin had proven over and over exactly what kind of man he was—and the lengths he would go to for power.

But no matter what horrors came to pass, we would face them together. My heart rate steadied, and I pulled Lorian close.

As if reading my mind, he shifted his hand to my chin, tilting my head back until I met his eyes. "I need you to promise me that you will never risk your life like this again. That you'll never almost throw your own life away to save mine."

"I can't do that."

"Listen to me, wildcat. Our story doesn't end when this life does. You'll be mine in the next life—and the life after that. If you hadn't wielded time, I would have waited as long as it took to see you again."

Tears rolled down my cheeks. I heard what he was saying. But every time I closed my eyes, I saw the moment Conreth's power hit him. And the way his body had just... shattered. He was there, and then he wasn't. For a few sickening, awful moments, he had left me.

And out of all the darkest moments of my life, those were the worst.

He sighed at my silence, gently brushing away my tears.

"What am I going to do with you?"

I reached for him, guiding his mouth to mine. "Love me," I murmured against his lips. "Just love me."

He let out a rough groan, gently biting my lower lip before laving the tiny sting with his tongue. My knees weakened, and he pulled me closer, deepening our kiss, his tongue stroking against mine.

I breathed in the scent of him, basking in the feel of his arms around me. A moment later, he was pulling me out of the cabin, ignoring anyone who attempted to talk to us as he dragged me back to our own.

He slammed the door in Galon's face and immediately locked it. I let out a choked laugh.

"Lorian!"

"He can come back later."

He pulled me close, his quick fingers easily unlacing the ties holding my dress in place, until it was only held up by his chest plastered to mine.

The dress fell to the floor, and he lifted his head. Sliding my hands up his chest, I unbuttoned his shirt, taking a detour to smooth my palms over the bumps and ridges of his abdominals. I let one hand dip teasingly low, and Lorian shuddered, pressing against me.

Shucking off his shirt, he pushed me back onto the bed, grinning down at me when I gaped up at him in surprise. I hadn't even been aware that we were moving.

His smile was wide, disarming, with that hint of vulnerability—one that reminded me he wasn't used to making such a joyous expression.

I was going to fill his life with so much happiness and joy, until I got to see that smile every single day.

His smile faltered, but his eyes remained filled with life.

"What is it?"

When I first met Lorian, I'd never imagined he could look like this. So open and at ease, despite all the reasons he had to be bitter and furious.

Lifting my hand, I ran my thumb along his lower lip. "I like to see you smile, that's all."

Sarcastic smirks, wicked grins, and the cold, feral smiles he so often wore right before he hurt someone. Once, I'd thought that was all Lorian was.

"You make me smile," he said, nuzzling my palm.

He caught my hand with his, brushing his lips against the sensitive skin of my wrist. I shivered, and he kissed his way up my arm, finding the spots that made me squirm. The places that made my thighs clench.

Even my arm felt sensual when Lorian was the one paying it this kind of attention.

Slowly, methodically, he stripped my remaining clothes from me, pausing to nibble at my hip, to caress my breast, to kiss a path from my collarbone to my belly button. I shivered and arched and urged him on, but there was no rushing Lorian when he was in this mood.

My head spun, and I realized he'd rolled us. I grinned, leaning down to kiss my way across *his* chest, moving down, down—

"What—"

"Here," he said, having lifted me as if I weighed nothing. "I've fantasized about this."

I blinked down at him. He'd positioned me above his shoulders, a knee on either side of his head.

"Ride my face, wildcat."

My cheeks blazed so hot, it was as if they'd caught on fire.

Lorian laughed. For some reason, he still found it both amusing and enticing when he managed to embarrass me. I wasn't a prude, but compared to his long-lived fae sensuality, I was still catching up.

I shifted, and he wrapped his hands around my thighs. "Let me make you feel good."

"Like this?" I bit my lip as I looked down at him. I wasn't ashamed of my body. If anything, I was feeling particularly proud of it recently after all the training I'd been doing. But…no one looked good at this angle.

Lorian lifted his head and nipped my thigh. "Be filthy with me."

"I just—"

He sighed. "Perhaps I'm not being clear. I want you to sit on my face until all I can taste, all I can smell, all I can *feel* is you. Now."

"Who put you in charge?" I muttered, slowly lowering my hips. "Arrogant—ohh…"

He chuckled against me, using his hands to urge me closer as his tongue swept across my clit, dipping down to my entrance, where he lingered before dancing that clever tongue around the most sensitive part of me once more.

My head fell back, and I groaned.

Lorian's hands tightened at the sound, a growl leaving his throat and sending the most delicious sensation through me.

I shuddered, head spinning, my breath coming in ragged pants. He just increased his pressure, seemingly insatiable for the taste of me. I looked down, and his eyes were dazed with feral pleasure as they met mine. I clutched at his forearms, desperate for something to hold on to.

Every muscle in my body tensed, my thighs tightening. He lashed his tongue along my slit, teasing me, and I broke out in a sweat, stomach clenching, rocking my hips for more, more, more.

I realized I was moaning the word, right as he circled my clit and then *sucked*.

Arching my back, I drew in a single breath, thighs quaking. Pleasure rippled through my body, and I shuddered with it, coming apart so completely, it felt as if I would never be put back together.

When I opened my eyes, I had slumped over, and Lorian was watching me with a strange kind of contentment.

"More," he said.

I shook my head, throat dry. He just laughed.

"In that case…"

Lorian flipped us, positioning me on my hands and knees, ass in the air. Smoothing his hands over my butt, he made an appreciative sound.

His hard length pushed against my entrance, sliding inside me. I was still sensitive, and I squeezed down on him, enjoying his low grunt.

He thrust achingly slowly, then stopped, buried within me, brushing one hand down my back, gently caressing my skin.

I was still shaking, I realized, my muscles trembling from the most incredible climax of my life.

And yet the feel of him, so deep within me, his hands teasing my body...

"Does that feel good?" he purred, leaning close as he thrust again. "You're so fucking tight, wildcat."

My nipples tightened, and I rocked back into him, bucking, desperate for more.

He increased the pace, driving into me, sliding one hand under me, finding my clit.

The sound I let out was half yelp, half moan, and he laughed. "Good girl."

I was writhing now, but he kept the same steady speed, fingers drifting over my clit just enough to keep me on the edge.

"Lorian..."

"Something you want, Prisca?"

I tensed in an attempt to flip us over and take exactly what I wanted. He just laughed again. "I don't think so." His hands found my hips, and he slammed into me, until my breaths came in rough pants and all I could feel was him urging me higher and higher...

Warmth swelled through my body as his movements became faster, harder, almost violent.

I *reveled* in it.

My climax hit me like one of his lightning bolts, until all I could do was moan, my hands fisting in the blankets beneath us. Lorian continued thrusting, then stilled, pushing deep within me and staying there for several long moments. A rough curse left his throat, and I smiled, dropping my head to the bed.

THE QUEEN

If I were a coward, I would leave right now.

I would take this chance—while Sabium continued his conversation with Zathrian and Eadric alone—and I would run for my life.

And then I would face the reality that I was alone, hunted, and practically powerless.

How would I live with myself if I didn't make the most of this opportunity?

Instead, I filled my pockets with jewels, added several necklaces and bracelets to those I was already wearing, and waited for the castle to fall silent.

Nelia was gone.

Pelysian could not help me.

But I was a queen. And one day, I would rule this continent.

Time crawled, until I felt as if I might peel off my skin for some relief. Finally, I cracked open my door, ignoring the night guards, and strolled toward Sabium's rooms.

I had every right to walk wherever I wanted.

Sabium was the only one who would question my presence.

I smiled at his guards, forcing a blush to my cheeks. Let them assume I was visiting him for sex.

Even if Alcandre was the one walking into his rooms each night.

Maroon and gold assaulted my eyes as I stepped inside Sabium's receiving room. His sitting room was also empty, but I could hear the sound of water splashing from his bathing room, the murmur of Sabium's servants. My heart pounded, and I scanned the room.

No, he wouldn't keep it here.

His bedroom was next. I stepped inside, and it felt as if the temperature plummeted several degrees.

There it was.

My vision narrowed until all I could see was the cover. The grimoire didn't look ancient, yet the god had likely protected it with his power.

Pure elation filled my lungs as I reached for it.

And Sabium's laugh rang out behind me.

I whirled, backing toward the door. He stood in front of his closet, Tymedes at his side, several guards next to him. And those guards held Lisveth, Caraceli and Pelopia in their arms, hands covering their mouths.

The bathing room had gone silent. Alcandre slipped from the room wrapped in nothing but a bath sheet, a tiny smile playing around her mouth.

She had done this.

Sabium watched me, his eyes dancing. Realization slid through me. This was exactly what he had wanted. If he'd killed me earlier, word would have spread about the slaughter of the queen he'd claimed to love. Now, he could prove I was a traitor, and his court would celebrate my death.

"Did you really think I didn't know you were planning to steal from me?" He smiled. "Who told you about the grimoire, hmm?"

Lisveth whimpered.

I would kill them all. My hands trembled as I opened the grimoire, scanning it desperately for the magic I needed.

Blank pages.

I froze.

Sabium chuckled. "Oh, Kaliera. You truly are the stupidest woman on this continent. Well, except for this one." He gestured to Lisveth, and I let out a choked scream.

"No, Sabium!"

The guard dragged his knife across Lisveth's throat. Blood spurted.

So much blood.

The room suddenly seemed to be painted red with it.

Lisveth's screams turned to a choking cough, and the guard stepped back, letting her slump to the floor.

My eyes met Alcandre's.

Her face had whitened, but her lips thinned as I stared at her.

She sauntered toward me, and Sabium allowed it. "You didn't protect us," she hissed, leaning close. "Every day of our lives revolved around serving you. You knew what was happening in this castle, and you left us to be preyed on. Now it's your turn."

"And Lisveth?"

"These fools won't survive what's coming. I'm

doing them a favor."

Cold rage swept through me. But I looked past her.

"Sabium, please."

"Call me by my name, my love."

I shuddered. "Regner." The word was almost soundless, my voice hoarse. But he smiled.

This had all been a game to him. He'd allowed me to eat with Zathrian, to learn of his alliance, and to know exactly how the barrier had fallen. Then he'd used Alcandre to trap me.

And Lisveth.

Poor, sweet Lisveth.

Tears were streaming down Pelopia's face. Caraceli was struggling in the guard's arms. They knew they were about to die.

I inhaled, sharp and quick, shoring up my resolve.

I couldn't help them.

My hands were moving before I understood what I was doing.

And I shoved Alcandre toward them, darting toward the door.

Sabium's laugh rang out behind us.

"Where do you think you're going, *Your Majesty*?" Tymedes taunted. "Our king allowed me the honor of finally killing you."

I ran faster.

The guards outside my room frowned at me, confused. "He has gone mad," I snapped. "Protect me!"

One of the guards pulled his sword. Ducking into my room, I panted for breath.

"Stand down!" Tymedes roared at the guards.

I hiccupped out a sob, lunging for my mirror. Tymedes's huge bulk swept into the room, just footspans behind me.

"Face your fate." Tymedes swung his sword, and I ducked, lunging into the mirror.

Tymedes's palm hit the glass. Our eyes met for a single moment, and his sword slammed into the mirror behind me, shattering the glass.

Would I be trapped here, in the between place?

My scream was ripped from my lungs as I lunged for the light on the other side.

Pelysian's mother turned, head angled, as if she had been expecting me.

And I dropped to my knees, staring at the black ruin of the mirror on this side.

Lisveth's trembling lips flashed in front of my eyes. The foolish child hadn't deserved such a fate. But women so rarely received what they deserved. And much would be sacrificed to kill Sabium.

Still, my stomach swam at the uselessness of it all. At the sheer waste. I hadn't stolen the grimoire. All I had managed to accomplish was allowing Sabium to know exactly how I had plotted against him.

Pelopia and Caraceli were dead, as were the others. Alcandre would die too, and hopefully, *her* death would be long and painful. It was only a matter of time.

Pelysian's mother seemed to be waiting for me to speak. Slowly, I got to my feet.

Despite what Sabium would do to those who remained loyal to me, a smile played around my mouth. For so long, he had imagined me caged. Declawed.

"I suppose there are worse things than being a monster. Such as being leashed by one."

Now, he knew better. I was no longer leashed by him. Had never truly been declawed.

I might not have the grimoire, but I was free. My son was free.

And now, I would ensure Sabium regretted everything he had done to me.

MADINIA

The temperature was cooler this close to the Normathe Mountains. That was a blessing as we tore through the forest in the heat of the day. But it would be a curse tonight when we were no longer moving.

I stumbled on some undergrowth, turning my ankle. I was too tired to curse. Besides, the young boy in my arms had begun to shiver. His burns must have been agonizing, but he was still in that deep, unnatural sleep.

A girl of around fifteen winters had taken the other boy, after breathlessly introducing herself to me as Narmena. Our group had been running for hours, although I could hardly call our stumbling trot a run. When we finally stopped to gulp at water from a stream, I removed my tunic, sank it in the cold water, and wrapped it around the boy.

"His name is Darnis," Whirna whispered, pushing his hair off his face. Her hair held the same dark hue, the occasional strand lightened by the sun. Most of their features were similar too, from their sharp chins to the scattering of freckles across both their noses.

A large part of me was worried about the trauma and the travel sending Whirna into sudden labor. If that happened...

"The fire came so quickly," she said, pressing a kiss to his brow. "I didn't have time..."

I didn't tell her he would be okay. But I spent several seconds brutally damning the gods for giving me the power of fire but not the power to fix burns.

I was a creature created for destruction, not healing. But that didn't mean I couldn't regret.

"Is everyone ready?" I asked.

Exhausted nods. No one complained. All of us were aware of what was at stake. The iron guards were coming. Some of those groups that'd fled would be found and slaughtered. It was inevitable, but my mouth flooded with rage and bitterness all the same.

I shouldn't even be here. This shouldn't be my problem. If not for the fucking barrier, I would have fled this continent the moment we'd escaped from Regner's castle.

I should be in some distant land, where my greatest issue was choosing which dress to wear to dinner. I shouldn't be feeling a young boy shiver his life away as I led a stunned, desperate group of hybrids through the forest.

This was all Prisca's fault.

That bitch got beneath my skin. She made me *care*.

Now, I would be forced to watch as these people

died one by one. Likely, I would bleed out in this fucking forest myself.

"Madinia?"

I forced some of the rage from my face. With a wave of my hand, we continued our desperate charge toward safety.

7

MADINIA

We buried Darnis in a small clearing close to a stream.

Whirna lay on the ground, clutched at the dirt, and sobbed. Most of the others were crying too. I stared at the tiny grave, throat tight, eyes burning.

Would he have lived if we'd made it to the Asric Pass? Vicer had almost certainly stationed healers there. I had simply been too slow.

The world spun dizzily around me, and I stumbled.

"Please, eat something," someone murmured, grabbing my arm to keep me steady.

"I'm fine." The other hybrids needed the food. And I felt too sick to eat. The woman pulled me until I was facing her. Her eyes seemed almost crazed, her face tight with desperation. "We need you. The remainder of these children need you." She shoved a few pieces of dried meat into my hand, and I didn't argue, simply lifted one to my mouth and began chewing.

I was so, so tired.

Part of me wished I'd killed Stillcrest

back at the camp. Likely, she'd been cut down shortly after we escaped. But if she was alive...she should have to live with what she had done.

And still, the guilt clawed at me. I should have insisted these people leave the moment I arrived at that camp. I should have made Vicer use his power. I should have—

"She's not going to leave him," the woman next to me said, nodding to Whirna's prone form. "You will need to do something about that."

I looked at her. She looked expectantly back at me.

"What's your name?" I asked.

"Glenda."

Her eyes were a blue so light, they reminded me of the fae king's. But unlike Conreth's icy gaze, hers was warm, despite our increasingly dire situation. Deep laugh lines had been carved around those eyes. This was a woman who enjoyed her life.

"Do you have children, Glenda?"

She nodded toward twin boys of around eight winters.

"Then you can imagine her pain much better than I can."

"Ah, but she doesn't need my empathy. She will have that when we find safety. Right now, she needs strength. Conviction. Force."

"You want me to bully a pregnant woman who has just lost her son?"

She gave me a steady look. "We took too much time here. We are not out of danger. You know this."

And Whirna would need someone like Glenda for

sympathy. For support. Glenda would be the one to make sure Whirna got up each morning and put one foot in front of the other. I didn't want Whirna to remember this woman berating her next to her son's grave. Not while she was mourning him in the weeks and months that followed.

If we lived that long.

Whirna had stopped crying. Now, she lay next to the grave, her eyes blank as she stared into space.

I crouched next to her. "I can't even imagine the pain you're feeling right now," I murmured. "It's inconceivable. But we need to keep going."

"Just leave me."

I reached out and touched the swell of her stomach. "You know I can't do that."

Her gaze dropped to my hand. When her eyes met mine, some of the blankness had slipped away, replaced by pure agony. "I promised him I would keep him safe. It was my job to keep him safe."

I had nothing for her except the thought of vengeance. "We're going to make them regret this," I swore to her. "We're going to kill Regner and wipe out his iron guards."

A tiny spark flickered in her eyes. Something nudged at my hand, and I yanked that hand away, gaping down at her stomach. There had been so much *force* behind something so tiny. The baby seemed to do what my words couldn't, and Whirna allowed me to help her to her feet.

"You will return to this place one day," I promised. "You'll visit your son."

She didn't seem to have the strength to reply, but as I tightened my hold on her arm, she took a few steps.

It was enough.

And so, we continued. Until screams sounded in the distance, piercing the stillness of the forest around us. My heart leaped, my pulse pounding in my ears.

Everyone froze.

I lowered my hand, gesturing for the group to crouch. The screams went on and on, and horror slid into the hybrids' eyes.

One of the other groups had been found. My power burst from me, and I forced the flame from my hands.

Perhaps I could give this group the exact directions to the next stop. I could go fight with the others and return—

"You can't save them," one of the older boys said bitterly as he watched me. "It's too late."

I'd once thought the worst feeling was terror. I was wrong.

The worst feeling was helplessness. Nothing could be worse than wanting to help someone—to save a life—while knowing it was entirely out of your control.

This was why it was better not to care about anyone than to end up in a situation like this, where there were no good choices left.

"We need to keep moving," I said.

"Why?" one of the older girls asked. "We're all going to die. You think the soldiers are going to stop?"

I caught two exhausted nods as I whirled to face her. "No. They're not going to stop. But better to die trying to live than to sit here and wait for death."

She stared at me for a long moment. Tears flooded her eyes, and she turned her gaze back in the direction we'd come. Where Darnis lay in a shallow grave.

I didn't give her any further encouragement. I didn't

have a single kind word left in me.

"Keep moving," Glenda murmured to her. "You can do it."

We made it to the first camp. I was too numb to feel anything close to elation, but logically, I knew we were in a better position now. The chest was where Vicer had described, and we pulled out the blankets and food we ideally would have used to spend the night.

But we couldn't. We had to keep moving. So we ate quickly and took whatever supplies we could carry with us. No one protested as we reburied the chest and began walking once more.

Our pace slowed until it was barely a shuffle. I used my power to light the way, dampening it whenever I heard a noise in the distance.

Eventually, we curled up deep in the forest, children stashed beneath bushes, adults pulling as much undergrowth over us as we could.

I couldn't sleep, my mind replaying every moment. But the rest would help.

Hours later, more screams cut through the night. To my left, someone's teeth were chattering. But all of us stayed still, attempting to keep the children quiet. By now, they were exhausted, a few of them even sleeping through the screams.

Finally, the sun began to rise, and I clenched my teeth. I refused to give in to the sick panic dragging vicious claws through my chest. These people would *live*.

Slowly, quietly, I woke the others. A few moments to duck behind bushes or gulp at water from a nearby stream, and then we were moving once more.

The forest around us was both sanctuary and adversary—the trees and brush providing cover, but the rustle of fallen leaves carving through the silence, each snapped twig underfoot as loud as a thunderclap to my ears.

Our progress was painstakingly slow. The younger children were carried in the arms or on the backs of anyone who could hold them, their weight slowing us even more. Tiny faces were smudged with dirt and tears, wide, fearful eyes looking to us for assurance. All I had to offer were weak smiles and hushed encouragement.

And then, in the distance, the haunting sound of hoofbeats.

My heart plummeted into an abyss. "Down," I hissed.

Everyone dropped.

By now, the children knew to stay quiet, although the youngest hiccupped through her suppressed sobs. If we'd had young babies in this group, we likely would have been found by now.

The hoofbeats thundered toward us.

"Run!" I ordered, handing the boy I was holding to an older girl. "You know the way."

My palms turned slick, my entire body went cold, and the metallic taste of terror flooded my mouth. I was all these people had. If I went down, they were next.

"Faster," I ordered desperately.

The forest around me erupted into a cacophony of sounds—the cracking of branches under the weight of heavy boots, the clanging of armor, the cruel laughter of one of the guards.

There was no outrunning them. I had to take a stand

here and buy the others as much time as I could.

An arrow whistled past my ear, embedding itself into a tree with a gruesome thud. Baring my teeth, I aimed my flames at the horse, begging forgiveness. I gave it a swift end, but its death caused further chaos, the other horses bucking desperately.

"Face your death with dignity, corrupt filth." The iron guard wore silver trim along his armor. The captain.

I hurled my fire at him. It crashed against his ward, but his pained grimace made it clear it had hurt.

Good. Every second I delayed them was another moment for the hybrids to escape.

I pulled my sword. "Fight me like a man."

Several guards laughed. Most of them were moving forward to surround me. Scanning them, I counted. Seven. More than enough to decimate every single group of hybrids currently fleeing.

Dark power swept toward me. This was it. I rolled my shoulders.

The power bounced off a ward so strong, it glowed silver.

I jolted back, brandishing my sword as another man stalked through the clearing toward me. Our eyes met, and his mouth dropped open.

"You," he snarled. "Why is it always you?"

"My thoughts exactly."

Calysian.

"You owe me a life debt," I blurted.

He smiled, ignoring the dark power hitting his ward once more. "I thought you didn't want my debt?"

"It's not up to me, remember? You said the debt

hadn't been satisfied. A matter of honor."

His teeth flashed as he laughed, and my stomach clenched. After a long moment, he heaved a sigh. "Oh, fine."

By the time he gave the iron guards his full attention, they had surrounded us. But at least that meant they hadn't yet gone after the hybrids.

The captain smiled, as if reading my mind. He gestured to two guards behind us. "Go."

Just as an arrow hit Calysian's ward.

Calysian gave the soldier a bored look. More arrows flew toward us, and I sent my fire twisting between them, igniting one of the guards who'd turned to go after the hybrids.

I blocked out his screams, watching the captain. He was tired. He couldn't hold the ward while his own men attacked, yet Calysian seemed as if such a thing was easy for him. It was the one advantage we had. I waited until the guard at his left fired another arrow...

Now.

I'd used this tactic on the iron guards at the hybrid camp. And just like those guards, two men clawed at their eyes, wailing for mercy as my fire engulfed them.

Calysian tutted as he lifted his hand, reinforcing his ward against a sudden barrage of dark power and fae-iron-tipped arrows.

I sent more power toward those arrows, and several of them dropped straight to the ground. "Feel free to help whenever you get tired of watching."

"There's that sharp little tongue. Do you ever get tired of wielding it?"

I ignored him.

"Ah, silence. Adorable. Tell me, just how did you end up here, Madinia Farrow?"

Grinding my teeth, I ignored him some more. A life-or-death situation, and he wanted to chat. Idiot.

I had no interest in people like him. People who took nothing seriously. I took everything seriously.

Every muscle in my body ached with fatigue. A guard to my left was attacking again and again, his movements almost too fast to see as he nocked his arrows. Those arrows slammed into our ward, until I could almost feel the headache it must have given Calysian.

The guard let loose the next arrow, and I waited. He lifted one arm to pull an arrow from his quiver.

Now.

I directed my flames toward a slice of skin I'd glimpsed along the back of his neck—between helmet and armor.

Calysian's ward was holding, and I used it for cover as I attacked again and again. He slid outside of the range of his ward, leaving it to cover me as he targeted that same slice of unprotected skin, his sword slicing through a guard's neck like a warm knife through butter.

Two left.

"Behind the tree," he ordered.

"I don't—"

"Now."

Darting behind the tree, I reached for the last of my power. Calysian's ward dropped. It had been impressive, but from the bitter frustration on his face, even his power wasn't enough to hold such a ward indefinitely against iron-tipped arrows and magical attacks.

I couldn't understand how he'd held it this long already.

The captain wasn't looking quite as smug anymore. He was staring at the death around him—and the last guard across the clearing—as if he was wondering just how it had all gone so terribly wrong.

Calysian could likely take the captain. Slowly, I began to creep behind the trees, toward the remaining guard.

A desperate scream sounded, and I whirled.

The captain lay on the ground, lifeless. His horse had bolted, while Calysian shoved his hands on his hips, shaking his head. It was almost as if he was displeased by how easily he had killed the captain.

An arrow flew toward his unarmed back.

I slashed at it with the last of my power—just enough to throw it off course.

Turning, Calysian raised one eyebrow as it dropped to the ground. His lips pulled up from his teeth in a snarl. Irritation gleamed in his eyes. "That's another life debt."

"You would have likely saved yourself."

"It doesn't matter. Intention matters. Make me owe you again, and I'll kill you myself."

I showed him my teeth. "Try."

His gaze narrowed on my face. Irritation gave way to languid amusement. I looked away.

"That one was free," I panted, the world spinning around me. I doubted I could call even a single spark to one of my fingers. "You don't owe me anything."

He shook his head. "Wait here."

I didn't argue, simply slumped to the ground with the tree at my back. A single muffled yell came from the remaining guard, and Calysian returned mere moments later.

He frowned at me. "You smell like death and sorrow."

"We lost one of the hybrids. A child." My throat thickened. He studied me, as if surprised I would care. I wanted to smash my hand into his face for that look.

Of course I cared.

I wasn't entirely a monster. Although, I was sure I was close.

I surveyed him. He'd once told me he'd become trapped on this continent when the barrier went up. Which made him over four hundred years old. He didn't seem like one of the fae, but if he was hybrid, he would have shown more signs of aging. So, what was he?

"What were you doing here?"

"I was attempting to travel to a northern village."

"Why?"

He gave me an amused look that silently asked me why I felt entitled to that information. "I will help you round up your lost sheep," he said.

I didn't bother arguing. Hopefully, the hybrids had continued moving in the direction I had instructed. I surveyed the carnage around us one last time.

They would have hunted every single fleeing hybrid until we were all dead.

I wished we could kill them all again.

THE QUEEN

Pelysian's mother stared at me. It had been hours since I walked into this hovel, and I'd been forced to sit here and watch her stitch. She hadn't even offered me sustenance.

Her gaze flicked to the mirror behind me, and I turned. Still black.

"Only two such mirrors in existence, and one of them was shattered under your watch," she said.

"I almost *died*, witch."

She just tutted at me.

"What is your name?" I asked, shifting on the uncomfortable wooden chair. It scraped against the earthen floor. Truly, it was barely a hut. And yet, I would need to get used to such poverty—at least until my son was crowned. Without the grimoire in my hands, making sure Jamic took his rightful place would be difficult. But not impossible. If Prisca killed Regner, Jamic and I would find a way to kill her and take the book.

The hag turned her attention to the shirt she was stitching. "How many times have we spoken before now?"

If she thought such a pointed question could embarrass me, she was mistaken. "Too many," I said.

She let out a chuckle that turned into a hoarse cough. "My name is Ravynia."

"Your power is vast. Why do you not use it to claw your way out of this poverty?"

"This is not poverty. You do not *know* poverty. You have not seen it, smelled it, lived it. I am content with my life and my home. Besides, if those in power were to learn of my gift, what do you think would happen to me?"

I knew what would happen to her, because I had plans to install her in the castle the moment Regner was dead. She would ensure I could always see my enemies coming. And forever outwit them. She would fight it, but I knew who her children were. And as I knew well, people would do anything for their children.

She gave a faint smile as if she was reading my thoughts. "Imagine if Regner had enjoyed my power," she said mildly.

I shivered at the thought. But her life would be much different under my service. Unlike my husband, I was not evil. Nor was I insane.

The afternoon passed achingly slowly. Finally, hooves sounded outside. I stiffened, but Ravynia waved her hand. "It is my son."

He took his time, likely untacking his own horse. When he finally opened the door, he didn't look surprised to see me.

A quick glance at his mother and then his eyes met mine once more.

"Your ladies are dead, aren't they, Your Majesty?"

I felt a pang somewhere in my upper chest at the memory of the terror in their eyes. "Yes."

Pelysian's gaze dropped to my hand, which was rubbing my chest. "And does it bother you?" he asked softly. "Knowing you're the reason for their deaths? Knowing they likely could have lived if you had given them a second thought?"

My throat thickened as a strange feeling burrowed

deep into my gut. Fury. It was fury. That's all it was. "In times of war, sacrifices must be made," I snapped.

Something that might have been grief flickered across Pelysian's face before his eyes turned cold. Remote.

"So be it." He took a step back from me. As if I were contagious. As if he were repulsed. Blood roared in my ears, until I barely heard his next words. "You are the second most recognizable person in this kingdom. I cannot keep you safe here," he said. "You must join with the hybrid heir."

I sniffed. I had no desire to go crawling to that little bitch, with nothing but the clothes on my back. But his declaration was not a surprise. I'd had hours in this place to ponder my options after all.

I had a choice to make. Bury my pride long enough to get close to Prisca, or hide somewhere until the war was over and my son was ready to take the throne.

The decision was easy, despite my distaste. It was finally time to see my son.

ASINIA

Torinth was alive.

Yesterday, we'd received the news from one of Demos's contacts in Gromalia. And Demos's expression had transformed into pure, unadulterated joy. That look on his face…it had made my knees turn weak.

But within moments of reading the message, he'd

turned silent once more—even though Tor had agreed to meet us. Ever since, Demos had become increasingly withdrawn as we traveled, his expression distant.

Already, we were traveling north through Gromalia toward Prisca and the others in Sorlithia—a city Tibris and I had never seen, and one Demos had visited when he was so young he could barely remember.

Not only was Tor alive, but he'd been living in Thobirea. And he'd agreed to travel west to meet us in one of the larger villages, where we would find a tavern grimy enough that four hooded visitors wouldn't draw any attention.

The rebels had begun evacuating before we'd left camp. Tibris had been busy up until the last moment, ensuring those who were leaving were in good health, and giving final instructions to the human healers traveling with them. I'd caught the last of his goodbye with Herne, their low, pained voices barely reaching my ears. I'd had to look away, unable to watch their faces, tight with suppressed grief and fear—not for themselves, but for each other.

Shockingly, Conreth had given permission for those who were heading toward the Asric Pass to travel within the fae lands, along the border—preventing the need for them to step foot into Eprotha. He'd even ordered a group of fae guards to meet the rebels and escort them—likely to ensure no one wandered off and stumbled across a wildkin.

When I'd expressed my surprise at Conreth's sudden cooperative nature, Demos had shaken his head. "The idiot killed his brother and almost killed my sister. This is likely a temporary lull in his bad decisions. But we need to take full advantage before he changes his mind."

As we traveled, we occasionally stopped at small villages to find supplies. There, we came face-to-face with signs mourning Eryndan's death. The Gromalian king's death had shocked his kingdom. Worse, there were also plenty of signs with Prisca's face, declaring her to be the king-killer.

Regner's lies had reached even here.

By the time we reached the village of Ardanor, none of us were speaking. Vynthar had disappeared to do whatever it was the Drakoryx did when he wandered off alone. Tibris was distracted—likely worrying for Herne and the other rebels. Demos was brooding and somber as he prepared to face Tor. And I was consumed by the thought that he might not help us.

I was also consumed by another thought.

The same thought I'd attempted to ignore even as it continued to poke at my subconscious.

A thought that felt like an itch I couldn't scratch.

A thought that intruded even into my dreams.

A thought that insisted I needed to be a larger part of ending this war.

One day, when this continent finally knew peace, I wanted my name to be mentioned in the old tales.

I wanted it written that while I might have been partially responsible for the start of this war, I was also responsible for ending it.

That I had been brave and loyal and true.

That I had been *worthy*.

"Asinia?"

I lifted my head. We'd reached the tavern, and Demos was waiting for me to dismount.

"Sorry."

His gaze had already turned to the sturdy wooden tavern door. Hopefully, Tor was waiting at a table inside.

Tibris slid Demos a concerned look. We'd told him what we knew of Tor, but it was clear he was also unused to Demos's grim silence.

The tavern door hung open, anchored by a large rock. Demos lifted his head, and we followed him inside. Nerves fluttered in my stomach.

Long tables, worn smooth by the passage of time—and countless elbows—were clustered together across the wooden floor, surrounded by smaller circular tables wedged against walls and windows. It was nearing the midday meal, and villagers and travelers alike had gathered to eat and lift a cup.

It felt strange, to suddenly be confined within a room of people after so long traveling and living in the camp. The noise seemed to swell, and I gritted my teeth through it as Demos scanned the room, his expression intent.

The bar itself—a solid slab of oak staffed by a scowling innkeeper—was lined with an array of mugs, continually lifted and carried by a tired-looking barmaid.

Demos turned away, and Tibris and I followed him to one of the small, circular tables in the back.

A cloaked figure waited. He lifted his head, and both men went still.

His nose had been broken at least once, his hazel eyes were shadowed, and he needed a shave. But I could make out smile lines around his mouth.

Someone burst into laughter a few tables to our left, the sound sudden enough that it seemed to snap whatever tension had caused both men to freeze. Tor got to his feet as we approached, clasping Demos's hand. After an awkward moment during which it seemed as if both men considered and rejected the thought of a hug, we were all quickly seated, and Tibris and I were introduced. I blew out an unsteady breath. So far, so good.

Tor nodded at us, but his gaze met Demos's.

"You're alive."

Demos nodded. "I didn't know it at the time...didn't know it until my sister appeared in the dungeon, but Telean had been forced to work as the queen's seamstress. She convinced her to let me live."

Tor nodded. But he didn't say a word. I shifted on my wooden stool.

It was Tibris who cleared his throat. "We're here to ask for your help."

Another nod.

We told him everything we knew.

"You truly believe I can help with Regner's wards." From the tone of his voice, Tor either didn't believe us or didn't *want* to believe us.

"I know you can," Demos said. "To this day, I've never come across anyone else with your particular power."

Tor took a deep breath. And his gaze was steady. "I can't fight in your war."

A leaden weight had taken up residence in my gut. One chance. We had one chance to kill Regner.

"You mean you won't," Demos said.

Tor narrowed his eyes, crossing his arms as he leaned back in his seat. "I have children now, Demos. Everyone we loved from that time is dead. You may have moved on, may have created a new family and forgotten what happened to the people who trusted you the most, but I haven't."

My nails dug into the wooden table beneath my hands. "Watch your mouth," I snapped.

Tor glanced at me. "It's only a matter of time before he gets you killed. You may be willing to lose your life for this, but my children need a father."

"And what will happen when war comes for your children?" Demos asked. "Do you think you'll be able to keep them safe? Your family could have a home. In our kingdom, Tor."

He shook his head, his mouth trembling once before he thinned it. "We spoke about that for years. And I never saw that kingdom. All I saw was our friends arrested. I heard their screams when they burned."

Demos flinched. This was *killing* him.

My hands began to shake, my entire body stiffening until my muscles felt frozen.

"And where were you when he was rotting in that cell?" I hissed. "*My* best friend broke in to the castle and saved our lives. What did you do, except turn and run? Did you enjoy building your new life, while knowing Demos would never experience such joy again? Did you even think of him?"

"Asinia." Demos's voice was as unyielding as iron.

"No. If he's going to blame you, then he can look at his own actions." I turned my attention back to Tor. "Or lack of them. Even Vicer never forgot about Demos. He made sure Prisca knew to get him out. Meanwhile, you moved on." I curled my lip at him. "Demos said you were once like brothers. If that's the case, I'm glad I'm an only child."

Tibris canted his head but stayed silent. Demos reached for my hand and rubbed his thumb over my wrist. His hand was so warm, his touch soothing. I took a long, deep breath and let the air shudder out of me.

Tor dropped his gaze to our hands, his expression contemplative.

Demos was silent for a long moment, and his words from the camp circled through my mind.

"I don't want him to join us out of guilt. I want him to join us because he has hope."

I didn't care why Tor joined us. Only that he did.

"I want you to understand the choice you're making." I met Tor's eyes. And now I could see the war that raged within him. "Without you, we have no chance of killing Regner. His wards are just too strong. All the people you lost? They'll never be avenged. And more will die. More and more and more, until this continent is steeped in death."

Tor watched me. And the barest hint of a smile flickered around his mouth. His eyes met Demos's. "Always knew you'd find a woman just like this."

I squinted at him. "Like. What?"

"Fierce."

I opened my mouth. Truthfully, I'd expected him to call me something much worse. And the way Demos had snarled told me he'd expected the same.

I shrugged.

Tor sighed. "At least tell me how it would work."

PRISCA

Daharak was taking no chances as we sailed north along the Gromalian coast. At least two hundred ships sailed with us. When I'd mentioned that this could be somewhat concerning to the Gromalians, who might fear an invasion, she'd shrugged.

"We've been in their waters since the barrier fell. If that spoiled prince doesn't know you're on the same side by now, then he's useless to us."

Thora's lips had curved at that.

When Daharak had learned who Jorvik was—and that he'd managed to get onto her ship under false pretenses—she'd practically breathed fire. Zathrian's little messenger was currently residing in the brig, where he would be staying. According to Marth, Jorvik hadn't had a chance to pass on anything that would harm us irreparably.

In the distance, the unmistakable green banners of the Gromalian fleet whipped in the wind, their ships cutting through the water and approaching us with a caution that bordered on hostility.

"What were you saying about the prince knowing we were on the same side?" I muttered to Daharak.

A smile played around her mouth, and she merely raised her hand. The air was thick with tension, and I licked my lips, tasting salt. A Gromalian ship peeled away from the others, slowing as it neared us. The Gromalian captain, tall and solid in polished armor, called out across the water.

"State your purpose in our waters."

Lorian watched him, seemingly unconcerned. Daharak squinted into the sun, holding up a hand to shade her eyes. "Idiot," she muttered to us. "You don't want to know the amount of armor we've found at the bottom of the ocean, their owners decomposing inside it." I wrinkled my nose, and she raised her voice. "We seek an audience with your prince in Sorlithia. He will wish to speak to us."

Silence stretched as the Gromalian captain considered her words. We would, after all, need to sail past the capital. And yet, the natural harbor protecting Thobirea made the city impossible to invade by water.

The captain's eyes met mine, before flicking to Lorian, Galon, and Marth.

"Let them pass," he commanded. "But your remaining fleet may not dock."

Daharak nodded easily. We hadn't expected to be able to dock. Not just because of the logistics of bringing this many ships with no warning, but because of our currently fraught relationship with Rekja.

Still, the threat of those ships should keep us safe as we made our way to Sorlithia.

The fleet continued northward over the next few days. As the coastline began to curve inward, the silhouette of the city started to emerge on the horizon, and we adjusted our course toward it.

The Gromalian captain had obviously been in

contact with the ships guarding Sorlithian waters, because those ships turned, granting us passage, and we prepared to dock, sails descending, ropes creaking, crew calling to one another in the language of the ship—one I was unlikely ever to understand.

Not long now.

A choking sensation tightened my throat, until I struggled for my next breath. So much rested on this meeting. On our ability to convince Rekja to go to war with us. Without him…

Even with some of the most powerful fae on the continent fighting on our side of the battlefield, they could only do so much against thousands and thousands of humans, many of them bloated with stolen power.

While many humans had received their power back when the barrier fell, too much of that power was still kept in oceartus stones, used for convenience in Regner's capital, and held by his most loyal people.

We needed boots on the ground.

I turned to find Daharak and the others talking a few footspans away. I hadn't even heard her approach.

"After we speak to Rekja, you should return to the rest of the fleet," I said to Daharak. "Keep your trowth stone by your side, and if you don't hear from us by nightfall tomorrow, move back south."

Daharak's mouth twisted. "I don't like it."

"It's unlikely Rekja will cause any problems once he sees Thora," Lorian said. "But if he does, you will need to meet with the others and continue with our plans."

From Daharak's expression, she didn't like that thought either, but she gave us a stiff nod.

I hesitated, and then the words spilled from my lips. "Please look after my aunt."

Her expression softened. "You know I will."

I did. One of her pirates had already saved Telean's life not long ago. My aunt would stay on the ship. We hadn't spoken since the morning I'd woken up. Truthfully, I didn't know when we would. For the most part, she'd locked herself away in her cabin. She was just as stubborn as I was.

Galon and a few of the other warders formed a barrier around our ship as we docked. Daharak was the first off the ship, sauntering down the ramp as if there weren't fifty guards waiting for her.

"Take us to your king," she said.

"Our king is busy," one of them called. Several others laughed.

Daharak gave him a wide smile. "And yet a captain of your fleet already allowed us through."

A heavily muscled guard stepped close, putting him just inches from me. "I suggest you get back on your ship—"

Lorian let out a low, vicious snarl. He was becoming a little...feral as time went on with no sign of my power.

The guard froze.

Daharak raised her hand, the silver coin gleaming in the sun. He reached for it, and she shook her head, tucking it away. "I don't think so."

The guard narrowed his eyes but sent a wary glance toward Lorian. "Let them pass."

"But—"

"Don't make me tell you again."

One of the other guards spat on the ground in front of us. But he stepped aside.

Sorlithia was much, much smaller than Thobirea. Small enough that Thora had suggested we walk from the dock to the city walls.

Where the Gromalian capital sprawled from the docks to the castle, Sorlithia was barely a large town in comparison.

Fortified walls encircled the town on all sides, rising high above the ground, designed for defense. Several guards strolled along those walls as I watched, eyes scanning anyone who approached. Every few footspans, crenellations rose like jagged teeth against the sky, providing cover and strategic points for archers and defenders. Towers, taller than the walls themselves, punctuated the perimeter at regular intervals, providing an even higher vantage point.

And yet, it didn't feel like a military town. Those walls seemed ancient, covered in a patina of time, with creeping ivy and blowing wild flowers softening their imposing structure.

The town unfolded like a tapestry of quaint charm as we walked through it, several guards trailing after us. The streets wound in lazy, meandering patterns, giving me an opportunity to study the buildings—their facades displaying an array of pastel colors, from warm peach tones to soft lavenders.

Residents wandered past, some of them stopping to stare, to whisper. But for the most part, they were wrapped up in their own lives, hauling baskets to and from the market, cajoling stubborn children, finishing the day's errands.

Like most cities, Sorlithia's heart was its market square, and the bustling hub somehow retained a relaxed atmosphere. Taverns and inns surrounded the market, while children splashed in a huge fountain.

This was a city of trees. Lush gardens sprawled every few blocks, attracting birds and butterflies. I could see why Rekja preferred Sorlithia to his capital.

And we were about to destroy whatever peace and solace he'd found here.

Next to me, Thora twisted her hands. I couldn't tell if she was nervous or trying to restrain herself from elbowing past us and running toward the castle as it came into view.

It was perched atop a gently rising hill—an unassuming yet undeniable presence. Unlike the castles in the Eprothan and Gromalian capitals, the castle of Sorlithia was all quiet elegance and understated strength.

Its walls were a light gray, with huge windows large enough for a man to stand in. The guards at our backs spoke to those at the castle gates, who gave us long, suspicious stares but allowed us to pass.

Gravel crunched underfoot as we strode toward the large wooden doors. Intricately carved with creatures I had once thought were nothing but myth, the doors were ajar, guards stationed on either side.

One of those guards spoke briefly to the guards escorting us, murmuring something that made Lorian's lips quirk. But the guard turned, gesturing for us to follow through the grand hall, which boasted a ceiling that arched high above our heads, painted in deep blues sparkling with silver—the night sky. Lorian took my arm as I almost tripped, my gaze stuck to that magnificent ceiling.

The guard turned left, and we followed him into a formal sitting room. I swept my gaze over the room, noting the plush silk chairs, the polished wood of the side tables. But my attention was caught by Rekja.

He stood by the window, his long red hair tied back as he gazed down at something out of sight. He wore casual clothes. But no one who looked at him would doubt he was born to wear a crown.

The Gromalian prince slowly turned, his eyes meeting mine, his expression unfriendly. "You. And just how did you get— Ah." Striding forward, he plucked the coin from Daharak's fingers. "Due to my respect for ancient traditions, I will give you five—" His hands fisted as Lorian and Rythos stepped aside, revealing Thora.

Her mouth trembled, her eyes flooded with tears, and she reached for him.

Rekja caught her hand, pulling her close. "How—" He cupped the back of her head in his hand as she buried her face in his chest, and a series of emotions flashed across his face. Incredulity, shock, and finally, a burning, endless wrath.

"You took her from me."

"We *saved* her," Lorian corrected.

Thora lifted her head long enough to pin me with a look. She knew we would have arranged for her kidnapping, regardless of the fact that she was already being hunted.

My heart sank. But she took a deep breath, clutching Rekja close. "They kept me safe," she said. "If not for their spy's quick thinking, Jinoran would have killed me."

Rekja's expression darkened. "He disappeared three nights ago. Gods, I thought you were dead." His gaze met mine, and his eyes were no longer unfriendly. No, now they shone with appreciation. "It seems I owe you my gratitude."

Thora sent me a warning look. It wasn't difficult to follow her thought patterns. If Rekja learned we were responsible for spreading rumors of their relationship, he'd be unlikely to work with us. Thora was keeping that from him in an effort to save both of our kingdoms.

One day, when all of this was over, I hoped Rekja made Thora his queen.

"You're aware that Regner is moving his army south through Eprotha," Lorian said.

Rekja nodded. "My scouts have reported signs of his regiments outside of Lesdryn. But...he sent this yesterday."

Releasing Thora, he swiped a scroll from a nearby table and handed it to me.

To His Majesty King Rekja of Gromalia,

Please accept my sincere condolences on the passing of your father. Occasionally, difficult choices must be made for the greater good—a reality I also understand all too well.

At this time, I find it necessary to remind you of the alliance forged between our kingdoms under your father's reign—an agreement witnessed and honored by advisers from both our kingdoms. This alliance promises to ensure the prosperity of humans across our continent. Any deviation from this agreement would be deeply regrettable and could be construed as a declaration of war.

It is my sincere hope that we continue to maintain the friendship and cooperation established between Gromalia and Eprotha.

His Majesty King Sabium of Eprotha

My lungs seized, and I lifted my head. If Rekja allied with Regner instead...

Lorian had leaned over my shoulder to read, and he plucked the message from my fingers when I was done, handing it to Galon and the others.

"Not-so-thinly veiled threats," he said.

Rekja nodded. "His decision to march some of his regiments south may merely be a way to warn me of the consequences of not cooperating."

I studied his face, but his expression gave no hint of his thoughts.

"And will you ally with him?" Marth asked.

"No," Rekja said. "But the situation is precarious. I am king in name only—I have not yet been crowned. And there are many in Gromalia who would prefer we committed to our alliance with Regner—and our fellow humans."

"He will not allow another king to live on this continent," Lorian warned.

Rekja nodded. "I know this." But his gaze was drifting over Thora in a way that was all too familiar. I glanced at Lorian, and his lips twitched.

"Perhaps we could give you some time to reacquaint yourselves," he said smoothly. "And we could discuss our mutual enemies after that?"

Rekja gave him an appreciative nod. "Actually," he said suddenly, as if the thought had just occurred to him. "There's someone you should meet."

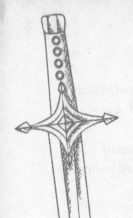

8

PRISCA

"You." I'd only made it one step into the doorway before freezing like a rabbit.

The woman squared her shoulders, holding my stare. She wasn't wearing her blue gown. Long, dark hair fell over her shoulders. No diadem held back her hair. But I would have recognized her anywhere.

I stared. And stared some more.

The last time I'd seen her, I was trembling, pressed up against Lorian in the hidden cavern beneath Regner's bedroom. I'd lost my grip on my power, and we'd been forced to hide. Terror had flooded my body when she'd nonchalantly walked into the cavern, stolen one of the empty oceartus stones, and strolled out.

Every hair on my body stood up. Lorian responded to my terror instantly, shoving me behind him.

"I mean you no harm."

"You're Regner's High Priestess. Forgive us if we choose not to trust you," I said. Since she'd made no threatening moves toward us, and I felt faintly ridiculous, I elbowed my way past Lorian. Daharak leaned against the nearest wall, watching the scene with clear interest, while Rythos and Galon spread out near the windows.

"You have Jamic," the priestess said.

"Yes. And he's safe."

She gave me a faint smile. "Surely he's mentioned me."

He had mentioned a priestess who was kind to him. Madinia had told me of their conversation. And the last time I'd seen this woman, she'd been *stealing* from Regner.

"That oceartus stone was for him," she murmured.

"You knew we were there?"

She nodded. "I knew most of what happened in that castle."

"You're lucky we didn't kill you," Lorian said.

She gave him a look that told him he was a silly little boy. It was a good look. Perhaps I'd try it out myself someday.

Lorian flashed his teeth at her. "Why did you need the oceartus stone?"

"Surely you saw the condition Jamic was in when you took him. Regner allowed me to see him regularly. To check if the amulet was still leaking power into him. When the guards weren't paying attention, I would use oceartus stones to siphon some of that power away. Otherwise, he would have slowly lost his mind."

"And what did you do with the power?" Rythos asked from near the window, his eyes narrowed.

She met his gaze coolly. "I walked through the slums and deposited it where it would do the most good. Healers, usually."

I wanted to think that at least one of Regner's priestesses was truly good. But from the sneer on Rythos's face, he was in no danger of believing her.

"As Regner's pet priestess, you would know just how to use those stones," he said. "Since you and every witch like you have gladly served him for so long."

The room went silent. It wasn't like Rythos to use his words to cut. But Lorian had once told me Rythos hated two creatures more than any other—priestesses and stone hags.

To her credit, the priestess didn't flush. She merely returned her gaze to me as if he didn't exist.

I wasn't surprised by her ability to suppress any emotions she might feel. Working for Regner would have quickly taught her such a skill.

"What is your name?"

"Mona."

"And how did you end up here? In Gromalia?"

Mona gestured to the table, and I sat with Lorian and Galon. Lorian was guarded but quiet, and I knew he was willing to hear her out. Rythos roamed the room, while Daharak continued leaning against the wall. "Now that is a long story," Mona said. "And I have a far more important story to tell. But I was born in Eprotha. My mother was a priestess, and her mother before her. My mother was almost shockingly intelligent. She struggled with people—with understanding their emotions and the nuances in their tones. When she couldn't see the logic in their actions, she was baffled by them.

"And while my mother had been raised to be an incredibly devout woman, she saw…flaws in what we were told." Mona's eyes shuttered, and for the first time, she lost some of her cool confidence. "Her mind was so sharp, she could find a way to solve almost any problem. And yet, even with her devotion to the gods, and her commitment to the king she knew as Sabium, she couldn't make her mind stop unraveling his lies. Slowly, she lost her ability to push the truth aside for the sake of Sabium's religion. And it began to make her crazed."

I couldn't imagine what that must have been like. The confusion turning to realization as she understood what was happening. "I'm sorry," I said.

Mona met my gaze. "Thank you. As you can imagine, her fury was endless. The thought that she had been used to cause so much harm to others was intolerable. And she turned that sharp mind to revenge. Slowly, she began to help other priestesses question our teachings. She had to be careful. So, so careful. But she learned of those who were fighting back, and she joined them. They gave her a task. Assassinate Regner."

I sucked in a breath so quickly I choked. "She attempted such a thing?"

She nodded. "Her power was one of sickness. An attack power that would rot an enemy from the inside out. Unfortunately, my mother did not know of Regner's ward. She did not know of the mirror or the grimoire. Her attempt failed. And she was slaughtered. I was arrested."

I flinched. "The truth-seekers…"

She gave me a faint smile. "My power allows me to evade the truth-seekers. I lie. I manipulate. I can hide my power from the assessors. I am everything my mother should have been. With her mind, she might have saved our continent."

"Then how do we know you are not lying to us?" Rythos demanded. I gave him a look, but…he had a point.

Mona sighed. "You don't. But if you believe one thing, believe this—I would never betray my mother. Before she attempted to kill Regner, she told me everything. And she asked of me only one thing. That I undo the evil Regner had forced his priestesses to commit in his name. I promised her I would succeed where she had not."

"How did you end up in Regner's castle?" Galon asked. He was studying her intently, but unlike Rythos, he didn't radiate suspicion.

"Regner found it amusing to put me in my mother's place. As far as he knew, I was the most pious. The most loyal. A woman ashamed of her mother's actions. And so he used me as an example to others. An example…and a warning."

It sounded like Regner.

"And yet you escaped the castle."

She nodded. "I escaped the day you attacked. But not before I caught a glimpse of what you did to that sanctuary." She smiled, and it was as if the sun had appeared from behind a dark cloud. "I knew I couldn't complete my task from within the castle. By then, I had learned of Regner's ward. While my mother had never been trusted to know the truth of what happened to the oceartus stones, Regner decided he needed my help. And he likely found it amusing to prove my mother right, all while making it clear that I could never avenge her. But I watched him. And I studied everything. I slipped around the castle and read the books he kept hidden. I overheard secret conversations, and when I realized you were finally going to wage war, I came to King Rekja."

Rythos pulled out a chair and sat, folding his arms as he watched her. "And what is it you have to tell us?"

To her credit, Mona answered his question as if it hadn't been dripping with sarcasm.

"You need to kill Regner, this is true. But when you kill him, you will have a task that is just as important."

Rythos opened his mouth, and she held up a hand. "By now, Jamic has told you of the dark god—and his siblings who planned to strip him of power. You know of the three grimoires he poured his knowledge and power into."

I nodded.

"You've likely been wondering how Regner has transferred his stolen power from the oceartus stones to the people he chooses."

"Yes," I said. "At first, we assumed he had some kind of magical device hidden somewhere. Until Jamic told us he used the grimoire to take the human's power with the oceartus stones."

"What we need to know is how to return the power to those he stole it from," Galon said.

"Through the grimoires. But it must be carefully done. So carefully. When the grimoires are used, whoever wields them becomes stronger. But with each use, Calpharos's memory and power return—the grimoires acting like a beacon in the night. Soon, the dark god will come for those books. And when he comes…there will be no hope for anyone on this continent."

The room seemed to tilt around me. I shuddered, and Lorian shifted closer, pulling me into him.

"What is it you want us to do?" I asked, my voice hoarse.

"The grimoire cannot be destroyed. To attempt to do so would only draw the dark god's attention." Some of the color drained from Mona's face.

"Clearly, drawing his attention isn't a good thing," Marth muttered.

"And the stolen power?" Daharak asked.

Mona blew out a breath. "No one knows. But when you kill Regner, someone must take the grimoire. Someone you trust not to be seduced by its power. They must take it and hide it where it will never be found. Or this world and every other world is doomed."

LORIAN

"We'll see you soon," Prisca murmured to Daharak as we stood at the city gates. The pirate queen was leaving to return to her ship. Now that she knew for sure Rekja wasn't about to declare war on us, she would sail south once more. Some part of me still wondered whether allowing the pirate queen to learn so much about the true history of this world—and the hidden power available—would one day prove to be a mistake.

For now, at least, she was bound to work *with* us.

A man stood at the gates waiting for Daharak. I

recognized him as one of her captains—a burly, somber man named Jasick, whom Daharak seemed to trust like no other. When a pigeon landed on his shoulder, he took the message automatically, still watching Daharak.

But when his gaze dropped to the message itself, he jolted as if I'd struck him with my power.

Daharak glanced over and instantly strode his way. He handed her the note, and when she looked up, her eyes were dead.

"What is it?" Prisca demanded.

"Regner must have used the grimoire to hide several flotillas. We've been wondering where all his ships are. And they were waiting for us. They attacked without warning. My people didn't have a chance."

The blood slowly drained from Prisca's face.

"How many?"

"They sank eight hundred of my ships."

Almost half of her fleet. Fuck.

"My people are saving anyone who hasn't yet drowned. Northin gave the order to deploy the ships still anchored near the fae lands, but…"

"This is a huge loss." Prisca nodded. "I'm sorry, Daharak."

I wrapped my arm around Prisca and pulled her close. Her eyes glistened, and I knew she was thinking of the lives lost. The families who would never see their loved ones again.

I was thinking about the war. About the eight hundred ships we desperately needed that were now gone.

"I told my people we needed to fight this war so the barrier could come down," Daharak said bitterly. "So we could be free. And half of them died for it."

Prisca looked as if she'd been punched in the gut. With my arm around her, I could feel her hunch forward slightly, protecting herself from an invisible blow. She opened her mouth, but Daharak had already turned and was striding away, Jasick by her side.

"I made that deal with Daharak," Prisca murmured. "I didn't tell her we had Jamic, so she made the blood vow under false pretenses."

"She wanted that barrier down more than anyone, wildcat." Turning her, I steered her back toward the castle. "If Regner used so much power to hide his own fleet, this was something he had planned for a long, long time. Even without Daharak choosing to ally with you, Regner was likely waiting for his moment. He simply couldn't afford to have Daharak and her ships as a threat to his own fleet."

The castle was quiet as I led Prisca back toward our rooms. One of Rekja's messengers had told us that the king would meet with us again in the morning to discuss the war. Impatience clawed at me. When I recognized one of the maids, I stopped her.

"Do you have parchment?"

She nodded, reaching into the pocket of her long gown. Leaning on the castle wall, I scribbled a quick note to Rekja, letting him know what had happened to Daharak's pirates. We didn't have time to waste here.

"Take this to your king. Tell him it's from me. Thank you," I said, and she bowed her head, walking off in the direction of what was likely the royal chambers.

I stifled the urge to stalk after her and interrupt Rekja and Thora's *reunion*.

But Prisca was silent next to me, staring out of one of the wide windows in the hall, which looked down at the castle gates.

I took her hand. "Come with me, wildcat."

"I asked Rythos to meet me in our rooms."

"Is this about the priestess?"

She glanced away, but her chin stuck out in the way I'd once found infuriating and now found adorable. "You don't think he'll talk to me?"

My instinct was to nod, but I thought about it. "His experience with the priestess was during a time when we were separated. There's a chance… I think some part of him may hold me responsible for the circumstances that led to it. I should have been there. But I wasn't. So he may be able to open up to you in a way he can't with me."

I hadn't thought about that period of our lives for a long time.

So much had gone wrong while we were separated—thanks to Conreth's punishment. While Marth's brush with death was some of the worst of it, Rythos had suffered too.

Prisca was studying me. "Do you need to talk?"

"No, wildcat. Talk to Rythos. I need to speak to Galon anyway." Opening the door to our rooms, I gestured for her to walk inside.

She was still looking at me, and I knew what she was going to ask next. So I followed her inside.

Prisca had been casting glances my way for days and then glowering around the general vicinity, as if warning the gods themselves to stay away.

"Do you still feel like you're being watched?" she asked.

I hesitated, and Prisca narrowed her eyes. I was the most powerful fae on this continent. I'd spent decades being known as the Bloodthirsty Prince. And yet, when my wildcat gave me that warning look, I had to fight the urge to glance away.

For a moment—just a moment—I could see her as a mother, giving our own children that exact expression. The look that told them they had better tell the truth. The thought of it warmed my chest.

"Yes," I admitted. "But I don't want you to worry, wildcat. I'm handling it."

She ignored that. "Do you think Mona would be able to tell us? If it was one of the gods taking an interest in you?"

I shrugged. "I've never been one to trust priestesses. And seeing what they've allowed Regner to do to this continent… We may need to take her advice, but I don't feel the need to tell her of my personal…issues."

Prisca smirked at my last words, and I pinched her nose.

She laughed, and I caught the sound with my mouth, pressing her against the door.

She opened her mouth, but the door vibrated beneath my arm as someone knocked.

"Do not enter," I growled, ignoring Rythos's low laugh. Prisca was already grabbing my hand in an attempt to pull me away.

I sighed, allowing it. Rythos strolled inside, giving me a nod.

"I'll leave you alone," I said. I could feel those eyes on me once more, and this time, they felt different. Malevolent.

I wanted them away from Prisca.

She studied my face. "I'll see you soon."

"Soon, wildcat," I promised.

Rythos heaved a sigh. "You'll be parted for an hour or two at most. This is getting ridiculous."

Ignoring him, I pulled Prisca to me for another kiss. Perhaps I could throw him out.

She poked a finger into my chest, and I raised my head with a sigh. "Fine."

Her laugh seemed to caress my skin as I closed the door behind me. Stalking down the empty corridor, I made my way toward Galon's rooms.

I was instantly surrounded. Jolting away, I drew my sword, sweeping my gaze over my attackers. The men wore maroon and gold, weapons in their hands. They'd clearly already come from a battle, all of them covered in blood.

If they'd taken the castle, they would be aiming for Prisca.

I slashed out with my sword...

And my blade sliced into one of Rekja's walls.

The air froze in my lungs.

My blade had also cut into the throat of one of the Eprothan soldiers. But where there should have been a man lying dying on the ground, choking on his own blood...

There was nothing.

I was completely, utterly alone.

9

MADINIA

Calysian helped me search for the hybrids. They had left obvious tracks—branches broken, footprints in damp dirt. And they likely hadn't managed to run very far. Without his help fighting the iron guards, all of the hybrids would have been slaughtered.

Perhaps I should thank him. It went against most of my instincts, but...

Turning to him, I found him glowering at me.

"What?"

"Where is the hybrid queen?"

"Busy calling our allies to war." I gave him a warning look. I was allowed to speak critically about Prisca. This man had not earned that right.

His dark eyes glittered. Either with amusement or annoyance, I wasn't sure. The man was irritatingly difficult to read.

Somewhere in the distance, a child was wailing. I barely hid a flinch.

"Thank you," I ground out, my gaze on the forest ahead as I picked my way over a fallen branch.

"Look at me."

My muscles locked up. This man needed to learn that I didn't take orders.

"Madinia," he crooned. "Look at me."

I took a long breath and turned, attempting to ignore the way his low voice had made my lungs squeeze. This man was a predator through and through.

He stared at me as if I were a pawn he was considering putting into play—his dark eyes filled with ruthless calculation.

"The fates have seen fit to push us together more than once. One day, when I need you, you will help me with my own goals."

It would be difficult for him to find me on another continent. But still, the entitlement in his voice infuriated me. I said nothing, and he seemed content with my silence. Likely, he'd decided I would fall in line with his decrees.

He truly was an idiot.

We plunged deeper into the dense forest. The sounds of the natural world enveloped me, a stark contrast to the turmoil and death we'd just left behind. My heart still raced, each beat a reminder of the gravity of our situation.

Even with tracks the hybrids had left, Calysian's keen eyes spotted signs of passage I would have missed.

The child's wailing began again, this time even louder. If not for the looming presence next to me, the child—and all the others in our group—would have been buried together in more unmarked graves.

"You saved a lot of lives today," I said.

That dark gaze flicked to me, a flash of something I couldn't identify in his eyes before he nodded curtly.

We approached the hybrids' chosen hiding spot.

Their fear was almost palpable, and it was evident that they hadn't been able to run any farther. This was where they had decided to take a stand.

My mouth watered as sickness crawled up my throat. They would have died screaming. All because Regner had twisted the minds of those he had raised as iron guards.

A dagger flew through the air toward Calysian. One of the boys attempting to defend the others.

Calysian caught the blade, a deep line appearing between his brows.

"Stand down," I sighed. "He helped me fight the iron guards."

The boy gulped. "Are they…"

"That group is dead. We don't know if there will be more to follow."

The hybrids gathered their meager belongings, their movements quick but shaky. Calysian watched the scene with an inscrutable expression. "I must leave now."

I wasn't surprised. In truth, I was only surprised he'd stayed this long.

His dark gaze speared into me. "Remember what I said."

I showed him my teeth. "If you attempt to force me into submission, you will regret it."

The group around us ceased speaking, and I could feel their attention on us. Calysian smiled. "If anyone could achieve such a feat as to make me regret my actions, it would likely be you."

Without another word, he turned and walked away, melting into the forest. Despite the fact that we no longer had the benefit of his power and sword, some of the tension dissolved from my muscles.

Turning back to the hybrids, I led them forward, toward our next hiding spot—a hidden cave nestled in a thicket. The moon hung in the sky like a gift from the gods, considering how dark the forest had become. Something unwound in my chest. The iron guards would have split all escape routes into sectors. With several of them lying dead in the forest, we likely had a little time to rest.

And we needed it. The supplies had been cleverly warded to keep animals away, and we pulled out more blankets and dried meat. It was too risky to light a fire, so we slept huddled together, the adults taking turns on sentry duty.

At least, the others slept. I couldn't sleep with the ball of dread heavy in my gut. Each time I closed my eyes, my body reacted with a racing pulse and tense muscles, alert and waiting for the next calamity.

We were up with the sun the next day, trudging through the forest. With its dense canopy and tangled underbrush, it seemed to stretch endlessly before us, various shades of green blaring into a monotonous march. Each step was a battle against the fatigue pressing down on my body.

Our progress was slow, hindered by the ever-present fear of discovery, even now. The constant vigilance, the hushed whispers, the wary glances—all of it combined to further steal what little energy we had left.

The path, strewn with twisted roots and fallen branches, seemed to mock our efforts, our steps becoming shorter, our feet often failing to lift high enough to remove the risk of stumbling. As the day wore on, the weight of exhaustion grew heavier. As did the weight of the children the adults carried. The young girl in my arms had somehow managed to fall asleep, her head nestled into my neck, even as I continually switched her from hip to hip in an effort to ease the weight in my arms and back.

The adults kept a stoic front for the children, but the strain was evident in the deep lines etched on their foreheads, the hunch of their shoulders, the exhaustion in their eyes as the hours wore on.

As the sun began its descent, painting the sky in hues of pinks and purples, I attempted to remember what came next. I knew we were traveling in the correct direction, but a dense, heavy fog had swept into my mind, and I couldn't lift the mist enough to determine where we were supposed to stay next.

There were safe houses in various villages, but we hadn't taken one of those routes. Or had we?

My mind whirled, until it felt as if the ground itself was shifting beneath my feet. I leaned on a tree to steady myself, and Glenda handed me a waterskin.

"Drink." Her tone left no room for objections.

I took a few sips, conscious of how long the water might need to last.

The last rays of light began to fade, casting long shadows in front of us. And then I heard it.

At first, I thought I was imagining the faint sounds of voices, a murmur of life in the suffocating stillness of the forest.

And then, a woman was standing in front of me, wide-eyed, a crossbow in her hand. "Come quick," she called to someone, and I wanted to tell her to shut her fucking mouth before she drew the wrong kind of attention.

"Survivors!" someone else shouted.

I felt my eyes roll back as I slumped to my knees.

PRISCA

Rythos folded his arms and gave me a dark look. "You wanted to see me?"

His tone was oddly formal.

I frowned at him. "Um…"

Realization slammed into me, and a sick feeling swelled through my body. It was because I'd summoned him. As if he were my subject.

I'd asked Rythos to meet me places before. But tonight, he was bristling from what he likely thought was my order. And I knew it wasn't truly about me. Knew that on any other night, he would have shown up with a grin on his face, eyes dancing as he made some teasing remark.

"I…I thought this might be a good place to talk. Lorian tested the silence ward on the balcony."

Some of the ire left his eyes, and he nodded. We looked at each other in awkward silence for a long moment. While technically he would be my subject when he lived in the hybrid kingdom, he had to know I wouldn't throw my weight around. And yet…

"Pris?" He smirked at me. "It's fine. Let's talk on the balcony."

I threw open the wide doors and stepped outside. It was cooler here at night, but the wind wasn't quite cool enough for me to need a cloak.

And I was still putting off this conversation. I needed to choose my words carefully.

"I noticed you didn't like the priestess." So much for speaking carefully.

Rage flickered in Rythos's eyes. "They're responsible for just as much pain and carnage as Regner's assessors. How many times did you watch them steal power from tiny, innocent babies, Prisca?"

The memory of the last Taking I'd seen flashed through my mind before I could stop it. The baby had screamed so loudly…

Forcing the memory away, I leaned on the balcony railing next to him. "You heard what she said. Some of the priestesses were working against Regner."

"Not enough of them."

We were both silent for a long moment. And then Rythos sighed. "You're right. I'm not…reasonable or neutral when it comes to those women."

"What happened, Rythos? You don't need to talk about it if you don't want to," I blurted. "But it might help."

He sighed. "It was during the time Conreth separated all of us. After Lorian refused to kill the wildkin. I was in northern Eprotha—not far from your village, although you hadn't yet been born." His eyes glittered. "It was before Regner truly knew just how dangerous Lorian and the rest of us were—back when we could still walk freely in our human glamour. I met a woman."

"Ah."

He slid me an amused look. "Yes. Ah."

"And you fell in love."

"Love?" He raised one eyebrow. "At the time, I thought it was love. Now, I know it was nothing more than infatuation. Seeing the way you and Lorian are together... it proves I didn't have anything real with her."

My chest clenched. "I'm sorry."

"Don't be. Your love gives me hope, darlin'. There's something so pure about it—even when you both want to strangle each other."

I laughed. One side of his mouth kicked up into a crooked smile, but it disappeared just as quickly.

"We were together for months before I realized she was a priestess. I was traveling often, completing various tasks for Conreth. I never saw her in her robes. I completely missed the signs."

Priestesses weren't celibate. It wasn't unusual for them to take lovers. So that hadn't been the problem.

"She didn't know you were fae."

Rythos slowly shook his head. "And then she realized she was pregnant."

My stomach twisted into a tight coil. But I waited for him to finish the worst of his story.

"For us fae...any children are a miracle."

I nodded. Their low fertility seemed to be a result of their long life-spans.

"When I learned she was pregnant, I was so ecstatic, I lost control of my glamour. She told me she would never subject herself to breeding with a monster. And she walked out. I gave her a few days, assuming she would calm down and we would talk."

Grief tightened the corners of his eyes.

"She…"

"Yes. She went to the stone hags, who used their power to…"

Heat seared the back of my throat. I'd seen Rythos with Piperia. He would have made an incredible father.

"I can't imagine how painful that was."

"The worst part was…she *wanted* a baby. She would have done anything to be a mother. Except have *my* baby."

His eyes turned bleak, and I reached for his hand. "I know it probably seems likely that Mona is just another coldhearted priestess. But believing that a group of people are all the same is one of the reasons this continent is the way it is. You don't have to communicate with Mona if you don't want to. But…you could find it healing."

He squeezed my hand. "You're right about believing people are all the same. I just… I can't ever see her in those robes, Prisca."

"I'll make sure you never do."

"Then I'll think about it."

The door swung open behind us, and Lorian stepped onto the balcony.

"Prisca." His face was tight with sorrow.

My lungs seized until my voice was barely a whisper. "What is it?"

"I just got a message. The hybrid camp was attacked. Most of them were slaughtered. Some are still moving toward the Asric Pass, but they are being hunted by Regner's iron guards."

Most of them were slaughtered.

My knees turned weak. Rythos caught my arm, steering me toward Lorian, who pulled me into his chest. "I'm so fucking sorry, wildcat."

"Madinia. Vicer."

"I don't know."

"She was right." I let out a laugh that came out more than a little hysterical. "When Madinia told Vicer to use his power on Stillcrest, I was against it. And now all those hybrids...the *children*."

My eyes burned, but I couldn't seem to cry. I didn't deserve the release of tears.

My people. The people I was supposed to keep safe.

Consequences.

Were these the consequences from the gods? I turned back time to save one life and lost hundreds or thousands more?

I was going to be sick. I was—

A scream cut through the night. Followed immediately by several more. My heart jumped into my throat, and I pulled away from Lorian as Rythos squinted into the distance.

"What can you see?" I demanded, wishing yet again for fae vision.

"Winged beasts. Heading this way. From the north."

10

PRISCA

Rekja's war room was a grand chamber that sprawled across the uppermost floor of the castle's east wing. Windows on each side offered views of both the city below us and the dock to the east.

The sky was filled with winged creatures. Likely, they were the same creatures that had attacked the rebel camp and almost killed Demos. They hovered at some invisible line in the distance, waiting to attack.

Outside the northern city gates, the ground was a sea of black. More creatures, only these were clearly confined to the ground. Behind them, soldiers hauled catapults and battering rams, while others built siege towers.

Flames flickered in the distance. They were setting up their encampment. I took a moment to reach for the threads of my magic, hope flickering in my chest.

But no. My power was still nowhere to be found.

I hadn't expected it to be back. And still, the disappointment engulfed me.

Inside, the room buzzed with an undercurrent of tense energy. Every chair around the massive oakwood table was occupied by Rekja's commanders, generals, and advisers, their expressions ranging from determination to weariness.

More soldiers lined the walls, their backs straight and hands clasped behind them, lined the walls.

"We need to send a message to Asinia, Demos, and Tibris," I told Lorian. "They're traveling this way."

"Already done. I told them to head toward Thobirea," he said, and some of the knots in my stomach unraveled. His gaze flicked to Rekja, who stood near one of the windows, gazing down at the city below him. I didn't ask why Rekja's scouts hadn't seen the Eprothans approaching earlier. If they hadn't sounded the alarm, it was because they were likely dead.

When his eyes met mine, they held grim acceptance.

"Regner isn't here. He sent his general, Tymedes. He has demanded I concede this kingdom to Eprotha."

For a long, hideous moment, I couldn't even speak.

Rekja glanced at Lorian when I didn't reply. "This would always have happened. My father clung to his ignorance, believing Regner would allow Gromalia to exist. And that together, human kings would rule all four kingdoms." His mouth twisted.

"This city is in a strategic location to take the rest of Gromalia," Lorian said. "Regner can't take the capital by water, but if this city falls, the Eprothans can use this as their base until they're ready to continue moving south."

Rekja said nothing. His eyes had turned empty, almost lifeless.

"Regner has decided to use the monsters he has been hiding," Galon said. "And that makes me wonder where he is positioning the rest of his human soldiers."

Rekja gestured to the monsters flittering back and forth above Regner's soldiers. "What are they?"

Lorian studied them. While Asinia had sent us a message describing them after their attack on the rebels, he hadn't wanted to give his opinion until he saw exactly what they were. And from the cold wrath in his eyes, he now knew. "The winged creatures are known as skyrions. The creatures on the ground are terrovians." He looked at me. "They have been twisted to obey Reiner's command, but their original home was within Sylvielle's territory."

And Regner had stolen them as babies, breeding them until they were a substantial part of his army. There were enough skyrions and terrovians here to rip everyone in this city apart.

"What do we do?" My lips were numb. My voice didn't sound like mine. I reached for my power, searching yet again for some tiny spark as I clutched my hourglass.

Nothing.

"This city isn't built for a prolonged siege," Rekja said. "Residents will begin evacuating through tunnels beneath the city. But there won't be enough time to get them all out. Sorlithia will fall. The most we can do is attempt to save as many lives as possible."

Across the room, Thora's bottom lip trembled. This was their favorite place. The city they likely escaped to often. I hadn't seen much of it, yet what I had seen, I'd loved.

And Regner would destroy it and everyone here.

The loss of my power was crippling. Without it, I would carry hundreds or thousands of deaths on my conscience.

"Where do the tunnels end?" I asked.

"Deep within the forest, along the border between both kingdoms."

I barely hid my wince. Between Regner's regiments and the hybrid camp.

"Tell them to move south," I said.

"Of course they will move south." Rekja gave me a look.

"Not to the next city," I said. "Not to the next villages. Regner will simply continue wiping them out. Tell your people to move toward central Gromalia."

Rekja hesitated. Clearly, while he was willing to ally with us, trusting his people to the fae still wasn't something that came naturally to him.

"We are moving our people out," I said. "Those who can't fight will be traveling to the hybrid kingdom through the Asric Pass. Those who can fight will join together— hybrid and fae fighting side by side. Fight with us, Rekja. Tell your generals to march your army all the way south. Our armies are setting up a camp there, ready to march on our orders."

His eyes flared. "And were you going to ask permission before marching into my kingdom?"

He was terrified for his people. And some tiny part of him blamed me and my people for Regner's actions. So I simply gave him a steady look. "Yes. That conversation was going to happen tomorrow."

His gaze held mine, before slowly shifting to Lorian's. But he knew he had no choice. At this point, he had nowhere else to move his army without putting them directly in Regner's path. And we needed to strategize before we met the human king in battle.

"Fine."

"How long did Tymedes give you?" Marth's voice came from behind us. He was leaning against the wall, sharpening one of his blades.

"Twenty hours."

Enough time to devastate morale. Not enough time to fully prepare for a siege. Enough time for thousands in this city to contemplate death. Not enough time for reinforcements to arrive.

If Daharak hadn't already sailed south, we would have had her ships. But this battle wouldn't be fought on water. And the skyrions would decimate her fleet. My heart tripped. What if she had been intercepted while leaving Gromalian waters? My aunt, the pirate queen, and the two hundred ships that sailed with us could already be at the bottom of the ocean.

If only we'd brought Jamic with us. The fae king had assured Rythos that he would teach Jamic to effectively wield the power that seethed within him. So that when we walked onto the battlefield, Jamic could access as much of that power as possible.

But we would have stood a better chance with him here.

"My father had never imagined Regner might attack this castle," Rekja said, and I forced myself to stop lingering on the what-ifs. "We don't have enough of a stockpile of supplies for long."

I didn't say what we were all probably thinking. With those deadly creatures waiting, this was unlikely to take long anyway.

"The skyrions attacked the rebel camp," I said. "They were able to fight them off. Tell your soldiers to aim for their wings or their heads."

"And you?" he asked, gesturing to the hourglass around my neck.

"I haven't been able to access my power since we took down the barrier." I fought to keep my voice steady. But I had to steel myself against the bitter disappointment in Rekja's eyes.

Around us, Rekja's people were murmuring, expressions serious. Lorian stepped forward, taking my hand. "If we have twenty hours, we need to use them to get as many people out of the city as possible," he said. "Without creating panic or alerting Regner's general to our plans."

And so, as the sun rose higher in the sky, we traveled along the beautiful Sorlithian streets I had admired. The streets that would soon run red with blood. Each of us carried a seal from Rekja, ensuring his people would believe us when we told them what was happening.

The evacuation needed to be quiet. Contained.

Just as the rebels had built tunnels beneath Lesdryn, some clever ancestor of Rekja's had done the same beneath Sorlithia. Perhaps he had known Regner. Known it was only a matter of time before the madman to the north turned on the Gromalian people.

Entire families took whatever they could carry and scurried into the tunnels. This wasn't something any of them had ever planned for, and yet they moved quickly. Perhaps more people would escape than I'd first imagined.

Still, I searched again and again and again for my power.

Please, I begged the gods. *Please.*

Where my power had one radiated deep within me, now there was nothing.

Some of the Sorlithians who were too weak to move were carried. But others couldn't be moved. They would stay with the human healers who refused to leave their patients' sides, defying orders from anyone who attempted to make them leave.

My eyes burned, the muscles in my chest clenching. Tibris would have stayed too.

Our own healer was on one of Daharak's ships—hopefully still sailing south.

Finally, exhausted, we returned to the castle to prepare our next move.

Lorian kissed my forehead. "I want you to try to get some rest."

I slitted my eyes at him.

He snarled back at me, clearly exhausted himself. "You're almost asleep on your feet."

I dropped my gaze. "My power still hasn't returned, Lorian. If all I can do is help people flee, then…"

His hand caught my chin, and he waited until I met his eyes. They softened. "Don't you dare believe for one second that your worth as a queen—or even as a person—depends on your ability to access that power."

A lump had formed in my throat. I heard him, but in this moment, when my power could save so many lives… It was difficult to believe I hadn't failed everyone who would die today.

"There are still people who were moving too slowly to evacuate," I murmured.

"It's too late," Rekja said behind us. "Tymedes has become impatient. Our time is up."

LORIAN

Regner couldn't have known that Prisca would come here. And yet, his general was likely rubbing his hands together at the thought of killing the hybrid heir and taking her body back to his king like a cat displaying its kill.

With a thought, I dissolved my human glamour and returned to my fae form. My teeth and ears lengthened, my body grew a little stronger, my senses heightened.

None of us was wearing armor.

Not even Prisca. She was too petite. Unlike in the hybrid or fae kingdoms, which recognized that women could make the most vicious fighters of all, most soldiers in Gromalia and Eprotha were men. The breastplates were too large, the gauntlets would prevent her from using her hands, and the chain mail would slow her down.

For Marth, Galon, Rythos, and me, the armor was too small. Even in our human forms, it would restrict our movements.

Prisca met my gaze, raising one eyebrow. Even if I could yank her out of here, she would never be the first to leave. I would have to knock her unconscious.

"Don't even think about it," she muttered. "I may not

have my power, but I have my brain, and I can still swing a sword."

She could. She was fast—even faster with her daggers than her sword. No one had trained harder than my wildcat, even while traveling.

"A moment," I said, gesturing to the door and glancing at Marth, Rythos, Galon, and Prisca.

Rekja nodded, turning back to stare out the windows.

I opened the door across the hall, finding a small sitting room.

Prisca walked ahead, murmuring quietly to Rythos. I grabbed Galon's arm. "I need you to—"

"I know. If you fall or if it looks like there is no hope left, I will get her out. I promise."

Some of the tension melted from my muscles. But I leaned closer. "You will need to hold some power back during the battle. And…if it comes to such a choice, Prisca will fight you."

His mouth twitched. "Let me worry about that."

Relief swept through me like a cool breeze, and we stepped into the room with the others, Galon pulling the door closed behind us.

"Rekja knows this city will fall," I said. "But while he may think he understands what that means, it will be very, very different when it actually happens."

Rythos nodded. "This is his first test as a king—not yet crowned. And unlike his father, he truly cares for his people. He will likely attempt to stay. If he dies, there is currently no successor to the Gromalian throne."

I nodded. I had seen it time and time again. Leaders who had stayed behind in a desperate bid to save their people. It never ended well.

"Which means his generals and distant relatives will be scrambling for power," Marth said. "Right while we need the Gromalians allied with us and focused on the threat Regner represents."

Prisca nodded, but I could tell it still bothered her—thinking this way. In her mind, we should want to save Rekja because he was a good man. And because no one should be left behind to die.

"So we haul him out of here," she said, meeting my gaze. There was a hint of challenge in her eyes.

"If it comes down to it, we knock him out and drag him out of the city," Galon said.

"That would be enough for him to declare war," Rythos warned.

I barely heard him. I was too busy staring at Prisca's unprotected body. As much as I still wanted to raid Rekja's armory, it would be useless.

Panic sliced through me like a blade, and my voice was just as sharp. "You stay next to me, wildcat. I mean it. If you go wandering away to save some unlucky soul, I'll cart you out of here myself."

Galon stood close enough to me that I could see his shoulders shaking out of the corner of my eye. Marth made a choked sound. Prisca narrowed her eyes at both of them before turning back to me. "Threats are unnecessary," she bit out.

Rythos burst out laughing. "With a woman as stubborn as you, threats are all Lorian has."

My entire body suddenly went cold. I could feel those eyes on me once more. The hair rose on the back of my neck, and I suppressed a snarl. If one of the dark gods wanted to drag me to Hubur, they wouldn't do it during this battle.

I would not leave Prisca alone. Not here.

Prisca sniffed at Rythos. "Traitor." Turning her attention back to me, she took my hand. Her skin was so soft, the bones of her hand delicate. Fragile. "I know I'm useless without my power, Lorian. I'll stay close. I promise."

I cast a single glance at the others, and they grabbed their weapons and filed out of the room.

I caught Prisca's chin in my hand. "You are not, and could never be, useless. If I have made you feel that way, then I apologize, wildcat. I merely thought we would have more time before…this. I knew you would fight, but I imagined you fully armed and able to access your magic, with enough armor to keep you as safe as possible…and our own armies at your back."

A sick kind of panic took up residence in my chest as I realized just how much danger she would be in.

Her expression softened. "This city will fall. I know this, Lorian. And I will leave when there is no other choice. But until then, we save as many lives as we can."

I stroked her stubborn chin with my thumb. "Deal."

PRISCA

My lungs burned, my heart raced, and I had yet to

swing my sword. Behind me, Lorian waited for me to climb up the internal staircase to the top of the northern city wall, following me up once I'd reached the top.

Rekja had stationed most of his soldiers here, where they could use the battlements and crenellations for cover while observing the battle. The air was thick with fear, anticipation, charged with the energy of a storm about to break.

The king himself wore silver armor, his helmet adorned with a green stripe worked into the metal. He stood a couple hundred footspans away, on the northwestern intersection of the city walls, his gaze on our enemy in the distance.

The scent of the sea mingled with smoke and iron. At our backs, the city stretched out, Rekja's people running for their lives.

The soldiers around us moved with purpose, armor clinking softly as they adjusted their helmets, checked their weapons, joked uneasily with those they would fight and die next to.

A horn blew in the distance, and the ground seemed to undulate as thousands of creatures shot toward the city. My teeth began to chatter. Lorian's hand found my shoulder and squeezed. He didn't say a word, simply stood next to me, a silent support.

Skyrions darkened the sky, flapping feathered wings as some of them split off, perhaps to chase after Daharak's ships. Fog rolled over my mind, until I could only think one word—Telean.

We weren't currently speaking. Neither of us had said goodbye before I'd left. By now, I should know better than to tempt fate that way. My aunt was on one of those ships, and—

No. If I thought like that, the terror would cripple me.

I caught a glimpse of one of the skyrions, highlighted by the moonlight. Long arms ending in clawed talons, a hunched spine, glowing red eyes... My stomach roiled.

On the ground, terrovians sprinted toward the walls. Their fur was dark, so sleek it seemed almost like oil dripping across the ridges of their muscles. The creatures' heads swayed, low and intent, sending a shiver down my spine. It was like watching shadows come to life.

I dragged my gaze away and caught a muscle ticking in Lorian's jaw. His hands fisted, and I could practically feel the frustration eating at him.

"You can kill them all, can't you?"

"The power that burns through me when you are in danger...I can access it once more. I can likely kill everything in the sky," Lorian said. "It's too difficult to differentiate targets on the ground, and the fae fire would spread, doing more damage to the people remaining in this city than Tymedes's army."

"You...you kept your fire contained in Eryndan's castle."

"Because it burned for mere moments in a confined space. This would ravage through anything it touched." His eyes turned intent. "I will be almost powerless if I do this. You currently don't have any access to your own power."

And the protective part of him that insisted he shield me from everything dangerous was urging him to conserve that power.

"Do it. Kill the creatures in the sky." Lorian was death with a weapon in his hand. But I'd heard from Asinia just how much damage the winged creatures could do.

The first skyrions reached the city walls, tucking in their wings and aiming for Rekja's soldiers.

"Fire," one of Rekja's generals screamed.

Arrows filled the sky. But where each skyrion fell, another took its place, slashing out with teeth and claws, lifting soldiers from the wall and throwing them to the ground. I reached for my power out of habit, uselessly watching as one of the soldiers went over the wall, his gaze locking with mine.

I grabbed Lorian's arm.

"Innocent people are dying!"

A muscle feathered in his jaw. I shouldn't have attempted that kind of logic. Lorian would save innocents whenever he could, but if it came down to me or them, he would choose me every time.

"I'll protect her," Galon said behind us. "You know I have enough power to do it."

Lorian turned and studied him. His cheekbones seemed even sharper than usual, his eyes wild.

"Please," I begged.

He gave a stiff nod, turning to the sky. His expression turned almost serene. Relaxed. As if it had taken everything in him *not* to use his power, and this was some kind of mental and physical release.

His eyes turned white, the way they sometimes did when his lightning had slipped free. But it wasn't that power that he aimed. No, it was fae fire that swept through the sky. Red, orange, yellow, and purple. My breath caught. It was as beautiful and deadly as the man himself.

Every skyrion in the air turned to ash.

Choked gasps sounded behind us. Footsteps sounded, as if someone had turned to run.

A man let out a sound like a squeak. "Bloodthirsty—"

"Don't you dare!" I whirled on Rekja's soldier.

Lorian's arm came around my waist, and he buried his head in my neck. His entire body was trembling with obvious fatigue. But after one long inhale, he lifted his head.

I cupped his face until he looked at me. His eyes were wild in a way that made my heart thunder. But he didn't need fear. Not from me.

Slowly, he came back to himself. His lips pressed to mine for the barest moment, and he inhaled again, as if my scent was clearing his head.

One of Rekja's soldiers turned toward us, his face white. "They're... Some of the creatures on the ground are fleeing."

I followed his gaze, my breaths stilling in my chest...

He was right.

Some of the terrovians that had been clawing at the walls were turning to run, their instincts likely screaming at them after Lorian's decimation.

But still more of them were digging their claws into those walls. And I let myself imagine—just for a single moment—what I could do if I had my power.

And then they began to howl.

The sound pierced the night, seeming to shake the

stone beneath my feet. The scent of fear and sweat curled up my nostrils, and my entire body went cold.

"Their howls increase fear," Galon said, plucking a crossbow from one of Rekja's soldiers—a young man who was shaking too hard to hold it straight. Galon's arrow lodged straight into the throat of the terrovian clambering up the wall, and the creature fell, taking several others with it.

Galon's no-nonsense refusal to panic seemed to help the soldiers around us reach for their own calm. They launched arrow after arrow, taking down as many terrovians as they could before the creatures reached the top of the walls.

Lorian wrapped my hand around my sword, gave me a look that warned me not to do anything that might cause him a single moment of concern, and turned to behead the first creature that made it up to the top of the city gates.

Next to me, Rythos sliced a terrovian almost in two. On his other side, Marth shoved his sword deep, before kicking the creature to the ground and swinging once more.

Something barreled at me, and all I could see were long, vicious teeth. I twisted, and the creature slid past my body, but it was breathtakingly fast, immediately righting itself with a fluid, menacing grace.

I lunged forward, driving my sword toward the creature. It moved with terrifying agility, but Galon's insistence on repetitive, never-ending drills had finally honed my reflexes. My sword found its mark, plunging into the creature's side. It howled, and the sound sent shivers down my spine, urging me to release my grip on the sword. I tightened my hand instead, and the beast thrashed, its movements becoming erratic, desperate. I held on, pushing deeper as its hot blood gushed over my hands.

But I needed my sword free. Ripping my blade from the creature, I turned, coming face-to-face with a terrovian that snapped at me, just inches away.

I let out a yelp. The terrovian's head hit the ground, and my eyes met Lorian's.

He scanned me for damage, his eyes feral. I gave him what I hoped was a reassuring nod, and he planted himself closer to me, turning to kick out at the next beast.

My breaths came in sharp pants, my hand slick on the hilt of my sword. It was heavier than anything I'd trained with, but I swung it again and again and again. One of Rekja's soldiers screamed, falling from the wall, his chest a bloody ruin. I caught a glimpse of the king himself, closer to us now as he lunged at the terrovian, before I was forced to turn and meet the next attack.

The creature died with my sword buried in its gut, and I had a single moment to glance below us as the gates shuddered. Eprothan soldiers had followed the terrovians. The humans slammed battering rams into the wall, the gate, anything they could. To our right, several of them were clawing their way up a siege tower. Galon waited until they were almost at the top before unleashing his own power, the water slamming into the tower and washing away any soldiers or terrovians within his reach.

Lorian leaned down, beheading another creature before turning to Galon with a snarl. He wanted Galon to conserve his power to get us out. And I knew if I'd had my power, that agreement wouldn't have been necessary.

The bitterness on my tongue tasted almost as bad as the terrovian blood that had sprayed my face.

Galon jerked his head behind us, and I followed his gaze. He'd bought us time. Time for oil to be brought from the kitchens. This city couldn't have been less prepared for attack. We would have to use the oil sparingly.

The scalding liquid gleamed ominously, and Rekja waited until the exact moment the gates were almost heaving with creatures and soldiers.

He nodded to one of his soldiers, who lifted his hand. The huge cauldron rose into the air, tipping slowly. And then it moved across the entire width of the gate, spilling oil over anyone—and anything—beneath it.

The screams were chilling.

But the oil bought us a few desperate moments to gulp some water as the terrovians backed away from the wall below us, snarling. I surveyed Lorian, Galon, and Marth. All of them were covered in blood, but none looked seriously injured.

"Rythos?"

Lorian nodded behind me, and I whirled, finding Rythos leaning precariously from the wall.

"Is he *talking* to someone?" I took a couple of steps closer, my head spinning. But it was a group of Eprothan soldiers hanging from the wall. The oil had missed them, and they'd aimed for Rythos. They'd made it close enough to him that he could use his power.

Within moments, they'd begun to turn on their own people, creating confusion and chaos. Rythos got to his feet and stumbled. Clearly, he'd expended a lot of power in a short time.

I launched toward him, but Marth was already there, preventing him from falling over the edge.

My gaze slid past the others, to Rekja's soldiers. And my muscles locked up.

I'd been fighting in the midst of deadly, experienced fae warriors. And so I hadn't noticed just how dire our situation had become. The soldiers Rekja had ordered to the wall had thinned significantly.

Even their best warders hadn't been able to hold the line for long against soldiers bloated with Regner's magic and arrows tipped with fae iron.

It was only a matter of time before the enemy made it through. Already, their siege ladders were being hauled close once more.

Despair slid into my chest like a finely sharpened blade. I pulled, automatically searching for the threads of my power once more. But it was as if those threads had been cut.

People were going to die here, and all I could do was kill a few terrovians.

Was this the price Telean had spoken of? Would the consequences of my actions be to watch innocents die one by one, until it was my friends and family who were the ones being slaughtered?

And then the creatures were upon us in a maelstrom of fur and fangs and fear, each terrovian a blur of deadly grace, and there was no time to rest, no time to think, as more terrovians made it to the wall—Eprothan soldiers following close behind. At some point, they'd already managed to get another siege ladder up.

I'd once thought I might find it difficult to kill humans. But the rage burning through me made it much, much easier than I'd ever imagined.

These soldiers were filled with blood lust, trained to attack innocents. They would kill everyone in this city if ordered.

When they saw Lorian and the others, many of the soldiers faltered. But with nowhere else to go, they attacked. Again and again.

Galon used his power to sweep more of them away, while I could practically feel Lorian itching for more of his own power. He was able to summon enough lightning to work with Galon's water, killing any soldiers unlucky enough to be touching that water, but frustration and fatigued warred on his face.

And yet, if he hadn't killed the skyrions, the city would already have been Regner's.

An Eprothan soldier lunged at me, and I met his sword. Fuck, he was strong. I slammed my foot into his knee, and he howled, swinging his sword again. But it was sloppy, his body unbalanced. Darting to the side, I tripped him, throwing him off the wall.

I turned just in time to block the next sword, twisting my body to protect my own blade—and arm.

This was nothing like training with Galon. Never could I have imagined having such little space to work with, the stone slick with blood and water beneath my feet. It was so crowded, I barely had room to move.

But every soldier and creature we killed was one less to kill the innocent people of this city.

Chaos reigned.

A blade slipped past my guard, slicing into my arm. Hot pain slid up my bicep, and a choked scream left my throat as my sword hand faltered. Lorian was instantly there, his own sword cleaving the soldier's chest.

"It's not bad," I protested, but he'd already ripped off a piece of his tunic to tie around the wound.

"Prisca." His voice was gentle. I knew what he was going to say.

"No."

"I want you to go," Lorian murmured, as if I hadn't spoken. His fist slid out and smashed into an approaching soldier's face. The man dropped to his knees with a grunt, and Rythos kicked him off the wall. The soldier screamed for a brief moment. "With Galon," Lorian continued. "Now."

"You know I won't leave you." It felt as if he'd been shattered apart yesterday, an hour ago, a second ago. When I looked at him, all I could see was ice.

He gripped my chin, his green eyes burning into mine. "All of us will leave at some point. They're going to take this city."

"We go together. I'm not leaving you here, powerless." Not after watching him die so recently.

"You make me insane."

"I love you too."

His lips twitched. Then I was in his arms, his mouth crashing down on mine. Within a moment, we were fighting back-to-back once more, the brief reprieve over.

I launched toward the soldier aiming for Lorian's back, a feral snarl leaving my throat.

And then Marth screamed Rythos's name.

11

LORIAN

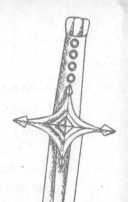

"*To your right!*" a voice roared, echoing through my head until I spun.

A voice that made my heart leap into my throat.

A voice I'd thought I would never hear again.

I searched for him frantically, my gaze snagging on Rythos, who fought with brutal ferocity against two of Regner's soldiers, his teeth bared, eyes alight with challenge.

But a third was approaching from behind. Next to him, Marth kicked out at one of the terrovians, burying his sword in another's eye.

One of them crouched, preparing to launch at him, but he was already moving, slicing his way toward Rythos.

Ducking beneath a soldier who wielded both a mace and a shield, I slammed my foot into the side of his knee and slipped around him, slashing out again and again.

Time slowed to the barest crawl.

Rythos whirled. His arm was already coming up, too slow to parry the attack from behind.

Marth was instantly there. He swung his sword. But the terrovian hit him from the side, pushing him off-balance.

My own sword was already whistling through the air, and the terrovian's head dropped to the stone, separated from its body. But Marth was too slow to meet the knife still aimed toward Rythos with his own blade.

So he met it with his body.

Rythos made a sound caught somewhere between a roar, a howl, and a sob. It echoed across the wall, until it seemed the fighting paused for the barest moment. He moved faster than I'd ever seen him move before, his dagger whipping out to slash the soldier in the throat.

Marth's hand had already reached for the hilt of the knife buried in his chest.

"Don't touch the knife!" Prisca screamed. She ducked around a soldier and crouched, slicing his hamstrings. He bent, already falling, and she ruthlessly kicked him in the ass, sending him careening off the wall.

My gaze met Marth's. He was still alive. But the fae iron so close to his heart…

Rythos clamped down on Marth's hand, preventing him from pulling the blade free—and bleeding out right here. "You know better," he growled.

Marth slumped. Rythos easily hauled him up, cradling him to his chest. "They've overrun the city," he said. "It's time to fall back."

I slashed my sword through the throat of a soldier who came too close and surveyed the city below us. Rythos was right. While we'd been guarding this part of the wall, Regner's army had merely attacked the weaker points.

Siege ladders were clustered along the north and west walls. Even as I watched Rekja's soldiers use what little power they had left in an attempt to bring them down…

It was far too late.

The soldiers had poured over the walls and were rampaging through the city. The screams carried over the clashing swords surrounding us.

We had bought the city as much time as we could. But now, we needed to ensure Rekja got out of here alive.

In the city at our backs, an Eprothan soldier dragged a Gromalian woman by the hair, a vicious smile on his face. Galon threw one of his daggers, and the soldier slumped, clutching at his throat as he bled out. The woman fell with him but didn't hesitate, scrambling to her feet and running for her life.

"Take Marth," I bit out. "I'm going for Rekja."

Galon cursed. But he knew I was right. Marth needed a healer, and I needed to ensure the Gromalian king stayed alive.

Marth's head lolled, but he raised his hand, pointing.

I spun, my gaze finding Rekja fighting on top of a battlement, Thora at his side.

Prisca darted close, lashing out at another soldier. But the Eprothan siege was a success. We'd saved as many lives as we could.

Galon's eyes met mine. "You need to take Rythos with you."

Rythos stared at Marth and opened his mouth, clearly torn. But his gaze shifted to Rekja, still swinging his sword, and he nodded.

If Rekja wouldn't leave, Rythos would use his power

to convince the Gromalian king it was the best action. It would kill a part of him to use his power on an ally. On someone he might one day have called a friend, but after everything we'd just learned about Stillcrest and Vicer and the carnage that had followed...

There would be time for him to face the morality of his actions after the war. If we lived long enough.

Rythos handed Marth to Galon. Marth let out a faint groan, more color draining from his face.

Prisca stared at him, her eyes filled with suppressed horror. My chest clenched. "You need to go with Galon, wildcat."

Prisca scowled but didn't argue. She'd turned her gaze to the soldiers pouring into the city, her knuckles white as she clutched the hourglass around her neck.

Galon squeezed my forearm. "I'll get them out," he vowed.

My throat thickened. Marth's eyes were closed now. Would they ever open again? Or, like Cavis, would his fate be to die by fae iron to the chest?

Galon moved toward the stairs, slashing out occasionally with his sword, but conserving his power for later, when they would need to get to one of the tunnels.

Prisca gave me a final glance. There was nothing we needed to say. But I memorized her face. "I'll see you soon."

Her mouth trembled, but she forced it into a smile. "Soon."

And then she was gone, guarding Galon's and Marth's backs.

PRISCA

Regner's soldiers had learned about some of the tunnels. It was evident from the windows smashed in the buildings that housed those tunnels, the people lying dead nearby.

Likely, they'd followed some of the Gromalians who'd managed to escape and were killing them at this very moment.

Chills broke out across my skin.

We'd already marked the tunnel we needed. The tunnel that would take us closest to one of the healers Rekja had ordered evacuated long before Tymedes's deadline.

Galon used his power again and again as we ran through the city. He flooded the river, sending it barreling toward a large group of soldiers intent on chasing several fleeing Gromalians. He poured water into mouths and eyes, leaving soldiers choking behind us as he strode down the streets he'd clearly memorized. He created waterspouts with so much pressure, they knifed through skin and flesh.

I strained, searching for my own power. All I found was a vicious headache. My hand tightened around my sword, and I guarded our backs against anyone who thought to follow us.

Galon's arms were full with Marth's limp body. And while one hand held his sword, I knew he wouldn't risk wielding it unless he had to. Not with Marth defenseless and so close to death. Even Galon's gait was smooth, ensuring he didn't jostle Marth too much.

And so Galon drained his power, because mine was nowhere to be seen.

By the time we found the correct street, his face was gray. He leaned into the shadows of a brick house, panting. "I'm out."

Helplessness tore at me. I couldn't carry Marth. He simply weighed too much. And if I dropped him, the knife in his chest could find its way to his heart.

A choked sound echoed in my head. The sound Cavis had made when—

No.

If I didn't focus, all of us were dead.

Around us, screams tore through the night. The soldiers had already begun sacking the city, and flames leaped in the distance, greedily eating through the homes and livelihoods of the people who'd lived here.

We needed to cross this street. And as we did, we would be perfectly silhouetted by the flames to our right.

"I'll go first," Galon said. "Wait until I signal you."

It was smart, and I understood his reasoning. If someone happened to look down the street, he would be the only one seen.

At least at first.

Since I couldn't contribute anything to our escape, I didn't argue. With a final glance at me, Galon strode across the street, ducking down behind an overturned carriage.

I almost followed him.

But some sense I couldn't define screamed at me.

I hesitated.

A woman sprinted past me, arms pumping, mouth gaping wide. Behind her, a soldier easily ran within touching distance, clearly enjoying the fact that he could catch her at any time.

My hesitation had saved my life.

The soldier grabbed her hair, and her scream became a choked sob.

Slowly, Galon began to lower Marth to the ground. He wasn't going to have enough time. Everything went silent around me as I bent just enough to lunge forward from my toes.

I sucked in a deep breath.

Another soldier sprinted past. I hit the ground and crawled toward the shadows of a horse cart on the side of the street, silently begging the gods for just a little help. Just enough that he wouldn't notice my movement out of the corner of his eye.

The soldier let out a wild laugh, and it was so out of place, for a second I didn't believe I'd truly heard it. But the laugh went on and on. Because he was having *fun*.

Heat began to burn in my gut. My hand squeezed the hilt of my sword so tightly, it felt as if my bones might crack.

Slowing to a walk, the soldier said something I couldn't hear to his friend. They both glanced around, and I froze like a rabbit, conscious of how little cover I had in these shadows.

I needed the element of surprise. I'd dropped to the right, and I could no longer see Galon. But he was likely readying himself to attack. If I just made it a little closer, I could take out the second soldier while Galon took the first.

And that was when I saw them.

Four children, huddled beneath the horse cart. The closest boy was pressed up against one of the wheels, his eyes almost as big as those wheels as he stared hopelessly at me in the dark.

My heart beat inside my throat. If the children made a sound, they were dead.

I held up one finger to my mouth, turning back to the soldiers.

The woman lashed out with a dagger she'd hidden in the hand at her side. It sank into the soldier's gut. He didn't hesitate. With a roar, he pulled the blade free and slammed it into her throat.

The world dimmed around me and did one slow spin. I blinked several times, as if I could clear my vision and undo what I'd just seen.

The woman was dead before her head thudded to the ground.

But so was the first soldier. He stared down at the blood pouring from his stomach in disbelief, slumping to his knees.

And *that* was why the blade would remain in Marth's chest until a healer removed it themselves. I glanced at the children. Their eyes were just as wide as mine likely were. One of the boys had thankfully covered the eyes of a little girl, and he stared helplessly at me.

I had to get them out of here.

Movement in the street. The second soldier spat on

the woman's body, picked up the knife from the ground, and added it to an empty sheath on his ankle.

One of the children sneezed.

I flinched as the sound carried through the night, and my heart thundered until I could feel it vibrating in my throat.

An older child had slammed a hand over the mouth of the younger child, and both of their faces were so, so pale in the dim light, it was as if they were already corpses.

The second soldier smiled. And then he turned toward the cart.

For the first time, hatred engulfed me until I could barely breathe, could barely think around my loathing for the soldiers. I'd hated many things since this war started. Regner and all he stood for. Eryndan and his useless arrogance. The fae wardens who'd refused to ally with us.

But this? This was different. I'd never felt this kind of hate for the soldiers before. For humans. The people I'd been raised among. Those who were here on orders.

But it wasn't those orders that made these soldiers steal and rape and kill. No, they did those things with a sick kind of pleasure—and that pleasure was evident in the whooping cheers of a group in the distance, followed immediately by terrified screams from several women.

The laughter grew even louder, drowning out the sound of the footsteps of the soldier who now stalked toward the children, his hand on his sword.

People who would do this—invade a foreign land for no reason other than they wanted what their neighbors had and felt entitled to it—people who would commit such atrocities and find them entertaining...

They deserved any retribution that came their way.

My own power was nowhere to be found. I might never find it again.

So I'd kill this man with my sword instead.

It was different now, without Lorian and the others standing with me. On the other side of the street, I could almost hear Galon grinding his teeth as I slowly got to my feet.

But the soldier didn't hear me. He was too busy taunting the children.

"Come out," he crooned. "I'll make it quick. If you force me to drag you out of there, it will be worse."

A dark, black feeling encompassed me, filling me as if I breathed it in with every inhale. It was frightening, how much hatred flowed through my veins.

Hatred and…rage.

I was tired. So, so tired.

But the rage was fuel. The hatred was speed.

The soldier was leaning down, still taunting the children as I leaped.

He must have heard me, because he began to straighten, to turn. He held his sword in his left hand, and I approached from the right.

He should have protected himself with his right arm. He'd have lost the arm, but he might've had a chance.

Instead, he made a stupid choice. He tried to switch his sword from his left hand, fumbling it. My sword sliced through his neck, and his body—already unbalanced— crashed into me.

I barely kept my feet. Below me, the children were as silent as the space between my heartbeats.

"Prisca," Galon hissed. He was already moving, storming toward the first soldier. It took me only a second to understand why.

The thud of boots on stone, each step perfectly in sync.

And they were coming toward us.

I kicked the soldier's head away from the children, and it rolled toward the other side of the street.

It hit Galon's shin, and he let out a disgusted growl as he dragged the first body into the shadows. I fought the urge to vomit as I grabbed the second soldier's shins and pulled with all my might.

He barely moved. Galon stepped toward me, and I shook my head, pointing at Marth. If he died, Marth died too.

Unsurprisingly, Galon was prepared to ignore me. He took another step. But I'd managed to get some leverage by squatting a little and taking long lunges backward. My thighs burned, but the boots were coming closer.

I managed to get the body into the shadow of the cart. My chest clenched at the horror the children had seen today.

But I couldn't think about that now.

There was a huge smear of blood on the cobblestones—a clear indication that a body had been dragged away.

The boots sounded like thunder now.

Seconds. They'd be here in seconds. I reached for an old blanket from the back of the cart, throwing it over the blood. Hopefully, it would look as if it had merely fallen from one of the many people the Eprothan soldiers had cut down.

A glint of light on the corner warned me it was too late, and I leaped for the shadow behind the cart, meeting a pair of wide, tear-filled eyes. Slowly, I lifted my finger to my lips once again.

All I could see were boots and calves, marching two-by-two, still in time.

The first soldiers to breach the walls had likely been given orders to create chaos. They'd been allowed free rein to do whatever evil they liked. These soldiers were highly trained and headed directly for the castle.

One of the pairs of boots stopped suddenly, and another pair slammed into it. I tightened my hand on my sword. Somewhere in the darkness across the street, Galon would be doing the same.

Sweat streamed down my forehead, stinging my eyes. I blinked as fast as I could, not even daring to move enough to wipe it away.

Galon and I could take out anywhere from six to ten soldiers. And by that, I meant I could take out two, and he would cut down the rest with his blinding speed.

We'd just watched at least fifty soldiers march past. And there were more to come. Not only were there just two of us—without access to power—but Marth was in terrible shape, and we had the children behind us to think about too.

I strained again, grasping for even the tiniest thread of my magic. Nothing.

And for the first time, I actively resented my own power. How could it have abandoned me when I needed it the most?

One of the soldiers cursed and muttered something too low to hear.

The other soldier turned his feet. Toward the cart. "But—"

My vision sharpened. I could smell the thick smoke pouring toward us, mingled with the sweat of the soldiers. Each scuff of boot on stone sounded like thunder in my ears.

The soldier resumed marching, and the others behind him ran a few steps, quickly catching up to the others.

I stayed where I was and trembled, watching the soldiers pour past us.

The Sorlithians would never forget what had happened here today. They would never forget the screams and the pain and the terror. Horror had warred with rage on the faces of every innocent I'd seen, and I knew if they ever got the opportunity for vengeance...

They would make these soldiers *suffer*.

And they deserved their vengeance.

Finally, when their footsteps were nothing more than a distant echo, I stood. My limbs were cramped, my foot had gone to sleep, and I shook it out, limping over to the children.

"Come out," I whispered.

As one, they shook their heads. I wished I had time to gently cajole them. But every second we spent on this street was risky.

And then Galon was there. He took one look at the children and sighed, shaking his head. But when he pointed at the spot next to him, they crawled from beneath the cart.

I frowned. And then it hit me. I was the one they'd watched behead a soldier and then drag the body away. I was still covered in his blood. Of course they were frightened of me.

"Marth?"

"Alive." Galon's voice was grim, and my mouth went dry.

He leaned down. "Parents?" he asked the children.

The oldest one, a boy, shook his head. "We don't know where they are."

"Then you're coming with us."

The boy opened his mouth as if to argue, but Galon was already turning away, lifting Marth back into his arms.

"We're going to take you somewhere safe," I said.

The youngest girl slipped her hand into mine. I glanced down at her tiny, pale face and glazed eyes. Clearly, she was no longer concerned about all the blood covering me. She just needed whatever comfort an adult could provide.

"Other hand," I murmured, switching sides with her. I needed my sword in that hand, but as long as she was close, I could push her free if we were attacked. She stuck her free thumb in her mouth, and I rolled my shoulders.

The entrance to the tunnel was on the next street. It was a bookshop, and someone had been smart enough to overturn several shelves, pushing them up against the door. The chain around my lungs slipped free as Galon led us down the side of the store, and we slipped through the back entrance, taking the stairs down to the cellar.

"I don't want to," the little girl said, attempting to

pull her hand free from mine.

I couldn't exactly blame her. I wasn't particularly happy about taking the ladder down into the tunnel either.

"We have to go, Celere," one of the boys told her. There were three boys, all of them older than her. "Don't be a baby."

"I'll carry you down," I said.

She nodded, lifting her arms, and I picked her up. She was surprisingly heavy for such a small child, but she immediately melted into me, her body going limp.

"Let me go first," Galon said.

He took the ladder down, Marth still in his arms. My pulse pounded in my ears, some part of me convinced there were soldiers waiting. But if that was the case, there would be clear signs in the cellar.

Still, I watched, openmouthed, as he somehow managed to keep his balance on the rickety ladder, leaning Marth against it.

When he was halfway down, he dropped, landing so softly, Marth likely hadn't felt a thing.

The boys went next, scampering down the ladder. They were watching Galon with big eyes.

I shifted Celere around until she was on my back, and she linked her hands around my throat.

"A little lower," I murmured.

She tried, but she was frightened as I moved down the ladder, and her hands squeezed, cutting off my air.

Finally, we made it to the bottom, following Galon through the tunnel.

It was clear that this was one of the few tunnels that had remained hidden. It was quiet, dimly lit by light orbs, and I could see obvious signs people had used it to flee—a child's blanket dropped next to one wall, a few pieces of fruit scattered several footspans later.

My body was still trembling, recovering from the fear and rage that had roared through me like wildfire. Now, I just felt drained, so exhausted I could barely put one foot in front of the other. The children spoke little— the boys introducing themselves as Jory, Roen, and Nyle and then falling silent, while Celere sniffled occasionally as she clung to me.

Thankfully, Galon knew exactly where we were going. The tunnel ended, and we climbed the ladder up into the forest, moving quietly, keeping our footsteps light. There were no signs of Gromalian soldiers this far from the city. But we were quiet and careful just the same.

Fresh air slid up my nostrils, dried the sweat from my face, and ruffled my hair.

As Rekja had promised, healers were stationed near where we climbed out of the tunnel. Two of them leaped toward us, and the blood drained from one of their faces.

"He's still alive?"

"Fae," Galon bit out.

The male healer tensed, as if that meant Marth had some disease he could catch. Out of all the fae men I knew, Galon was probably the most patient. And yet, today had been long, with much of it outside of his control—something the fae struggled with at the best of times. When the male healer leaned closer to Marth as if studying a strange insect he'd never seen before, a low growl slid through the clearing.

No one moved. I reached out and grabbed Galon's

hand. The growl abruptly cut off.

The female healer immediately shoved the male aside. "My name is Rhea. Lay him down. Carefully."

Her hands swept over his chest. And her easy confidence made my own hands relax.

"Hit a lung. Due to his fae healing, the lung has healed around the knife. It's the only reason he is still alive."

Tiny dots appeared in front of my eyes at her words, and I placed Celere on the ground. The children were quiet. Likely, I should take them somewhere away from this. Just as I had the thought, the male healer gestured for them to follow him, promising them food. Thankfully, he seemed able to behave normally with the children, and they followed him.

Rhea looked up at us, and her lips thinned. "I need to remove the knife. And he's not going to like it."

Galon gave a sharp nod. He knelt on Marth's thighs, holding his wrists down.

Marth made a low, rough sound. I slapped my hand over his mouth, and his eyes were wild and unfocused as they met mine.

He bucked, but he was likely weak from blood loss, and Galon easily held him in place.

"Healer," I said, leaning down so he would hear me. "We got you to a healer."

I wasn't sure if it was understanding and relief that made his eyes close, or if he'd simply passed out once more. His blond hair was tangled around his face, and I pushed it back, my heart aching.

He was alive. He hadn't joined Cavis.

Rhea was panting when she was finished. "I've closed the wound, but he'll need to see another healer soon to help with the remaining healing and blood loss."

"But it's safe to keep traveling?" Galon asked.

She nodded. "If you managed to get him here in that condition, you're safe to continue."

"Thank you," he said. I nodded to her, scanning the clearing for the children.

They were drinking water, bread in their hands. When Celere noticed me looking, she nudged Nyle, who said something to the healer and herded the others toward us.

A little food and water had been good for them, and they followed after us for a while with no complaints. Celere ended up on my back once more and somehow managed to fall asleep, her head lolling on my shoulder.

A few hours later, we made it to a temporary camp. Demos and the others had clearly received Lorian's message, and a few hundred of our people had traveled north to meet the Gromalians. Both the hybrids and fae were handing out food and water, giving medical attention when necessary, and leading Gromalians to makeshift tents.

I'd attempted to force my brain from thoughts of Lorian and Rythos. From thoughts of my brothers and Asinia and Madinia. But now, those thoughts beat at me, a constant refrain of loss and death.

Galon took Marth to a group of healers, while Celere clung to my hand. Then she let out a cry.

"What is it?" I asked, crouching, but she was already running.

A woman ran toward us, a man quickly catching up to her. The woman's arm had been bandaged, and tears rolled down her face as the boys followed, launching themselves at the couple.

Within moments, the woman was sobbing, Celere in her arms. The man spoke to the others in a low voice, lifting his head to meet my gaze.

"You saved our children."

"They were clever. They'd managed to find a place to hide."

"We were going to die," Roen said. "The soldier said so."

The remaining color drained from the man's face. "The children were in front of us when we were moving toward the tunnel," he whispered. "A group of Eprothans attacked, and we lost the children in the chaos. I didn't know they hadn't made it to the tunnel until the entrance had been barred behind us. I don't know how to thank you."

My throat clogged. This was one bright spot in an otherwise horrific night. "Knowing you're all together is enough."

"Is there anything I can do for you? Anything you need?"

I shook my head. "Just look after one another."

The woman smiled at me, still clutching Celere to her. I watched them walk away, almost swaying on my feet.

Warm arms encircled me. I tensed, then instantly relaxed as Lorian's scent wound toward me. Turning in his arms, I laid my head against his chest for a long moment.

And just like that, I could breathe freely again. The world fell back into place.

"You found me."

"I'll always find you. You're so tired," he murmured.

When I lifted my head, his lips met mine, hard and possessive. I was suddenly drunk on the taste of him. The feel of him. And at the same time, I felt as if I could focus once more.

Our kiss turned gentle. Tender. Lorian brushed his mouth against mine. Once. Twice.

"I was so worried about you," I admitted.

His eyes were heavy-lidded, and he ran his hands up and down my back, as if still soaking in the feel of me.

"I just talked to Galon. You were the one truly in danger."

"Rythos? Rekja? Thora?"

"All safe. Rekja suffered heavy losses. But we managed to convince him to leave. Thora was helpful there." His gaze flickered, eyes turning feral.

And then, in a movement so fast my head spun, he shoved me behind him, his sword suddenly in his hand.

I pulled my own sword. Had iron guards found us? Were the Eprothans sneaking up on us even now?

A woman carrying a cup of water dropped it and stumbled backward with a yelp. Somewhere, a child burst into tears. One of Rekja's guards palmed a dagger, searching the crowd for a threat.

I peered around Lorian. Nothing had changed. No soldiers had burst through the tree line. No arrows were ripping into our people.

There was no threat.

Silence rippled across the camp. Lorian's face was corpse-white.

"Lorian," I murmured quietly. "What is it?"

He sheathed his sword, but his hand remained on the hilt, knuckles whitening. When I stepped in front of him, his eyes were dazed, confused.

And then, they filled with wrath.

"It's nothing," he said, and his voice carried over the crowd. His gaze swept the camp, and suddenly, everyone decided they had something else they needed to do.

"Lorian—"

"I'm fine, Prisca." His words were carefully neutral. He didn't snap or snarl or sneer. But I flinched all the same.

Because he was lying to me.

Removing his hand from his sword, he held it out, waiting until I put my own hand in his. He led me toward the tent that had been designated for us, and my gaze slammed into Galon's.

His eyes were dark with concern. Concern and fear.

12

PRISCA

We stayed at the camp for three days before packing up and traveling toward Thobirea. Rekja and Thora had left two days earlier to meet with his generals in a bid to shore up their defenses. But it seemed it was only a matter of time before Regner continued moving south, farther into Gromalia.

Daharak lost twenty ships to skyrions that had been deployed after her before Lorian had killed them. I could practically feel her fury dripping from the terse words of her messages. But she'd also kept my aunt alive, and for that, I would be forever thankful. She wasn't happy about meeting us in Rekja's castle, but she understood the need for a strategic conclave.

A day into our own travels east, I finally received a message from Madinia. The thought of her lying in the forest somewhere, dead by an iron guard's blade... I hadn't been able to stand it. I'd sunk into a denial so complete, that even if someone had told me she truly had perished, I don't know if I ever would have accepted it.

She'd led a group of hybrids to safety

but had fallen unconscious and butted heads with an "overbearing healer who needed to learn her place." When she'd finally left the gathering hybrids at the beginning of the Asric Pass, she'd begun working her way south through Eprotha, carefully staying clear of Regner's soldiers.

I scribbled a quick message back, letting her know she should meet us in Thobirea.

Tears rolled silently down my cheeks as I watched the pigeon dart into the sky. Lorian wiped them away with his thumb, then leaned down, rubbing his nose gently against mine. "It would take more than Regner's iron guards to kill Madinia," he murmured wryly.

I shook my head. "Don't jest. She's fast and strong, but she was traveling with a group of hybrids. And we've still heard nothing from Vicer."

"It'll likely take him some time to come to terms with the attack," Rythos said from his horse. We'd stopped to eat, and Lorian handed me up to my own horse before mounting his own.

"It wasn't his fault," I said.

"No," Marth said. He was healed but tired easily, and as the shadows grew longer, he slumped in his saddle, leaning forward in a way that made it clear we would need to stop soon. Rythos wasn't speaking to him—still livid about the way he had taken the knife for him. But Lorian had told me to let them discuss it when they needed to.

"It was Stillcrest's fault," Rythos said, not looking at Marth. "But Vicer will still wonder every day for the rest of his life if the hybrids who died were worth her free will."

The thought was a depressing one. *Just let him be alive. Alive and miserable is fine for now, just as long as he is breathing.*

Lorian was growing increasingly quiet and refused to speak about the incident at the camp. I'd attempted to talk to him over the past few days, but he'd shut down. It had shaken him. I'd known that much by the dazed look in his eyes in that clearing.

Perhaps he'd just been...spooked. Perhaps his mind had simply struggled to accept that we were no longer in danger. But even now, while we were traveling, he continued to turn his head, as if he could hear something even the other fae could not. This was no longer about feeling watched. Something had changed.

The days were long. By the time we began approaching the Gromalian capital, any semblance of a cheerful mood had deserted us.

We stopped one final time on our way to the castle, and I stood by the river after filling my waterskin. A hand clamped down on my shoulder, spinning me. I let out a surprised yelp, almost falling into the river, my hand sliding down for my knife. But it was Lorian who'd grabbed me. Lorian, who was edging me back along the river, his sword in his hand.

An ambush this close to the capital? Where were Rythos and the others?

Darting to the side, I drew my own sword. And stared.

Lorian stood, teeth clenched, realization dawning in his eyes.

There was no one there.

But he was still looking at something. A strange, uneasy feeling took up residence in my gut.

"What is it, Lorian?"

He opened his mouth, and I sheathed my sword. "Don't tell me it's nothing."

Lorian sheathed his own sword and turned to face me. His expression was stony, his eyes distant. And I knew what he was doing.

"I know you think I can't handle it—"

"Stop." He was clutching my arms in a moment. "That's not it, and you know it. I didn't want to worry you. But you're already worried. And I'm...concerned."

He was more than concerned. I could still see the restrained panic in his eyes. But the fact that he was allowing me to see it meant more than I could have explained.

"What's happening, Lorian?"

"I..." He set his jaw. "I think I'm seeing the dead."

I stared at him. Of all the things I'd thought he might say, that was nowhere on the list.

"It started with voices," he said. "Strange words hissing in my ear. They turned to threats. And then I was seeing soldiers charging at me. Humans, mostly. They were so vivid...they're *still* so realistic, it's difficult to determine what is real and what isn't. And then I realized that many of those soldiers were covered in blood, the walking wounded. And some of them shouldn't have been able to walk at all, let alone handle a sword. I think...I think they're some of the people I've killed."

His expression changed into something I almost didn't recognize. "Do you ever think about it, wildcat?

Just how many people I've killed? The lives ended? The families missing loved ones?"

I buried my hands in his shirt, as if I could keep him here with me. As if the action could prevent him from lingering on the past.

"No," I said. "Not anymore. You've saved a lot of lives too."

Lorian just shook his head. "Thousands, Prisca. And already, the ones I've seen have begun to talk to me."

A hot ache burned through my chest, working its way up to lodge in my throat. "What do they say?"

"Threats, mostly. The voices seem to happen more often, almost like the sound of leaves rustling in the trees—a constant noise in the background of my life. But the visions come suddenly. So suddenly, that I'm not sure what's real and what isn't."

"We'll fix this," I said. "We'll find a way to make it stop."

He gave me a faint smile. "I heard Cavis. He was the one who warned us of the soldier attacking Rythos."

I broke his hold on me and reached up to twine my arms around his neck, searching for a reply.

"I'm not losing my mind," he said.

"I don't think you are."

He lifted his head, green eyes searching mine. Some of the tension disappeared from his face. "I appreciate your faith in me. Truthfully, it feels as if my sanity is trickling away, drop by drop."

I didn't want him to give me that look, so filled with love and trust. Because my grandmother's voice was playing through my mind.

"In the unlikely event that you don't join us in the afterlife, there will be consequences. Grave consequences. You think you know what it is to suffer. You will live with the repercussions of this choice for the rest of your life."

I stared up at the man I loved more than anything or anyone. And my throat was suddenly so thick, I couldn't breathe.

"Wildcat, I promise I'll get better. I'll stop reacting like this. I'll learn what is real and what isn't." Lorian's voice was a low growl, tinged with desperation. He cupped my face, and I realized the color had likely drained from it.

"It's…it's not that. I think this might be some of the consequences from the way I…"

"Brought me back."

I nodded, my eyes stinging. "You *died*, Lorian. You might not remember it…" He stared at me, and I realized he did remember some of it.

"This… The gods know I would find it worse for *you* to suffer. To watch you deal with the repercussions of my choice." I dropped my gaze. I couldn't even look at him.

Lorian's hand slid to my chin, holding tight until my eyes met his once more. "I would take any consequences to be here with you. Any repercussions. Any punishment. *Anything*. You think I wouldn't make the same choice a million times, even knowing the outcome? I would let my brother shatter me with his magic every day for the rest of my life as long as I got to see you in those moments before my death."

Taking my hand, he pressed a kiss to my knuckles. "Now, let's go."

Approaching the city gates was a completely different experience compared to the last few times we'd traveled here. This time, the guards were clearly expecting us, and they bowed low, instantly allowing us to pass.

Which was a good thing since I still couldn't access my power.

I strained, searching for it constantly. But at this point, I had to accept that it likely wasn't coming back. I had angered the gods and depleted not just my own power, but a piece of my mother's and grandmother's souls.

Panic writhed through my gut like a deadly snake. Who would follow the hybrid heir if they learned the time power she wielded no longer existed?

"Prisca." Lorian's voice was soft, and I arranged my expression into something neutral. We were already approaching the castle.

Our welcome was similar to the one we'd received at the city gates, and I studied the statues in the courtyard as one of the stable hands took my horse. It felt as if it were only yesterday that Rekja and I had stood here, his father still alive and unwilling to help us. I'd threatened Rekja then. Threatened him with Thora. And then I'd ensured the Eprothan ambassador had seen us together, close enough to give value to the rumors we'd started. Then, I'd thought those were some of the worst things I could do. I'd had no idea just what lengths I would go to for my people.

Now, Rekja's father was dead. He'd killed him—and I was partly responsible.

Several servants leaped forward, greeting us as if we were old friends and leading us to the same rooms we'd stayed in last time.

"We have others who will be arriving soon," I said. "My aunt Telean, Daharak Rostamir—"

"Oh, we know." One of the women smiled. "His Majesty has instructed us to prepare rooms for all of your friends and allies. And Madinia Farrow arrived just a few hours ago."

I let out a shaky laugh. Madinia was finally safe.

Marth muttered something and stalked away. Lorian was staring at a spot by the window, his expression haunted.

"I think we'll take some time to freshen up." I attempted a smile. As much as I wanted to see Madinia immediately, I wouldn't leave Lorian with that look in his eyes.

"Of course, Your Majesty... Only..."

I took pity on her. "What is it?"

"Regner's queen." Her nose crinkled and was brought under control immediately.

"She's here?"

"Yes, she arrived yesterday. His Majesty said you would likely wish to speak to her at your convenience, so she is currently under strict guard. But I believe she has somehow heard of your arrival and..."

I sighed. "I can only imagine how demanding she is being. I'll see her as soon as I've changed out of my traveling clothes."

Kaliera would, after all, sniff out any hint of weakness.

Lorian stepped up next to me. The color had returned to his face, but my instincts screamed at me. Which of the dead were torturing him now?

"I'll come with you," he said to me. "First, I want to speak to Rekja."

If Lorian wanted to speak to Rekja alone, it wouldn't be about war strategy. He would never enter those discussions without my input.

As curious as I was, I was more desperate to bathe properly for the first time in days.

I pondered Kaliera as I bathed. There were only two reasons she would be here. Either she'd decided to work with Regner to infiltrate us, or he had discovered just how duplicitous she truly was. If it was the first reason, I felt relatively confident we could keep her from learning anything crucial. If it was the second, I couldn't understand how she could possibly still be alive.

By the time the water grew cold and I'd forced myself out of the tub, Lorian had returned. His gaze was a caress as I stepped into the room, a silk robe clinging to my damp skin.

He'd also found somewhere to bathe and change, and I allowed myself to wander closer, until he snatched me up and attacked my mouth with a fierce need I hadn't expected.

I sank into him, my head whirling as all thoughts and reason disappeared. It wasn't just my head that was whirling—the room was moving around me because he'd picked me up and was stalking toward the bed.

I yanked my head back.

"I don't think so. As much as I enjoy the thought of Kaliera waiting for us, I'd be too...distracted."

He gave me a wicked grin. "I bet I could convince

you to change your mind."

I'd bet he could too.

I hesitated. We hadn't had enough time together while we were traveling, and I missed him. Missed being close. I was incredibly tempted to try to lock out the world.

But Lorian was already switching course, placing me on my feet and practically dragging me toward the closet.

"Let's get this over with," he growled.

My core ached with the same frustration, and I pulled on the first dress I saw, found some shoes with a low heel, and followed Lorian out the door.

"I need to ask one of the maids where they've stashed her." Lorian took my hand.

"You're back," a cold, irritated voice said.

I whipped my head to face the door so quickly, I gave myself a headache.

Madinia wore leather leggings, a white men's shirt, and a dark scowl. But she was alive.

Her eyes met mine, and she gave a faint smile at whatever she saw on my face. Some of the ire left her expression.

I didn't attempt to hug her. Something about the stiff way she stood made it clear she wouldn't welcome any affection. Not that she was the kind of person who welcomed it most other times.

"You're alive." I kept my tone light, placing my hands on my hips. Next to me, Lorian gave her a nod. But I knew him well enough to see the hint of relief in his eyes. If only because he knew we needed her power.

She just nodded. "You're going to see her."

"Yes."

"She's been asking for me. But I wanted to wait for you."

I couldn't blame her. Kaliera had a way of getting inside your head—especially when you weren't at your best. And it was clear from the strain in Madinia's eyes that she wasn't even close to her best.

"Well then, let's see what she has to say."

She fell into step on my other side. "I know where she's staying."

It turned out, Kaliera's rooms were disturbingly close to our own, although Rekja had thankfully stationed two guards on the door. They straightened as Lorian approached, the guard on the left casting a wary glance at his pointed ears.

I raised my eyebrow, and when his eyes met mine, his cheeks heated.

Lorian and the others had ceased using their glamour, for the most part. Everyone knew they weren't human, and as I'd commented recently, if we truly wanted peace when this war ended, humans would need to get used to working and living with the fae.

The first step meant no longer hiding what they were. Hopefully, the humans who had been taught to fear the fae would see they were just…people. But it would take time.

The guard on the right nodded at us, leaning over to throw open the door. Lorian went first—a clear indication of how little he trusted the human queen.

Kaliera was wearing a green dress. It fell elegantly to the floor as she stepped toward us, her gaze scanning me from head to toe. I'd left my hair down, not even taking the time to dry it.

As usual, she looked perfect. Not a hair out of place. But her displeasure was evident in the thin line of her lips. The slight tightness around her eyes.

She studied Madinia, who stared blankly back at her. When Kaliera let out a tiny, dismissive snort, I thought she might burst into flames right there.

Lorian must have imagined the same, because he wedged his body between Madinia and Kaliera.

The queen smirked. "I met your cousin," she said, returning her attention to me. "He said you turned back time."

Her words took all of the air out of my lungs, as if someone had shoved their fist into my gut. She'd met Zathrian. It wasn't surprising, considering I'd seen him working with Regner. But...it was strange. I'd never even had a conversation with the man, who was related to me by blood, and yet Kaliera had met him.

Still, I knew better than to let her see any kind of reaction.

I raised one eyebrow. "I met your general. He laid waste to an entire city."

"Regner's general," she ground out.

Finally, she was calling him Regner. Was it because he was now hunting for her?

"What happened?"

"I attempted to steal Regner's grimoire. Alcandre betrayed me." One hand buried itself in her dress. "You don't seem surprised."

"You taught those women everything they knew."

"The rest of them are dead."

She'd said it to shock both me and Madinia. And

it worked. My eyes stung, and Lorian wrapped an arm around my shoulders. Next to us, Madinia let out a small, broken sound. But I was watching Kaliera, and while her words might have hurt us, they hurt her too.

Still, I'd learned enough about this woman to know that didn't mean she would change a single decision she'd made. Even if those decisions had led to their deaths.

"I want to see my son," she said.

I wasn't surprised by her demand, but I squared my shoulders. "He's currently busy."

"You will allow me to see him." Her voice was imperious, the tone insisting she would accept no argument. It wasn't unlike Madinia's tone when she was in a mood. Of course, this was the woman she had learned such behavior from.

"He's not here. Unlike his mother, who is only interested in saving her own skin, Jamic will use his power to save innocents whenever he can."

She didn't bother denying my accusation. But her lips tightened. "When will he return?"

"Soon."

Kaliera's eyes glittered. "I know where the last amulet is."

I forced my expression to remain neutral, even as my heart began to race. "And?"

"And I know how to get to it."

"How?"

"I went searching for it. Before I attempted to steal the grimoire. But I was unable to retrieve it." Her tone was neutral, but I caught the flicker of fury in her eyes.

"How convenient," Lorian rumbled. He'd pinned her

with a hard stare.

He had a point. The queen had allegedly attempted to find the two artifacts we needed the most. She'd found neither and had instead turned up here empty-handed.

"It is in the same place he has been breeding his monsters. A mine named Lyrishade."

Now, my heart began beating faster. If Regner kept his monsters there, we could kill them at the same time as we stole the amulet.

"Tell us what you know."

"As soon as I see my son."

I laughed. Kaliera's nostrils flared, and I took a single step closer to her. "Let me be clear. We do not trust you. How do we know Regner did not send you here with this story? Even if he truly did turn on you, this may be the way you decide to reach his inner circle once more. I'm not risking my people on your word."

She opened her mouth, and I shook my head. "You will see your son as soon as we have the amulet and I know for sure our people aren't going to end up trapped."

"You'll tell us every detail, or I'll make sure your son dies," Madinia said. "I could probably make it look like an accident. Jamic likes me, you know. He thinks we're friends."

I hid my wince. Madinia didn't make idle threats. But of all of us, she was the one Jamic trusted the most— especially after she'd saved his life.

She wouldn't. I couldn't believe she would kill someone who thought of her as a friend. Not in cold blood.

But Kaliera certainly seemed to think she would. She stared at Madinia for a long moment.

"I'll tell you everything you want to know," she said. Finally, she'd lost some of her confidence—false as it might have been.

Some part of me almost felt sorry for her. It didn't feel good to deny anyone access to their family or to allow Madinia to threaten their lives. But I knew what it was to lose the people I loved now. And I would never risk those people based on Kaliera's trustworthiness.

"And if I find out you're lying, I'll kill you slowly," Lorian said.

Her eyes narrowed as she faced Lorian, but the color left her cheeks. Not only would he happily use her son as leverage, but he'd kill her without a second thought. It was clear by the cold promise in his eyes. And from the single, sharp nod she gave, she knew it too.

"I learned something else that may be of some importance," she said quickly. "I will tell you now to prove that you can trust me."

"Fine," Madinia said. "Tell us."

"When I was hiding in the mine, I overheard two Eprothan guards speaking about the origins of the monsters."

"Regner stole them as younglings when their parents left to hunt," Lorian said.

Kaliera shook her head. "You don't understand. There were so many monsters in that mine. Thousands. Plus, I heard you were attacked by thousands more. Servants talk." She waved her hand. "The guard said one of the fae wardens—a woman—has been giving Regner creatures from her territory." She met Lorian's eyes. "He laughed and said you have no idea what's coming for you."

Lorian's expression didn't change. "That was all he said?"

Kaliera nodded. "I have...someone I can put you in contact with. Someone else who has traveled into the mines. He knew where the amulet was."

"And just who is he?" I asked.

"The pirate queen's brother. His name is Pelysian. He wants Regner dead too."

"Fine," I said. "Write down how we can contact him and give the information to one of the guards on your door."

Lorian held out his hand for me, and I took it. Together, the three of us walked out.

I could hear voices in the room next door. Marth said something, and Galon and Rythos laughed in response.

"If she's not lying, she's just saved Conreth's people days of searching for the amulet," I said.

"Lyrishade was the next place we were planning to check after a small village nearby. Conreth no longer has many of our people that far north," Lorian said. "It sounds as if we will need to send a highly trained group of our own."

Madinia didn't say another word. Just turned and stalked away. I couldn't even imagine the horrors she'd seen. Perhaps...perhaps she would just need some time.

"And the warden?"

Lorian's eyes turned flat. "Kaliera might be attempting to make us turn on one another. Sylvielle has powerful allies—something Regner would know if this is the truth. If Conreth makes a move on her without proof, her allies will refuse to march with him."

"She refused to join with us at the summit."

"Yes. And now, that choice looks much more suspicious. I will send a message to Conreth. Unless she is an idiot, she will agree to join us on the front lines instead of risking a full investigation."

I knew Conreth well enough by now to know he would still make sure that investigation happened.

"There's something else," Lorian said. Stepping forward, he cupped my chin, gazing down at me. "I want to marry you."

His words were so unexpected, I blushed, glancing at the guards. They stared straight ahead, pretending they'd lost all hearing. Grabbing Lorian's arm, I pulled him down the hall.

"Haven't we already had this conversation?"

He allowed me to direct him to our rooms, but the moment we entered, he pressed me against the wall with a grin. One of those wide, happy grins I so rarely got to see. I memorized the sight of that grin and tucked it away.

"I want to marry you here."

I blinked. "In…Gromalia?"

"If you'd prefer to wait until we're in our kingdom, we can," he said. "But everyone you love will soon be gathered here. They'll all be together for the last time—likely until this war is over."

My mouth had gone dry at the thought. He was right. "You want to make sure everyone can attend." Because there was a very real chance that we might lose more people we loved.

"I would marry you anytime, anywhere," he said. "But we deserve one day of joy and happiness before we face whatever is to come."

I peered up at him, my gaze sweeping over his sharp cheekbones, those piercing green eyes so intent as he watched me. His mouth was curved, but the tiniest line had formed between his dark brows.

He wanted me to say yes. This mattered to him. Greatly.

I realized then that somewhere along the way, I'd stopped picturing a future. I'd stopped contemplating *our* future.

And so, even as I'd nodded along while others talked about what would happen after the war, and I'd made plans out loud, a large part of me didn't truly believe I would be here to see it happen. Especially now that I had no power.

It seemed almost as if I was testing fate to assume I would survive. After everything I'd done. All the people I'd killed, all the ways I'd defied the gods.

Lorian knew.

I wondered how much of that knowledge had gone into his insistence that we be married now and not wait until after the war. He was trying to make me picture our lives together. Trying to bring that numb part of me back to life.

And he was succeeding.

"If Rekja agrees…" I began, then narrowed my eyes at him. That was why he had disappeared. "You've already asked him, haven't you?"

He dropped a kiss to my forehead, lingering for a long moment. "Of course I have."

13

PRISCA

Telean and Daharak settled into Rekja's castle the next day. It was oddly disconcerting to see the pirate queen away from her ships, and from the nonplussed expression on her face as she stalked around the castle, she felt the same.

I'd wrapped my arms around Telean the moment I saw her. There was much we'd left unsaid, but I'd never forget the sick feeling of dread when I'd thought either of us would die with harsh words still between us.

She'd petted my back then stepped away to murmur with Lorian. Our relationship was still fractured, but it would be fixed. I'd make sure of it.

The word had gone out to all our allies. We would meet at Rekja's castle to finalize our plans and prepare for war.

Four days later, Tibris, Demos, and Asinia arrived early in the morning. With them, they brought a man they introduced as Tor. Demos had found the only chance we had to weaken Regner's wards enough for us to kill him.

I launched myself at Tibris, tears sliding down my cheeks as I hugged him. He clutched me to him, only letting go when Demos muttered something I didn't catch beneath my breath.

Demos squeezed me so tightly, I almost couldn't breathe. Had he somehow packed on *more* muscle?

Asinia looked healthier than she had in years. Her skin had darkened with the sun, and she moved easily—as if she'd reached a new level of comfort with herself. She wrapped her arms around me, and we held tight, rocking from side to side for long moments.

I glanced around. "Where's Vynthar?"

A cloud rolled over her expression. "We don't know, Pris. The last time we saw him was in Ardanor, and then… he hasn't appeared since."

My stomach roiled. Vynthar had terrified me the first time I'd met him. But now…now, I considered him a friend.

"Do you think he's…"

"I'm sure he's fine," Demos said.

If he *was* fine, then he'd just…left.

Perhaps he'd decided he had done enough. Given enough. He'd saved lives when the skyrions attacked the rebel village. He'd gone with Asinia and Demos to keep them safe. He'd done so much more than I could've ever hoped.

But I wished I could have thanked him. Wished I could have said goodbye.

Tor disappeared to take a nap, and the rest of us ate together, sharing stories and laughter. By some unspoken agreement, none of us talked of the horrors we had seen or the death we had dealt—that afternoon, we would meet to talk about war and plan our strategy. While we ate,

Lorian told the others about the time he'd found Marth sleepwalking on Daharak's ship, headed straight for the railing. Galon told them of the time we'd been training on the deck, and I'd fallen against an overturned barrel—disturbing a rat. The rat streaked toward me, and with nowhere else to go, I went *up*—scampering up the closest rope, which had swung wildly. Losing my grip, I'd used my hands to slow my fall, giving me a wicked case of rope burn.

Asinia told us how Demos had decided he was tired of lying around after he'd almost died. My stubborn brother had made it two steps out of the tent before falling unconscious. He'd dropped like a log, ensuring Tibris had to heal his hard head once more.

Tibris grinned, bringing up the time one of the rebels—a soldier who'd defected from Regner's army—had loudly declared that women shouldn't be seen on a battlefield. Asinia had calmly picked up her crossbow and shot the cup of ale straight out of his hand.

Hours later, when the others had returned to their rooms to rest before the meeting, Tibris found me. "When was the last time you took a walk?"

I frowned.

"You're coming with me."

I laughed as he grabbed my hand, pulling me through the castle. Several people approached, and he cut them off each time. "Ask Lorian," he instructed.

No one looked pleased at his words. I couldn't blame them. Lorian was doing everything he could to lighten the load for me, but he had a tendency to snarl when asked stupid questions.

And he considered a lot of questions to be stupid.

I shook my head at Tibris, but my brother had no hesitancy with taking charge when it came to the overall health of those he cared about. His healing instincts were often impossible to ignore.

Rekja's gardens were a serene haven that felt worlds away from the strife and politics of the castle. As Tibris led me through the winding pathways, the lush tapestry of colors and scents enveloped me, pulling some of the tension from my muscles.

Tall, elegant trees formed a leaf canopy above our heads, their branches swaying gently in the breeze. Beneath them, flower beds burst with a riot of purples, reds, and yellows. I sucked the earthy scent of damp soil into my lungs as we meandered along the cobblestone path.

I'd needed this.

By the time we made it to a private corner of the garden, Tibris was frowning down at a rosebush as if it had personally offended him. He glanced up, meeting my eyes.

Gods, it was good to be able to look at him again. To hear him. To see he was alive and unharmed.

"You scared me," I said. "When I learned they were holding you."

"I know. I'm sorry."

Tibris's voice was oddly flat, and I peered up at him. "What is it?"

"There's something I need to tell you."

My heart thundered. His expression was guarded. Eyes grave.

"You can tell me anything," I said. "You know that."

Swallowing, he nodded. But he glanced at his feet.

My palms went damp. Was he sick? Had something bad happened to him at that camp?

Tibris met my eyes. And it was as if he was steeling himself to deliver news he thought I wouldn't like. "While I was at the rebel camp, I met someone."

The fist squeezing my heart unclenched. "Is that all? Gods, Tibris, you scared me."

His gaze stayed steady on mine. "It's not that simple, Pris. It's Herne."

"Herne…the camp leader?"

He nodded stiffly, shoving his hands into his pockets.

My chest tightened once more, joined by a sickly sensation in my stomach. I could see it now—from the look in his eyes, the longing on his face. My brother was in love. And instead of the supportive response he deserved, he expected me to be displeased by the political implications.

Was that who I was becoming? My eyes burned.

Tibris stiffened. "I'm sorry. I didn't plan this. Gods… he didn't either. I know it's inconvenient, but he's on our side, Pris."

Tears spilled down my cheeks. Tibris looked like I was torturing him. "If it's impossible for us to be together, just tell me."

"And you'd let him go? Just like that?"

A muscle ticked in his jaw. No, my brother wouldn't let Herne go. But if he thought I didn't approve, he would remain torn between us.

"I'm sorry, Pris. I didn't mean to fall in love with

him. Just like you didn't mean to fall in love with Lorian. I understand you're angry—"

"Stop."

He shoved his hand through his hair,

"I'm not angry. I'm not annoyed. I'm happy for you."

He narrowed his eyes at me. "You don't seem happy."

"I'm also…hurt," I admitted. "Because you thought I'd put politics ahead of you. And at the same time, I understand why you would think that. I've made choices that will haunt my dreams for the rest of my life." My stomach churned. Those choices had ensured almost an entire village of hybrids had died. Those choices had left me without my power at this crucial moment during this war. I dropped my own gaze, unable to meet his eyes. "Why wouldn't you think that?"

"Herne's people shot me," he said. "He decided to keep me as a hostage so he could make you do whatever he wanted."

Despite his words, I smiled. It was as if he needed to get all of Herne's bad deeds out into the open so I could decide if I would accept him.

I'd accepted Herne the moment Tibris told me he was in love.

My brother had never said that word before. Never even implied it.

"He kept the rebels alive and made it almost impossible for Eryndan to strike at their camp. He's a good leader, Tibris, even though he almost got you killed. I still want him on our side. And…if he's the one for you, I'll support you both."

His grin lit up his whole face. It hit me then. In the

middle of this war, I was so, so grateful I could have this moment with my brother. There was still good in this world. Love still existed, and it was everywhere.

I grinned back. "Will I like him?"

He shook his head. "No. Not at first. He's stubborn, arrogant, hotheaded… You know, he's not unlike Madinia."

I groaned. "Two of them. Just what we need."

Tibris only laughed. "We'd better get back for the meeting."

Which meant getting back to the reality of our situation. I sighed. "Let's go, then."

Tibris turned quiet as we walked back toward the castle.

"What is it?"

"It's Vicer. Do you think he's dead, Pris?"

"No. I think Vicer is smart, and he's lucky. He's managed to survive all this time, after all." I'd gone straight to denial. But I truly couldn't imagine Vicer being struck down in that village.

By the time we made our way up to the large sitting room we were using for most of our meetings, we were the last to arrive, and Lorian gestured at the seat he'd saved for me. He looked rested, almost relaxed, but he scanned every inch of me as I sat down.

Tor's eyes were wide as he glanced around the sitting room.

I watched his gaze sweeping across the wood of the table between us—polished to a gleam, the thick curtains framing windows overlooking manicured gardens—held in place by jeweled ties, and the plates of dainty pastries placed on the table by uniformed servants.

The look in Tor's eyes reminded me of my first few days in Lesdryn. I'd been torn between awe and disgust as I'd compared the differences between those lucky enough to live in the cities and those from villages such as ours.

When he finally glanced back at me, Tor's gaze lingered on my gown, his expression tinged with disgust. There was no use telling him this gown was borrowed or that I felt just as uncomfortable sitting in it as he did looking at it.

Galon, Rythos, Marth, Lorian, and I sat on the long side of the table. Daharak, Telean, Demos, Natan, and Asinia sat across from us. Natan and Demos were speaking quietly, and the ghost of a smile drifted over Demos's face. Madinia prowled the edges of the room, occasionally gazing out the window.

Blynth and Hevdrin were deep in conversation down at the other end of the table, with Rekja and several of his advisers across from them. Conreth had also sent one of his most trusted advisers—a man named Meldoric.

Tibris took a seat next to Demos, and I took mine next to Lorian. Everyone fell silent.

I took a deep breath. "Let's get started."

I told the others of the priestess we'd spoken with in Rekja's castle. And how she'd turned on Regner. Daharak chimed in with the belief that if Regner was killed, all the stolen magic would be returned to those from whom it had been taken.

"You truly believe that?" Madinia asked from her spot near the window.

Daharak shrugged. "We have to try. The grimoire

can't be destroyed, so it's our only hope."

She told the others of the dark god Calpharos, and the importance of taking the grimoire from Regner and hiding it—before this world had no hope of peace.

"Well, that's depressing," Tibris muttered.

Rekja sent him an amused look. "Where are we with numbers?"

"I have less than fifteen thousand people in fighting condition," Daharak said grimly. "Regner planned his ambush well."

My heart sank. When I'd first learned of who Daharak was, my aunt had told me she commanded eighty thousand men. I'd since learned that number wasn't quite correct. She'd had eighty thousand people before Regner's attack, including women and children, along with those who were too old or young to fight. It took thousands of people just to move her fleet into place.

"We have approximately seventeen thousand fae and hybrids in the hybrid camp, ready to fight," Blynth said, drawing me from my grim thoughts. "More are joining every day."

Hevdrin nodded. "The fae numbers are fluctuating as Conreth works to negotiate with Verdion, Caliar, and Sylvielle. As it stands, we have almost twenty thousand fae readying themselves for battle."

Twenty thousand fae. Hope stirred in my chest. Even with all the fae iron and stolen power Regner wielded, one fae would be worth at least two human soldiers on a battlefield.

All eyes turned to Rekja.

He sat straight-backed in his chair, his expression solemn.

"Now that Regner is marching on our lands, I will not be able to spare as many soldiers as I had hoped. We will need to ensure enough are well positioned to protect our people."

My heart sank. Another reason why Regner had chosen now to march on Gromalia. So Rekja would have fewer people to contribute to our armies.

He nodded at whatever he saw on my face. "We will march with you to war. But I can only spare thirty thousand soldiers."

"Just under eighty-five thousand total," Lorian murmured next to me.

I didn't enjoy talking about people as numbers. Each of these soldiers had a family and friends who loved them. And we were speaking of them as if they were tools.

Was this the reality of royalty? Of power? People became little more than pawns that were moved into place with no regard for the lives lost or changed forever?

The thought sickened me.

If we lived through this, I would do whatever it took to ensure this never happened again.

"Zathrian still has twenty thousand hybrids," Galon said. "Camped near the Cursed City."

"And Regner?" I asked into the silence. "What are his final numbers now?" No matter what those numbers were, they could have been worse, I reminded myself. If he'd allied with Gromalia, we would have been decimated.

"One hundred sixty thousand, plus however many creatures he can wield against us," Demos said quietly. "I got the final estimate this morning."

"Plus Zathrian's army," I said bitterly.

Demos nodded, his expression tight. Next to him, Tibris tapped his fingers on the table, a crease forming between his brows.

"One hundred eighty thousand soldiers," Natan said. "It will be a slaughter."

"We need Zathrian's hybrids," I said. If we could get our numbers to one hundred and five thousand, plus Herne's rebels, along with any extra fae Conreth could negotiate for, we might have a chance.

"Whatever your elder said has helped. Orivan has agreed to read a message from you," Blynth said.

Zathrian's general, the one Blynth had said was a good man. A loyalist. Potentially our only hope at wresting that army from my cousin. And Tymriel had finally proven useful.

I stared at Blynth. He gave me a faint smile. "If you send him a message, he will keep its contents to himself."

"I will write to him today," I said. It would be the most important message I would ever send.

Blynth leaned forward intently. "Even if he will ask his men to stand down within your cousin's camp, you'll still need to be able to get through Eprothan waters and dock near the camp. If they recognize you, you won't get within shooting distance of your cousin."

"Leave that part to me," Lorian said.

I turned to Tor. "Did Demos explain why we need your help?" I asked.

"He did. But your plan sounds thin."

It was a fair enough summary, given that he would be expected to have one of the most important—and riskiest—roles in that plan.

"We're out of options," Madinia said. Her eyes flashed as she stared at Tor, disgust clear in the wrinkle of her nose.

"And I'm to be your last effort."

"Would you like to hear exactly what Regner just did to an entire hybrid camp in Eprotha?" Madinia purred. "Would you like me to tell you about the small boy I helped bury, his pregnant mother who was so grief-stricken she had to be half carried through the forest while we waited to feel arrows in our backs at any second?" She stalked closer. Everyone had gone silent. "Perhaps I should tell you about the screams that echoed through the forest as the iron guard hunted any who thought to flee to safety."

"N-no." Tor swallowed. But he raised his head, staring her straight in the eye. "But you're expecting me to risk my life, and you don't know if it will even work."

I opened my mouth, but Marth was already speaking. "No, we don't. But we do know that if we do nothing, we are dooming every hybrid and fae on this continent to horror and death. If you can hear all of that, if you can lose your family and friends to Regner's dungeon and know they were starved and tortured before they died…if you can know that there are people risking everything to save the lives of strangers…" His voice trailed off, and then he angled his head. "If you can hear all of these things and refuse to help—and still meet your own eyes in the mirror for the rest of your life, however long it would last—then you don't belong in this room."

Tor's face flushed. I sucked in a breath, but Marth merely leveled the other man with a glare, folding his arms over his chest.

Demos stood. "Enough," he said. "The fact that Tor is willing to hear us out is courageous in itself."

Tor ignored him. And Asinia's hand twitched like she might grab Demos's.

Rekja stood, and Tor's gaze jumped to him. "Make your decision fast. All our lives may depend on it."

It wasn't fair, what we were doing to him. No one deserved the weight of so many lives on their shoulders.

Rekja turned to me, his long red hair falling over his shoulders. "Two things. First, when my father met with Regner, he mentioned a deal with the ruler of the fae island close to the southern tip of our lands."

It took me a moment to understand. But Rythos let out a strange sound from the back of his throat. "Quorith."

"Yes. The ruler of that island made a pact with Regner. This was discussed at a dinner between Regner and my father before the barriers fell. My father wanted the island for himself after the war. Regner had told him he could take it."

Hot fury pulsed in my veins. Verdion was a fool. A fool who was going to have the blood of thousands on his hands.

Rythos looked as if he had been punched in the gut. His hands began to shake, and he buried his face in them, silently removing himself from the conversation.

Rekja flicked his glance back to me. "I will take my leave to meet privately with my generals."

I glanced at Demos. He was watching Rekja stride out of the room with his advisers, his expression thoughtful. When he returned his gaze to me, it was instantly evident that I wouldn't like whatever he said next.

"You need to make a choice, Prisca."

"What kind of choice?" Sometimes it felt as if my days were made up of nothing but choices. And each of those choices had brutal, often immediate, consequences.

"Vicer. At this point, we haven't heard anything from him. The last time Madinia saw him…" His gaze flicked to her.

Madinia nodded, her expression blank. "He left to fight the iron guards. Alone."

My eyes stung. "You believe he's dead."

"We need to assume he's dead until we learn otherwise," Demos said. "Vicer is smart, and he knows that area of Eprotha well. There's a chance he's still alive, wounded, or busy helping other hybrids get to safety. But we can't rely on him until we know that's the case."

I forced myself to pretend Vicer was just another person. Not someone I knew. Someone who'd helped save hybrid lives for years.

If we were to assume Vicer was dead, then we would need to move forward without him. But for the hybrids we were attempting to save, Vicer was the person many of them knew or, at least, had heard of. They knew he had been fighting for them in the city for all those years, and his contacts stretched throughout Gromalia and Eprotha.

"Give me your suggestions for people whom his contacts would trust, and if we haven't heard anything from him three days from now, we will choose someone to…"

I couldn't say the word *replace*. Next to me, Lorian wrapped his arm around my shoulders. "Someone to temporarily fulfill his duties until we learn more," he said.

I glanced at him. It was clear he assumed Vicer was dead. But he was being very careful to spare me from that assumption.

Tibris cleared his throat. "Where do you want me to go, Pris?"

I'd already thought about this. "I want you to go to the pass. The hybrids who have already been fleeing toward the camp... I know Vicer said they have their own healers, but as soon as we have everything in place, we will be sending as many hybrids as we can off this continent. Many of them will need healing."

He narrowed his eyes at me, and I knew what he was thinking. That I was sending him away to keep him safe. Because he was human.

I shook my head at him. "There's another reason. I'm hoping that if you go to the Asric Pass, Herne will go with you."

His eyebrows shot up. "You want him there? Why?"

"From what you said, the rebels were exceptional about hiding their tracks and ensuring their camp was almost impossible to spot. As more and more people travel to that camp, they will begin leaving signs of that travel."

Tibris's expression cleared. "I'll send a pigeon to Herne."

A knock sounded on the door. Madinia stepped over and opened it.

"Message for someone named Marth," the messenger said. He had a long cut across one cheek. "And your pigeon needs to be replaced. Almost took out my eye."

I sighed. Trust Marth to have a vicious pigeon.

He slowly uncoiled his huge body, strolled across the room, and plucked the message from the man's hand, giving him a gold coin. "Thank you."

Marth read the message, and his face drained of blood. A chill slid over my skin, my heart stumbling on its next beat.

His eyes met mine. "I know what Rothnic has been working on. Our spies have finally learned the information. One of them was caught and killed. But two managed to escape Eprotha."

Lorian tensed, and I could feel the impatience rolling off him in waves. Regner's favorite Patriarch had a gift for creating horror with his magic.

Finally, Marth shook his head, as if attempting to clear it. "The weapon they've created...it takes down wards. All kinds of wards."

Oh gods. The fae lands, Quorith, *Lyrinore.*

We needed those wards. Without the wards, the sea serpents wouldn't attack, and the hybrid kingdom would be invaded. So would the fae lands. And our people would die.

It was as if history was repeating itself.

"Regner is going to attack us on all fronts, isn't he?" I said, my lips numb. "He'll split our forces, use whatever weapon Rothnic has come up with, and take down all of our wards. We'll be so busy defending our lands, we won't be able to strategize."

Silence.

"I don't understand," Asinia said. "These wards are ancient. How could Rothnic have found a way to bring them down?"

"According to our spies, the wards won't remain down. They'll merely be temporarily shifted into another world."

Madinia scoffed. "Another world?"

Demos raised one eyebrow. "You may imagine yourself the center of this world, but it makes logical sense that there would be others."

I sighed. Just as the sky was blue, Demos and Madinia would always dislike each other. Next to Demos, Asinia gave him a warning look. His mouth twitched, his eyes heating.

Now, *that* was interesting.

"If I may reclaim your attention?" Marth bit out.

I looked at him, and something inside my chest cracked. Not long ago, it would have been Marth teasing the others, keeping the atmosphere light, not allowing us to give in to dread and fear. Since Cavis's death, he was a grim, joyless version of himself.

"This is the ward." He swiped an apple from a bowl of fruit on the table and placed it on a piece of parchment to his right. Our world. "Rothnic uses his weapon." He placed the apple on the table, away from the parchment. "The ward still exists, but it's no longer in our world. It's temporary—power is always drawn back to its origin."

"So Rothnic shifts our wards. How long will they stay that way?"

Marth shrugged. "I don't know. It depends on the power of the weapon and the one wielding it. Likely, Regner will have infused both with as much stolen power as he can."

Dread hollowed my stomach, and panic slid neatly into the gap.

Slowly, I got to my feet. "It's time to clear the Asric Pass of Regner's soldiers. And then we will begin moving any hybrids who want to leave the fae lands—or any other kingdom—toward the Pass."

Regner would learn those soldiers were dead and instantly retaliate, but we had no choice. We had to protect the innocent.

Rythos swept a hand over his jaw, his expression grave. "Without the wards, he will take Quorith. If only to disable our ships. I need to go. I have to tell our people what my father has done—and what the consequences will be."

I nodded, but my chest tightened. "I don't want you to go alone."

A hint of impatience flickered in his eyes. "Pris—"

"Please, Rythos."

He frowned. "Fine."

"I'll go with him," Madinia said.

She stood near the door, leaning against the wall, arms crossed. Perhaps volunteering to go with Rythos was a way for her to avoid so much…togetherness. If I knew one thing about Madinia, it was that she preferred to be alone. And she'd been different since she returned from the hybrid camp. Before she'd left, it had seemed as if she'd softened in some ways. Now, her walls were firmly in place once more.

"Thank you."

Rythos didn't argue, just gave a stiff nod.

"I told you we should have killed Rothnic," Madinia mused.

Lorian pinned her with a look. "If Rothnic had died that night, we wouldn't have been able to free Jamic."

Hevdrin had been mostly quiet up until now, but at that, he cleared his throat. "We need to split our forces."

He was right. I knew he was right. That didn't make me any happier about it.

Lorian nodded. "We need the last amulet. If we're going to trust Kaliera—and we know for sure she wants her son—then we'll need a larger group to go into the mine."

Demos leaned back in his chair. "If it truly is where Regner has been breeding his monsters, we also need to find a way to wipe out as many of them as possible."

"By now, he will have moved many of them out," Galon said. "The attacks against both the rebel camp and Sorlithia made it clear he's already using them."

"Agreed," Demos said. "But we can still deal him a blow." His gaze met mine, and my stomach tensed before he even said the words. "I want to go."

It would be so, so dangerous. "You don't think you would be of more use elsewhere?"

He shook his head. "For now, our strategy remains the same. I'll get the amulet and meet you after you've taken care of Zathrian. Because that's what you're planning, isn't it, Pris?" One side of his mouth curved, but no humor glinted in his eyes.

The room had gone silent.

"Yes," I admitted. "The time for wishing things could be different is over."

Demos gave me an approving nod. "Hevdrin is

right," he said, glancing at the other man. "We can't afford for Zathrian to turn our own people on us. But with Regner attacking on all fronts, we also can't afford to just be on the defensive. Without the amulet, this can't end."

Surprising no one, Asinia got to her feet. "I'm going with him."

Demos leveled her with a long stare, but he didn't argue.

"Pick ten people to take with you," I told them. "Powerful fae and hybrids."

No one spoke. But a new energy had entered the room, and my skin prickled with it. It almost felt like the way the air crackled before Lorian used his power. It was a feeling of anticipation mixed with dread, mixed with something else. Determination, maybe.

"I'll do it," Tor said into the silence. His face was gray, and his lower lip trembled before he firmed it. "I'll help you."

I met his eyes. "Thank you."

He just shook his head, turning away.

He'd made his decision. I shifted my attention to Blynth. "I need you to return to our army and ensure they are ready for battle."

He nodded. "Done."

Lorian got to his feet. The room went silent again.

"There's another reason we wanted to bring you all here together. Even in the midst of war, it's important to make time for joy. To allow hope to be our light in the dark. The day of the summit, I asked Prisca to marry me. We don't know what will happen in this war. But we have to make time to celebrate our lives—or Regner wins."

Lorian looked at me then, and I blinked back tears.

"We want you to celebrate with us," I said. "Tomorrow, before we all separate."

Smiles unfurled, a few cheers broke out, and some of the quiet dread disappeared from the room. Warmth spread through my chest. This was why Lorian wanted to get married now. A chance to enjoy one another's company one final time before we were all separated. To celebrate love and to celebrate one another.

Rythos and Galon slapped Lorian on the back. This announcement hadn't come as a surprise to them, but they grinned at me.

Surprisingly, it was Marth who hugged me first. "I'm happy for you, Pris."

"Thank you. And thank you for surviving Sorlithia and being here."

He gave me a faint smile, stepping away to let the others congratulate us.

I'd asked Asinia and Madinia to stay, and they waited, one wearing a bright smile, the other a glower.

"Tomorrow, for our wedding...I want you to stand with me. Both of you."

Joyful tears filled Asinia's eyes. A cold rage filled Madinia's. My heart sank.

"Of course, Pris," Asinia said with a wide grin. "I'm honored."

Madinia slowly shook her head, and my heart plummeted. "I never asked to be part of your little group. I'm here to win this war and leave. So stop trying to make me care about you. All of you."

She turned and stalked out.

MADINIA

My mood was dark as I strode through the castle, searching for some distraction—a way to replace the image of the disappointment in Prisca's eyes.

She had no business asking me for such things.

Darnis's tiny face flashed before my eyes. And I was suddenly back in that forest, the weight of a child in my arms and the weight of the lives I was responsible for on my shoulders.

A cold sweat broke out on the back of my neck. I couldn't linger on it. There were more important things to think about. Such as my plans after this war.

It was time to talk to the pirate queen.

Rekja had put us all in the same wing, but there were enough rooms to search that by the time I found Daharak, the sick feeling in my gut had almost dissipated.

She sat in an elegant sitting room with a view of the ocean. She stared at the water with longing. But her face was bloodless.

"What is it?" I asked.

Daharak's eyes stayed on the majority of her fleet, anchored close to shore. "You mean other than the thousands of my people lost to the sea?"

I studied her face. Since the moment I'd seen her in this castle, she'd been quiet, solemn, withdrawn. But this reaction was different. She looked as if she'd been gut-punched, slapped across the face, and thrown into a cold lake all at the same time.

"I can't use the weapon," she said when I didn't respond. Her voice was hollow, empty.

The memory of our conversation on her ship trickled into my mind. "You're speaking of the weapon you used your blood vow with Prisca to find."

She nodded. Daharak was usually someone who commanded attention. When she walked into a room, people noticed. Now, though, she seemed somehow diminished. Her shoulders slumped and she looked smaller, as if some of the life had been drained from her.

I sat next to her. "What's so special about this weapon?"

Reaching into her cloak pocket, she pulled out a blue orb. It looked as if it was made of glass, but something about it made me shiver. I was both drawn to it and tempted to demand Daharak put it away again.

"Rumors are that the orb is gods-touched. My father searched for it, and his father before him. We have enemies, and the weapon can do almost anything. There are limits to its power, of course, but…with the barrier down, it is only a matter of time before our ancient feud is reignited." Daharak lifted her hand, and the sunlight spearing through the window made it appear as if a blue fire burned within the orb. "It would have finally finished things."

I listened to what she wasn't saying. Daharak had clearly planned to use the weapon to wipe out her enemies as soon as we won this war.

"Why can't you use it?"

"I made a deal with someone for the location of the weapon. After years of keeping the location from me, he finally told me—on his deathbed. What he failed to mention was that only someone pure of heart can wield it."

I bit my lip, attempting to hide a smirk. "You don't believe you're pure of heart?"

Daharak gave me a poisonous look. "Pirate. Queen. The things I've done would give you night terrors. Which means I can't use this unless I feel like sacrificing my life to it." Her mouth tightened in a grim smile. "And as much as I'd like my enemies to pay, I plan on being around to see it."

Moments like these made me certain the gods were playing with us. A weapon powerful enough that Daharak Rostamir had hunted it all these years and she couldn't even use it on her enemies.

Worse, none of us could use it either. Pure of heart? All of us had killed. I'd killed and enjoyed it. Wished I could repeat it. Likely, I would again.

I sighed. "Don't tell Prisca."

That caught her attention. Daharak's brow lifted, her gaze settling on my face. "Why?"

"Because the idiot will do something stupid like attempt to sacrifice herself for the good of everyone else, and Lorian will finally lose control and lock her away somewhere. I don't want to have to deal with the dramatics."

Humor flickered in her eyes. "Fine." Daharak placed the orb back in my hands, and I frowned at her. "Perhaps your new life will give you an opportunity to find someone who can use this weapon for good."

"We're not going to pretend I'm pure of heart?"

Daharak snorted.

I sensed movement by the door. I snapped my head around, and Daharak launched herself to her feet with a curse. Asinia narrowed her eyes at me, and her gaze lingered on the orb in my hands. "Keeping important information from Prisca isn't going to help us."

Fury bit at me with sharp teeth. "Eavesdropping now, Asinia? Do you think the gods would allow Prisca to escape their wrath after she stole Lorian's life back from them?"

The blood drained from Asinia's face. She knew as well as I did that none of us could use the weapon.

With a curse, she kicked the chair in front of her and turned, stalking toward the door.

I raised my eyebrow. I hadn't seen much of her temper. Clearly, I wasn't the only one feeling the pressure.

"Speaking of that new life, I want to talk about what happens after this war," I said when Asinia had slammed the door behind her.

Daharak angled her head. "You really think we'll survive?"

"Only idiots march into battle believing they will die."

She laughed. "Wise words for someone who has never battled."

I shrugged. While traveling through Eprotha, I'd come to a sudden, unwelcome realization.

I was penniless.

While I'd sold Kaliera's jewels in the fae lands—something I hadn't gotten nearly enough credit for—those funds had been gradually eaten away by the many costs of outfitting our armies. Lorian had contributed, as had his friends, and I was relatively sure even Conreth had dug into his own coffers at this point.

But the fact remained—wars were expensive. Armies needed weapons and food and tents. By the time this war ended, there would be little coin left.

I wanted a new life on a new continent. But I was most assuredly *not* suited for poverty.

"Now that's a calculated expression," Daharak mused. "You'll need to work on that."

I scowled. Not long ago, hiding my true feelings behind an expressionless mask had been second nature for me. Clearly, spending this long away from court hadn't done me any favors.

"It's not enough to set foot on a new continent if this godsforsaken war ever ends," I said.

Daharak watched me, her dark eyes cool. "What is it you want?"

"I want to earn some kind of living. By the time I step off your ship, I need to have enough coin to start a new life."

"Strangely, I can't exactly picture you scrubbing my decks. You'd likely become irritated and set the entire ship alight."

My nose wrinkled before I could control it. Daharak grinned at me. "Don't fret. I have a need for someone of your talents. By the time you're ready to start your new life, you'll have a purse full of coin."

This time, I let my lips curve. But Daharak's grin disappeared. "Heed my words, Madinia Farrow, for I have a tiny drop of my mother's sight. If you refuse to open your heart to those who would lay down their lives for you, you will not arrive on the eastern continent with just a purse full of coin. You will also carry with you a heart full of regret. And that heart will be much, much heavier than any coin you can imagine."

"I have no idea what you're talking about."

She gave me a sharp smile. "You think feelings are a weakness. And sometimes, they are. Sometimes, those feelings eat at everything you thought you were. But a life refusing to feel, to love? That is worse than a weakness. That is a travesty. To refuse to feel the full range of emotions, to deny yourself joy in an effort to protect yourself from the loss? I may not know much—may have no true glimpse of the future the way my mother does—but I know without a doubt that one day, the tiny moments of joy you keep turning your back on? They're the moments that will keep you alive."

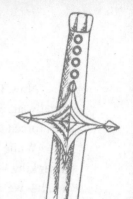

14

PRISCA

Conreth arrived the night before our wedding. And he brought Jamic with him. Clearly, Jamic's training had gone well. He'd regained some color in his face. He'd lost the haunted look in his eyes, and he no longer flinched at odd moments.

He'd also asked to see his mother. Lorian didn't like it. Truthfully, neither did I. Kaliera was dangerous. But when Jamic had gravely requested to spend some time with her, I hadn't had the heart to say no.

Lorian hadn't been sure Conreth would be able to make it to these meetings, but the fae king could achieve almost anything when properly motivated.

And he wasn't the type to allow everyone else to make war plans without his input—even with his generals and advisers speaking in his place.

Of the five wardens who ruled their individual territories within the fae lands—with Conreth as monarch—Thorn and Romydan had agreed to join us. Both had also fought with us to bring down the barrier.

Sylvielle, Caliar, and Verdion had not.

Now, Conreth brought welcome news. Sylvielle had finally agreed to fight with us. Caliar and Verdion had reinforced their refusal.

While the Arslan had ignored the summons from their king—something Conreth had told us through gritted teeth—we were hoping Rythos would finally be able to convince his father of the seriousness of our situation.

But today...today, I would attempt not to think of war—as much as one could while in the midst of it.

Because today was my wedding day.

Rekja had given us full access to his castle, instructing us to make the most of this day. I'd immediately handed all of the details over to Lorian, who had handed them over to someone else.

Conreth came to our rooms after we broke our fast.

Lorian and Conreth had an unspoken agreement to stay away from each other except for war strategy. If Lorian was surprised by Conreth breaking this agreement, he didn't show it. But I caught the wariness in his eyes as he watched his brother.

Conreth turned to me. "I owe you an apology."

Unfortunately, I wasn't as used to hiding my expressions as Lorian. The corner of Conreth's mouth tipped up.

"Me?"

"Yes. Because of my actions, you watched Lorian die in front of you."

I flinched. I couldn't help it. Just the words, and I was back on that ship. Lorian snarled at his brother, pulling me close.

"I'm fine," I told Lorian, driving my finger into his

ribs. He gave me a doubtful look but turned back to his brother.

"Because of me, you had to use your power in a way that was forbidden. And now, you can't use that power," Conreth continued. He attempted to keep his expression stoic, but it was clear he was bothered by this. At least, it was clear to *me*. Who knew what Lorian was thinking?

Conreth seemed to be waiting for me. I nodded.

"Lorian was correct. If we had worked together, I might have killed Regner's general. Perhaps I might have even managed to kill your cousin. Instead, I allowed my fury and frustration to take over, playing right into Regner's hands. You deserved better. Both of you."

For the first time, I felt a tiny drop of hope. Perhaps one day, Lorian and Conreth would truly be brothers again.

"I would like to attend your wedding," Conreth said. "I know I don't deserve it. But I would like to watch my brother on one of the happiest days of his life."

A lump began to form in my throat. I hadn't realized Lorian hadn't formally invited his brother to our wedding. I'd thought it was a given that he would be there, if only because he was an ally.

I glanced at Lorian. He was watching Conreth with a calculating look in his eyes.

Uh-oh.

"Yes," I said.

"On one condition," Lorian murmured.

Conreth's expression turned guarded, but he nodded.

"I need Renit."

Conreth's brows drew together like two white

caterpillars about to fight to the death. He opened his mouth, eyes firing at his brother.

But he paused, took a deep breath, and considered it.

I didn't know what Renit was, but from the intensity in Lorian's eyes, it was crucially important.

A tense silence claimed the room. Lorian's expression was relaxed, his hands in his pockets. But I was relatively sure he was holding his breath.

Conreth's mouth twisted. "Fine. Temporarily. *Very* temporarily."

Lorian smiled, and he seemed lighter somehow. "In that case, brother, I will see you at the ceremony."

Some of the tension disappeared from Conreth's face. He nodded at both of us and walked out.

My gaze met Lorian's. As much as I liked the thought of the brothers reconciling, I didn't think Lorian bargaining with Conreth in order to allow him to attend our wedding was necessarily a step in the right direction.

"Trust me," Lorian said, leaning close and nuzzling my ear as his hands began to wander. "You'll thank me in a few days."

Someone knocked on the door. I sighed, wishing we had time for those clever hands to continue wandering. Lorian let out a low growl, and I untangled myself from him. "That will be Telean."

My aunt had insisted on working with Rekja's seamstresses to create my dress. Likely, that had been what she had been whispering about with Lorian.

Clearly, she had decided we were taking too long to open the door, because she opened it herself before standing there silently, her hands on her hips.

A single wordless look was enough to reinforce her impatience. My chest lightened. Despite everything that had passed between us, she seemed willing to put our disagreement aside for today.

I gazed at Lorian. The next time I saw him…

"Go, wildcat. The quicker you get ready, the sooner you'll be in my arms again." He pulled me close, pressing a gentle kiss to my mouth. I soaked in the feel of him.

Telean cleared her throat, and I laughed against his lips.

"You better let me go."

Lorian sighed, and I wiggled free, following Telean from our rooms, down the hall, and into hers.

My breath caught.

Three dresses hung near the window. Mine was a stunning amber, while she had chosen emerald green for Asinia and Madinia. Clearly, Lorian had told her I'd asked both of them to stand with me.

Looking at one of those dresses made disappointment curl in my gut. So, I focused on my dress. And on Asinia's.

Telean crossed the room and stood next to them, watching me silently.

For all of her fury about the way I'd used my power to bring Lorian back, she'd clearly worked with him before he'd even asked me to get married here. And she'd chosen the colors of both of our eyes.

"They're beautiful. I don't know what to say."

She sighed. "I won't apologize for the things I said."

I flicked my gaze toward the dresses hanging like a silent apology.

She ignored me.

"I suppose you believe I am too old and bitter to know anything about love."

I frowned at her. She'd made it clear how much she loved both Demos and me, even in her no-nonsense, gruff way. "No. I don't think that at all."

Reaching out a hand, she checked the hem of one of the green dresses, releasing it with a pleased hum.

"I had a great love once too. I don't talk about him. I try not to think about him. And then I feel the guilt of that decision." She smiled at me, and her eyes lit with a joy I'd never seen from her. "Yorin would be severely unhappy about that. The man was beautiful, and he knew it. He would have expected me to tell everyone of my loss."

My lips curved, even as my chest ached for her. "What happened?"

"He died during the invasion. He was supposed to meet us—to escape with your parents. Instead, he went back in an attempt to protect a group of hybrid children. I didn't learn of his fate until weeks later. Each day, I had woken with the hope that he would join us." Telean's expression turned lost, and for a moment, she looked much older than her years.

My throat clenched tight. "I am so sorry. He sounds like an incredible man."

She nodded, her eyes bright with tears she refused to shed. "Even when I learned of his death and was forced to accept he had been gone for days...if there had been any way to bring him back——no matter how forbidden——I would have done it. Without hesitation. Perhaps...perhaps that was why I was so hard on you. Because I knew I would have chosen the same path, and I know you will suffer for it."

I had been forcing myself to block out the knowledge of what was coming. I believed Telean when she said the magic I had used was forbidden for a reason. And that the gods would demand a steep price for it. At first, I had assumed the price was the decimation of the hybrid camp. But… I knew there was worse to come. How long would Lorian be haunted by the dead? Would their presence slowly chip away at his sanity?

"Nelayra?"

I took a deep breath. "I…I saw my mother. When I turned time backward. And my grandmother."

Telean's eyes filled. And I told her everything. When I got to the part about the tiny lights they had given me, her mouth dropped open, until my voice trailed off.

"If not for that, I would think you had imagined it. That your air-starved mind had merely given you the hallucinations you needed in that moment."

"What did they do?"

"You said pieces of yourself were…disintegrating."

I nodded, and she sucked in a rasping breath. "You were losing your soul, Prisca. Your mother and grandmother gave you enough of their own to keep you alive."

My mouth trembled, and I clamped down on it with my teeth, struggling to keep from bursting into tears. "Did… Do you think it hurt them?"

She gave me a shaky smile. "I don't know. But they clearly believed this was the right choice. They obviously wanted you to return to your life and save the man you love."

Tears rolled down her cheeks. "Forgive me," she said. "I miss your mother. She was my best friend. We were supposed to have centuries."

My own eyes burned, and she shook her head, wiping away her tears. "Your power?"

"I still can't feel it," I admitted.

I didn't say how useless I felt, in the midst of a war without my power. How it had killed me when Rekja had leveled me with that disbelieving stare while Tymedes waited to attack.

Telean sighed. "You are more than just your power, Prisca. Look at how much power Regner has. And look at what he has done with it." My aunt cupped my cheek, smiling up at me. "Even if your power never returns, I have no doubt that you will be a glorious queen."

I hadn't known just how much I'd needed to hear those words from my aunt. I was still desperate for my power, but Telean had taken the worst of the ache from my bones. At least for today.

Telean smiled. "Enough of this for now. Today is a happy day. Now, let's get you ready."

ASINIA

The day Prisca helped us escape Regner's dungeon, Demos had begun to change.

He didn't just transform physically—although watching him eat three or four courses for each meal, his muscles straining against the seams of his clothes, had been…interesting.

No, he'd also changed in other ways. Those changes might not have been as obvious, but they were the important changes.

Gradually, he'd begun to let go of some of the bitterness I'd so often seen in Regner's dungeon. The rage had transformed into a quiet peace—with occasional glimpses of his sly sense of humor. He still planned Regner's murder with a single-minded focus that occasionally made even Lorian raise an eyebrow. But he'd seemed to find some measure of joy in life as well.

Tor's presence… It had smothered that joy, strangled that humor, and turned any contentment into self-loathing. Gone was the wicked gleam in Demos's eyes when he looked at me. Now, those eyes were blank, dark shadows beneath them.

I hated it. Hated that Tor had brought all of Demos's guilt and self-contempt back to the surface. Hated that instead of talking to me, he was pulling away.

His conversations with Tor were short and clipped. The other man hadn't attempted to rekindle their friendship, although I'd caught him staring at Demos occasionally while we traveled.

Now that we were in the castle, with plenty of room to avoid each other, Demos did exactly that. But Tor wasn't the only one he avoided.

And gods, it hurt.

Pushing the thought from my mind, I pasted a bright smile on my face, making my way toward Prisca and Lorian's rooms. This was my best friend's day, and if she hadn't yet noticed just how Demos was struggling, I wouldn't be the one to point it out.

She deserved at least one day of true happiness.

Knocking on the door, I cracked it open, following the voices I could hear into one of the bedrooms.

Telean stood behind Prisca, fiddling with something in her hair, and when she stepped aside, I let out an audible gasp.

Prisca looked ethereal. Her long blond curls had been left loose, tiny white flowers woven into the strands. But it was the diadem she also wore that stole my breath.

I'd seen it once before—when she was preparing to meet with Eryndan. Prisca had been uncomfortable, still fighting against her role as hybrid queen.

The band was made from twisting white-gold vines and dotted with diamonds, while the emerald centerpiece dipped low, to the middle of her forehead.

Telean had obviously known this announcement was coming—and who Prisca would ask to stand with her, because she'd worked magic of her own, procuring dresses for Prisca, Madinia and me.

Clearly, no one had told Telean that Madinia had refused.

Prisca's dress hung on the closet. It was a color I couldn't name—not gold, not bronze, but something in between. Two other dresses hung close by, with flower crowns waiting on the vanity.

Once, long ago, Prisca and I had planned our weddings. I'd told her I would wear whatever she liked, so long as she crowned me with flowers.

Now, it seemed ludicrous. But even while we were at

war, when this wedding would be nothing like she'd once imagined, Prisca had still remembered.

Telean nodded at the dress on the right. "Go on, then. Put it on so I can take a look."

I complied, and Prisca's eyes shone as Telean stepped behind me to button the silky material.

"It fits well," Telean remarked, and I gazed in the mirror.

The dress was a dark green that shimmered when the light hit it. The material gently cupped my breasts, tucked in at my waist, and fell elegantly over my hips, the long train sliding fluidly across the floor.

I grabbed the flower crown and placed it on my head. Prisca grinned at me. "Happy?"

"Of course."

Telean smiled at us. "You both look beautiful." She was clearly being careful not to mention the other dress, still hanging nearby. Occasionally, I wanted to slap Madinia. But I hadn't been there when that hybrid camp was attacked. And after what she'd said to Tor…

She was suffering.

"Now, I believe I'll go find my seat."

Prisca leaned down and kissed Telean's cheek. "Thank you."

Telean's eyes gleamed, and she turned, bustling out.

"It feels like tempting fate to be this happy," Prisca said. "To celebrate anything. But…in the days after Lorian asked me to marry him, I kept thinking about how Cavis should have been there with Rythos, Marth, and Galon. And I kept wondering who else wouldn't make it to our wedding. If we would even get to be married."

I took her hand. I hated that those were the thoughts she was thinking on her wedding day. "These moments are reminders, Pris. Reminders of what we're fighting for. They give us hope. *You've* given us hope."

Prisca squeezed my hand, her eyes glistening. "Thank you. And...I never got to thank you properly for keeping Demos alive."

"You know you don't have to thank me for that."

"Yes. But I'm doing it anyway. Having both of my brothers so far away...it was awful. I had to actively force myself not to spiral, thinking about all the things that could go wrong. But knowing all three of you were together, and that you would keep one another safe...that was enough to get me through the fear."

The door opened. I turned, meeting Madinia's eyes. And I gave her a warning look. If she dared to upset Prisca today...

Madinia's gaze slid past me. "I'll do it," she muttered. "I'll wear the stupid dress. I'll even wear...*that*." Her nose wrinkled at the flower crown on my head, and I attempted to stifle my grin.

"Are you sure?" Prisca arched an eyebrow, her voice cool. "I wouldn't want to *force* you to be my friend."

Madinia curled her lip. Stalking to the vanity, she picked up the flower crown and shoved it on her head. It leaned drunkenly to one side. "Happy now?"

Prisca smirked. "You know, I am."

Madinia looked like a cat who'd been dunked in a barrel of cold water. But her hands moved to the back of her tunic, and she pulled it over her head, further jostling the flower crown. I would've offered to help, but she likely would have snarled.

Her leather leggings were gone a moment later, and she reached for the dress Telean had designed for her, completely unconcerned by her nudity.

If I looked as incredible as Madinia did while naked, I would be unconcerned too.

Prisca's mouth curved into a full-fledged grin. And then she reached for her own gown.

I held out my hand, and she gave me the gown to hold.

I didn't know how Telean had accomplished it, but she'd managed to ensure the material matched the amber of Prisca's eyes.

Prisca dropped her robe, displaying the glimmering bronze lace she wore beneath. "Well, well, well," Madinia said, voice dripping with amusement.

Prisca's cheeks reddened, but she winked at me as I held the dress for her to step into.

I stared hopelessly at the back of it. Even as a trained seamstress, I would need a moment to understand how the ribbons interconnected to hold the dress in place.

"Let me," Madinia said, and for once, her voice was soft.

I stepped back as Madinia easily discerned which ribbon needed to cross in each place. The dress glowed, cascading down and clinging gently to Prisca's form. The bodice, adorned with tiny, iridescent jewels, sparkled in an elaborate, swirling pattern. The neckline dipped low, while the gauzy layers of the skirt fluttered with her every step, falling in gentle, undulating folds to the floor.

Prisca turned, and I surveyed the back of the dress.

It was daringly bare, save for the intricate ribbons that crisscrossed over her skin. Those ribbons played a tantalizing game of both highlighting and concealing, adding an element of mystique to the overall design.

It was, without a doubt, the most beautiful dress I'd ever seen.

Prisca wrapped her arm around each of us. It occurred to me now that other than Telean, no older women were here on this joyful day. No one to pass down wisdom about marriage or life or love.

All three of us were motherless. Was it easier for Madinia, who'd never had a mother? Or easier for me, who at least had my memories? Or perhaps it was easier for Prisca, who could mask her sorrow with rage at the only mother she'd known before she'd learned the truth.

Pushing the thoughts from my mind, I studied our reflection. We had each other. Even Madinia had suppressed her instincts to shove everyone away. At least for today.

Prisca's thoughts seemed to be similar to mine, because her eyes met Madinia's in the mirror. "I'm not sorry that you care, Madinia. Because when someone like you takes an interest...worlds change."

Madinia sighed. Then she pushed a curl away from Prisca's face and fussed with her hair. "You look breathtaking," she declared. "Now, go marry that possessive fae before he comes in here and drags you out."

Prisca laughed, and together, we walked out of the room. Outside, Demos and Tibris waited in the hall, both of them wearing perfectly fitting pants and jackets, their hair neatly combed. Demos… When I caught sight of him, my breath caught. I attempted to hide it with a cough, and Madinia gave me a knowing look.

Both of Prisca's brothers held out an arm, and she stood between them, linking her arms with each of theirs.

Leaning over, I wiped the fresh tears from her face.

My eyes met Demos's. His gaze slowly traveled from my feet, up the length of my gauzy dress, to the tops of my breasts, and lingered on my painted mouth. Finally, it reached my flower crown. His lips twitched.

I sent him a killing look and his smile widened, but he didn't say a word.

Madinia went first, and I followed her along the hall and down a set of long, sprawling stairs. The doors at the bottom of the staircase had been flung open, and we stepped out and into the waiting carriage.

Prisca and Lorian had asked for only one thing—that their ceremony be in the forest, where they had spent so much time soon after they'd met.

All of us were quiet as the carriage left the city gates. Prisca seemed both nervous and oddly peaceful, her hands trembling while her eyes were calm.

Finally, the carriage stopped, and Madinia slid out.

I leaned over, squeezing Prisca's hand. "I love you."

She gave me a trembling smile. "I love you too."

Someone began playing a breathtakingly haunting melody, and I stepped out of the carriage.

Sunlight flickered through the branches overhead, dancing across the grass, which had been carpeted with flower petals. The scent of earth mingled with the fragrance from countless wild flowers adorning the clearing, and the breeze teased my hair, fluttering the ribbons hanging from branches above our heads.

Madinia began her walk down the aisle, and I craned my neck, peering past her.

Lorian stood next to Marth, Rythos, and Galon. He shifted his gaze to his left, as if someone were standing on his other side.

My heart clenched. He was picturing Cavis next to him.

And I watched as his eyes gleamed with a flicker of amusement—as if his dead friend had made some pithy remark.

A hint of disquiet fluttered through me. Did Prisca know Lorian was walking the thin line between what was real and what...wasn't?

I began my own walk. Lorian shifted on his feet, clearly impatient, and I grinned as his eyes met mine. He wore a deep midnight-blue coat that caught the light with every movement. Golden embroidery adorned the edges, while a vest of silken silver hugged his torso, its buttons gleaming like polished stars. Beneath both, he wore a crisp white shirt. His trousers were perfectly cut, the dark fabric complementing the splendor of the coat, and part of me wondered if Telean had paid him a visit to ensure the fit was perfect.

Madinia stepped to the side. But I was still watching Lorian as he glanced past me and his gaze landed on the love of his life.

Words failed to capture the essence of that look. My heart seemed too small to contain the joy that surged through me at the sight. It was a look of bewildered adoration and tenderness, as if Lorian couldn't quite believe Prisca was his. The love was tempered with a healthy dose of possessive lust that made it clear he would do whatever it took to keep her.

Prisca beamed back at him. And in that moment, I could briefly forget about death and war.

15

PRISCA

Lorian's eyes met mine, and I lost the ability to breathe.

I'd seen so many expressions on his face when he looked at me. Irritation, humor, bemusement, lust, a love so deep it made me question if I could ever be worthy of such adoration.

But now, he looked at me as if I was the last star left in a sky filled with darkness. He looked at me as if he was drowning and I was the only one who could give him air. It was a desperate, possessive, love-stricken look.

And I was pretty sure I was gazing at him the exact same way.

My heart had been galloping in my chest, my hands shaking. But the moment our eyes met, all nerves faded away, until there was only room for joy.

I was already mated to this man, and I was beginning to understand just how deep that bond went. But he'd wanted to give me this. A ceremony that told me without a doubt that he was mine and I was his. Across every kingdom. Throughout every world.

Galon had agreed to marry us. And it felt right that the man who'd been Lorian's father in every way except blood—and the man who'd saved my life that day by the river—would be the one to make us husband and wife.

He said something that made everyone laugh, but I was too busy staring at Lorian. He gazed down at me, that half smile on his face, and my heart flipped in my chest.

Galon raised his voice. "Today, we gather here during a time of war to celebrate one of the great milestones of life. I have been blessed by the gods to have witnessed Lorian and Prisca's love since the moment they laid eyes on each other. Although…both would have sworn to all of the gods that love was the very last thing they could have imagined feeling."

Galon was usually a man of few words. But today, he told our friends, family, and allies the kinds of stories that made them roar with laughter.

From the time Lorian caught me attempting to steal his horse, to the time I finally managed to use my power on him by the river—and slammed my knee into his balls. Galon had clearly spoken to some of the others as well since he was sure to mention how jealous Lorian had become while watching me dance with another man in Regner's castle.

Tears filled my eyes as his stories reminded me of the way Lorian had stayed at my bedside when I was poisoned. Of the way he'd relentlessly bullied me until I emerged from the shell of fear and apprehension and self-doubt. Lorian had seen the truth within me—that I was strong and determined, and that I didn't have to let my past determine my future.

"Like the ancient trees surrounding us, your love

will endure times of storm and serenity, weathering the fiercest winds of adversity, and enjoying the gentle breezes of peace," Galon said.

"Your love will prevail through times of sun and frost, basking in our warmest, brightest days, and enduring the icy touches of our hardest nights.

"And your love will stand strong through drought and abundance, through parched summers and bountiful springs, growing deeper with each passing year."

Galon handed the marriage bracelet to Lorian. "And so you shall vow."

Lorian took my hand, and the feel of the warm strength of his palm beneath mine seemed to settle something deep within me.

He stared intently into my eyes. "I vow to be the roots that ground you, the branches that help you reach for your dreams, and the shelter that forever keeps you safe. I will love you in every life."

My lips trembled, but I managed to swallow past the lump in my throat, repeating his words. My voice cracked on the last sentence, and Lorian pulled me close.

"Not yet," Galon said. As usual, Lorian ignored him, gently pushing the bracelet over my hand until it encircled my wrist. The magic woven into the metal instantly shrank the bracelet until there was just enough room for my wrist to be comfortable, but it could only be removed with tools.

"Fine," Galon said with a wave of his hand that made everyone laugh. "Just as you are mated, so shall you be wed. I now pronounce you husband and wife. You may…"

More laughter.

I barely heard it, because my head was whirling as Lorian's mouth met mine. I soaked in the feel of him. The taste of him. The scent of him.

He let out an exultant laugh, pulling me to him and spinning me around until all I could do was hold on, my chest lighter than air.

LORIAN

Prisca was my wife. She was also my mate. She was my *everything*.

I barely tasted the wedding feast Rekja had provided, too busy focusing on the way Prisca beamed as well-wishers approached. She licked her lips, and my gaze caught on her mouth.

A cheery tune began playing, the musicians drawing couples from their tables. Rekja had even managed to arrange for music on such short notice. I owed him my gratitude.

Catching Prisca's hand, I brought her knuckles to my mouth. Her eyes met mine, and I basked in her attention.

"Dance with me, wildcat."

She smiled at me, allowing me to lead her from the table. Several people had been approaching from various directions. I sent them a warning look, and they immediately found someone else to talk to.

Prisca squeezed my hand until I glanced back at her. "Are you terrifying our guests during our wedding feast?"

I gave her my most charming smile. "I missed you."

"I was sitting right next to you."

"You were looking at other people."

Her laugh rang out, and I drew her to the far edge of the tent, close to the musicians. When the music turned slow, I pulled her into my arms, kissing my way up her smooth, warm neck.

She let out a hum, tipping her head back, and I caught her lips with mine.

Gods, the taste of her.

I forced myself to lift my head, almost throwing her over my shoulder when her glazed eyes met mine.

"Are you happy?" I murmured.

She grinned up at me. "I'm so happy, I feel as if we got away with something we shouldn't have. This feels like a dream."

The music ebbed and flowed as couples danced around us. I drew her even closer, and she nestled her head on my chest. Pride swelled within me. Not long ago, the thought of being tender with anyone was unfathomable. The thought of risking my heart, untenable. Now, it was the thought of being away from this woman for even a few days that seemed unbearable.

"You clawed your way under my skin, wildcat."

She angled her head, smirking up at me. "You deserved it. You were so grumpy and mean with your orders and threats." She gave a mock shiver. "Very scary."

I leaned down and kissed the shell of her ear, enjoying the way her breath caught. "You had no problem standing up to me."

"Oh, there were problems," she muttered, laughing

when I nipped her ear.

"Hey, darlin'," Rythos said behind us. "Can I cut in?"

Ignoring him, I nuzzled Prisca's cheek. She pinched me.

I heaved a sigh. "Fine. But then we're leaving. I'm tired of everyone talking and looking at you. I want you to myself."

"Possessive man."

I stepped away, but not before giving Rythos a warning look. He would never attempt anything with Prisca. But it was good to remind him of the immediate consequences, just in case he ever lost his sanity.

Both of them rolled their eyes.

I stepped away, prepared to at least find something to drink if I couldn't dance with my own wife at my own wedding.

"Pouting, brother?"

Conreth gazed at me, hands on hips. For once, his words didn't carry any true animosity or mockery. His eyes danced, inviting me to join him.

Despite the people clamoring for Prisca's attention, I was in a good mood.

"Rythos," I grumbled, and Conreth grinned, handing me a drink.

"Thanks."

We watched them dance for a moment. Rythos said something to make Prisca laugh, her smile lighting up the entire room.

"You seem happy," Conreth murmured.

"I am."

"If that ever changes…"

Our eyes met. His expression was casual, but I saw the offer for what it was. He was saying I could come back. That everything could return to the way it was.

I stared straight into his eyes. Our father's eyes.

"An accident of birth made me a fae prince. And I gave up that title because I could never have stayed by Prisca's side otherwise. I regret nothing."

He frowned. "You say that now. Titles aren't meaningless, Lorian."

I shrugged. "I was a fae prince, and now I'm Prisca's mate and husband. I know which titles mean more to me. Which titles I wear with pride and will until the day I die. Besides, she has a title of her own."

"Her title as the hybrid heir?"

"No." I bared my teeth. "Mine."

After a long moment, Conreth offered me a smile. "You have something special. Thank you for allowing me to be here today."

I nodded. I didn't point out that I was getting something in return, and Conreth chose not to mention it either.

But his hand slid to his neck. And I tensed as he slowly removed one of the amulets, holding it out to me.

"What are you doing?"

"It doesn't make strategic sense for me to have both of them."

"So give one of them to a fae you trust."

"You are a fae I trust."

"My loyalty is to the hybrids."

He gave me a faint smile. "Yes. But we are still allies. This proves such a thing to any of our people who might doubt the strength of that alliance."

Slowly, I took the amulet, pulling it over my head, where it pulsed warmly.

"Fine."

Conreth's smile widened at my curt tone.

Asinia walked past, her expression unreadable. I watched her. Everyone Prisca cared about was mine now too. That had been the case for a while now, but today, it felt even more important.

"If you'll excuse me," I said.

Conreth replied, but I was already striding away, grabbing Asinia's hand.

ASINIA

A warm hand clasped mine. For a moment, my heart leaped.

But it wasn't Demos.

"Are you happy, Asinia?" Lorian guided me back toward the musicians, seamlessly transitioning me from the direction I'd wanted to travel to the direction he chose.

He was waiting for me to reply. This seemed like an unusual conversation for Lorian's wedding day. Still, I supposed we were all leaving tomorrow. We no longer had the luxury of waiting for the right time. For anything.

"What do you mean?"

He shrugged one shoulder. "Prisca considers you to be her sister. That makes you mine as well."

Despite the strangeness of this conversation, I smiled. "Don't you have enough people to manage, Lorian?"

From the arrogant arch of one eyebrow, he likely believed there were no limits to the people he could manage. I laughed.

Lorian spun me, but he was still waiting. "I'm... I...I feel like happy isn't the right word. I feel so many emotions right now, all of them constantly warring within me. On days like today, a word like *happy* seems almost...tepid. What I feel today is a kind of defiant joy. It's a feeling that lies. A feeling that whispers that everything is going to work out. Because how could it not?" I waved my hand to encompass the area where everyone was dancing.

Both of us turned to watch the others.

Prisca was beaming up at Rythos—right before Demos and Tibris cut in—one on each side—and swayed with her to the music. Until Demos said something that made all three of them howl with laughter. Nearby, Daharak and Madinia were drinking copious amounts of wine and...*cackling.*

One of Daharak's pirates had dragged Marth toward the dancing, and he peered down at her as she gave him a bawdy wink.

Rythos had joined Galon, and together, they watched Marth with wide smirks on their faces. Everywhere, fae and hybrids and humans danced and ate and laughed together—a glimpse of what the future could look like if we won this war.

"Today, we're creating memories," I said around the lump in my throat. "Memories we can hide away and cherish. Memories we can take out and examine as we march toward battle. Memories that might briefly keep us warm on the loneliest, coldest nights if we lose all of this." Lorian's gaze burrowed into me, and I shrugged self-consciously. "I've heard... I've heard that when you die, your memories make the dying a little easier. That those memories play through your mind and give you some comfort. If that's true, and the fates decide it is my time, I hope those memories include this day." I waved my hand again, before moving it back to Lorian's shoulder.

He let out a hum, but it didn't sound like agreement.

"When you... Did you..."

His mouth twitched. "When I died, did I see my memories?"

My face flamed. "Right. Prisca turned back time. So you wouldn't remember."

"That's not entirely true." Amusement flickered through his eyes, and I realized my mouth had fallen open.

"What happened?" I breathed.

His expression turned serious. "One moment, Prisca was running toward me, and then my vision turned white. I caught sight of Cavis's face, briefly. But it was immediately followed by Prisca. She was all I saw. All I wanted to see. And then the next thing I knew, we were in the water. I have no recollection of the dying itself. But I know I felt regret. So much regret." He paused, his brows lowering. "I think that has to be the worst part about dying. Leaving the people you love and regretting."

It was the most Lorian had ever said to me, and I considered his words. He turned us again, his gaze flicking behind me and firing with that possessive light. I didn't need to glance over my shoulder to know who he was looking at.

He met my eyes once more. "I don't think it's the memories of your life that you see when you die. I think it's the people you'll miss the most. The people who made your life worth living. And sometimes, if you're lucky, you see the one person you would defy the fates and stay for—if you could." He gave another languid shrug, but his eyes turned intent, the light dancing across high cheekbones and pointed ears. "Thankfully, you don't need to preoccupy yourself with such thoughts of death. You won't experience it for a very, very long time."

That seemed unlikely, given the current state of this continent. I raised one eyebrow. "And why is that?"

"Prisca needs you." He gave me a teasing grin, and I marveled at the sight of it. Just months ago, I would have laughed at the idea of seeing such a happy, relaxed expression on his face. "Besides, I quite like the thought of having a sister," he mused. "That means you will live a long, happy life."

I rolled my eyes, but I couldn't help but grin back at him.

"Now, if you'll excuse me, I need to go reclaim my wife."

I smiled. "If I were you, I'd sneak her out of here."

"Planning to." He stalked away.

Since Demos obviously wasn't going to ask me to dance—and I ignored the pang of hurt that thought caused—I held my head high, walking toward the edge of the tent—and the forest beyond it.

"Where are you going?" Tibris stepped in front of me.

"I want some air."

"Dance with me first."

I heaved a sigh. "Is this a pity dance?"

"Yes. Herne isn't here. Take pity on me."

I grinned at Tibris. He knew what I'd meant. But I took his hand anyway, allowing him to lead me back toward the music.

"I...questioned this, when Lorian announced it," he said. "It seemed almost ludicrous to celebrate anything when we're about to go to war. But as usual, he was right." Tibris rolled his eyes.

I laughed. "It helps that I've never seen Prisca so happy."

Tibris shifted us so we could both watch Prisca laughing up at Lorian as he snatched her hand. "Gods, I hope they get a future," he said. "I hope we all do."

"We will. We have to believe that, Tibris."

Nearby, Rekja spun Thora, and she nimbly ducked beneath his arm, swaying her hips as she caught the beat of the music.

"You think he'll marry her?" Tibris asked, following my gaze.

"I think if he doesn't, he's an idiot."

Tibris tensed. I hadn't realized he was that close to Rekja. But my eyes followed his gaze and locked on the man stumbling in through the open doors, two Gromalian guards close by.

My heart thundered in my chest, and my cheeks suddenly ached from my grin. Immediately, Tibris and I were walking toward the group.

Vicer was bruised, thin, and covered in dirt and old

blood. A woman followed him into the ballroom, hair tangled, clothes in the same condition. She looked so uncomfortable, so entirely miserable, that I was relatively sure I knew who she was.

Vicer looked around the ballroom as if he was struggling to understand. Heads were turning, and Demos appeared next to him, slapping him on the back as he murmured something I couldn't hear.

Vicer seemed like he hadn't heard him. He still looked stunned.

The musicians clearly sensed something was wrong, because they stopped playing. And Vicer's words carried over the crowd.

"You're...celebrating?"

Prisca whirled. Her eyes widened and flooded instantly as she hurried toward him. "Vicer. You're alive."

He waved his hand at the celebration. "What is this?"

"Our wedding," Prisca said carefully. "Since we will all need to separate tomorrow, Lorian and I decided to get married now." She scanned him, shifting from bride to queen. "We have a lot to talk about."

Vicer nodded absently. He looked vaguely shocked, as if all the sights and sounds were too much for him.

"And who is this?" Lorian asked, nodding toward the woman.

"Stillcrest and I made a deal," Vicer said, seeming to come back to himself. "I bring her to you, and she never speaks to me again."

Stillcrest flinched, immediately attempting to hide it within a shrug. But everyone had caught it.

"And why would you want to see me?" Prisca asked

the woman, her expression as cold as I'd ever seen it.

Stillcrest took a step closer. And then Marth was there. "Careful," he snarled.

I doubted Stillcrest was attempting to assassinate anyone, but I could see the wisdom of watching her closely.

"I come to join your army. To fight by your side. If you'll have me. There is nothing I can do to remove the stain on my soul from the choices I have made." Her chin wobbled, and she managed to firm it, meeting Prisca's eyes. "No way to bring back the innocents lost through my own audacity. But I ask that you allow me to fight with you to make those who took their lives regret their actions."

Prisca's eyes burned. It was rare for her to show her fury these days. She was learning to control her expressions. She stalked close to Stillcrest…

And slapped her across the face.

Stillcrest's head whipped to the side, her cheek stained red.

I jolted, taking a step forward automatically. I didn't know exactly what I was planning to do, but Lorian and Marth had done the same thing.

And then Prisca wrapped her arms around the woman responsible for the deaths of hundreds of hybrids.

Kaelin Stillcrest lowered her head to Prisca's shoulder and cried like a baby.

My breath shuddered from my lungs, and my eyes burned. I understood.

Kaelin wasn't going to forgive herself. She wouldn't have believed Prisca's forgiveness or respected her if she hadn't shown some sign of her displeasure. The slap was a public humiliation that said everything that needed to be said. Prisca didn't need to tear into her with harsh words. The woman was clearly doing that to herself every moment of every day.

The slap was the displeasure of a queen who knew Stillcrest wanted to feel some kind of punishment.

But the hug...

That was my best friend. The girl who had sat next to me on the roof of the bakery in our village as we made our own clumsy blood vow. The woman who had tricked her way into Regner's castle and saved me from certain death. The person who loved those around her with such intensity, the thought of them in pain was intolerable to her.

And even though part of me felt Stillcrest deserved worse—deserved to be turned away, her offer of help denied...

Prisca released Stillcrest, who wiped at her eyes, her head low. "I believe there are a few rooms left near our chambers," Prisca said with a glance at Rekja, who gave her a nod.

Stillcrest bowed her head, sidling away. But she raised her gaze, staring defiantly at anyone who glowered at her.

"How could you consider forgiving her?" Demos bit out.

"I'm not forgiving her," Prisca sighed. "Not truly. But it's not my place to punish her either. I could have been Stillcrest, Demos. I've made decisions in this war that have cost people their lives. I'll likely do it again.

And again. And despite my desire to blame her for what she did, I'm the hybrid queen. That camp was my responsibility, and I failed. What kind of hypocrite would I be to turn her away now?"

There was no use telling Prisca the camp wasn't her responsibility. I understood her reasoning, even if I disagreed with her logic.

Demos shook his head. But he clearly knew he wasn't going to change her mind about Stillcrest.

"I don't want to argue," Prisca said, and her voice was low. "Let's just enjoy every moment we have together. Please."

Demos slung an arm around her shoulders and rolled his eyes at Tibris, who grinned at him.

The musicians resumed playing, and Lorian swept Prisca into his arms once more. Demos murmured a few words to Vicer, who nodded, yawned hugely, and wandered away in the same direction Stillcrest had gone.

Demos's eyes met mine, and he stepped closer.

"Dance with me."

I wanted to make some pithy remark about how he'd suddenly remembered I existed. But he was finally looking at me, and the way he was looking at me prevented me from being able to say anything at all.

The musicians switched to a slower song, and Demos pulled me close. My heart ached. When I pictured my future—if we all got to have one—it was this man who I could see by my side.

But...something in him had broken. And I didn't know if it could be repaired. Because I was relatively sure he didn't want it to be repaired.

His nostrils flared. And then he gave me one of those looks. The look that left me trembling at night. Yearning for him.

Not that I'd ever let the stubborn bastard know that.

"Why did you volunteer to come with me, Asinia?"

I tucked away the anguish that he would even ask that question after the kiss we'd shared. Perhaps what I'd thought was a life-changing kiss had meant nothing to a man as handsome as Demos. He'd likely had women tripping over themselves to kiss him before he was imprisoned. I was merely the one who'd been with him since Regner's dungeon.

And so, I didn't answer his question. Because I wasn't sure my heart could take the vulnerability of it. "Why did you allow me to come with you?"

His lips tightened. "Because I want you where I can see you. Alive."

"I want everyone in this ballroom to stay alive, Demos. If that's truly the depth of your feelings for me, then that's all I need to know."

I attempted to shove my way out of his arms. His grip on me tightened. But then he let me go.

I turned and walked away.

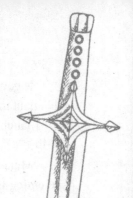

16

PRISCA

"I'm sorry," Lorian murmured as Kaelin Stillcrest walked away. "I wanted this night to be perfect for you."

And that ugly scene had been far from perfect.

But it was reality. We were at war. Besides...

"Vicer is alive, Lorian. That's all that matters."

He took my hand, and then he was tugging me toward the side of the tent, where cooler air danced toward us. Several people nearby whistled, and Lorian smirked, sweeping me out of the tent and into his arms.

Someone had arranged for a carriage to meet us directly outside the tent. The driver bowed his head in greeting, and I stepped inside as Lorian helped me with my gown.

He followed me, his huge body taking up most of the space, and I nestled under his arm as he leaned close, pressing his warm lips to mine. Something bumped against my chest, and I shifted away long enough to take in the amulet.

"Conreth gave that to you."

He gave me a grumpy, put-upon look. "I don't want to talk about my brother."

I laughed, nuzzling close. "This was the best day of my life."

"Mine too. I know it's a human custom, but...it means something to be your husband as well. Mates don't often marry. They don't need to. A mating is for eternity, and none would disrespect it. But our wedding wasn't just so you could feel we were bonded together in your culture as well as mine."

"Is that so?"

He angled his head, watching me closely. "It was another way to tie you to me. Another way to make it clear to everyone that you're mine."

"Well," I said, doing my best to keep my face blank. "Now that is truly shocking."

He narrowed his eyes, and I burst out laughing.

The carriage stopped, and he helped me down, murmuring a few words to the driver.

Inside, the castle was quiet. We'd snuck out of our own wedding, and we didn't see a single person as we made our way up to our rooms.

Someone had left light orbs glowing dimly, along with a platter of food waiting on a table near the window.

Strangely, something was fluttering in my stomach. Lorian leaned over and wrapped me in his arms from behind, pressing a kiss to my temple.

"Nervous?"

"A little. Is that strange?"

"Nothing you feel is strange."

His voice was a low rumble, and as he turned me to

face him, my nerves disappeared. Anyone who had heard of the Bloodthirsty Prince would never be able to reconcile the fact that this was the man with that reputation. The man who looked at me with so much tenderness, my eyes stung.

"Do you trust me, Prisca?"

"With my life."

His eyes glittered with male satisfaction.

"Will you trust me now?"

I peered up at him.

My stomach fluttered again—this time in anticipation. I nodded.

Lorian smiled. One of those slow, brilliant smiles that made my heart flip in my chest. He reached behind me, and at some point, he'd studied the back of my dress. His clever fingers plucked the ribbons, and my dress fell to my ankles.

I stood in front of him wearing nothing but a few scraps of bronze lace and gold shoes. The material seemed to glow in the candlelight, and Lorian's breath whooshed out of his lungs.

His smile disappeared, and he took a step closer, gently tracing the edge of the lace along my breast.

"There's something I've been wanting to do to you for a very long time," he said, and my heart stopped as his eyes met mine. They gleamed with a feral possessiveness. "Something I've dreamed of doing to you since the moment you stopped time when we were below Sabium's rooms."

My breath hitched. "You were so angry."

"I was furious. I looked up, and you had disappeared, reappearing near the top of the stairs. It was then that I realized that you could leave me at any time. If you wanted to escape me, you could." He leaned down until his lips were almost touching mine. "I wanted to tie you to my bed. To look at you and know that for at least that long, you couldn't leave me, even if you tried. I wanted to make you lose your mind with pleasure, so that when you were finally free, all you would be able to think about was me and the way I felt inside you."

My thighs tightened, my nipples hardened, and my core ached for him. Lorian smiled. He knew.

But he waited.

It was the ultimate act of trust. But I already trusted him with my life. With the lives of everyone I loved. And the thought of being tied up, displayed for him...

"Yes."

Lorian's nostrils flared. And then I was lying on the bed, and he held up four long, thick black ribbons.

"You were planning this."

"Wildcat, some part of me has been planning this since the moment I caught you attempting to steal my horse." He dropped a kiss to my nose and then gave me a wicked smile as he took my left hand.

My heart pounded, and he pressed his lips to my racing pulse, his mouth lingering along the sensitive skin of my wrist. I shivered, and his mouth curved against my skin.

"If you want me to stop..."

"I don't."

"If you do, say the word 'valeo.'" He stretched my arm above my head, wrapping one of the black ribbons around my wrist. I craned my neck, but the headboard was flat. And yet, I could no longer raise that arm. It was as if my wrist was stuck to the mattress above me.

"I don't understand."

"They're enchanted," Lorian murmured, pressing another kiss below my ear. "You can struggle as much as you like. But you won't be going anywhere."

I was so wet, my thighs had dampened. So aroused, I was already trembling. Lorian let out a low laugh.

"Is it any wonder I'm convinced the gods created you just for me?" he breathed, his tone full of wonder.

I frowned at him. "Perhaps the gods created *you* just for *me*."

"They created us for each other."

"I refuse to give them that much credit," I muttered as he took my other wrist.

He hummed, pressing kisses along my inner arm, wrapping that black ribbon around my wrist.

When my arms were immobile, he lifted his head. His eyes glowed.

I shifted my legs restlessly, and the smile he gave me dripped with dark promise. "They're next."

My body shook as he slowly tied my left ankle, pausing to kiss his way back up my leg, nuzzling at my inner thigh. When he kissed his way down my other leg, I arched, already desperate.

Gods, he made me *want*.

A low chuckle, and then that foot was caught too.

Lorian shifted until he stood in front of the bed. And he just looked at me.

I squirmed. "What are you doing?"

The look in his eyes was all dark promise. "Memorizing this sight." His gaze caressed every inch of me, as hot as his mouth had been on my skin.

"Lorian..."

He crawled onto the bed, hovering over me. When our eyes met, I sucked in an unsteady breath. His pupils were encircled by the tiniest slice of green, his eyes glazed.

"I could tease you for hours…"

"Don't."

"Why not?" His voice echoed strangely, and I shivered. The movement seemed to please him, and he dropped his head, lapping at my skin.

I gasped as he found my nipple. "Because I need you inside me."

"Do you know how many times I dreamed you would say those words to me?" He shifted until I could feel him, hot and heavy and so *thick,* positioned right at my core.

"How many times?" I whispered.

"Countless. And each time, I loathed myself for it, because you could never be mine."

Slowly, he began to push into me. I angled my hips, but he placed one hand on my hip, easily holding me in place.

"But you're mine now."

Twisting his hips, Lorian pulled back. Then he plunged into me with one long stroke. I gasped, my hands automatically straining with the need to do *something*.

And the fact that I couldn't…

"You are so, so wet," he whispered.

I was also on the edge, my body trembling. Lorian's eyes flared as he felt me tightening. "Well," he purred. "That was easy."

"You smug bastard."

"I have another ribbon. For that beautiful, vicious mouth."

I clamped my lips shut, and he laughed, lowering his head to thrust his tongue between them. I moaned into his mouth, panting, and he thrust forward, still holding me in place as I attempted to buck up into him.

All I could do was take what he chose to give me. My limbs turned weak, and I let out a low groan.

"There you go." Lorian slipped his hand down to caress my clit. Once. Twice.

My vision went dark, every muscle in my body clenching, shuddering as my climax tore through me.

I was still trembling when I came back to myself to find Lorian still hard within me.

He simply gave me a pleased smile and continued that slow, steady thrusting.

I was so sensitive, I shook my head, and he just laughed. "Valeo?"

"No. But—"

"Then I get to do what I want."

The hand on my hip slid to my butt, angling me for him. And he drove into me, each thrust hitting that spot within me. Every inch of my body was suddenly too sensitive, even as I craved more, more, more.

I strained against the ribbons, and Lorian's eyes turned wild as he watched me.

"Come for me."

I clamped down around him, waves of pleasure overtaking me, pouring from my core, through each of my limbs. It went on and on, pure euphoria choking a moan from my throat as he pounded into me. And then he stiffened, and I could feel the length of him pulsing inside me as he buried his head in my neck and shook.

The ribbons disappeared. Sliding my arms around him, I panted, vaguely shocked.

Slowly, Lorian lifted his head, his green eyes gleaming in the dim light. "Did you enjoy that?"

"You know I did."

His smile was satisfied and vaguely smug. "I can't wait for hundreds of years just like this."

Rolling to the side, he lifted each of my limbs, studying them carefully.

"What is it?"

"The ribbons are enchanted to never hurt you. But I wanted to check."

My heart melted. "I'm glad we were married here. You were right. It was perfect."

"Repeat the part about how I was right."

I poked him in the ribs, and he pulled me down until I lay across his chest—his favorite relaxed position.

I'd almost drifted off when he kissed my head. "I heard Cavis today. I saw him too."

Lifting my head, I stared down at him.

Lorian smiled at me. It was a devastating, heartbreaking smile. And yet there was a touch of joy in it. "If I am to be haunted by the people I have killed, so be it. But I didn't kill Cavis. And seeing him on my wedding day...*hearing* him...it was a gift, Prisca."

My throat swelled. "What did he say?" I whispered.

"He said you looked beautiful. And that I had better treat you well."

My eyes filled, and he kissed the tear that rolled down my cheek.

THE QUEEN

They'd celebrated today. A *wedding*.

I'd caught some of it from my window. Had even heard the guards murmuring, mentioning the fae prince had ensured they each received a plate of food from the wedding feast.

My food had been the same chicken and root vegetables as yesterday.

The door opened, and I whirled.

"Mother." Jamic smiled, and it was wide and familiar. There was no sign of his suffering on his face or in his eyes. But it would be there, burrowed deep within him. And he would carry it always.

The guards closed the door behind him, and I opened my arms. He'd grown so tall, and he strode to me in just a few steps, patting my back.

Finally, I was touching my son. I could feel him, warm and alive. No longer was he suffering each day while I paced my chambers, powerless to save him.

"Where were you?" I asked.

"In the fae lands. Learning how to wield my power properly."

My mouth wanted to twist, and I forced my expression into neutrality. Of course the fae would attempt to use Jamic for their own gain.

"Have they treated you well? Are they giving you enough food?"

Jamic's expression turned puzzled. "Of course."

"And your power." I lowered my voice. "Do you retain everything Regner gave you?"

He stiffened. "You mean everything he forced upon me? It was not a gift, Mother."

My cheeks heated. "Of course not. No one knows that more than I. You were nothing more than a vessel. One he would have killed when it suited him. But my question remains. Do you still have that power?"

His gaze searched my face, but he gave a single, sharp nod.

My body suddenly felt lighter than air, and my smile felt foreign—too wide for my face. "Good. When all this is over, we will rule Eprotha together."

Jamic stared at me. And for a moment, I had a flash of the tiny boy he had been on that day when I had hissed at him that I was not his mother. It was a look almost like… betrayal.

I cupped his face. "We will undo all of Regner's evil," I promised. "Our people will thrive."

Jamic still didn't speak. What had happened to my son? Had Regner's evil caused so much damage to his mind that he now trusted no one? Or had that hybrid bitch turned him against me?

I hadn't seen him for too long. He had grown into a man. And he had forgotten that I was the one who had ensured he would do so.

My mind raced. It wasn't too late. I could turn him back to me once more. But it would take time and a soft hand.

"I'm sorry," I sat down on the nearest sofa, patting the

space next to me. "You probably don't want to talk about such things. Why don't you tell me about the fae lands? I've always wanted to visit."

The tension left his face, and he walked over to me, the hint of a smile softening his features.

LORIAN

Prisca shifted in her sleep, a tiny sound leaving her throat.

I opened my eyes to slits. But that sound hadn't been what woke me.

No, it was the screaming in the distance.

Prisca shifted again. I wasn't surprised she hadn't yet woken. I could barely make out the sound with my fae senses.

But it was getting closer.

Rolling out of bed, I pulled on my pants, reaching for my sword. Crossing to the balcony, I looked down into the gardens.

Nothing.

From the front, then.

Regner had learned of our wedding night. And he'd waited until we were the happiest we could be. Until Rekja's guards were tired. Until there were more people moving in and out of the castle than usual. People he could use.

The screams had cut off. A bad sign. Likely, Regner's

iron guards were sneaking through this castle, slicing throats and dragging bodies into the shadows.

Prowling back toward our bed. I placed my hand over Prisca's mouth. She came awake swinging, and pride flashed through me even as her fist caught the side of my face.

"We're under attack," I whispered into her ear. She tensed, pushing against my arm, and I let her sit up.

"Lorian." The word was almost soundless, but confusion flickered across her face.

"I know. It's too quiet. But I heard screaming. We need to get to Galon and Marth." Without her power, Prisca was too vulnerable here. They could guard her while I went hunting.

Something that looked almost like despair flickered across her face, and I knew she was mourning her missing power. Knew she loathed that we had to make allowances for it. But she didn't argue when I threw her my shirt— simply pulled it on, grabbed a knife from the bedside table, and slid from the bed, moving almost as soundlessly as I had.

We took two steps toward the door…

And soldiers burst into the room.

All of them wore Eprothan colors.

Grinding my teeth, I reached for my control, refusing to allow myself to end each and every one of them. If I used all of my remaining power here and now, I would be drained when I needed to get whoever survived this attack out of the city later.

So I shoved my power down deep. So deep that it felt as if it might burn me alive. And I tightened my hand around my sword.

Gods, I hoped the others were still alive.

"You made a mistake coming here," I said, pushing Prisca behind me, toward the bed. And I didn't miss the confusion on her face. I couldn't blame her for that confusion. She'd trusted me, and I'd let this happen. On our wedding night.

"The Bloodthirsty Prince," a man hissed, stepping forward.

I no longer saw him as human. I simply saw him as a target.

Until I looked at his face. His *ruined* face. A face that had been melted.

The realization slid into me slowly. My head spun. I'd already killed this man. I was sure I had.

To my left, several soldiers snarled at me, stab wounds leaking blood down their chests. To my right, another lifted his dagger with a hiss, the bottom half of his leg missing.

These were the dead. And they wanted their revenge.

A man stumbled toward me. A man with no hands. A man I'd killed in an inn far from here, when he'd dared put those hands on my wildcat.

He gave me a nasty grin and held up his stumps. "Oh, how I've wanted to pay you back for this. You and that little bitch."

A woman laughed as she slunk closer, a sword in her hand, one eye gazing at me. Her other eye was gone, an empty hole remaining. "Are you pleased by the horror you've wielded?" she purred. "You hold the title of one of the deadliest creatures to ever walk this continent."

Fae fire filled my hands.

"Lorian, no."

I blinked. And it was Cavis who was standing in front of me.

He should have moved on. Should be at peace. Was I keeping him here?

"No," he said, reading my mind. "You'll know when it's time for me to go. If you survive that long."

The soldiers moved toward Cavis, and the sound that came out of me was animalistic. A snarl that ripped through the room.

They would come no closer to him. Or I would make them pay.

The dead paused. But I had a feeling they wouldn't stay that way for long.

"You're not holding me here," Cavis said. "But you're holding them here. You have to choose, Lorian."

"Choose?"

He gave me an impatient look, his gaze steady. And he pointed to the bed, where Prisca sat, staring wide-eyed at me.

This war didn't get to take what we had.

It could take everything else, but it couldn't take that.

The Bloodthirsty Prince, the dead had hissed. That was the title I heard over and over. I'd once said the title didn't matter. Perhaps it hadn't. Until I'd met *her.*

The woman who'd made me want to be a better man. The woman who made me care.

"Choose, Lorian," Cavis demanded once more. "*Now.*"

And I understood.

I might have been given the ability to see the dead, but

I didn't have to see these soldiers. I saw the people I killed because I harbored guilt for those deaths. Because despite my pretense at accepting my title of the Bloodthirsty Prince, I'd always loathed it. And I'd allowed Prisca to defend anyone who dared to name me as such.

It was a weakness—that guilt.

Each and every person I'd killed had deserved to die. They'd threatened my people. Or worse, they'd threatened Prisca.

The man with no hands would have left her hanging in that inn.

The soldier with the gaping wound in his throat had kept her caged in Regner's cell.

That one there—with half his face missing—he'd leaped at her in Sorlithia, swinging a broadsword at her back.

Realization came swiftly. The name held no power over me anymore. I would no longer feel ashamed of it. I *was* the Bloodthirsty Prince. And I would keep that title until the day I died.

To keep her safe.

The dead disappeared. Cavis winked at me.

And then he was gone.

"Lorian," Prisca said carefully. Gods, she was white. And she trembled in our bed. Swallowing self-disgust at the way I'd frightened her, I placed my sword on a chair nearby and strode to her.

She leaped into my arms, burying her face in my neck.

"It's better. I'm better now, wildcat. I promise."

17

PRISCA

Transitioning from the best day of my life to the reality of war was a shock—even knowing it was coming.

First, Madinia and Rythos left. Madinia submitted to my hug, and for some reason, her compliance made my stomach twist.

Rythos pressed a kiss to my cheek. "I'll see you soon, Pris," he vowed.

There was nothing left to say. And I refused to send my friends away with tears streaming down my cheeks. So, I forced a smile, clutching Lorian's hand as they said their goodbyes to the others before getting into the waiting carriage.

The carriage would take them to the dock, where they would board a ship south to Quorith.

Please let Verdion listen for once. Please let him ally with us.

Natan approached next. He'd already spoken to Demos, and I'd agreed to talk to him now, with no one else around. While he'd given Lorian one long-suffering look, Natan seemed to accept that he could be trusted.

"What is it that you're doing?" I asked.

He gave me a faint smile. "We're

infiltrating Regner's ranks. Our people may be human, but that's what will make us the most dangerous. We'll do whatever we can to slow him down." His eyes filled with a mixture of sorrow and pride.

Reaching out, I took his hand. Looking into his eyes, I acknowledged the sacrifice Natan and his people were making. The sacrifice they would have to live with after this war was over.

The sacrifice that would no doubt haunt them.

It was one thing to kill your own people in defense.

It was another to sleep next to them, to train with them, to eat with them, and then turn on them.

Of all of us, Natan's role in this war might be the hardest. And yet it was one of the most important.

"Thank you."

"You don't have to—"

"I know. Your people. You have to live on this continent. But thank you, Natan."

His eyes softened as he nodded, and I was once again forced to acknowledge just how much this war had already changed him.

"Goodbye, Prisca."

"Goodbye, Natan."

Lorian and Natan nodded at each other. And then he was gone.

Swallowing around the lump in my throat, I held it together until it was time for Demos and Asinia to leave. Demos slapped Tibris on the back as Asinia hugged me. "Be careful," I told them, swallowing a sob. "Look after each other."

Asinia glanced at Demos, and some of the tension

drained from her face. "You know we will," she said. "We're going to find the amulet, Pris. We'll see you soon."

And then they, too, were gone, traveling north to the Lyrishade mine.

I stood in Rekja's courtyard long after they were gone, as still as the statues surrounding me.

My chest was raw, as if I'd been flayed open. Lorian didn't say a word, just stood by my side, a silent support.

Early this morning, I'd received a note from Conreth's wife, Emara. It had been impossible to tell if she knew what had happened between Lorian and Conreth, who was still mostly a silent presence whenever we gathered. In her message, Emara had congratulated us on our wedding. And she'd said she had plans for after the war. Plans that involved opening their borders to humans and hybrids. Those who wanted to study, to explore, to live side by side with the fae.

This was what I needed to focus on. The things that would come after the blood and death.

And yet...

When I looked up at Lorian, my eyes hot with unshed tears, he cursed, pulling me into his arms. "I'm sorry, wildcat."

Sniffing, I nodded. But I had no time to fall apart. We'd already met with Rekja earlier today, and the rest of us would have one final meeting before leaving.

Vicer had already left with one of Rekja's generals, and they would meet with three thousand hybrid soldiers. I'd questioned whether he was ready after his experience at the hybrid camp, and he'd simply shaken his head at the suggestion he needed time to grieve.

Truthfully, there was little time to give him. So Vicer would bring extra supplies to ensure the hybrids who were readying to travel across the pass would be well-guarded, warm, and fed.

"How are you feeling?" I murmured. "After last night?" Lorian had explained what had happened. His guilt had been a weakness that the dead who'd meant him harm had taken full advantage of. And together with Cavis, he'd found a way to banish them. I was hoping that banishment would last.

"I'm perfect, wildcat. I promise."

He did seem lighter. No longer was he staring into the distance or slowly turning his head to glower at things we couldn't see. But it hurt my heart to know Cavis hadn't found peace.

And I knew it hurt Lorian's too.

Lorian took my hand, leading me back to our rooms, where Marth and Galon were waiting to discuss our own plan. Surprisingly, Marth took one look at my face and dragged me into his arms for a hug.

When we were all seated at the table in the main room, Marth drummed his fingers absently on the arm of his chair. "How exactly do you think we're going to get close to Zathrian? Even if Prisca had her power, he has nulled it before."

Rage cut through me, thick and deadly.

Zathrian nulling my magic had allowed Lorian to die.

"You're looking a little scary, Prisca." Galon nudged me. I attempted a smile.

"Simple," Lorian said. "We'll use Renit."

Galon's eyes flashed. "Conreth gave you Renit?"

"Temporarily."

Enough was enough. "Exactly what is Renit?"

"Not what," Marth said. "Who."

"Renit is a person?"

"Not just any person. Renit has the power of mimicry."

I waited for him to explain. Marth raised one eyebrow, drawing out the moment. Despite my annoyance, I would take any hint of playfulness from Marth at the moment.

"Renit can make someone appear to be someone else."

My mind whirled with the implications of that kind of power. "Why didn't you use his magic to get into the castle?"

"Two reasons," Lorian said. "First, his power is extremely limited. It lasts an hour at most. And it cannot replicate someone entirely. The most it can do is an imitation that would be just passable—mostly from a distance. I needed a glamour that would allow me to stroll around Regner's castle. One that I could wear sitting footspans from Regner until I found what I needed."

"And the other reason?"

"Conreth," Galon said. "Renit is usually kept in Aranthon, close to Conreth. When he travels, he is disguised and slipped into one of the carriages trailing the king."

It took me a moment to understand. "In case there's an assassination attempt," I said, my words dripping with the disgust that crawled through me. Every time I thought I was close to understanding—if not entirely forgiving—

Conreth, I learned some new, unwelcome information about him.

"Yes," Marth said. "If anyone attempts to kill Conreth, Renit will be right there. Very, very few people know about his power."

"Which means if there were an assassination attempt, he would make someone else look like Conreth and create confusion."

"He could make up to four people look like Conreth," Lorian said. "But the disguise would only hold from a distance. Anyone who had met my brother even once before would immediately know they were looking at an impostor."

"But it could still save Conreth's life," I said. I could imagine just how confused attackers would be if there were suddenly four or five Conreths to attack.

"Yes."

I understood then, just what Conreth was sacrificing. Renit's constant presence must have felt like an irreplaceable layer of security. The fae king was incredibly strong—I'd seen exactly how strong when we took down the barrier. But his father had been strong too. And that hadn't saved him. Or his mother.

I pushed those thoughts away and considered why exactly Lorian had bargained for Renit. And why Lorian was insisting on bringing Kaliera. And the blood began to drain so quickly from my face, I was suddenly dizzy.

"You don't think we should sneak into Zathrian's camp at all," I said, and my hands began to shake.

"No," Lorian said gently, taking both my hands in his. "We're going to walk in."

ASINIA

There were too many soldiers guarding the mine.

They crawled across the landscape like ants working within a colony.

According to Lorian, when his people had first spied on this place months ago, it had had just a few guards. Enough that anyone who happened to travel through the area wouldn't become suspicious. Wouldn't ask any deep questions about exactly what could possibly be being guarded with such ferocity.

There were only two possible reasons for Regner to have ordered this much security.

Either it was in direct response to his queen's little visit, or it was in preparation for our own.

If there was one thing the human king was particularly good at, it was anticipating the actions of his enemies.

Few safe routes were left for us to make our way north. Demos's contacts had come through, giving us continual updates about the movements of Regner's regiments and the routes of his scouting parties. Still, we'd had to backtrack multiple times when we'd come too close to groups of soldiers that had inexplicably moved into new positions.

As much as Demos would have liked to create some chaos and carnage, we couldn't afford for Regner to know we'd slipped past his borders and were moving north.

Thanks to Madinia and Vicer's campaign to educate the

populace, getting across those borders had been a matter of waiting until the right guards were on duty—and sympathetic to our cause. They'd allowed us to stroll into Eprotha with a nod.

Still, some part of me wondered if Regner did know we were here. From the intent look in Demos's eyes as he watched the soldiers, it was clear he was also considering the possibility of a trap.

We'd spent the morning slowly exploring the area. The terrain was unstable, making it a difficult place to set up a permanent camp. Demos had disappeared to spy, confirming our suspicions when he returned—the guards had chosen a second location with higher ground, allowing the guards who weren't on shift to monitor the mine from a distance, along with the surroundings.

A sensible plan, although it would make things more difficult for us. If there had only been one or two of us, it likely would have been easier to get into the mine. But we needed all of us inside to find the amulet.

The guards stationed their horses in a corral near the mine's perimeter for a swift response, but their barracks were set up on sturdier ground. While it was a strategic location, it left them with a predictable routine.

We'd arrived early enough to watch the day shift tie up their horses and walk directly to their posts—swapping with the bleary-eyed night shift.

Gwynara sidled closer. She was short for one of the fae, but from what I'd seen so far, she was well respected. When she'd made a suggestion while we were traveling, the others had usually agreed.

"There are too many of them. Do we still go in?" she

whispered. "It could be a trap."

We watched the soldiers for another few hours. There was no way we could get this many people into the mouth of the mine without alerting those guards. Besides, we couldn't risk them coming in behind us. We needed them dead.

Between us, we had plenty of power. But we couldn't risk exhausting ourselves before even entering the mine. Who knew what we would find in there, or how much power it would take to get back out? After what Demos and I had experienced with Prisca and Lorian when we'd searched for the hourglass, neither of us was pleased at the thought of being underground once more.

There was one upside, though. While the labyrinth of caves hiding the hourglass had been filled with fae iron that had gradually drained not just our power, but our strength, Kaliera had insisted that wasn't the case here. And while I hadn't been inclined to believe her, Marth had pointed out that Regner wouldn't have been able to keep the fae creatures alive while they were young if he'd cut off their connection to magic.

At one point, I was so tired of waiting, I began fantasizing about nocking an arrow and taking out the four soldiers I could see.

These soldiers weren't particularly alert. They strolled across the areas they'd been assigned to guard, their steps shortening as the afternoon dragged on.

I calculated I could hit three of them before the fourth noticed. He would turn to run, but as long as the wind didn't change suddenly, my last bolt would hit him in the spine.

Demos caught my hand and gave me a look. I'd been stroking my crossbow, I realized. He shook his head at me, but amusement gleamed in his eyes.

Likely, he was fantasizing about his own attack. While he could be patient when necessary, he preferred to act quickly.

Already, I was learning just how much of war involved anticipation. Long hours of boredom on sentry duty or spying or waiting for someone else to do their part first. The boredom was occasionally broken by moments of heart-pounding, palm-slicking terror that dumped adrenaline into my bloodstream and left me shaking afterward.

Sometimes, I wondered if there was something wrong with me—because I was beginning to prefer those moments over these long hours of waiting.

With nothing else to focus on, my mind continually returned to our friends. If Madinia and Rythos couldn't get the fleet...if Prisca's cousin was strong enough to kill her...if Telean was discovered at the tiny inn where we'd left her writing messages and organizing escape routes for the hybrids, based on the information Demos's spies had smuggled to us.

Finally, at Demos's signal, we melted back through the forest, far enough away that we could have a short, hissed conversation.

"I say we wait until just before the next shift change," Amalra said, flicking her long, dark hair over her shoulder. "It'll mean another few hours, but they'll be tired and slow."

"We don't need to wait," her sister Elysanth muttered. Where Amalra was lithe and dark-haired, Elysanth was curvier and blond. "As long as we make sure we've taken out all the sentries before we attack, we can use those hours to strike. By the time the next shift arrives, everyone here will be long dead."

"The problem is the other guards," I said. "The ones above us. Demos said they have a relatively good view of the camp. If one of them happens to be looking, they'll see what's happening, no matter how quiet we attempt to be."

"Asinia is right," Nyrik said. "We need to take care of them at the same time, before they can alert anyone else."

Demos was quiet, his brow furrowed. My hand itched to stroke over the strong lines of his brow, and I shoved it into the pocket of my tunic.

"We need a distraction," Demos finally said. "And I know where to find one."

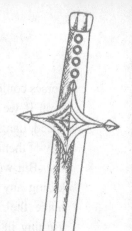

18

ASINIA

The horses were wary of us from the moment we approached. We were strangers, and we didn't have time to croon into their ears or stroke their fears away.

Besides, in order for our plan to work, we *needed* these horses to be spooked.

Demos had already taken care of the guard nearby—silently slitting his throat and leaning his body against a tree. I'd glanced away at that part. I could kill without a second thought during the heat of battle. But I still hadn't reached a point where I could kill in cold blood.

Horrison untied the horses, and Gwynara stepped forward. Her main power was similar to Madinia's. Except when she cupped her fire in the palm of her hand and then blew on it, the fire spewed from her hand, the warmth drifting close to several of the horses' rumps.

As expected, the horses were unhappy about this turn of events. Two of them bucked, one reared, pawing the air, and several shot forward, driving into the other horses, who immediately bolted.

More fire—close enough that a few of the

horses could see it—and there was no holding them back, even if we had wanted to. They galloped at breakneck speed, dangerous enough in a forest that I was worried a few of them might really break their necks.

But we had no time to waste. The others would be killing any remaining sentries while Brinlor and Nyrik made their way to the guards who weren't on shift. Turning in the opposite direction of the horses, we cut through the forest toward the mine entrance, not even attempting to be quiet.

My blood pounded in my ears until it drowned out every other sound.

The guards had drawn their weapons by the time we got to the edge of the forest. One of them pointed up at us, but it was too late.

Gwynara had driven the horses into such a frenzy, several of them hurtled down the steep embankment, straight for the guards.

One of the guards whirled, raising his hand, but it was too late. The horse rode straight over him.

"Nice," one of the fae whispered. I winced.

Another guard turned to run, clearly following his instincts. But there was no hope, and he likely died the moment the horse's hoof smashed into his head.

A guard with gold thread wound into his uniform finally used his power, slamming it into one of the out-of-control horses.

The horse went flying, rolled, and stumbled to its feet. It stood there shaking, its head low. My chest clenched, but I couldn't take the time to feel sorry for the poor thing. Demos and the others had already made it down the embankment. I nocked my first arrow, sending it straight toward the guard who'd pointed at us. He ducked out of sight behind a rock. My teeth clenched until it felt as if my jaw would crack. This had to be quick, before they sounded an alarm.

I waited until Gwynara aimed her power at one of his friends and he lifted his head to use his own power on her, and my next bolt hit him between his eyes.

By the time the guards were dead, the others had returned. "We got them all," Nyrik said. "We've got three hours to get in, find the amulet, and get out. By then, it's likely whoever these guards report to will begin getting suspicious when they don't hear anything."

Demos glanced at a burly hybrid named Yan. "You need to conserve your power for after. Stay on watch, and don't use it unless absolutely necessary."

"Understood."

Yan and Demos each took a trowth stone, so we'd be able to communicate.

And then it was time.

No part of me wanted to go into the mine. I wasn't claustrophobic like Pris. But my body remembered what had happened the last time we were below the earth. Thol had died in front of me. Cavis took Prisca, and that was the last time we saw him alive. Lorian, Demos, and I had fought our way out of those caves, only for me to be hit in the head by one of Regner's monsters,, the bleeding almost killing me before they got me to a healer.

"Sin."

Demos was waiting. The others had already begun walking into the entrance. He held out his hand.

I took it. The feel of his warm hand engulfing mine seemed to anchor me, and I could focus once more.

The others had waited inside for us, and I pulled my knife with my free hand. My crossbow would be useless in such a confined space.

Demos waited until we were all close enough that he only needed to whisper. "According to Kaliera's spy friend Pelysian—who I still struggle to believe is Daharak's brother, by the way—we need to walk one hundred footspans. Once we get near the monsters, there will be a false wall hiding another tunnel. From there, we move down."

We all nodded, and then we were moving as one.

It smelled like death. The fae creatures could likely scent us, because their furious screams echoed through the mine toward us, making me fight the urge to cringe. It was even colder than I'd expected, the chill leaching the energy from my muscles.

My eyes struggled to adjust to the sparse, flickering light from the orbs hanging sporadically along the walls. With the others in front of me and Demos by my side, I could at least focus on the uneven ground beneath my feet as we inched forward.

One of the hybrids knocked into the skeletal remains of a scaffold, cursed, and continued walking. The foul odor intensified, clinging to the back of my throat. Everyone seemed suddenly on edge as the light began to change, taking on a sinister, greenish hue.

The monsters were snarling—deep, vicious sounds that made my heart slam against my rib cage. The closer we got, the louder they became, until they were suddenly howling, as if they might rip themselves free from whatever kept them trapped. When we were in the right place, Demos gestured to the walls, and all of us began desperately searching for the entrance. I ran my hands along the rough surface, looking for anything that didn't feel like it should be there.

Unsurprisingly, it was Demos who found it. Regner had used a natural fissure in the rock—widening it just enough that it was possible to traverse the narrow path.

The ground sloped down, gradually becoming steeper until I had to dig in with my toes, my thighs burning. No one spoke, and the fire in Gwynara's hand was our only light. The air grew even cooler and damper as we descended, the echo of dripping water now louder than the snarls above us. Every step was a battle against the slippery terrain, and I fought to keep my balance, my fingers continually scraping against the cold, wet stone.

Our footsteps began to echo. We'd entered some kind of cavern.

With so many people walking ahead of me, it wasn't until they shifted aside that I saw it. A vast, underground lake lay before us, its surface perfectly, eerily still. Stalactites hung from the ceiling like jagged knives, some of them so low they nearly reached the water's surface.

The presence of so much water made sense, given how close we were to the Dytur River. Likely, water had infiltrated the mine tunnels at some point, forming the lake we stared at now.

Still, it was yet another complication. Yet another problem to solve before we could find the amulet and leave this place. Along with Gwynara's fire, there was a single light orb high above our heads, casting just enough light to get a glimpse of its width.

Seemingly impassable, the edges faded into the darkness. There was no way to tell how deep it was—or where it ended.

"The bitch tricked us," Horrison muttered.

Someone else cursed. I was pushed a step as someone jostled the person in front of them. Demos let out a rough, impatient sound, and everyone went silent.

I barely noticed. I was too busy watching the subtle ripple on the surface—in one particular spot. It was barely a hint of movement in the depths of the water. And it was only every so often. I counted to ninety before the next ripple. If the rest of the lake hadn't been so still and I weren't paying excruciatingly close attention, I would've missed it.

"Look," I said, pointing.

Nothing happened.

I glanced at Demos. "I promise I saw something. Just watch."

His gaze locked on the area I was pointing to. And his expression turned calculating.

"So that's how he has done it," he said. "Good catch, Sin."

I didn't preen, but it was close.

Now we needed to debate who would go in. The water was so incredibly still, I had no doubt Regner had planted something in the depths, just waiting for whoever was foolish enough to risk the water.

Unfortunately, we were the fools in question.

"Who is the best at sensing and breaking wards

around physical objects?"

Brinlor raised his hand. We hadn't spoken much, but from what little interaction we'd had, he seemed to be a steady, dependable man.

He stood and watched the water intently for several long moments. Then he closed his eyes. "There's definitely something heavily warded in there," he said finally.

"Can you remove the ward from here?"

Brinlor shook his head. "It's too strong. I need to go in. And I'll need someone to watch my back," he said, already removing his shoes. "If I'm focusing on breaking the ward, I won't have much concentration left for whatever beasties Regner has left for us."

The thought of those beasties turned my blood to ice. But I opened my mouth.

Demos's head snapped around. "No."

"I'll go in," Gwynara volunteered.

"I'm going in too," Demos said. I tamped down my instant denial, even though I'd expected this from him. Demos didn't let anyone do anything he wasn't prepared to do himself.

Except me. I ground my teeth. But this was not the time.

Three others spoke up. Horrison, Firion, and Nyrik.

"We'll need you here," Demos said to me. "With Amalra and Elysanth shooting at anything that moves."

"Everything except us," Brinlor said cheerfully.

I couldn't argue with that. My arrows could at least distract anything that attacked the others.

I felt as if my fear might tear me apart. Demos was already stripping off his shoes, most of his weapons, his cloak. He glanced at me, and I grabbed his hand, unsure exactly what I was doing.

His expression softened. "I'll be fine."

I nodded, but it felt as if I'd swallowed a small orange and it was now stuck in my throat. With a squeeze, he removed his hand from mine and dove into the water.

PRISCA

The ship creaked around me, and I forced myself to take a long, slow breath. Even after so much time spent on the water, it was unlikely I would ever become truly comfortable with this kind of transportation—although I only needed the occasional seasickness tonic these days.

But there had been only one way for us to travel through Eprothan territory—on one of the few Eprothan ships Daharak had liberated during the battle to take down the barrier. It was the gold gleaming along the prow of Regner's ship that had sickened me when we'd boarded. The thought of the wealth he wielded while those in his villages starved... it made my stomach churn.

Now, we'd gathered in the largest stateroom, sitting, once again, around a circular table.

When Lorian had insisted we needed to bring Kaliera, I'd hesitated. I'd liked knowing she was tucked away in Rekja's castle, the door to her rooms locked and securely guarded. Still, if she'd wanted to escape us, she wouldn't have come to us in the first place. Since she wanted to see Jamic—and he'd asked her to cooperate—she was forced to work with us.

I'd questioned whether Zathrian would believe Regner would simply arrive with no warning. The answer to that question from anyone who either knew Regner or had studied him intently had been a resounding yes. Arriving unexpectedly to observe one of his allies—and to determine whether that ally was complying with his orders—was exactly the kind of move Regner would make.

As Lorian had pointed out, we didn't need to fool Zathrian himself. We simply needed to be able to travel unimpeded through Eprothan waters to get close enough to the tip of this continent where we could dock and travel to the Cursed City. It wasn't entirely surprising that my cousin had chosen to make such a place his base. Not after everything I'd learned about him.

Easily defensible, the Cursed City was located on the northwest coast in Eprotha—directly across the Sleeping Sea from our kingdom.

We'd made it past the Frosthaven Isles—several of our people strolling the deck while dressed in Eprothan colors in case any of Regner's lingering ships thought to approach. But that hadn't happened. Something told me most of Regner's captains and generals were focused only on their orders. It was a small comfort.

I'd longed to pace along the deck, but I knew better than to risk being seen, so I'd hidden away down here— Lorian and Marth keeping me company.

Now that we were approaching my cousin, I was so

antsy, my entire body felt as if I were the one with the lightning power and my muscles were barely containing the deadly strikes.

And yet my own power was still nowhere to be seen.

Lorian eyed me. "You want to fight, wildcat?"

Marth snorted.

I got to my feet and pulled my darkened hair back into a braid. My blond curls were too distinctive, so I'd had one of Rekja's maids help me with them before we left.

Reaching for my dagger, I grinned. Fighting with Lorian would help disperse some of this restless energy. We might not be able to fight on the deck where Galon had insisted on training each day we'd been at sea, but if we pushed this table up against one wall, I could still likely exhaust myself enough that I'd have no room for any other thoughts.

"That's exactly what I want."

A knock sounded on the door. I cursed.

"We can wrestle later," Lorian told me with a predatory grin.

Marth opened the door to reveal Galon. A thin man stood behind him, and Lorian sighed.

"It's time," Galon said.

The man followed Galon inside, bowing to me. "Your Majesty."

"You must be Renit," I said. He was on the shorter side for one of the fae, thin in stature, but he walked with purpose.

Renit nodded, giving me a shy smile. His hair fell over his eyes, and he brushed it aside. But he straightened his shoulders as he turned his attention to Lorian.

"Your Highness."

Lorian shook his head. "No."

Renit gave him a stubborn look. Lorian ignored it. "What do you need from me?" Lorian stood, his head nearly brushing the ceiling of the cabin. It had been clear from the moment we boarded that this ship was built for human-sized men.

"Shift to your human form. It also helps if you picture Regner in your mind. Use your own focus and power to boost mine." All timidity had vanished from Renit now that he was focused on his task.

Lorian nodded.

It happened so slowly, it was as if nothing happened at all. And then I noticed Lorian's cheekbones had flattened. His nose was thicker. His hair gradually lightened. His cheeks turned a ruddy color.

I was suddenly staring at Regner.

He got to his feet, moving toward me.

I skittered away instinctively, my back hitting the wall.

Lorian froze.

"I'm sorry," I breathed. "Just give me a moment."

A muscle feathered in his jaw. In *Regner's* jaw.

My breaths were coming faster.

Regner's hand—no. *Lorian's* hand fisted at his side, as he was barely restraining himself from reaching for me.

Galon grabbed my shoulder. "Pris," he said gently. "Look at his face."

I forced my gaze up, meeting Lorian's eyes. They gleamed at me, emerald green and filled with concern and frustration.

Renit's power hadn't been able to touch his eyes. Relief warred with worry inside me. Those eyes would make it more difficult for us to get close to my cousin. But knowing I would be able to see Lorian next to me...

It helped.

"I'm sorry."

"Don't apologize, wildcat."

It was Lorian's voice too. Something in my chest unlocked, and I could suddenly breathe properly. Now that I was looking at him, I could see his cheekbones were still too sharp to fit Regner's face, his jaw too wide.

"Your disguise will be relatively easy, Prisca," Galon said. "Regner does, after all, travel with servants. You'll stay a few steps behind the rest of us until we're close enough to strike."

After that, things moved quickly. Someone found a uniform that looked just like the one Tibris had worn while working in Regner's castle. I pulled it on, scraping my dark hair into a bun and burying it beneath a maroon hat.

We weren't attempting to fool Zathrian or Eadric, I reminded myself over and over. All we needed to do was get past the hybrid guards and into the camp. Our disguise only had to be good enough to last for a few minutes. Enough time for our ship to dock.

Only moments passed before I was standing on the deck of Regner's ship as we approached the Cursed City. Someone had ordered Kaliera to join us, and she stood in full view of anyone who could see our ship. She wasn't happy that Conreth had taken Jamic with him once more.

But I was pleased they were separated. According to Marth, Jamic had defended his mother's actions when we were in Thobirea.

"She has already suffered more in her life than most would suffer in several lifetimes," he'd said. "Few could truly blame her for grasping at whatever power she could. For trying to control anything that could make her own life a little easier."

In reality, many, many people could blame her for exactly that. And Jamic's defense of his mother was concerning enough that all of us had agreed to keep them apart.

It was natural for him to want to see the good in Kaliera. Unfortunately, she would destroy any good in *him* if she could.

The ship rolled beneath me, and I grabbed the rigging, turning my attention to the dock in the distance. Zathrian had been busy rebuilding it, but it was already falling apart in places, wooden beams straining against gravity—likely thanks to our grandmother's curse, which continued to prevent anyone from building on this land.

"The hags must be working with Regner and Zathrian," Galon said as we approached. It was strange seeing him in Eprothan colors. "They hold the remains of this city, and they wouldn't allow Zathrian to build his camp directly outside it without some bargain in place."

Marth's lip curled. "It's a good thing Rythos isn't here to see this. He'd befriend the bitches and create chaos like they'd never seen. On second thought…it's a shame he couldn't attend this little meeting."

Guards converged on the dock as we approached.

The captain roared orders, his voice carrying over the wind as he stood at the ship's wheel.

I studied the faces of the guards below us, ready to order our retreat if necessary.

But while many of them stared at Lorian and Kaliera, those glances were fearful and rage-filled...not suspicious.

This was good news. If the hybrids here hated Regner, it would be easier to convince them to march with us.

A crewman with the agility of a cat perched at the bow of our ship, casting a thick hemp rope toward the dockhands below. They caught it with ease, securing it swiftly to one of the wobbling bollards.

By now, messengers would be taking the news of Regner's arrival to my cousin. Since he'd spent so much time with the human king, I had no doubt Zathrian would immediately see through Lorian's disguise. That was expected. We simply needed to get close enough to him to strike.

My palms turned damp. I stood a few footspans behind Lorian since Regner wouldn't surround himself with servants unless he needed something. His shoulders tensed slightly, and he smoothly launched into motion, strolling down the gangway.

Fuck.

Lorian was attempting to tamp down his natural fae grace. But it was like watching a leopard imitate a sheep. Galon let out a string of quiet curses, realizing the problem, and managed to walk more like a human. Kaliera shot me a scathing look, lifted her head, and walked down after him.

Unfortunately, Marth could have been walking along

a tree limb for how gracefully he strolled. Clearly, he hadn't recognized any problem at all. He was too busy sweeping his gaze over the guards, searching for threats.

A soldier approached, walking with the stiff formality of the highly ranked. His gaze slid over Lorian's and met mine as I trailed after them, making a point of stumbling on the ramp like the human I wasn't. As if I could somehow make up for the fae grace he'd just witnessed. He pressed his lips together.

"Your Majesty." He bowed to Lorian. "My name is Orivan."

His eyes slid over to me again, and I shuddered with relief. Blynth and Tymriel had assured me he was sympathetic to our cause, but there had always been the chance we were walking into a trap.

Orivan nodded at my unspoken question. "I will take you to the hybrid heir," he said loudly. "He will wish to receive you immediately."

"I suggest you focus on walking like a human," he said under his breath, and Marth glanced bemusedly at his feet, as if wondering how exactly he was supposed to achieve *that*.

Smoke curled into the air from the campfires in the distance. The Cursed City sprawled out to our left as we walked along the coast. Rounding the western edge of the city, I held my breath as I approached the guards stationed at the entrance.

Instinctively, I reached for my power. But the guards bowed their heads to Orivan, who swept past them with a nod. I kept my own head down, expecting one of them to yell out at any moment.

But…what were the chances most low-level guards would accuse the Eprothan king of duplicity? Would accuse one of Zathrian's trusted generals of leading his enemies into their camp?

From the incredulous look on Galon's face, it was clear he would have expected exactly that from any soldiers he had trained.

I caught up to the others, still trailing behind them. "I hope you are everything Blynth and Tymriel said, Nelayra Valderyn," Orivan murmured.

"I don't know what they said about me, but I promise I will prove myself to you," I said, keeping my voice barely above a whisper.

He gave a sharp nod. We rounded one more corner, where a huge training arena sprawled across the landscape. Zathrian stood next to that arena, Eadric by his side.

My heart kicked in my chest, my blood turned to ice, and the world receded as I stared at my cousin.

Eadric took one look at Lorian and raised his hand, stabbing his finger toward him.

"Lies," he hissed.

Zathrian's eyes met mine. And he grinned.

19

MADINIA

While Conreth was undisputedly the king of the fae lands, his kingdom was divided into territories. And the island of Quorith was ruled by Verdion. I'd learned all I'd needed to know of Rythos's father at the fae summit. He was a ruthless, bitter man who refused to cooperate, comply, or concede power—all because his family hadn't been chosen to guard one of the three fae amulets gifted to them by the god Tronin so long ago.

According to the little Rythos had told me while we traveled to the island, while Verdion was the ultimate authority of Quorith, he still answered to a council. If every member of that council unanimously agreed, their votes could override him.

Unfortunately, Verdion was so determined to stay out of this war that he had refused to even take the evidence to his council. And I was betting he hadn't told them about his little deal with Regner. He'd been willing to break Quorith's own laws in order to disregard Conreth's wishes.

Spare me from these powerful men and their ancient grudges.

Prisca had once told me that Rythos and Verdion did not speak. All she had said was that Verdion was threatened by his son, even though Rythos had no intention of fighting him for power.

Sounded similar to a certain fae king we all knew.

I glanced at Rythos. While Cavis had been the kindest to me, Rythos had been a close second. Right now, however, he was lost in grim silence, his gaze on the blurry, warded island in front of us as our small boat was rocked by the waves.

Perhaps a distraction that could also help with my own curiosities was warranted. "Do you know anyone pure of heart?" I asked him.

Surprise flashed across his face.

"What exactly does that mean?"

"I don't know," I admitted. "Probably someone who doesn't enjoy killing bad people."

"You know," he said, running his hand over his face, "I don't think I do. That probably says a lot about the people I surround myself with."

I couldn't help but smile at that. Rythos raised his eyebrows, and I turned it into a scowl.

"Why do you need someone pure of heart?"

"Daharak's weapon." I explained the orb to him, even taking it out of my pocket. "You seem…nice. Occasionally."

He just shook his head at me. "Not nice enough for that."

I sighed, tucking it back into my cloak pocket and returning my attention to the island. "Verdion has been alive for a long time, I'm assuming."

"Yes."

"So why would he believe Regner when he said he wouldn't strike at Quorith if he remained neutral?"

Rythos snorted. "The same reason Eryndan believed him when Regner said the human kings would rule together. They trust him because they love power, and they can't imagine losing it. And…they want to keep their people safe."

I shivered as we approached the island. Quorith's wards were stronger than any other, built with a kind of magic that made the skin on my arms prickle. Rythos stood, murmured a single word in a language I'd never heard, and the ward disappeared as if it had never been there at all, shimmering back into place once we had passed.

I hadn't visited when the others had stolen a ship to take Prisca to the hybrid kingdom, and I swept my gaze greedily over everything I could see as Rythos docked our boat. The island unfolded before me like a promise of untold stories and uncharted paths. The lush greenery and vibrant flowers dotting the landscape weren't just splashes of color but markers of a culture steeped in beauty and a love for the wild. Laughter spilled out of the taverns across from the dock, people speaking in languages I didn't understand but longed to learn. And the air…the air was rich with the scents of freedom—wild flowers, exotic spices, the sea…the very essence of a life where I could slip into place without anyone knowing who I was.

Rythos held out his hand, and I realized he'd already stepped onto the dock. I allowed him to help me out of the boat, studying the grandeur of a distant building as he stepped away to talk to someone. It was undoubtedly an architectural marvel, with its towers and bridges, the marble and stone weaving together to create something strange and unique.

"I've never seen that expression on your face before," Rythos said.

I instantly controlled my features. "What expression?"

He flashed his teeth in a brief smile. "Something like awe. Or wonder."

I cleared my throat, forcing myself to tear my gaze away from a group of women dancing in the street. "When all this is over, I'm leaving this continent. I want the life that was denied to me for so long. This island...it soothes some part of me. It reminds me that there's more out there for me. And that one day, I'll find it."

The corner of Rythos's mouth tipped up. "I didn't want to return here," he said. "It holds mostly bad memories for me. So thank you for allowing me to see it through your eyes."

I nodded, and he took a deep breath, his gaze lingering on the white building in the distance.

"Let's get this done."

No one attempted to stop us as we made our way along the bustling streets. Perhaps because everyone seemed to know who Rythos was—people either waved and called out to him or gave him narrow-eyed stares, whispering to those next to him.

By the time we approached the white building I'd admired from the dock, I was tired of the eyes on us. Rythos appeared completely at ease, although in his fae form with his expression blank, it was almost like looking at a different man entirely.

I, too, had slipped on my court mask, and we strolled through the courtyard as if this were just another day.

No one greeted us at the door, although the guards bowed low at his appearance. Rythos wandered, ignoring the fact that the main hall was almost deserted. Like everything else I'd seen here so far, it had been designed with care—wide windows allowing sunlight to pool on the marble floors, recessed nooks with benches for seating, finely crafted rugs that were likely much, much older than I was. Gesturing for me to follow him, Rythos climbed the long staircase to our left.

I recognized Verdion's voice the moment I heard it. His low baritone set my teeth on edge. Rythos didn't hesitate at the closed door, simply pushed it open and stepped inside. Lifting my head, I pasted a cool smile on my face and followed him in.

Verdion glanced up from where he was seated at the head of a long, oval table. He didn't look at all surprised to see his son, but his eyes fired with wrath at the interruption.

"How dare you?"

Rythos ignored him, scanning the room. I counted twelve other Arslan men and women, all of them staring at Rythos. Clearly, we were interrupting a council meeting. How convenient for us.

"Out," Verdion snarled.

"I don't think so." Rythos crossed his arms. "Where is Brevan?"

"Your brother is away. He will return later today."

"And was he away for the summit as well?" Rythos

lifted one eyebrow and turned to the council. "Has my father told you all about the deal he made with the human king before this war even began? That Regner would choose not to attack this island as long as we *cooperated*?"

A woman with long, dark braids murmured something to the man at her side, her eyes wide. Meanwhile, Verdion's lips pulled back from his teeth. "The council knows everything there is to know."

"And did they know that Regner has never kept his word to his allies—not once—and thanks to our wards, he believes we attacked him during the battle for the barrier?"

"I heard what happened with those wards," Verdion said quietly. "I know that hybrid bitch interfered."

"That hybrid bitch is already twice the ruler you'll ever be," I snapped.

Rythos nodded his agreement. "Not to mention, the ward you think you can hide behind? Regner knows how to shift it. At least long enough to attack all of us."

"Nonsense. Our ward can't be shifted anywhere."

"It can be if one of Regner's pet Patriarchs developed a weapon that can temporarily remove wards from this world," I said.

His expression stayed entirely neutral, but I glanced at the council. Several men were frowning, while an older woman with deep laugh lines had shakily gotten to her feet. Perhaps this wouldn't be the battle we'd prepared for. Perhaps they would actually listen.

"We can no longer afford to be neutral," she said. "It is now a matter of honor. If we're attacked, no one will come to our aid."

"We won't be attacked," Verdion ground out.

I angled my head. "Oh yes, you believe you can go crawling back to Regner and bargain with him. Tell me, will you fall to your knees for the human king?"

Verdion's mouth dropped open, but he quickly recovered. "How dare you come here. You shouldn't even have stepped foot on this island, and yet you believe you can barge into this meeting and attempt to convince our people to go to war for you?"

"The Arslan were a great people once," Rythos said quietly, turning to face the council. "We weren't just known for our expertise when it came to inventions like our ships. We were known for our compassion. For our willingness to welcome people who were searching for a new life."

"You know nothing."

Rythos continued as if his father hadn't spoken, his gaze sweeping each council member. "What will you tell your children if Regner wins this war? How will you explain to your children's children that you had a chance to fight on the right side of history, and you chose not to get involved? Will you look them in the eye and tell them you allowed innocents to be slaughtered because it was politically convenient? War will come to this island. Already, Regner has invaded Gromalia. Yes, his creatures—creatures he took from the fae and twisted—have slaughtered almost an entire city of men, women, and children. And still, you would do nothing?" He let out a bitter laugh. "Do you know what happens to those who allow innocents to die for their own convenience? They soon find that convenience is replaced by the cold fingers of guilt tightening around their throats each time they attempt to sleep."

"Humans," Verdion snapped. "There are too many of them already. Perhaps this is nothing more than population correction."

Rythos bristled. "That population correction will come here. It is a fact."

"Allow us to think on this and vote," the woman with the laugh lines said. She had enough courage to carefully ignore the furious look Verdion shot her. "We must deliberate."

With a last look at the council, Rythos nodded. I followed him out. I didn't like leaving them where they could listen to Verdion's poisonous words, but we had no choice.

"What do you think they will do?"

Rythos shook his head, his face tight. "I don't know. Likely, they will deliberate for hours. Their decision won't come down to what is right, or good versus evil. They will spend their time poking at one another, using their political power to irritate those they despise, and questioning if we speak the truth."

Frustration clawed at me. Rythos nodded at whatever he saw on my face. "Pray to any gods you believe in that they choose to ally with us. Because if they don't, this island will become nothing but rubble, and the ships that could give us a fighting chance in this war will be little more than debris at the bottom of the sea."

ASINIA

For a few moments, it seemed as if perhaps we were wrong. As if perhaps the monsters lurking beneath the surface were merely created from our overactive imaginations.

A dark, scaled creature leaped across the surface of the water—shockingly fast—and aimed for Demos.

My bolt arrowed through its open mouth, and it silently dropped back into the water with a splash—just footspans from Demos's head. Cool waves of terror swept through my body, my muscles turning liquid.

He sliced a single glance at me, and then he was turning, paddling toward the area we'd first seen rippling. I nocked another arrow and waited.

Next to me, Amalra and Elysanth had done the same. All three of us were utterly silent.

Demos, Horrison, Gwynara, Firion, and Nyrik all circled around Brinlor, guarding him from every side as they swam toward the ward.

My lungs were burning, and I slowly let out the breath I was holding, rolling my neck. If I was too tense, I was more likely to shoot early. Which meant I was more likely to miss.

I had to—

There!

Another flash of something long, dark, and scaly, only this time, the creature didn't leap from the water. It swam up next to Firion, who responded by slashing out with his dagger.

Fighting in the water couldn't have been easy. Especially knowing lethal creatures were watching their every move. A flash of teeth, and Gwynara used her power, slamming her fire into the side of the creature.

Even though Gwynara was fae, I was relatively certain that Madinia's fire was much, much stronger. If she were here, she could have turned most of these monsters to ash.

The lake creature made a sound that caused goose bumps to break out on my skin. But it lunged again. This time, it was Demos who slashed out, catching it across one of its red eyes.

Brinlor had reached the ward. It must have taken an incredible amount of courage for him to close his eyes the way he did, trusting that the others would keep him alive. He was murmuring something under his breath, and a white glow began to spread beneath the water.

The lake suddenly teemed with life.

It was as if Brinlor's efforts to break the ward had woken every creature in the vicinity. I had to ruthlessly keep myself in check, suppressing the instinct to throw my crossbow aside and jump into the water in an attempt to save Demos from the creature that was now almost on top of him.

There was no intelligence in these creatures' eyes. Regner had somehow tied them to his ward, and there was nothing left of them except pure rage and the desire to kill.

I fired again and again and again, the others doing the same. But eventually, we had to stop. The chances of hitting one of our own were too high. All we could do was watch, guts twisting, hearts pounding triple time.

It was time for me to get into the water. I pulled my dagger from its sheath.

"Don't even think about it!" Demos roared.

To everyone else, it likely seemed as if he was screaming at the scaled monster attempting to get past him to Brinlor. But I'd caught the furious glare he'd aimed my way.

Even while fighting for his life, he was attempting to prevent me from risking mine. I ground my teeth but focused, waiting for the moment I could do something— *anything*—except stand here watching.

Firion and Nyrik were fighting the same creature, attempting to lure it away from Brinlor. The ward glowed brighter, which sent every living thing in that water into a frenzy. Gwynara was aiming her power at them, while next to me, Amalra sliced her hand through the air, stunning the closest creature. It slid down into the water.

One of the other fae aimed a dark ball of something that terrified me. It hit the creature, which instantly froze, splashing down into the lake.

The ward was glowing brighter and brighter, and the others were managing to prevent Brinlor from being jostled too badly. I caught sight of Horrison continually diving beneath Brinlor, likely guarding him from anything that was considering grabbing him from below.

Perhaps we really could do this.

Someone screamed. I scanned the water. I'd been watching the others, and I'd lost track of Demos.

I'd lost track of him.

Dread threatened to drop me to my knees.

Please don't let it be Demos. Please.

Nyrik's arm was missing.

It was the first thing I saw as my gaze caught on the other man. He screamed again, the water darkening around him. And the creature was coming back.

My skin turned clammy, and I sighted my next arrow.

But it wasn't interested in Nyrik anymore. His flailing had left a gap in the shield around Brinlor. And the creature dove into the gap.

I shot at it, missed, and almost hit Nyrik. Frustration burned through me. The others were using their power, but the creature was both larger and faster than those in the water. The attack on Nyrik seemed to have emboldened its little friends, and they attacked at once, the water churning.

I couldn't do it. I couldn't stand here uselessly and watch them lose their lives one by one.

"We need to go in!" I yelled.

"We die, and there will be no one left to get that amulet back to the others," Amalra ground out.

Demos was already barreling toward Brinlor, his muscular arms slicing through the water. My breath caught in my throat as the largest creature aimed at him.

The ward lit up the entire cave.

And then it darkened once more.

"Got it," Brinlor yelled, his voice hoarse.

"Go!" Demos hollered.

I lost sight of him in the sudden chaos. The water became a seething cauldron, turbulent waves crisscrossing over the surface of the lake as everyone hurtled toward us.

The creatures were gaining on them, and my heart beat in my throat, my entire body shuddering. Brinlor threw the amulet to Demos, who ducked beneath a long, serpentine body as it leaped through the air. The moment it was free, he hauled back his arm, and the amulet shot toward us.

Elysanth snatched it out of the air beside me, but I couldn't celebrate. I was too busy watching as Horrison dragged Nyrik through the water, the other man's struggles slowing them both down. Demos saw it too. He turned, going back for them.

My boots were off, my bow dropped next to them within a moment.

Swiping an arrow from my quiver, I leaped into the lake.

20

MADINIA

The council voted against us.

It wasn't even a close vote. Verdion sat at the head of the table, a small smile playing around his lips.

Thousands—perhaps hundreds of thousands—of people would die. And he was perfectly content. No, he was smug.

My hands burned, but I was getting better at controlling the fire that sparked within me.

"Why?" Rythos demanded.

"It's simple," a man next to Verdion said, stroking his dark beard. "While His Majesty may have broken our laws by not bringing such an important decision to the council—" he leveled Verdion with a long look, which Verdion ignored "—his logic was sound. Despite your passionate argument for us to involve ourselves in a war not of our own making, to do so would needlessly risk our own people. The Arslan will renegotiate with Regner. We will explain how our wards work and communicate our expectation not to be involved in this war."

The stupidity of his words stunned me into speechlessness.

A muscle twitched in Rythos's jaw.

"Leave," Verdion said.

I planted my feet. I wasn't going anywhere. I opened my mouth, but Rythos's expression had…changed.

This time, fire truly did burn in my hands, my power automatically leaping to protect me from the threat. Several Arslan glowered at me. But it was Rythos they should have been paying attention to.

His expression was perfectly pleasant. His eyes sparkled, and his head tilted in that strange fae way that never failed to make the hair rise on the back of my neck.

My hands burned hotter. But he wasn't looking at me. He wasn't even looking at his father. No, he was looking at the council.

And every one of them had stopped talking. They were looking back.

My heart thundered in my chest, and I took a step closer to the door. But I couldn't stop myself from watching, even as my instincts screamed at me to run before I was caught up in it too.

"This makes me sad," Rythos said. "I've come here to extend the hand of *friendship*."

Verdion choked. "Don't you dare."

Rythos didn't even spare him a glance. I could feel his power, the tendrils of it sweeping through the room, searching for the weakest—

"I'll be your friend," the woman with the braids spoke up.

"Silence!" Verdion roared, but it was too late.

"Don't choose her," the bearded man at Verdion's side snapped. "I would make a much better friend."

Rythos smiled, and it was terrible. "We can all be

friends, don't you think?"

"If you do this, it is a declaration of war." Verdion was trembling now.

Rythos spared him a single glance. "This is the reason you decided I was too much of a threat to be able to live here, isn't it, Father? I do so love being able to prove you right." He turned to the others. "I have a suggestion."

"What kind of suggestion?" one of the men asked.

"I think we should help my other friends."

"Your *other* friends?" Jealousy smothered the man's question. My stomach swam.

Rythos grinned. And even without the power dripping from it, it was an impressive grin, his teeth very white against his dark skin. "Yes. I'm hoping, one day, we can all be friends. But for that to happen, we need to share."

"Share?"

"Yes. Remember the ships I asked for?"

Slowly, methodically, Rythos guided them through what he wanted. His power didn't completely replace their will. No, that was Vicer's power. But now that the council members each considered him to be their best friend, they were willing to listen to what he had to say. They were willing to think logically and to put their political aspirations aside. They cooperated with one another because Rythos asked his *friends* to work together.

I felt the threat of his power, but he was being very careful to keep it focused away from me. And yet I couldn't allow myself to relax, couldn't seem to kill my instinct to prepare to defend myself.

The use of so much power was costing him. A bead of sweat appeared at his temple, signaling the strain. I could understand why. Rythos had to ensure these people would want to cooperate even after we left the island.

Verdion's eyes were bulging, but he seemed to be unable to speak, as if it was taking all of his power not to be swept away in Rythos's *friendship*. But he was the only one who had any such immunity. Horror flickered across his face as he watched his council vote unanimously for the Arslan to join the war.

"You will pay for this," he hissed through his teeth.

"Likely I will. Cheer up, father. You're getting what you wanted. After all, this was what you always feared. The reason you never trusted me. I'm pleased I could prove you right."

"Never return," Verdion gasped out.

One corner of Rythos's mouth kicked up. "Once this war is won, I have no plans to." He turned to the general. "We will meet to discuss our approach within three hours. Gather anyone who should attend such a meeting."

Turning, Rythos stalked out, ignoring the council members who implored him to stay.

My hand was shaking as I closed the door behind me, following him out. I'd seen him use his power on Regner's guards at the castle, but this...

He was ignoring me, his strides long as he slammed open a door. I followed him inside what looked like a series of rooms for guests. Within a moment, Rythos had disappeared through another door, and I stood in the entryway, heart pounding.

Retching sounded. It went on and on as Rythos vomited, the sound broken only by what sounded like rough sobs.

I strode to the window and stared sightlessly out at the city, grinding my teeth. Prisca should be here. I wasn't exactly someone who knew what to do or say under such circumstances.

Finally, what felt like hours later, Rythos stepped back into the room. He strode toward the window where I stood, and with every step, the lines of grief carved into his face faded, until his expression was carefully blank.

"Are you…"

"I'm fine."

I nodded, returning my attention to the city below us. If he wanted to talk about it, he would. I wasn't going to push him.

We stood in silence for a long time. Long enough that my feet began to ache. Perhaps I should leave him alone.

"Prisca was my first true hybrid friend," Rythos said, and I almost jolted at the suddenness of it. "She wanted nothing from me except friendship. The kind of woman she is…the loyalty she exudes…there are very few things I could do to lose that friendship. And I would never risk it."

"She is annoyingly persistent, isn't she?"

His mouth twitched. "That's one way to describe her. Once, when Lorian and Prisca first met—when they were still at each other's throats—Lorian implied to her that I'd used my power on her." I shook my head, and Rythos laughed. "Yes, I should have known then that they were mates. The move was so beneath him. So utterly unlike the man I knew."

"He'd never done such a thing before?"

He shook his head. "Lorian isn't known for his subtlety. When he wants something, he goes after it. Until

Prisca. She was the one thing he wanted but couldn't let himself have. And it tortured him. At the time, Prisca and I weren't even truly friends yet. But the betrayal in her eyes…it was devastating. I would never want to see that expression and know I had caused it. Not on Prisca, and not on any of my friends."

I couldn't have understood this just a few months ago. Now…now, I was beginning to.

"But you used it on your father's council."

Our eyes met. My voice held no judgment, and something in his expression relaxed when he realized I wasn't being malicious. I was, after all, the one who had insisted Vicer use his power against Kaelin Stillcrest. If he had…

A tiny grave appeared in my mind, Whirna lying next to it, her voice agonized.

"I promised him I would keep him safe. It was my job to keep him safe."

Rythos was still watching me. I cleared my throat. "I don't blame you. I would have done it too."

"I wouldn't have," Rythos said. "Just months ago, I never could have imagined I would have done such a thing. I was enraged at the mere suggestion from my father that I was too dangerous to be allowed access to his council. And I spent years believing he had unjustly banished me from our territory." He let out a humorless laugh. "I could have saved myself years of angst and rage by simply admitting that he was right. I was a threat."

I rolled my eyes. "Yes, you were a threat. And if Verdion had behaved as a true leader should, instead of holding on to pettiness over ancient grudges, you likely never would have acted on that threat."

He went still. "It's that simple to you?"

Impatience swept through me. "I'm not Prisca. If you want soft words about how this one choice doesn't change anything about your worth, talk to her. People who question their decisions and refuse to act based on preconceived ideas about right and wrong are useless in this war. If we're going to win, we need to use every weapon available to us. Vicer…Vicer didn't use his power, even when his instincts likely screamed at him to do so. And hundreds of hybrids paid for it with their lives." I pushed the image of that tiny grave out of my head once more and focused on Rythos. "Do you believe the gods give us our powers for a reason?"

He shrugged one shoulder, turning to watch a group of Arslan walking below. They looked so…carefree, laughing as they strolled toward the water. Had I ever been that carefree?

"I never used to believe such a thing," Rythos said. "I thought our powers were nothing more than coincidence. And then I met Prisca. I saw what she could do, and I realized we might truly have a chance to win this war."

If there was one thing Prisca was good at, it was getting people to believe in her. I'd once dismissed the power of hope. But that hope could be what made us survive this war.

"I don't think the gods make mistakes. I believe they take too much of an interest in some of our lives, but nothing is accidental. Why else would Lorian have the kind of power he does, when it would make more sense for it to belong to the fae king? You were given your power for a reason. Perhaps it was all for this."

"Perhaps it was not," a frigid voice said from behind us.

I whirled. The man standing in front of us must have moved incredibly quietly for Rythos's fae senses not to have noticed him. And I was betting I could guess how.

He was taller than Rythos, although not quite as broad. He had the same wide mouth, but his eyes were cold.

Rythos stiffened. "Brevan."

The Arslan heir swept his gaze over me dismissively before returning it to Rythos. But I wasn't interested in him either.

I was far more interested in the guards gathered behind him.

ASINIA

Gwynara swam toward me with the fluidity of a fish. I barely dodged her as she hurtled for the shore.

"Get out," she gasped, but I was already diving deep, knife in one hand, arrow in the other.

It was dark beneath the surface—pitch black, as if we were inside the belly of some vast, lethal monster. The only light came from the dim light pooling above us, casting shadows into the depths. I caught movement out of the corner of my eye and turned, but it was gone before I could strike out.

A moment later, I could see the men, three of them together, their legs powering them toward the shore. But

Nyrik's blood continued to darken the water around them.

More movement. And this time, I caught sight of the creature—about three times the width of the largest eel I'd ever seen, its open mouth displaying rows of vicious teeth. Teeth that still held pieces of Nyrik's flesh trapped between them.

My lungs had already begun to ache. But I could see what would happen. The monstrous eel was waiting below, and any moment now, it would approach diagonally, shooting up from the depths of the lake. Right before Demos and the others made it to shore.

I gripped the hilt of my dagger tightly, curled my knees in, and thrust them out, crossing the water to meet it.

The serpent creature was much, much faster than I was. But I was closer to the others. And I shoved my body in front of them, striking out with the knife.

It dodged me so easily, that if it could have laughed, it probably would have sniggered at me. It reared, shooting toward me, but I'd kept the arrow carefully hidden, and the moment it crossed within distance of my left arm, that yawning mouth open and ready to pluck my limbs from my body…

I shoved the arrow deep into the giant red hole of its open mouth.

It let out a noise so loud, I could even hear the muffled sound of it underwater. Another creature approached, darting toward me, and Brinlor met it with his sword, his frantic gaze telling me without words to *swim*.

My lungs were screaming at me now.

Air. Gods, I needed air. I could see the surface above

me, the dim light so close and yet somehow thousands of footspans away.

Strong fingers caught my wrist, pulling me up.

I surfaced with a sob-like gasp, and Demos's eyes met mine.

A series of emotions flickered across his face, almost too quickly to see. Relief, terror, fury, a strange, desperate need. Almost immediately, though, he turned his head and began yanking me toward the shore.

A single glance behind me told me the others were close. Together, we swam desperately. My teeth chattered with a mixture of cold and fear.

Shouts sounded. Demos and I both turned, and he pushed me behind him, shielding me with his body.

"Swim," he ordered.

But I couldn't. Because one of the creatures had surfaced like a dolphin, flying through the air toward Horrison. He bared his teeth, readying his sword. But a scaled monster was approaching from his left.

Demos swam back toward them, his knife in his hand. Brinlor approached on their right, flailing through the water desperately in an attempt to shield Horrison.

But it was Nyrik who used his one good arm to punch Horrison straight in the jaw. Screams sounded from the fae and hybrids behind us.

Horrison fell back, and Nyrik took his place, his expression grim as he met his fate.

The creature clamped its teeth around his throat, the force of its leap taking Nyrik down into the depths of the lake below.

Demos struck out at the creature on the left, his

sword slicing deep into its head. His blade was so sharp it slid through scales and flesh, and I let out a tiny sound as the force of his blow pushed him beneath the water.

I made it perhaps two footspans closer to him before he surfaced, whipping his head toward the space where Nyrik was no longer swimming.

"Everyone out of the water!" he ordered.

I doubted it was just water that rolled down Horrison's face as he swam toward me. Brinlor followed him, while Demos waited, covering their backs. He sliced a furious look at me, and I turned, heading toward shore.

The stubborn bastard wouldn't get out of the water until I did.

By the time we hauled ourselves out and lay gasping for air, I could have kissed the hard rock beneath us. But Demos was already pulling me to my feet and backing me away from the others, behind one of the rocky crevices.

I waited for him to snarl at me.

Instead, his mouth slammed down on mine.

Demos's kiss was a punishment. He bit my lip, soothed it with his tongue, and then swept that tongue deeper, demanding entrance to my mouth. He slid his large hand into the wet tangle of my hair and held me in place as his lips ravished mine. My entire body heated, turning relaxed, languid, until all I could do was open for him and follow where he led.

And then his mouth gentled, his tongue stroking mine teasingly. His other hand came up to cup my cheek, before sliding down to encircle my throat.

He didn't tighten his hand, but the threat was there.

He leaned back, and I swayed into him, wanting

more. When I opened my eyes, he was glowering down at me, his eyes still holding a feral gleam.

I shivered, and his frown softened. "You need to change out of those wet clothes." His voice felt as intimate as a warm hand sweeping across my bare skin.

I placed one hand against his chest, feeling the steady beat of his heart. "You're angry with me." I told myself I didn't care. At least he was alive.

"I am. When I saw you get in that water, I wanted to strangle you myself." He tightened his hand a little, then released me.

And just like that, all relaxation disappeared.

"You're welcome," I snapped.

"Thank you," Demos said gravely. "Please don't ever do that again."

"I won't."

It was quite unlikely we would ever be in a situation that involved a dark lake, a fae amulet, and vicious, deadly serpent creatures.

Demos narrowed his eyes, opening his mouth.

Someone let out a string of curses, and we both turned.

Gwynara lifted her head, tears running down her face.

"It's not the real amulet," she said, her voice cracking. "It's a fake."

21

PRISCA

"Cousin," Zathrian said, that wide grin never leaving his face as he ran his gaze over me. "Was this disguise truly supposed to work?" His gaze drifted to Lorian, and I stepped closer to him, noting the way Lorian's ears had already begun to turn pointed, the way his cheekbones were beginning to sharpen. But something that might have been surprise flickered across Zathrian's face when he spotted Kaliera.

"No," I said. "I merely wanted to visit. And something told me you wouldn't allow us to stroll through the gates otherwise."

Eadric snarled. "Kill them."

Crossbows were suddenly pointed at us from all directions. Lightning cracked the sky as Lorian tensed in response.

My mind suddenly threw me back to that moment outside Lesdryn, when Regner's men had pointed crossbows of their own at us. Lorian had made them very, very sorry.

Orivan held up a hand. "This is not the way of our people," he said to Zathrian. "If you were to kill the only other heir to the hybrid throne without a fair fight, things would not go well for you. In fact, I would wager that you would find it very difficult to convince these regiments to march beneath your flag."

"You are a traitor. And you will lose your head for this," Eadric vowed. But most of the guards dropped their crossbows and swords at Orivan's words, many of them staring intently at me. Zathrian's grin turned tense around the edges.

"Cousin," I said. "I challenge you."

"*You* challenge *me*?" he laughed. "And am I to believe that the fae bastards next to you won't become involved the moment it looks like you're about to die?"

I smiled at him. "Lorian, Marth, Galon," I said, never taking my eyes off Eadric's, "this is the man who killed Cavis."

Three feral snarls sounded behind me. "I challenge you," they said in unison.

Movement beside me. Lorian was slowly turning his head. Galon rolled his eyes, waving a hand. "Fine."

Marth had gone still, and his gaze was stuck to Lorian's.

"He's mine," Marth said.

"I don't think so."

Eadric's eyes glittered, as if this was all just too much fun. But tense lines bracketed his eyes as two of the most powerful fae in existence jostled for the pleasure of killing him.

He'd been more than happy to torture me and Cavis when we were chained. When we were imprisoned.

Lorian leaned over and murmured something to Marth. Marth stiffened. But after a long, tense moment, he nodded.

My own gaze slid to the man standing a few footspans behind Eadric. The man who had weakened both Cavis and me until we hadn't had a chance.

Soltor.

I gave him a slow smile. He attempted to ignore me, his eyes darting away, but the color had drained from his face.

"A true challenge must be fair," Orivan said, drawing my attention. Several soldiers nodded firmly. "That means no use of your power." He waved his hand at Lorian and me, then flicked his gaze to Eadric and Soltor.

"Fine," I said quickly. No one needed to know I currently didn't have any power available.

Orivan looked at Lorian. Lorian nodded. "I agree."

Zathrian's grin widened as he stared at me. "This is truly how you want to die, cousin?"

Lorian angled his head. A predatory gleam entered his eyes, his expression tight with feral wrath. The air around us seemed to go still.

For a long moment, it felt as if he wasn't human, fae, or hybrid. As if he were some other strange, lethal creature that was longing to be unleashed.

Behind us, Marth let out a low, threatening growl.

My cousin's smile had disappeared.

Lorian addressed Eadric. "Will you face the repercussions of your actions?"

Eadric sneered at him. "Out of all the fae I've killed, and I've killed many—" he winked at Marth, who took a step toward him "—your death will be my favorite."

This man…this man had made me watch while Soltor cut into Cavis. He'd ensured my friend's last moments were filled with fury and pain and fear.

I wished I could be the one to kill him.

"In that case," Orivan said. "Step into the arena." He glanced at me. "I hope you know what you're doing," he murmured.

I hoped I did too.

Galon leaned close. "I wouldn't let you do this if I didn't know you could kill him. And you can. I know you can do this, Pris."

Galon's steadfast confidence helped. Blowing out a shaky breath, I nodded. Lorian leaned over and pressed a gentle kiss to my temple.

"Remember what I told you when we traveled to the hybrid camp the first time, wildcat."

"When it comes to your survival, you cheat. You cheat and you lie. You fight dirty. And you do whatever else it takes to stay alive."

I squared my shoulders. I might not have access to my power, but Zathrian would have nulled it anyway. And this? This was personal.

I could sense Lorian's fear. Not for himself. For me. But I knew he believed I could do this. And he knew I *had* to do it. For our people.

"Make them pay," Marth muttered, slapping Lorian on the back. He reached out and squeezed my shoulder. And then I was following Lorian into the arena.

The word had spread while we were talking. Soldiers had gathered, standing shoulder to shoulder along the outside of the arena. They jostled for space, their eyes wide. I saw several passing each other coin, betting on the outcomes of the challenges. Likely, the odds of me winning weren't considered high. Good. I hoped whoever bet against Zathrian raked it in after this.

Lorian and Eadric stepped to one side of the arena. Eadric said something I couldn't catch to Lorian, his voice a low taunt. Lorian just smiled. A pleasant, unconcerned smile.

I shivered.

"You came here to take my army," Zathrian said when our eyes met once more. He drew his sword.

I said nothing, merely drew my own.

"I was trained from the moment I was born for that throne. *I* had time magic. *I* was supposed to be king."

I watched him. He held his sword loosely, his stance easy. My only chance was to use his confidence against him. "Your parents wanted my grandmother and parents dead so you could rule. And you would have happily allowed such a thing?"

"They had ignored the threat Regner presented for decades," he hissed, swinging his sword. His arms were thick slabs of muscle, and his taller height would give him more reach. If it came down to pure strength, I was dead.

I was fast, but I was betting he was too. He had decades of training on me. I knew how to fight dirty, but he likely did too.

And if I let myself continue this line of thinking, he would take my head before I got close to killing him.

He was cool. Calm. He watched me with relaxed certainty. I had to shake him up. Unnerve him.

"So, Regner was the threat, and your parents decided to allow him to invade. That sounds like some clever thinking right there."

He lunged at me, swinging the sword. I whirled away, but the lunge had been a chance for him to study my footwork. And he'd watched closely.

Zathrian sneered at me. "Do you know what happened when my parents realized I wouldn't be king? That your mother could become pregnant after all? My father almost killed me."

My breath caught. Did this mean I had another, older sibling?

Zathrian leaped at me, swinging his sword again and again. Across the arena, I heard Lorian let out a low grunt. But I couldn't afford to glance his way.

"Don't worry, cousin, this fight for the throne remains between us. That baby died before taking its first breath."

Something in my chest wrenched, but I shoved the emotion down to address later.

"How could your father have possibly thought it was your fault?" The question was partly to unnerve him, but another part of me simply didn't understand it.

"He wasn't like your father. Your father would have loved you if you were completely powerless. Mine wanted to rule our kingdom through me."

"I'm sorry."

I…was. It must have been awful, growing up like that. It didn't justify any of Zathrian's choices, didn't give him the right to ally with Regner and attempt to take my crown. But maybe, if not for his father, Zathrian would have been a better man.

His laugh was hollow, and he gave me an incredulous look. "You're sorry? Just when I finally began to get the elders to listen to me, they learned you were alive.

I'd spent my entire life honing my magic and planning for how I would save our people from Regner, and the moment they learned you existed, none of it mattered."

He attacked again. His sword slammed into mine, the force of it making my arm ache. I couldn't continue to meet his strikes with my own sword. But I needed a better tactic. He was too strong.

"Do you think I wanted this?" I snapped. "I wanted to give the crown to you the moment I learned it was mine. I never wanted to be queen. All I wanted was family. Even if the elders hadn't chosen you, I would have supported you. I would have abdicated the moment our people were safe."

His mouth dropped open, and for a moment, he looked truly stunned. I let out a hoarse, bitter laugh. "But you never came to me. Instead, you killed the man we sent, let Eadric work with Regner to kidnap me, and made sure he killed my friend. And then...then you killed Lorian. Even if I could forgive everything else, I could never forgive that." Rage curdled in my gut as memories assaulted me. Zathrian, standing on that ship, holding up that fucking mirror. Lorian, shattered to pieces, along with my ability to reason.

Zathrian's expression hardened. "Then let's finish this, cousin."

He struck fast and hard, his sword slashing in a wide arc. But I'd been expecting that. Galon had, after all, prepared me for such attacks over and over, until my response was rote. I leaned backward, the sword whistling above my head. And then I dived low, slashing out at his thigh.

He bellowed a curse. My blade gleamed red with his blood.

"You want to know what I think? I think you're a coward. A weak-minded brat who could have had family but chose power instead. It didn't have to end this way. But it will. And Demos and Telean and I will never think of you again."

Zathrian snarled at me. He struck fast, bringing his sword down on my left. I had no choice but to meet it with my own blade.

But he was strong. So, so strong.

And I dropped my sword.

Fuck.

Zathrian's eyes lit with triumph. "Do you know what I'm going to do to your brother? I'm going to make your death look peaceful compared to his."

I laughed at him. The sound was difficult to force out with my lungs frozen, my heart galloping in my chest. "We both know Demos will kill you. All the guards in the world won't stop my brother from taking your head."

Slash, slash, slash. Zathrian swept his sword toward me, and I dodged each strike, until it looked like I was running from him. I had a sudden memory of another arena and another man who'd been certain I would never be the hybrid queen.

That time, I'd used my power.

This time, I would prove I didn't need it.

Sliding to the side, I shoved Zathrian's sword arm away from me and punched him in the throat. It was a perfect punch, my first two knuckles sinking right into the spot Galon had taught me. My cousin gaped like a fish on land, one of his hands clutching at his neck. But he recovered faster than I'd expected, thrusting out one leg to trip me.

I went down. But I took him with me.

He lost his own sword. Together, we rolled several footspans to the right, almost slamming into Lorian and Eadric.

And Soltor.

The crowd roared. I'd blocked out everything but my cousin, well aware that Lorian could more than handle himself and I was the one who was most likely to die here.

But there had been no chance of Eadric fighting fair. Not against Lorian. And Lorian was sticking to the plan. If he came in and used his power to kill Eadric and Zathrian, there was almost no chance that the hybrids here would follow us.

I couldn't help but watch as Soltor opened up a deep slice across Lorian's neck.

And I was suddenly standing in that cell again.

It wasn't Lorian being sliced to pieces. It was Cavis.

Cavis who was bleeding and *dying*.

"Prisca!" Lorian roared.

Hands clawing at my throat. Zathrians hands.

I took a frantic gasp of air and swung my elbow, smashing it into his chin. He cursed, and I used his moment of inattention to wiggle free, making it to my knees.

Until he viciously pulled my hair.

"Hair-pulling?" I snarled, kicking out at him like a mule. "Seriously?" He dodged my first kick, but my second caught him in the chest.

There wasn't much power in it, though. And he'd

grabbed my hair again, yanking my head back. If I lived through this, I was cutting it all off.

He leaned over me. His eyes had turned crazed. Time seemed to stop as Zathrian stared down at me, and for one moment, his eyes cleared.

And then they narrowed.

Eadric began to laugh. Soltor was hurting Lorian. I didn't have to glance to my right to know that much. Lorian would never use his power here after agreeing not to.

But Zathrian glanced to the right. Still holding my hair in his tight fist, ignoring the punch I slammed into his nose, he leaned down, his hand groping for his sword.

Every time I'd escaped certain death, every person I'd killed to save my own life, every near miss and lesson learned…all of them had led up to this.

It was me or him.

I moved the fastest I'd ever moved in my life, sweeping my dagger from its sheath.

And I plunged it into his gut so hard, the cross guard bruised my knuckles.

For a second, our eyes met. And something that might have been betrayal slid through Zathrian's gaze. But it was immediately followed by a chilling acceptance.

"Do better than me, cousin. Be the ruler I wished I could be. Bring our people home."

He closed his eyes.

His body began to slump backward, his hand releasing my hair.

I could hear someone screaming in my head. Someone who sounded a lot like my grandmother. The screams were wordless, horrified, enraged.

I made it to my feet. My head spun. And against all of my best interests, against all sense of logic…it was *my* turn to begin screaming. For a healer.

Distantly, I was aware of several healers rushing toward Zathrian. But I was already turning, desperately looking for…

Lorian was covered in so much blood, it took me a moment to recognize him. The soldiers had stopped cheering at some point, and a hushed silence had claimed the arena.

Soltor opened another deep cut along Lorian's neck. It poured blood. He didn't react, but I knew it had to be hurting him. Weakening him.

Eadric laughed. "No longer the Bloodthirsty Prince. Now you're just bloody."

He slashed out with his sword. Lorian stepped to the side, the movement casual, inconsequential even. But it was still breathtakingly fast. Fast enough that Eadric stopped laughing.

He waved his hand, and Soltor slashed out at Lorian again.

A cold, unrelenting rage slid through every inch of my body. Freezing my bones. Numbing my skin. Dancing across my nerves.

I picked up one of the knives Eadric had dropped.

And threw it at Soltor.

I had none of Asinia's power. None of my own. But it was as if the gods themselves guided the blade.

And lodged it straight into Soltor's neck.

His eyes met mine. "That's for Cavis," I said.

Soltor gaped. The light left his eyes. And his body hit the ground.

Something tight in my chest unraveled, and it felt as if I could take a full breath once more.

Lorian looked at me. His wounds were likely agonizing. But he waited.

Yes, I'm fine.

His eyes glittered with joy and relief. And he turned back to Eadric.

Eadric barreled at Lorian, his face a mask of loathing. Lorian stepped to the side again. The movement easy.

And I understood.

He hadn't finished with Eadric yet because he'd wanted to make an example of him. He'd wanted every hybrid watching to see that even with Soltor cheating, Lorian would refuse to use his own magic.

Because he didn't need to.

He slashed with his sword, his speed and aim breathtaking as the tip of his sword cut a path across Eadric's face. Eadric screamed, clutching one hand to his ruined cheek.

"This is also for Cavis."

As Lorian carved into him, again and again, the way Soltor had cut both Cavis and himself, Eadric's words played through my head, his voice a low taunt.

"You're sitting there, half drugged, clamped in fae iron, yet you're actively planning my murder, aren't you?"

Lorian sliced Eadric's arm. Eadric roared and launched himself at him.

"You just don't know when to yield, do you?"

Lorian smirked, his sword easily parrying Eadric's.

And as he pushed the other man's sword away, he reversed the movement, carving his blade through Eadric's thigh.

Eadric howled.

"I will break you."

Lorian gestured for him to attack again. Eadric hesitated. Glancing around at the soldiers watching, he launched at Lorian once more.

Lorian raked his sword along Eadric's ribs. Another shallow wound. But I knew from experience just how much it would sting.

"I don't just mean physically. I'll break your mind. Break your spirit. It's the least you deserve."

Lorian glanced at me. Whatever he saw on my face made his expression crease with concern. Eadric took advantage of his distraction and swung his sword, opening a wound of his own along Lorian's sword arm.

"There's no limit to the pain you will suffer. The pain your lover will suffer. We will heal you again and again and again, and it will be your mind that breaks before your body. It's far more enjoyable that way."

Lorian was moving. I heard Eadric scream. But I was back in that cell. And Eadric was pointing at Cavis.

"Hurt him. Hurt him so badly, she has no choice but to tell us what we want to know."

"I don't like when my time is wasted. So that little lie is going to cost you."

"If you're going to act like an animal, you'll be treated like one."

And then Cavis was moving toward him. His expression peaceful. Filled with acceptance. *"Tell them I love them, Prisca."*

I choked on a sob, and it was enough to bring me back to the present. I couldn't fall apart here. Not in front of the people I was hoping to lead.

So, I raised my head and watched. And slowly, methodically, Lorian took Eadric apart.

Whoever said vengeance didn't help was lying. Watching Eadric stumble and gasp was delicious. When his eyes widened and he realized he was about to die, something within me began to heal.

It wouldn't bring Cavis back. But all of us could look his daughter in the eye and tell her the men who had killed her father were dead. And that they had suffered.

But Lorian's expression had turned cold. Remote. Something within me ached. "Finish him, Lorian," I said.

His blade was a blur. And Eadric's head rolled from his body.

Exhausted, I raised my gaze.

"As you wish, Your Majesty." Lorian's voice echoed over the crowd.

He dropped to one knee, bowing his head.

And so did everyone else.

22

LORIAN

Lifting my head, I swept my gaze around the hybrids. All of them had fallen to their knees, bowing to Prisca. No one moved.

My eyes found hers.

She stood in the middle of the arena. Her face was bruised, one eye swollen. Her skin was concerningly pale, the blood splattered across it serving as the singular splash of color. Her lip gave the tiniest tremble, and for the barest moment, she looked so fucking lonely, I wanted to scoop her into my arms and carry her out of here.

Instead, I steeled my spine and slowly bowed my head again.

"Your Majesty," I repeated.

And I watched as she rebuilt herself once more. Her chin jutted out, her head lifted, and her shoulders squared.

"Rise," she ordered.

Everyone stood.

Prisca was silent for a few moments. But she had everyone's attention.

"There are better ways to live than wrestling with constant terror. Than being lied to and stolen from, imprisoned and murdered. And there are worse ways to die than fighting for freedom, next to the people we love. Our people deserve a different life. A better life. Each and every one of you deserves to live in freedom. You deserve to watch your children learn how to use their magic as they grow. You deserve to live in peace."

Pride roared through me until I almost shook with it. This woman. She was everything I could ever want. She was so much more than I deserved.

And I'd keep her safe until the day I died.

Cheers broke out. I noted those who didn't cheer. And I knew Galon and Marth were doing the same.

I walked to her, and she held out a hand. It trembled slightly as I engulfed it in my own.

"You left Zathrian alive."

She swallowed. "We will see if the healers can keep him that way." Her gaze searched my face, a tiny wrinkle appearing between her brows. "It was a mistake. I know it. But I couldn't seem to kill him. After everything he has done…I was too weak."

"No. You were merciful. They are very different things."

She shook her head, and I tightened my hold on her hand. "If he were to pick up a sword and lunge at my unprotected back right now, what would you do?"

That line between her brows deepened. "I'd watch you cut him down," she said, as if I had suddenly become very stupid and she was worried about my mind.

"I'm wounded."

Panic flared in her eyes, and I grasped her hand tighter. "In this situation," I clarified. "I'm wounded and slow and won't see him coming. What would you do?"

"I'd kill him."

I nodded, lifting my other hand to run my thumb along her brow until her frown disappeared. "That is the difference between weakness and mercy, wildcat. Even after everything you have seen, and everything that has been done to you, your heart is still so big. You're still kind. You still see the good in people, no matter how little of it there is."

A hint of color crept into her cheeks. She opened her mouth, and then her eyes widened once more as her gaze landed on my neck. I knew what she could see. Soltor had struck particularly deep along the side of my throat. "You're still bleeding, Lorian. You need a healer."

She glanced around, just as Galon and Marth approached.

Galon wrapped his arm around Prisca. He wasn't someone who hugged others often, but he squeezed her close. "Proud of you," he murmured into her ear.

Marth slapped her on the back, cleared his throat several times, wiped at one eye, and ducked his head.

I surveyed the soldiers standing in groups around us. Many of them stared, while others spoke in low voices. We had this army, but after Zathrian's poison, the hardest part would be keeping it.

Orivan strode toward us. When he glanced in Zathrian's direction, his gaze lingering on the healers who fought to save his life, something that might have been sorrow slipped across his face.

Prisca might have Orivan's loyalty now, but it had belonged to Zathrian first. I would be keeping a close eye on the hybrid general.

"I would like a tour," Prisca said before Orivan said a word.

He glanced down at her tunic, still stained with her cousin's blood. But he didn't argue. "Of course."

Next to me, Galon nodded approvingly. Prisca was young, female, and everyone knew she had been raised human, in one of Regner's villages. She couldn't afford to show a hint of weakness.

Already, the soldiers were dispersed back to their tasks, and as we left the arena, many of them immediately filed in to resume their training, the healers moving Zathrian away to work on him elsewhere.

The camp sprawled efficiently across a wide, flat expanse of land—the perfect spot for such a gathering, given how close we were to the Cursed City to our north and the Normathe Mountains in the southeast. The command tent was stationed a hundred footspans to the left of the arena, in the center of the camp, its canvas walls taut against steel frames. Around it, the tents for the high-ranked soldiers were meticulously aligned and equally spaced.

Farther out, the soldiers' tents were arranged in neat rows, creating a uniformity that spoke of order and control. The pathways between each row were straight and clear.

Conreth would approve.

Orivan led us toward the periphery of the camp—past the blacksmith's area, where the ring of hammer on anvil filled the air. Through the cook's section, where smoke wafted from the fires, and alongside the medical tents, where healers bustled to and fro, likely attempting to save Zathrian's life.

While Orivan droned on about the facilities, the schedule, and the training, I surveyed the armory and supply tents. They'd been strategically placed for easy access, and guards were stationed outside each of them. Nearby, well-fed horses were led to and from the temporary stables.

I glanced at Galon, who gave me an approving nod. If there were sixty thousand hybrid soldiers in this camp, I would feel confident that we would win this war. But at least the twenty thousand we did have appeared well-trained and disciplined.

Orivan led us to tents that had been set aside for Eadric and Zathrian. They were currently being hastily cleared of their personal items, new linens brought in. Prisca kept her gaze on Orivan.

"The decision to work with Regner has never been popular among the hybrid regiments," he said. "While your cousin may have had every intention of turning on Regner at the end, he obviously couldn't inform our people of his planned duplicity. And many of them are old enough to remember that day when his parents ripped down our wards. There will, of course, be grumbling from those who support him as king." He hesitated. "A display of your power could be exceptionally helpful there."

Prisca's hands curled at her sides, but she nodded. The time would come when she would have to tell Orivan about the loss of her power. But both of us had agreed that our grasp on this army would be too unstable to risk such a conversation until we had to.

"For now, I need a healer for my husband," she said,

glancing at my neck. A flash of satisfaction arrowed into my chest at the term.

Orivan nodded. "Done."

After a moment, he hesitated, opening his mouth, but I was also done.

Done watching the fine trembling beginning in Prisca's hands. Done watching the way her gaze darted as if it couldn't quite decide what to land on.

She had played her part perfectly. But she was in shock.

I would step aside in whatever ways Prisca needed as she ruled our people. But when it came to her health, I would make no such concessions.

"Her Majesty needs some time to recover. She will meet with you later."

Taking Prisca's hand, I led her into the tent.

ASINIA

"It's a fake?" Amalra demanded.

Demos went completely, utterly silent. When he held out his hand, Gwynara placed the amulet into it.

"How close of a match is it?" he finally asked.

"It's perfect. If I couldn't feel that it has no magic, I would have thought it was the real thing. If Brinlor were fae, he would've been able to tell." She sent him an apologetic look. Brinlor shook his head, staring into the water as if still hoping Nyrik would surface. Heat seared the backs of my eyes.

"Is it possible it *is* one of the amulets, but it has been already drained?"

"No," Gwynara said. "If Regner knew how to completely drain a fae amulet, there would be no war, because all of us would already be dead."

Some of the color disappeared from Demos's cheeks. His hand curled into a fist at his side, and he carefully handed the amulet back to Gwynara. I had a feeling he was restraining himself from throwing it back into the water.

"I know of only one person with the ability to replicate something this well," he said. "And he is a hybrid who has helped us many times before. If Regner has gotten to him, anyone around him is in deadly peril."

My gaze met his. He was thinking about Finley. I didn't want to believe it. And I knew it would break Prisca's heart.

"We need to get out of here," Brinlor said. "The others will be ready to strike."

"Are we certain the amulet isn't hidden somewhere else in here?" I asked. "If we bring down the mine…"

Sound suddenly rattled from the trowth stone in someone's pack. Gwynara leaped at it.

"I don't know where the rest of you are," Yan's voice echoed through the cave. "But I can only hope you're still alive. Our spies sent me a pigeon. One of Regner's carriages was spotted close by, surrounded by guards. Something tells me the amulet is in that carriage."

"They took it out through a hidden tunnel," I said.

"We thought we were creating a distraction. But we were our own distraction." My breathing had turned shallow, and I forced myself to unfist my hands.

"Where are they?" Demos demanded, holding up a hand as we waited for the reply.

"They're moving southeast. Toward Mistrun."

"We'll never cut them off," Gwynara said, her face bloodless. "This was all for nothing…"

"We *will* cut them off," Demos declared. His words, the strength in his voice, the steady look in his eyes… they had an instant effect. Gwynara's lips firmed, and she nodded, reaching for her pack. Brinlor straightened his shoulders, tearing his wandering gaze from the water. The others seemed to unfurl from where they'd been frozen in pained disbelief.

Gathering our packs, we moved as fast as we could. No one was worried about hiding our tracks or staying quiet on our way back to the entrance. Every second we delayed was also another second that the real amulet was traveling closer to Regner.

How had it come down to this?

We might have Tor to help with Regner's wards, but without the amulet, we had no hope of killing Regner himself. Somehow, the fate of the four kingdoms depended on whether we could make up the lost distance and steal the amulet from the carriage without dying in the process.

And so, we ran.

I was lucky that I was shorter than most of the others, although even I nearly slammed my head into a particularly low part of the rock above us.

Somewhere in front of me, someone was using the

trowth stone to communicate with Yan.

The stench from the monsters assaulted my nose as we were suddenly just footspans from where they were being kept. My eyes watered, but I kept moving, until finally, *finally*, we stumbled out of the mine.

Beautiful, life-giving, fresh air caressed my face, and I took a single moment to suck in a steadying breath.

But the others were still running until they'd scrambled up the bank and were looking down at the mine below them. I raced after them, and Demos leaned down, offering his hand as I slid a few steps. I slapped my hand into his, allowing him to pull me up next to him.

Gods, my lungs ached.

"Now you'll see why Yan's orders were to conserve his power," Demos said, nodding toward the mine. He didn't even sound out of breath.

Placing my hands on my thighs and leaning over slightly to catch my breath, I watched.

At first, nothing happened. But then, slowly, my skin prickled. Several birds suddenly took off from the trees behind us with a wild flap of wings.

It started as a low rumble, quickly escalating as the ground began to tremble beneath us. The trembling turned to a sway, which became the awful sensation of the world moving beneath my feet. As one, we all backed away from the bank.

Ancient rocks groaned beneath the strain.

I glanced around, but everyone was focused on the mine.

The trembling turned to a sharp motion back and forth. I reached for Demos's hand instinctively, and he gripped mine tightly. A deafening crack echoed, followed by several more. Rock crumbled, the mine collapsing into itself, until all I could see was a cloud of dust.

The moment the ground ceased shaking, Demos was pulling me after him.

Our group fell into place around us, sprinting into the forest.

"How did you know that would work?" I panted.

"The way the queen described the mine. It sounded as if too much of the rock had been hollowed out—and something told me Regner wasn't too concerned with support structures. Yan is able to make the earth move—not for long, and he will be drained for days now—but it seemed the easiest way to kill what needed to be killed."

So many creatures that had been living and breathing just moments ago were now gone. But so were the claws that would have torn into us. The wings that would have carried us high before dropping us to our deaths.

Someone was yelling something, and Demos held up a hand.

"Iron guards!" Yan was screaming through the trowth stone. "They had a group of them waiting nearby. They're coming after you."

My entire body was instantly coated in a greasy sweat. But Demos just held out his hand. "Map."

Someone shoved it into his hands. He lifted it, narrowing in on our area and waving us away when we crowded too close, blocking his light. His finger jabbed into the parchment and then trailed down.

"We'll travel by river," he said. "It's fast, it's close by, and it'll get us to the only road they can take south with a carriage. The iron guards won't expect it. They'll stick to the forest trails, and if the gods are smiling on us today, they'll miss us entirely."

My heart stuttered. "Prisca nearly died in that river."

"It was much colder months ago when she went into the water," Demos pointed out. "I know this area, and the river isn't as fast here. As long as we stay together, we'll be fine."

It was dangerous, but it was our only hope. And I trusted Demos to make the most strategic decision.

Brinlor heaved a sigh. "Perfect," he said. "I was hoping to spend some more time in cold water."

Demos was already handing back the map. "Let's go."

We ran until I could hear the water even over the heavy pants of our breaths, our footsteps thumping along the forest path. My stomach churned, but within seconds, we were heading downhill. I stumbled, regained my footing, and we burst through the tree line and onto the riverbank.

Here, the Dytur River flowed quickly, but it didn't hold the same mortal peril as the section near our village. There, the water had been white in places, filled with rocks, and flowing so fast, I was still sometimes shocked that Prisca had survived. Here, the river was moving quickly, steadily, but it wasn't wild. We were farther from the mountains here, and I couldn't remember the last time it had rained.

Demos didn't hesitate. Within a moment, he'd grabbed my wrist and was wading in, pulling me with him into the water.

My teeth chattered. The river wasn't as cold as I'd imagined—compared to the lake within the mine, it was almost tepid—but my body was struggling to handle the constant rush of adrenaline.

With a single glance at the others, Demos nodded, kicking out and pulling me farther into the water.

Not for the first time, I was forced to admire his strategy. I knew some of it was his magic, but much of it was also his mind.

The river swept us along—pushing each of us into the occasional rock, but that was to be expected. Demos and Brinlor were watching each bend carefully, likely comparing it to their mental images of the map.

The guards were traveling down the main road toward the south. Which meant, depending how fast we traveled, there was a chance we could be lying in wait.

If we missed them...

If we missed them, our only shot was Yan. Perhaps he could create some kind of distraction or find a way to slow the carriage down. My heart tripped at the thought. The soldiers guarding the amulet would be some of Regner's best.

Anyone who slowed them down would die.

The river was cool, then cold, then frigid. I shivered, focusing on staying close to the others. I touched the bottom a few times, using my legs to push off from the riverbed. No one spoke, all of us grimly silent.

Regner had outwitted us yet again. I was glad Nyrik hadn't known the amulet was a fake before that creature had pulled him down into the depths of that lake. At least he'd died believing he was a hero. That he'd done something incredible for the war. That his actions had mattered.

A thick, dark cloud seemed to invade my head, turning it foggy. And it suddenly felt as if a heavy weight had been dropped on my chest. Demos moved his body closer. He didn't say a word. He didn't need to. But one of his arms came around me, and we floated together, both of us lost in thought.

As we rounded the next corner, Demos jerked his head, and then he was steering me toward the riverbank. Obviously, he'd seen some landmark he'd recognized. All I knew was I was more than ready to get out of the water.

It felt as if we took half the river with us as we crawled out, water streaming off our clothes. It was even colder out of the water, but Demos grabbed my hand and immediately broke into a run.

"You don't have to drag me with you," I muttered. "I'm not going to get lost."

"If I don't keep you close enough to touch, you might risk your life again."

Who needed dry clothes? It turned out, fury could keep you just as warm. I opened my mouth to snarl a reply, but someone let out a bird call, and Demos dropped into a crouch, yanking me down with him.

I glanced around me. Everyone else had hit the ground at the same time.

"The carriage is approaching," someone murmured behind us. "We have to get to the road now."

At that, we sprinted, all of us tripping and stumbling and hissing frustrated curses. There would be no time to strategize. No time to carefully weigh up potential plans.

The thought of what that could mean made me nauseous with terror.

The moment we made it to the road, Demos crouched behind a thick, leafy bush. Several others melted away, while still more crossed the road.

Demos finally released my hand, pulling his sword from his sheath. "Stay here," he said.

When I didn't immediately reply, he turned to face me, his eyes wild. "Please."

Frustration warred with logic. Logic won, and I nodded. I would use my crossbow and do what I could from here.

The carriage was moving toward us down the road, pulled by four horses, with ten guards surrounding it, also on horseback.

Impossible. It was ludicrous to think we could do this in our current condition.

Crack!

One of the fae had felled a tree in front of the carriage. Rough male curses sounded, and a horse reared, diverting the guards' attention.

Our people didn't hesitate.

They didn't let fear swamp them, didn't let the un-likelihood of their survival make them question this attack.

Not for one second.

They attacked like a storm, surrounding the carriage on all sides, working together as if they'd practiced this attack a thousand times before.

A guard with a power similar to Galon's sent a flood of water into Gwynara's face until she dropped to her knees.

The others covered Demos as he moved closer, clearly targeting the carriage. I reached over my shoulder for my crossbow, cursing as I nocked an arrow. The wood was swollen and warped, while the bowstring had sucked in enough river water that it wasn't stretching the way it should.

Fuck.

I aimed anyway, unsurprised when my shot went wide. I'd prepared for this possibility, ensuring it wouldn't hit any of our people. And thankfully, the guards were currently too busy to target me.

Taking a deep breath, I centered myself, focusing on the strange place inside me—the one that allowed me to make the kinds of shots that shouldn't be possible. It was a feeling of complete peace. As if I were floating somewhere soundless, where nothing else existed.

The next guard swung at Demos, who dodged to the side, swinging his own sword. My arrow hit the guard in the throat, and he dropped. Warmth spread through my chest. My crossbow might be warped, but I could still make a difference.

Demos sliced a single glance my way, before ducking beneath a flash of light. I wasn't sure what that power was, but it came close to hitting the carriage. My pulse raced, and I forced myself to slow my breathing once again.

Several guards cursed at the tall, bearded guard who'd clearly come too close to risking the stolen fae amulet with that strange light. I shot another guard while they were distracted. But my arrow drove into his shoulder instead of his throat. His sword arm, so he was at least incapacitated, but I cursed the diminished tension in my bowstring.

While the guards were bloated with Regner's stolen power, they were still only human. And I'd underestimated the fae and the hybrids. Underestimated the icy fury that drove them now, after they'd watched Nyrik die.

I scanned the road. Two of the guards were dead. Eight of them were left, and they fought with vicious determination, teeth bared, swords swinging.

Gwynara shot fire toward one of the guards, and Amalra followed it with a wide swing of her sword.

He ducked neatly out of reach, the sword whistling past his head.

I aimed. Fired. Missed.

Fuck.

With a smug smile, the guard lashed out, burying his sword in Amalra's chest. No. Gods, no.

Elysanth's scream carried over the battle. My hands shook, and I lowered my crossbow long enough to take several long, deep breaths.

Steady arms. Steady hands. Or I would be useless here.

The guard kicked Amalra off the end of his sword, spinning to meet Gwynara. But Elysanth was already there.

She ducked low, driving her sword up into his groin. He opened his mouth, and nothing came out.

Where was Demos... Where was he—

There.

He'd leapt toward the roof of the carriage. But his body slammed into an invisible barrier, which shoved him backward with brutal force. Twisting in midair, he kicked out, clipping one of the guards in the face. Brinlor slipped up behind the same guard and slammed his dagger into the spot where the bottom of his head met his neck.

The ward around the carriage was one that actively repelled any who attempted to get near it. And I'd seen it before. Regner's assessors often traveled with shield guards who prevented anyone from even getting close to them.

The only way to break it would be to kill the guard who was using his magic to keep it in place.

My eyes darted. Six guards left. But which one of them held the ward?

Horrison and Firion had ducked behind one side of the carriage and were using it to shield themselves from an unrelenting attack from a guard who was sending some kind of destructive power toward them. Firion leaned around one of the wheels, and the guard's shoulders stiffened. Firion's eyes widened, and he slipped back behind the carriage, just in time for the guard's power to slam into a tree off the road behind him, blowing it to pieces.

He wasn't the shielder.

Nocking another arrow, I waited, poised. A huge, broad guard with a thick neck was fighting Demos with his sword. I hesitated, my crossbow raised. But as much as I wanted to shoot him, that guard wasn't the shielder either.

Shielders required concentration. Focus. Even if he'd been given stolen magic, it was unlikely that guard would be able to fight someone like Demos while keeping that shield in place.

Elysanth raised her sword, guarding her injured sister. One of the guards lunged toward Elysanth, a wide grin on his face. My heart leaped into my chest.

Brinlor was there to meet him, and their swords clashed.

Relief coursed through me. I continued scanning. And my gaze caught on the guard toward the back of the carriage.

Smaller than the other guards, he wielded a sword that was awkwardly long for him, as if he was attempting to overcompensate. As I watched, he took several steps toward Horrison, who'd lost his sword and was fighting hand to hand with a guard who still had his.

He was going to attack Horrison from behind. I bared my teeth.

But he scuttled backward, closer to the carriage once more.

"I've got you." I'd just found their shielder. And he didn't exactly seem to be overflowing with courage.

The rough plan leaped into my mind, fully formed. I didn't have time to second-guess myself.

Demos—

I caught sight of him just as he buried his sword in the larger guard's gut.

"Demos!" I screamed.

He turned, wide-eyed. And his eyes sparked when he saw I wasn't hurt or bleeding, but was instead distracting him.

My crossbow was in my hands, my bow poised, so I couldn't gesture properly. I had to hope he would get it.

And so I exuberantly jerked my head toward the guard with the too-long sword. The guard who'd turned toward me as I'd called Demos's name.

I gave him a dark smile that I hoped was dripping with ill intent. He swallowed, moving back toward the carriage. But he couldn't go any farther without running into Firion and Brinlor, who had just killed another guard.

Movement.

Demos, prowling toward the amulet. I couldn't risk looking at him.

And so, I widened my smile, letting my arrow fly toward the guard.

He did what I'd anticipated he would do. What almost anyone would do, even if they wouldn't admit it to themselves.

My arrow came within inches of his face and was repelled so violently, it almost hit Gwynara as she fought hand to hand, her own power clearly drained.

The guard had ripped his ward from the carriage and wrapped it around himself.

My chest tightened until I could almost taste each heartbeat.

But Demos was already launching himself through the door he'd opened. I nocked another arrow, aiming at the guard, who gave me a smug grin as it hit his shield once more.

Demos wasn't out yet.

I needed to keep distracting him.

My next arrow went wide, and the guard's grin grew.

Good. Just keep looking at me, you idiot.

Keep looking at me and not at Demos, who was

jumping free, a box in his arms. Pure, unfiltered joy swept through me at the sight.

Demos disappeared, and I continued to fire on the guard, distracting him from the fact that Demos now had the amulet.

But Firion kicked the guard he was fighting into one of the carriage wheels. And the guard slammed into the wood. He let out a curse, calling out someone's name, and the shielder shifted the ward from himself to what he was supposed to be guarding.

But it was too late.

Demos was already rolling free from beneath the carriage. And when he threw the precious artifact, Gwynara's hand was already in the air, waiting to catch it.

The moment she slipped the amulet over her head, Regner's remaining guards went up in flames.

MADINIA

Rythos's brother ordered us to be chained in his dungeon. I sneered at him, my palms heating, even as my heart tripped in my chest. I could take out a few of the guards. Perhaps even Brevan himself, depending on his power. But they would kill us directly after.

Still, perhaps that was a better end than one that involved fading away in his dungeon until war found this island and Regner's soldiers arrived to kill whoever was left.

"Madinia," Rythos said.

I looked at him. The expression on his face urged me to cooperate. "Use your power," I said.

"He's out." Brevan's expression was terrible as he watched the flames burn in my hands. "If not yet, then he will be soon. I suggest you think very, very carefully."

My flames burned higher. "Perhaps you are the one who should think carefully."

One of the guards took a step forward, his eyes intent. Rythos caught my wrist. "Please, Madinia."

Fury burned through me, hotter than the flames in my hands. "You're seriously going to let him lock us away?"

Rythos's jaw tightened. "I'm going to trust that my brother will eventually begin to think logically."

The brother in question gave him a cool smile.

I gave him my most poisonous smile in return. "Something tells me he wasn't born with that ability."

Brevan's smile disappeared.

"Walk," he said. "Or my guards will make you."

I gave Rythos one more look. He just stared me down.

I didn't trust easily. And ignoring every single instinct roaring at me to flee this island…

It could be the biggest mistake of my life.

But if Rythos was convincing us to cooperate with his brother, he must have some kind of plan. So, I walked.

I'd expected a cell like the ones I'd heard about beneath Regner's castle. And I was relatively sure such a dungeon could be found on this island. But Rythos's station clearly entitled him to a slightly more tolerable cell. And I was pushed inside the cell with him.

Approximately twenty footspans wide and long, it contained two beds, a couple of wooden chairs and a table near the bars of the cell, and a room divider that could be dragged open, separating the beds for some semblance of privacy—at least from each other. A tiny bathing room, also divided near the back of the room. One of Brevan's guards leered at me in a way that warned me I wouldn't be receiving much of that privacy.

"Will you at least listen to what we have to say?" Rythos demanded as the cell clanked shut behind us.

Brevan studied Rythos. And there was something disturbing in his gaze. This was the kind of fae I'd been warned about, even as a child. Remote, emotionless, cruel. His eyes were chillingly blank.

"No," he said. "I don't believe I will."

Rythos's mouth fell open, and understanding dawned in his eyes. I wanted to punch him in the throat. He'd believed his brother would listen if only he played along and allowed him to lock us down here.

"You're going to die," I said.

Brevan's gaze flicked to me. "I suggest you refrain from threatening me."

"Oh, *I'm* not going to do it." Although I was fantasizing about doing exactly that. The bars on this cage had tamped down my magic until I could barely feel a single ember. "Your coward father has brought this upon himself, but all of you will pay for it."

Brevan glanced at Rythos once more.

"Brother," Rythos said hoarsely. "Please."

Brevan turned and walked away.

23

THE QUEEN

No matter the man, and no matter his loyalties, eventually, he could always be bribed, blackmailed, or beguiled.

The guard on my tent was no different.

He was young, with a sparse beard and a voice that broke when I called to him hours after the Bloodthirsty Prince had ordered me to be chained in this tent.

"Yes…your…Your Majesty?"

I offered him a gentle smile, gesturing to the chains on my wrists. "Surely there would be no harm in allowing me a brief walk?"

He swallowed, glancing around. "I'll have to ask my superior, Your Majesty."

I gave him a nod filled with sorrow and forced a blush to rise to my face. "At the very least…I need to take care of some personal needs."

His blush matched my own.

A hybrid soldier blushing like a nervous bride. I barely suppressed an eye roll.

"Of course, Your Majesty."

His large hands shook as he pulled out the key, unlocking the heavy manacles from one of my hands. With an apologetic glance, he ensured the other manacle stayed clamped around my left wrist, the chain dangling free.

I didn't say a word. Although I itched to order somebody to slit his throat.

Small steps.

I couldn't use my power with the fae iron encircling my wrists. But at the very least, I could determine which tent they were keeping Prisca's cousin in.

I'd watched the fight between them. One of Lorian's fae lackeys had ordered a guard to watch me, but I'd still seen the way Prisca had wrestled and rolled across that arena in order to prove herself worthy of the hybrid crown.

Meanwhile, the Bloodthirsty Prince had once again lived up to his name.

Prisca had looked utterly ridiculous, standing in that arena, dressed in servants' clothes, her face pale, hands covered in blood. And yet the hybrids had knelt to her.

But what choice had they had? Zathrian had been bleeding out behind her.

The hybrid heir was proving herself to be little more than a savage—as I'd always known.

"This way, Your Majesty."

I ignored the sneers as the guard led me to the latrine. My cheeks burned with fury as I took care of business like an animal, the guard standing several footspans away, gazing at the sky, his cheeks red.

If I had been born a man, with a man's strength, I could have used the chain dangling from this heavy manacle to strangle him.

Instead, I delicately cleared my throat, allowed him to lead me to a station to wash my hands, and gazed up at him with wide eyes.

"Please...my legs are cramped. Would you be so kind as to escort me on a short walk?"

He hesitated, glancing around. After a long moment, he caught the other end of my chain, holding it in his hand.

Like. A. Leash.

"I suppose that would be okay," he said with a decisive nod.

I imagined his head rolling free of his body.

"Thank you," I cooed.

I let him choose the route, gazing up at him as if I had no true destination in mind and simply wanted to stretch my legs. "What is your name?"

"Previs, Your Majesty."

"My name is Kaliera."

His blush traveled from his neck up into his cheeks. I glanced around. "This camp seems well organized."

"It is." He didn't say anything else, his gaze constantly scanning for higher-ranking soldiers. It was clear I wouldn't be getting any further information out of him until later.

But something far more important had caught my eye.

Several rows of tents to our left stood one of the fae...Galon.

He said a few words to a hybrid soldier, who gazed up at him like a dog hoping for a treat from its owner.

The hybrid soldier nodded, replying with a few words of his own. And as Galon stalked away, the hybrid soldier stayed posted outside the tent, his hand on his sword.

I ducked my head as Galon disappeared.

My mind was racing as Previs led me back to my tent, again chaining me to the thick, fae-iron pole shoved deep into the earth.

This wasn't over yet.

I simply needed to talk to Zathrian.

MADINIA

It had been two days. I only knew this because our cell was close to the main, locked door. And each time the guards brought our meals, I could catch a single glimpse of freedom when they opened that door.

So far, they weren't attempting to confuse us by giving us meals at strange times.

Rythos said little. I was the one who paced for hours. The one who wrung my hands, left my meals uneaten, and gulped for air—my chest so tight it felt as if I couldn't get a full breath.

"You should try to eat something," Rythos said when the next meal was delivered.

My stomach twisted, and I gazed at the bread, fruit, cheese, and sweet cakes that had been brought for us.

Royals.

Something told me Prisca hadn't eaten like this when she'd been captured by Regner's men.

Still, she'd at least been given chicken bones to aid her escape. Our cell lock could only be opened by a specific key, infused with magic. I knew because I'd questioned Rythos relentlessly about potential escape routes.

He cleared his throat, and I whirled to find him gazing expectantly at me. He nodded toward the food.

I barely resisted the urge to throw it at him.

"Perhaps you shouldn't have stopped me from getting us out of here," I snapped.

Rythos scowled at me. "The guard who stepped forward has a unique form of magic. He would have drained your strength until you were unable to walk properly."

I shuddered at the thought.

Then I turned to pace some more.

"They could be dead," I said conversationally. "All of them. They'll die, waiting for us to arrive with Arslan ships. Their last thoughts will be wondering where we are—"

"Enough!" Rythos roared, jumping to his feet.

I swept up the cheese knife and held it tightly in my hand, refusing to allow that hand to shake. I might not be able to access my power, but I would—

Rythos's lips twitched.

Disgusted, I threw the cheese knife back onto the table.

"What is your plan?"

"My brother is going to return," Rythos said calmly. "And I will talk some sense into him. He's a logical man."

"That's your plan?" Expecting his brother to be logical was the very reason we were in this cell.

He met my gaze, and fury burned in his eyes. "What would you like me to say, Madinia? I fucked up. And everyone we love is going to pay the price. Well, everyone *I* love. You don't care about anyone but yourself."

His words took the air from my lungs more effectively than a punch in the gut.

Rythos's expression immediately turned contrite. "I'm sorry. That was out of line. And entirely untrue. I don't even know why I said it."

Ignoring him, I walked over to my bed and lay on my back, gazing up at the ceiling as I began to rebuild my defenses.

And if my eyes burned like they were on fire, that was no one's business but my own.

ASINIA

Traveling through Eprotha sent chills along my skin.

The regiments that we'd been so careful to avoid...

They were no longer there.

Regner had moved his army. Likely, they were already marching south into Gromalia.

All we could do was hope Rekja's army could hold them off. And that by the time we reached our own army, we would be able to meet them.

If Herne and his rebels would join our numbers as promised. If Conreth would bring more fae from his lands. If Pris and Lorian and the others could use Daharak's ships as planned to transport as many of the hybrids as possible to meet us.

If. If. If.

Demos had written to Vicer, ordering Finley to be arrested, making it clear that he expected him to be treated with care and respect. Vicer was a good man, and he would ensure Finley wasn't targeted by anyone looking for revenge.

I'd been so, so sure that Demos was wrong about Finley being the one to replicate the amulet. There *had* to be someone else with a similar power.

But when we received a message back, stating that Finley was nowhere to be seen, I couldn't deny it any longer. Three days later, we received another message. Finley had been found walking north along one of the main merchant roads and was finally arrested by our people.

Even more worryingly, Vicer's message confirmed he hadn't yet reached the Asric Pass—even though the small battalion sent by Prisca and Demos had already eliminated the soldiers Regner had positioned ready to ambush any hybrids who'd attempted the pass. The three thousand hybrids Prisca had sent with Vicer had been plagued by bad luck, slowing them down significantly. Apparently, anything that could have gone wrong had. While Vicer had previously created a temporary camp at the entrance to the pass, it was not going to be well supplied enough for the number of hybrids who would now be arriving every day. The hybrids needed to arrive with food, tents, and, of course, weapons.

By the time we met Telean in the tiny village we'd agreed upon, she was practically vibrating with impatience.

All of us had been more than ready to enjoy a warm meal that wasn't cooked over a fire. But I'd mostly been too on edge to enjoy it. Even knowing that Regner had moved his armies elsewhere, I was aware there was always the chance that one of the humans here would recognize one of us and turn us in.

But Telean had chosen this village well. I'd already heard rumblings about Regner's lies, and the sanctuary had been turned to ash. There were no signs of any guards, assessors, or priestesses.

We stayed one night in the village, and despite my anxiety, I fell into a sleep so deep, when Gwynara woke me the next morning, I blinked at her for so long, she laughed at me.

We continued traveling. Demos wore the amulet around his neck, and the sight of it had at least drawn the ghost of a smile from Telean. But all of us were more than ready to meet up with Prisca and the others.

Three days later, Telean demanded we find a sanctuary.

"A sanctuary?" I asked. "Why?"

"That is my own business." She frowned at me.

"Many of them have been burned," Demos muttered, adjusting one of his stirrups.

"Not all of them."

"If they're not burned, it's likely because they are guarded," he countered, rounding his horse to check the other stirrup.

"I know how to avoid drawing attention," she snapped.

I opened my mouth, and she leveled me with a hard

stare. "We are about to march into battle. If I wish to speak to the gods, that is my right."

The likelihood of Demos allowing Telean to march into battle was about the same as me learning to fly. I glanced at Demos in time to catch the tiny smile playing around his mouth.

"I hadn't realized you'd become so pious recently." Demos arched one eyebrow.

Telean just stared at him until his smile became a full-fledged grin. "We'll find you a sanctuary, aunt." Something in my chest relaxed. I hadn't seen that grin for too long.

As promised, Demos found her a sanctuary. My breaths were strained and shallow as Demos and I huddled in the forest near the sanctuary, watching as Telean approached. This village was larger than most, and Regner's guards had a strong hold on the people here. They shuffled around, eyes darting as they went about their day, not daring to do anything that would draw the wrong kind of attention.

It was a village of women and children, with most of the men conscripted for Regner's war.

Horrison had declared Telean's excursion an unnecessary risk and refused to have any part in it. He wasn't wrong. Firion and Brinlor were arranging for fresh horses so we could travel more quickly, while Elysanth was likely in the nearest tavern.

We'd been forced to leave her sister with human healers in Eprotha. Demos knew they were loyal, but there was no way Amalra would have survived long enough for us to get her to a fae or hybrid healer.

The guard who'd stabbed her sister had used fae iron. Demos had told Elysanth to stay with Amalra, but she'd refused, stating that her sister would want her to get their vengeance.

Demos glanced at me, and his eyes dropped to my mouth. This was the first time we'd been alone in days. At night, I slept next to Gwynara, while he occasionally caught a few hours' sleep and then insisted on staying up as sentry.

I...missed him. We'd spent most of our days together in Herne's camp, and I missed those long walks. Missed making plans for the camp. Missed watching him look at me the way he sometimes did...

Focus. I had to focus. The guards near the sanctuary looked bored. My arrow was already nocked, and I aimed directly at the guard closest to Telean.

But they both ignored her as she shuffled through the wide wooden doors. I blew out a breath.

"Of all the times for my aunt to find her faith," Demos muttered.

"I'm sure plenty of people find their faith during war."

He sent me an amused look. "Have you found yours?"

"No," I said immediately. "You?"

Demos seemed to think about it. "I've never had a problem believing in the gods. I just struggle to believe their existence is of any benefit to us."

Despite my insistence that I hadn't found any kind of faith, I found myself glancing around, as if the gods could hear us and were about to strike us down. Demos shifted closer, lifting my arm to study a bruise near my elbow. The feel of his large, calloused hand on my skin made anticipation shiver through me. Made my heart race and my chest warm. When he released my arm, I instantly craved his touch once more.

Telean stayed in the sanctuary for a long time. Long enough that I had to fight with the voice in my mind. The voice that insisted some kind of harm had come to her. Already, Demos was tense, likely planning how we would kill the guards. His gaze remained pinned to the doors, as if willing his aunt to walk out.

A flap of wings sounded above my head. I froze. A pigeon was fluttering down from the sky, directly toward where we were hidden.

Demos let out a string of low, violent curses. But we were trapped. One of the guards was frowning, watching the pigeon dart toward us.

As long as there weren't any wards blocking our location from them, the fae-trained birds could find us with their own strange magic. Unfortunately, they had no understanding of the importance of subtlety. And anyone watching a pigeon fly purposefully toward a clump of bushes on the edge of a forest near a sanctuary—which was being guarded due to a number of attacks on others just like it...

I wasn't a warder.

Neither was Demos.

But I wouldn't allow Telean to die here.

The guard angled his head.

And Telean stepped out of the door.

The guard was still looking at us. My hand tightened

on my crossbow, and I aimed at his throat. Telean summed up the situation with a mere sweep of her gaze.

And then she clutched her chest, dropping to her knees.

"Why, why, why?" she wailed.

Every hair on my body stood up, as if Lorian had directed his power straight into me.

"What do I do?" I gritted out.

Demos was silent. I pulled back the string of my crossbow. "Demos!" I hissed. "Do I shoot?"

"Hold."

His tone was as unyielding as the rock I was balancing on.

The guards were watching Telean. She babbled something about her lost daughter. About the evil hybrids and the wicked fae.

The first guard glanced our way once more. But Demos was clutching the pigeon in his hand. I barely breathed.

"Get up," one of the guards snarled. The other guard said something too low for me to hear, but I could hear his mocking laugh. And that laugh told me Telean's distraction had worked.

She staggered to her feet, wiping her face with her hands. And then she stumbled off in the opposite direction from us, still weaving unsteadily on her feet. My hands shook at how close we had just come to fighting for our lives.

Demos and I slowly melted back into the forest. Both of us looked down at the pigeon in his hand.

He nodded, and I untied the message from its tiny

leg, unrolling it. Demos leaned close, and I couldn't help but breathe in the scent of him.

The message was from Rekja. Our generals had been moving our own army north. And Rekja's regiment had managed to push Regner's soldiers out of Gromalia. This war would be fought in Eprotha and not Gromalia.

I grinned, raising my gaze to Demos's.

But he wasn't smiling. Instead, a muscle ticked in his cheek, and his eyes were hard. "It doesn't make sense," he said, and his tone made a ball of dread expand throughout my gut. "It just doesn't make sense."

24

PRISCA

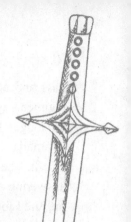

Asinia and Demos had found the amulet. From the tone of Asinia's letter, it had been even more difficult than expected. But it provided all of us with some much-needed hope.

We spent several days understanding everything we could about the army that would now fight for us. Each morning, Lorian, Galon, and Marth trained with them, analyzing the four thousand soldiers who made up our vanguard, the three thousand archers, the siege unit, and the remaining foot soldiers of the infantry.

In the afternoons, we learned logistics. According to Orivan, the elders had ensured that this army was well supplied and organized before allowing Zathrian to take control.

Within three days, we would be moving south, prepared to attack Regner's army from the north, while Daharak attacked from the sea and the fae, hybrids, and Gromalians marched through Gromalia. She had left to meet with her captains and solidify their own orders, leaving us the ship we'd arrived on.

It would take weeks to move this many soldiers all the way through the Normathe

Pass and across Eprotha. But according to Asinia, the regiments we would have fought on our way south were no longer there, having already begun marching into Gromalia.

In the morning, I was sitting outside our tent, answering Asinia's message. Some sense made me look up, and I found Lorian prowling toward me.

It must have been later than I'd expected.

"How was training?"

"They're in good shape. Galon's expecting you in an hour."

I nodded. "Any news from the Arslan?"

As expected, he shook his head.

Our messages to Rythos and Madinia either weren't being delivered, or both of them were in serious trouble. Lorian's jaw clenched. Panic wound through my gut.

Marth had stopped sleeping. He'd practically begged Lorian to send him after Rythos. But if his people had turned on them, or if Regner had set up some kind of trap, Marth would fall into it too.

I held up my most recent message. "Conreth is hoping to march soon. Apparently, he had some disputes with territory wardens that needed to be resolved in order to get the soldiers he needed."

As Lorian's skin sparked and his eyes turned half wild, I was glad none of those wardens was here at this moment.

If they were the reason Conreth's army didn't make it in time...

Marth strode toward us. Sweat dripped down his face, and he wiped at it with the back of his arm.

"Your cousin wants to speak with you. He says he has information you need to hear."

Zathrian had lived. The healers had gotten to him in time. I didn't know what I would do with my cousin. Perhaps I was merely prolonging the inevitable—and the best thing for all of us would be for him to die. Soon.

But...

"Do better than me, cousin. Be the ruler I wished I could be. Bring our people home."

I sighed. I was once again attributing good qualities to him that he didn't actually have.

Zathrian knew it was over. He knew he would never be king. Talking to him was like handling an angry viper and expecting it not to strike.

"What do you think he wants?"

Marth shrugged. "Whatever it is, I'm happy to torture that information out of him."

Lorian leaned close. "You don't need to see him, wildcat. I know it hurts you."

If Zathrian truly did have information that would help us win this war, I had to talk to him. If he was playing with me, so be it.

"I'll do it."

Lorian's eyes glittered. "I'll come with you."

"No. I'll talk to him alone."

I knew enough about powerful men to know their egos only became larger when men with even more power were around. Zathrian would be more likely to let something important slip if I poked at him, while Lorian's presence would either enrage him or turn him sullen. And...some part of me needed to face Zathrian alone.

Or perhaps it was simply because I knew Lorian wanted Zathrian dead almost as much as he'd wanted Eadric to die.

And I couldn't blame him.

Lorian studied my face. Whatever he saw there made him give me a nod.

When Galon noticed I was heading toward Zathrian's tent, he jerked his head at the soldier currently standing guard and took his place. If Galon was tired, there was no sign of it on his face. I might have thought it was overkill having one of our strongest fae warriors guarding a man who was clamped in the same fae irons I'd once worn, but clearly, Galon wasn't taking any chances.

He frowned. "Are you..."

I nodded. "I'm fine."

He glanced past me, as if searching for Lorian, and I shrugged. "I need to do this alone."

"I don't like it."

"I'll call if I need anything." My tone was unyielding. Galon heaved a sigh, but he nodded.

"Cousin," Zathrian said when I stepped inside.

They'd chained him to a thick metal pole in the ground. I knew without looking that it would be made of fae iron, as would the chains leading to the heavy manacles around his wrists.

My own wrists ached at the sight.

I met his gaze. "What do you want?"

His nostrils flared, and he gave me an impatient look. For a single moment, he reminded me so much of Demos, I had to glance away.

The two men didn't look alike. Demos had dark hair

and amber eyes, while Zathrian was blond with blue eyes. Demos had a larger build, while Zathrian looked like he could run for days.

But some of their mannerisms were so similar...

"You may not believe me, but I have our people's best interests at heart."

I choked out a laugh. "Is that why you allied with Regner?"

He gave me a patronizing sneer that made me want to reach for my knife. "We both know I was planning to turn on him when the time was right."

"But first, you'd wipe out the fae and any hybrids who didn't cooperate?"

Silence. I shook my head. "If you'd succeeded when we brought down the barrier, Regner would now be as powerful as a god. What were you planning to do then, Zathrian? How would you have stopped him?"

This time, he was the one to glance away. I let out a bitter laugh, and his eyes sliced to mine. "You want to know the truth? The truth is, I knew we didn't have a chance of killing Regner. My entire plan was to wait until he was busy killing the fae and get as many people back to our kingdom as I could."

I stared at him, stunned. "Then what? You'd raise the wards and no one could ever leave? And anyone who didn't make it would be stuck here, waiting to be slaughtered?"

"It wasn't a perfect plan," he ground out. "But if the elders had cooperated, I would have ensured they helped me get as many hybrids home as possible while Regner was distracted. As long as he thought I was allying with him, he didn't see me as a threat."

"It wasn't just the fae he would kill, though, was it? I would also conveniently end up dead, and so would Demos—ending anyone who could challenge you for the throne. And anyone who fought under our banner would die on this continent too."

His mouth tightened. "Yes," he conceded. "That was my plan."

"Great." Stepping back, I glanced around his tent. "I hope it was worth it."

"You're not listening, Nelayra," he snarled when I backed up a step toward the entrance. And then he frowned. "Where is your power?"

The question was so unexpected, I barely hid my flinch. But his eyes widened.

I cleared my throat. "I'm not sure what you're talking about."

"My power allows me to feel time magic in order to…nullify it. And yet I never felt your power when you arrived…" The back of my neck itched at the way his voice trailed off.

"It's gone." There was no point in lying. My allies knew I couldn't access my power. And soon every hybrid here would too.

"It's *gone*?" He let out a choked sound somewhere between amusement and disgust.

"Yes. Likely because of what I did when…"

"When I helped kill your fae mate."

"Yes." I studied Zathrian's face. I wasn't sure what I was looking for. Whatever it was, I didn't find it.

He was silent for a long moment. "This was the

biggest logic flaw in Regner's own lies, you know."

"What do you mean?"

"The idea that the gods could take our power—even if we offered it."

I sat in the wooden chair next to the tent entrance. "I don't understand."

"The gods are bound by their own laws, just as we are." He gave me another one of his disparaging looks. "Of course, since you were raised human, you only interacted with those with far more limited life-spans, which meant they were easily misled by Regner's lies. But the gods can't take that which they have given."

He was playing with me. But some part of me couldn't help but ask, "If the gods can't take my power, then where did it go?"

"I didn't say they can't hide magic. They can, after all, play with us in all kinds of diabolical ways." He raised his chained hands. "As this experience has already proven," he said bitterly.

I rolled my eyes. "Yes, *you* are the true victim in this war. You're saying the gods hid my magic from me?"

"I'm saying that is the most they could do. But that which can be hidden can also be found. Perhaps you didn't truly want to find it. Or perhaps you just didn't try hard enough."

My stomach twisted, tiny spots appearing before my eyes. "I don't believe you."

He shrugged. "You don't have to. But you know what I think? I think you woke up without your power, and you subconsciously latched on to that as the punishment the gods gave you for turning back time those few seconds.

Some part of you was relieved at the thought that the loss of your power was your punishment. Because it meant your punishment wouldn't involve losing anyone else you loved in this war."

Bile crawled up my throat. Stumbling to my feet, I turned to go.

"Wait."

I shook my head. Behind me, his words came faster.

"Yes, I might have gotten tangled in my own desperate need to rule. Yes, I may have almost cost you the man you love. And I'm sure you hate me for that. But you have to listen. For our people." His voice was desperate now, cracking on the last word.

Slowly, I turned. "You have two minutes."

And he began to speak.

Realization trickled into me. Slowly, my limbs became heavy, as if the dread had seeped into them. It felt like I was sleepwalking from his tent. Distantly, I heard Galon's voice. But all I could think about was getting to Lorian.

And then he was there. His huge body surrounded mine, pulling me into his arms.

"What happened?" he rumbled.

I gave myself a single moment to press my head to his chest, soaking in some of his strength.

"It was a trick," I whispered. My eyes met Lorian's, "Regner moved his forces down into Gromalia and let our spies learn of his weapon. He wanted us to think he was attacking on all fronts to remove our wards, so we would split our attention. In reality, he was readying his armies, gathering his monsters, moving the last amulet to the capital—" My voice broke.

Lorian's face turned stark. It was as if even those dark-green eyes lost some of their color.

"He's going to the pass." His voice was hoarse as he made the connection. "He's going to kill all of the hybrids who are attempting to get back to Lyrinore."

Sickness rose, clawing at my throat. I panted through it. "Anyone who can't fight. Women with young children. The sick. The old. He's going to murder them all."

The horror of it engulfed me. Regner would deal a blow that would not only kill our most vulnerable—the people we'd sworn to keep safe—but...how would our soldiers find the strength to fight, knowing they had lost everyone they loved?

"Do you believe Zathrian?"

"In this? I do. He said...he said something strange has been happening in the sea. What if...what if Regner's using the same magic that hid his fleet from Daharak to get his people into position?"

Lorian cursed, rubbing a hand over his face. "We need to check," he said. "Let's get messages out to our spies immediately. While we're waiting to hear back, we need to warn the others. But Prisca...there's not enough time."

My throat was so parched, I could barely speak. "Asinia, Demos, Telean...they need to know. We need to tell them to get to the Asric Pass. The soldiers guarding our people will be expecting Regner to have left a regiment or two to cut them off. They won't be prepared to meet all of his forces. We need to get a message to Tymriel and the rest of the elders as well. If they truly want to help our people, this is their chance."

Lorian pulled me along suddenly, until we were stepping into one of the central tents. A large map had been hung on one of the canvas walls, and I stared at the Asric Pass. I should have sent more soldiers. Why hadn't I sent more?

Lorian pointed at the center of Eprotha—and the regiments Regner had stationed there. "We'd thought they were going to move south." He ran his finger toward the fae lands. "But they'll attack from behind." He shifted his finger to the entrance to the Asric Pass, between Eprotha and the fae lands. "I kept wondering what Regner was waiting for. Now we know. He was waiting for our order to evacuate. When our people would be moving toward the pass."

My head spun. Thousands of our most vulnerable, along with a third of our army...they would be trapped between Regner's forces.

"Vicer only took three thousand hybrid soldiers to help with the evacuation."

"Regner will position more soldiers on the coast."

"Yes," I said. "As soon as he kills us, his plan is to use the ships he has kept hidden to invade the hybrid kingdom once again, wiping out every single hybrid still alive."

LORIAN

Orivan was grim. Silent. We'd immediately told him what Regner was planning, and he stood, hands on his hips as he contemplated the hybrids going about their day around us. Prisca looked shellshocked, as if she was unable to reconcile what she had just learned. I couldn't blame her. Even after everything I'd seen and done, some part of me refused to believe the extent of the evil Regner had committed.

I squeezed her hand. "I want to find the hags. They allowed your cousin to set up his camp this close to their territory for a reason."

And the stone women were known to be close to the dead. There was a chance one of them could help reverse whatever was happening to me.

As much as I wanted to be able to see Cavis, I couldn't afford to be distracted by the death I had wielded across this continent. Not with Prisca surrounded by those who could prove to be enemies. If Cavis were here, he would urge me to do whatever it took to keep her safe, just as he had done for his own wife and child.

Her gaze darted across my face. I couldn't tell her about the hags' connection to the dead. Not in front of Orivan. But after a long moment, she nodded. "Do you want me to come with you?"

Yes. I wanted her with me every second of every day, with a ferocity that occasionally disconcerted me, even now.

But the dark circles beneath her eyes contrasted concerningly with the wan appearance of her skin. She was so pale, it cut at something inside me.

"Stay here, wildcat." I glanced at Galon, who nodded at me. "Try to get some rest. I won't be long."

She frowned, her teeth worrying at her lower lip. But she didn't argue. That, more than anything, encouraged me to hurry. If she wasn't resting by the time I returned, I'd haul her to our tent myself.

"I'm coming with you," Marth said.

I frowned, but Galon could more than handle anyone who attempted to strike at Prisca. And she had just proven she could more than handle them herself, even without her power.

Orivan arranged for a couple of horses for us.

"The hags are dangerous," he said as we walked toward the camp's stables. "Allow me to send a few of my best men with you."

Marth snorted—likely at the idea that I needed the protection of hybrid soldiers. I sent him a killing look.

"We can handle the hags. Thank you."

Surprise flickered in Orivan's eyes, making it clear he hadn't expected basic manners from the Bloodthirsty Prince. But within a few minutes, we were mounting a couple of saddled mares and heading back toward the Cursed City. There was a chill in the air this close to the mountains, and my neck itched from the feeling of thousands of eyes watching us leave.

We rode in silence for a while. Marth scowled into the distance. He'd been deeply unhappy for a long time now. And it was time to talk about it.

My neck itched some more.

"Will Eadric's and Soltor's deaths be enough?" I asked him. "Will Regner's?"

He didn't ask me what I was talking about. He knew. And he didn't lie to me either.

"No. It will never be enough."

"Because you blame yourself."

He shrugged, refusing to look at me. My temper stirred.

"I've seen Cavis," I bit out. I hadn't told Galon this yet. It was a conversation I'd wanted to have when we were somewhere quiet. Somewhere we could mourn. But Marth needed to know now.

Slowly, Marth turned his head. And his eyes were a wasteland.

"I'm not jesting," I snarled. "You know I would never jest about this."

Understanding dawned across his face. Even at his most depressed, Marth was quick. "Because you died. And Prisca brought you back."

"I didn't just die. I shattered. My heart didn't just stop, it ceased existing completely. Perhaps that is why I'm now seeing and hearing the dead. Or perhaps it is because Prisca enraged the gods by her actions, and this is the consequence."

Marth gazed at me hungrily. "Tell me."

"I heard his voice at first. The night you were stabbed in Sorlithia." I scowled at the reminder. "And then the day I married Prisca, he stood next to us briefly."

Marth looked away, but not before I caught the wetness in his eyes.

"He was mostly focused on Prisca. But he looked at you. And he smiled that crooked smile. You know the one."

Marth pressed his lips together and nodded, still staring straight ahead. I steered my horse around a chunk of stone lying on the trail. We were already close to the city.

"He didn't say a word about blaming you. He didn't frown or scowl. He wore that expression. Half impatient, half amused. It was the same look he wore each time you were late to meet us because you were rolling out of some woman's bed."

Marth's shoulders slumped.

"And then on my wedding night." I wouldn't tell him all of it. That was for me. "I was haunted by the dead. Cavis helped me come to terms with my actions. And that night, after Prisca went to sleep, he came once more." I leveled Marth with a stare. "Cavis doesn't forgive you," I said, and his shoulders tightened once more. "Because there's nothing to forgive. I'm not sure why he hasn't moved on to whatever comes next, but it's not because he needs anything from you except for you to stop blaming yourself. You do him a disservice when you reduce his sacrifice to something you could have prevented."

Marth looked at me now. And his eyes were wet. "I don't know how to move on. I don't—"

"You start by mourning Cavis. You've been so busy blaming yourself for his death, you haven't celebrated his life or come to terms with the fact that it has ended. There's only one thing he wants from you. One day, when this is all over, he wants you to teach Piperia how to skip stones. The way he taught you all those years ago."

His lips tightened, but he nodded.

Hopefully he would think about what I had said. It was all I could do.

Besides, we'd reached the entrance of the Cursed City.

The last time we were here, all four of us had bargained with the stone hags for a special kind of moss that would help with our plans to sneak into Regner's castle. Nothing much had changed. For the Cursed City, at least.

Once a grand capital, it was now reduced to a haunting vista of decay and desolation. I'd heard of the majestic buildings that had once stood here, the lively streets and prosperous people. Now, it was nothing more than a wreckage of crumbled ruins, the skeletons of buildings jutting from the ground like broken bones.

Bones and wild foliage that had reclaimed the land, creeping over much of the fallen stone. The air was heavy with dust still, and a mournful wind whispered through the remnants of the city. I would die before I admitted it to Marth, but this place had always made the hair on my arms stand up.

The hags knew we were here. They always knew. Unlike our last visit, they didn't play games.

They appeared from the ruins, their gray skin matching the stone that remained as they lumbered toward us. Just as before, one of them wore a crown made of tourmaline.

Beneath me, my horse shifted uneasily as I surveyed the hag. This was not the same queen I'd originally bargained with.

Because that queen was standing to our left, screaming soundlessly.

"You killed the one who previously wore that crown," I said, my gaze lingering on the tourmaline

"She broke her word." The hag turned her face to glance at one of the others, and I recognized her then. This was the one who'd whispered into the queen's ear when she'd resorted to extortion at the last moment during our deal. It was this stone hag who'd convinced the queen to change her mind and honor the original deal.

"And were you involved with the plan to tell Regner who he was?" Marth asked.

"No. When I learned of her duplicity, I challenged her for the crown."

"And why would you do that?"

The tourmaline in her crown glinted as she angled her head in that slow way the hags moved.

"Because I hear the stones lying in the rivers. The stones used to cobble streets and build homes. I hear the whispers from the stone you call trowth, and I hear the stones used to build castles and armories across this continent."

"You hear our messages?" Irritation flickered through me. Irritation, and something darker. Something that made the hag blink at me, an expression that might have been fear slipping across her gray face. I'd often wondered at the hags' abilities to somehow know exactly what it was that a bargainer was looking for before they approached them. But knowing they'd been listening to everything our people said while using trowth stones…

Suddenly, they'd become much, much more of a threat.

"Only one who wears this crown may listen," she said quickly. "And I know only what the stones choose to pass along to me. There are two reasons why you have come here today."

"Yes."

"You can see the dead."

I nodded.

"And even though you have blocked those who wish you harm, you still want to know how to make it stop."

Several hags muttered. Marth's horse shifted to the left, and I caught Marth glowering at them.

"They merely wonder why you would reject such a gift," the queen said.

"For the most part, it is not a gift. The dead appear without warning, and they seem as alive as you and I. They're…a distraction."

That was an understatement.

"There is one who can remove that power from you," she said. "One day, he will come to you for help. But it will not be for many years. In the meantime, I give you this advice… The dead have only the power you give them."

Marth gave a slow clap. "How profound." The hag queen ignored him.

I buried the disappointment that clawed at me. As soon as Cavis found his peace, I would find a way to reverse this curse. And if not, I would live with it. In the meantime, we had a war to win.

"And Regner?" I asked.

"The human king will attack your most vulnerable."

"Yes."

"You want to know his plans."

"Yes."

"Then let us bargain."

25

THE QUEEN

It took time to move an entire war camp. Still, the hybrids were working quickly, the noise rising to a crescendo throughout the day as soldiers called to one another, horses and carts clattering past my tent. From the constant sound of rustling around me, it was clear some of the other tents were already being packed away.

I would likely only have one chance to speak to Zathrian. Once we left this place, we were marching to battle. Prisca leaving her cousin alive was foolish but entirely expected. And she would live to regret her mercy.

Thankfully, Previs was still the posted guard outside my tent during the day. At night, another guard took over—a grim-faced, gruff, older hybrid with a gray speckled beard who refused to even acknowledge me.

Previs had continued to lead me to the latrine and had even taken me to stretch my legs purely for some exercise. At one point, Marth had stomped over, leveling the guard with a cold look.

"What are you doing?"

"T-taking her to the latrine."

Marth's cold eyes had met mine. "I'm

watching you."

I'd angled my head, looking back coolly. When I didn't reply, he snorted, stalking away.

But the other soldiers grew used to seeing me walking through the camp, Previs by my side.

Twice now, we'd walked directly past the tent I was sure was holding Zathrian. Different guards had been posted outside, and all of them had looked at me as if I were a snake in the grass.

The bare bones of a plan came to mind.

Previs had grown lax, unlocking the manacles from my wrists and leaving them behind entirely. I'd made a point of letting him see the chafing and bruises they had caused when we'd walked a day earlier, wincing as I'd stroked the tender skin. And I'd kept my arm wound through his while we strolled, as if we were two friends taking a walk in a garden.

The idiot seemed to like that.

Fae iron didn't affect humans the same way it did hybrids and fae. So, while the manacles were heavy and unwieldy, they didn't dampen my power. The tiny amount of magic available to me remained entirely consistent.

But I could work with that.

As far as Previs was concerned, I had the smallest bladder in four kingdoms. But I needed each walk to plan my distraction. And he seemed more than happy to lead me to the latrine—as opposed to standing outside my tent in the sun.

All I needed was a simple diversion. For two days now, I'd been waiting for the tiniest distraction. Something I could do to draw the soldiers' attention.

Each time we took our little walk, my gaze darted in every direction, my hold on Previs's arm tightening until he cast me a concerned glance.

Panic began to burn a hole in my chest. I was running out of time. A flurry of activity had transformed the orderly encampment into organized chaos. The large command tent was already coming down, soldiers working in unison to fold heavy canvas and disassemble the supporting frames.

Most of the tents around us were being collapsed, each piece of canvas, every peg and pole were being efficiently packed, the hybrid soldiers' movements precise. Bedrolls and personal belongings were being rolled up and stowed in packs, while tents and other supplies were loaded onto waiting carts. Soldiers yelled orders at one another, their booming voices carrying over the clanking of equipment and the rustle of canvas.

Of course, no one had seen fit to tell me when we would be marching. But it was evident that soon, we would be on the move, and I would have no other opportunity to put my own plans into place.

"Your Majesty?"

I turned to offer Previs a gentle smile, keeping my gaze low so he wouldn't see the fury that likely burned across my face.

Someone began cursing roughly. I lifted my head.

A soldier had been leading his horse toward the stables. It was easy to see what had happened, a tent flap broken free, flying in the wind.

As I watched, the horse threw its head so hard, it yanked its lead rope from the soldier walking with it.

A hoof made contact with the soldier's shoulder as it reared, sending the soldier flying. The horse bolted toward us, careening down the row of tents.

The yelling turned to panicked shouts. Which turned to curses and—in one case—a high-pitched scream.

Previs attempted to pull me to the right. I slipped my arm free and dove to the left. And then I rolled.

I wouldn't get another chance like this. This was a distraction provided by the gods themselves. Proof that my planned path was one that they approved of.

At one point, the hybrids had swapped my filthy gown for some soldier's castoffs. I'd been thoroughly disgusted at being forced to walk around dressed in long pants and a tunic. Now, I more than appreciated the fact that I wasn't forced to contend with all that fabric while crawling through the gap between two tents.

The horse hadn't yet been caught, but it would be soon. And those soldiers would turn their attention to the fact that I was missing.

I wiggled faster, keeping my head low. By now, I knew the exact route to get to Zathrian's tent from anywhere within this camp. When I was several rows away, I could no longer crawl without drawing attention. Here, soldiers glanced with interest at the chaos to our right but continued to go about their tasks.

Getting to my feet, I strode purposefully but not too quickly. My heart was in my mouth as I beelined toward the row that would take me behind Zathrian's tent. But everyone was too wrapped up in both their tasks and the distraction the horse had caused to pay me much attention. It likely helped that they'd seen me walking this way many times with Previs.

I almost tripped on a rope holding one of the tent pegs in place, but I took it as a sign, dropping back to my knees as I approached Zathrian's tent. The canvas was so taut it was difficult to lift, and I was forced to wrestle with it, a sweat breaking out across my forehead as I shoved one arm beneath the tent.

No sound came from inside the tent. My blood turned to ice. Had I chosen the wrong tent? I would have only one chance at this.

I lifted the canvas high enough to shove my head beneath it, conscious that if a jumpy soldier was waiting in this tent, it could be the last thing I ever did.

"Well, well, well." Zathrian smirked, lounging on one elbow as if he were choosing to lie down and not because he was chained even closer to the long metal pole than I had been. "Why am I not surprised to see you stealing into my tent?"

At that, I shoved with all my strength. If anyone saw my legs hanging out from the side of this tent, I was dead.

"We don't have much time."

Zathrian lifted one eyebrow as he took in the dust that covered me. "I'm sure."

"Do you still wish to take your crown?"

All amusement left his face. "You came here to taunt me?"

"No. I came here to bargain with you. It's still possible for you and me to be the ones left ruling at the end of this."

He angled his head but stayed silent.

I gave him a cool, calm look. The look I'd perfected

in Regner's court. "I spoke to my son. He will use his power for the correct purpose when it is time."

Zathrian sat up. "I'm listening."

ASINIA

Demos had been right.

The fact that Regner had allowed Rekja to push his soldiers out of Gromalia didn't make sense.

Until we received Prisca's message and the pieces suddenly fit together.

The soldiers Rekja had thought were retreating were really moving west, toward the Asric Pass—where they would slaughter the hybrids who had been traveling toward the pass for weeks.

Regner had waited like an insidious spider himself, as we'd moved our people into his web. How he must have laughed when we finally began sending our people to the pass.

Right where he wanted them.

That heavy cloud had settled over me once more, my mind slow and thick as fog.

It was up to Demos to tell his aunt of Regner's true plans. And as usual, he didn't hesitate. Didn't put off the task. Didn't even attempt to truly soften the blow. Because that wasn't who Demos was.

And still, sorrow darkened his eyes when Telean turned white. She swayed, and he caught her hand, leading her to a chair in her room.

"Of course," she said, and her voice was drained of life. "Of course, he would kill the most vulnerable of us first. So that the rest of us lose all hope."

Standing next to the window, Gwynara was pale. "All those children…"

"Map," Demos said.

Gwynara opened Telean's door, calling to Brinlor. He appeared back with a map in his hand, and together, we helped him roll it out on the low table.

"When we traveled toward the mine, Regner's regiments were here, here, and here." Demos stabbed his finger into several spots within Eprotha. "They've moved locations since Lorian went on his killing spree when Prisca was taken, but I could never understand why Regner was gathering his soldiers in central Eprotha."

I nodded. "When we traveled back to meet Telean, there were no signs of those regiments."

"Yes," Demos said. "If he'd moved them south, our scouts would have noticed them. Not to mention, Rekja would have sent messages, begging for aid. But instead, Regner pulled his soldiers *out* of Gromalia."

"Our own army was marching north to meet up with Rekja's regiment," I pointed out. "Perhaps Regner was unprepared."

Demos shook his head. "We have twenty thousand soldiers in Gromalia at most. A third of them are fae, but Regner would have made allowances for that with his stolen magic."

"He knew we were moving our armies into position in Gromalia," I said.

"Yes. And his spiders are everywhere. Regner had to know Conreth would also be joining our armies. Not to mention Daharak's fleet moving south…" Demos's voice turned cold with rage. "He's only sending some of his foot soldiers to the Asric Pass. The rest of them will be moving northwest toward the Normathe Mountains. Thousands of his soldiers will take the fucking Normathe pass and prevent our people from using the hybrid tunnel to Lyrinore. Our people will have nowhere to go."

My lungs seized, and the room seemed to recede, until the map was all I could see.

"We need to move our army," Telean said. She sounded as if she'd aged ten years. My heart ached.

I studied the map as I held my side down. "Where to? If we're moving the hybrids through the Asric Pass, they'll end up on the western side of the continent. Prisca thinks Regner will attack from the Sleeping Sea, which means our people will be pinned down between his ships and his army marching from the east through the pass. If our army marches in behind them, we can kill Regner's soldiers at the back of his lines, but our people will still be slaughtered."

Demos just nodded. His eyes darted over the map.

"We order them to travel through Eprotha and over the Normathe Mountains before Regner's army can take it," Demos said.

"Are you out of your mind?" His words brought Telean back to life. "They can't march through the middle of Eprotha."

"Why not?" Demos stabbed his finger into the middle of the human kingdom. "As we've just seen, Regner's regiments are now nowhere to be found."

"Because they're going to be traveling through the Normathe Pass," I said, staring at him.

"They are. But I think we can beat them there."

"How?"

"It takes time to move fifty thousand human soldiers. They need to rest more often and for longer than the hybrids and fae. Regner already has a problem with morale. And we're going to slow them down much more. It's time to send a message to Natan."

My heart raced. "He wanted to slow down the army, but he also wanted to use his people during battle. To create chaos in Regner's lines…"

I let my voice trail off. I didn't need to say the next part of my sentence. That if Natan's people were successful, they would likely be caught and killed long before we faced Regner.

"If we don't slow down that army, there won't be a battle. There will only be a slaughter. Natan's people have already been spreading misinformation, inciting infighting, and disrupting communications. Now, they'll begin sabotaging equipment, tampering with supplies, and targeting generals."

A slick sweat broke out on the back of my neck. If they were caught, they were dead. And yet, if their tactics could buy us even a few hours to get our army to the Normathe Pass first…

"It will still take time for our army to travel north," Demos said. "So, we need to get to Vicer and the three thousand hybrids with him. We'll guard the mouth of the Asric Pass and buy our people as much time as we can until help arrives."

Silence claimed the room.

It was insane. At the very least, it was audacious, risky, and dangerous.

But it was our only chance. There was no other way to position our army along the coast to protect our people.

"Logistics," Telean croaked.

Demos sighed. "Kaelin Stillcrest said the pass through the Normathe Mountains is more dangerous than the Asric Pass, but it was her only plan if they were ever attacked. Of course, that plan relied on their scouts noticing that Regner's guards were on their way several days before they actually attacked." His expression darkened, and his hand tightened slightly on his corner of the map before he released his fist, smoothing the parchment back out.

"We need Rekja to march the rest of our army," Demos said into the silence. "Now. If they cut west through Gromalia into Eprotha—near Crawyth, they'll avoid Regner's regiment. From there, they head north."

"They're going to be exhausted," Telean said, her eyes stark.

"They will," Demos said. "We're scrambling to get our armies into place. And once they arrive, they'll be tired from traveling so quickly. Morale will be low, and so will supplies. Regner is getting exactly what he wanted."

26

ASINIA

It took us another day and a half to meet up with Vicer and the hybrids. We'd traveled through most of the night, stopping only to allow the horses to rest and grabbing a few hours of sleep ourselves.

We found their camp a day's ride from the foothills of the Asric Mountains, along the Eprothan and Fae border. The circles beneath Vicer's eyes were so dark they looked almost like ink, and I wrapped him in a hug. He patted me on the back. "Good to see you, Asinia."

"Where can we talk?" Demos asked.

Vicer led us to his tent. Firion created a sound ward, and Demos gave him a nod of thanks. The rest of us sat on the ground. Even the fae seemed exhausted from how hard we'd pushed ourselves to get to Vicer.

But Demos turned and poked his head out of the tent. "I need Stillcrest," he said to someone. "Bring her here."

When he turned back to face us, his gaze found Vicer's. "What happened?"

Strands of Vicer's hair had come loose from the low ponytail he usually wore, and he shoved them off his face.

"Finley wasn't the only spider in our

ranks. Weapons began going missing, horses were suddenly lame, porridge caused a food-poisoning outbreak so extensive that we lost an entire day of marching. The weather turned, and everyone seemed to become sick again at once. We attempted to keep those who were coughing separated from the others, but..." His voice trailed off.

"Do you have your suspicions?" Demos asked.

"Yes. I've got my most trusted people watching anyone suspected of being one of Regner's spiders, but I have to be absolutely sure they aren't arresting the innocent." He let out a bitter laugh. "You'd think it might help that Regner's webs usually appear on faces, necks, and throats once his spiders begin carrying out their orders. But it's horrific for morale. Soldiers have begun harboring distrust for the people they sleep and march next to. When the porridge was fouled, one of the cooks slit his own throat right after everyone had been served. And every inch of his face was covered with a black web."

My head spun at the image his words conjured. Demos had once told me that trust was everything in war. You had to trust that the soldier next to you would hold the line until the moment he died. If he turned to run, so would others, and all would be lost. Battles across our history had been won and lost based not just on weapons, weather, or location. But also due to courage, friendship, and bravery.

Demos's lips thinned. "Send a message to Rekja," he ordered Firion. "Tell him to protect Tor with everything he has. I don't want anyone near him except Rekja and Thora."

My mouth turned watery. Of course. With so many spiders beginning to reveal themselves, it was likely one of them was close to Tor. And any who were magically bound to protect Regner would know that Tor was currently the human king's biggest threat.

Firion nodded, stepping out of the tent as Kaelin Stillcrest walked in. I hadn't thought she could look much worse than the last time I'd seen her. But I'd been wrong.

Oh, she'd put on some much-needed weight since Prisca and Lorian's wedding. But her cheeks were sunken, and she appeared as if she were sleepwalking. There was no life in her eyes. Nothing except cold determination.

Stillcrest didn't say a word, and Vicer didn't look at her.

Demos told them of Regner's plans to attack the hybrids at the pass.

Stillcrest closed her eyes, her face draining of color.

And Vicer...

He folded like a puppet with its strings cut. His knees weakened until Demos leaped forward, guiding him down until he sat on the ground. Vicer's eyes filled, and for the first time since I'd known him, his face was a mask of pure, unrelenting hopelessness. My gut clenched. After everything Vicer had seen and done for hybrids across Eprotha and Gromalia, this was the moment that might break him.

"We haven't had enough time," Vicer said dully. "As soon as Regner's soldiers were dead, the elders began leading anyone who made it through the pass to the tunnel that would take them home. But the journey to the first camp was long and dangerous. And the rain made the pass itself treacherous. Less than half of the people we'd thought would have made it through the pass have relocated to the other side of the mountains. The rest have been waiting at the temporary camp at the mouth of the pass. And more hybrids are arriving there every day."

Urgency pushed me to my feet, and I gazed down at him. "You need to get word to the hybrids waiting at the mouth of the pass. They don't have long to get to the tunnel before Regner's fleet arrives."

Demos turned to Stillcrest. "I need you to tell our generals everything you know about the pass through the Normathe Mountains. Any details you can remember. Anything that could help our people travel through the range more quickly."

She nodded. Her gaze darted around until it met mine. The sudden intensity in her eyes was almost shocking.

"We're all going to die, aren't we?"

I jolted. She was still looking at me, as if she couldn't trust anything Vicer or Demos would say. I opened my mouth.

And it hit me.

Yes. There was a good possibility we were going to die. When I was trapped in Regner's dungeon, I'd had nothing to focus on but my looming death. But now...now I'd turned my attention to everything except the reality of the battle to come. I hadn't let myself understand the reality of what our numbers meant compared to Regner's.

Until this moment.

Stillcrest's gaze burned into mine. I swallowed, and her expression turned blank.

"We're going to get to the pass before Regner's

regiment. And we're going to hold the line until help comes," Demos said.

Stillcrest nodded. But her gaze dropped to the ground. He hadn't answered her question. And that was an answer itself.

"I know you've been traveling as quickly as possible, given the circumstances," Demos said to Vicer. "But we need to have this camp moving again at first light. Any who are unable to travel will stay behind, but they will be expected to follow tomorrow. We have no time to waste."

Vicer nodded. "We were planning to leave at first light anyway. There are a few empty tents for you. I'll show you where they are."

I followed him gratefully, more than ready to try to block out the world and get a few hours of sleep. The tents were close to Vicer's own, and I wasn't entirely surprised when Demos took my hand and led me inside the tent he'd been designated. He sat on the small stool, and his head fell forward, until it was resting against my stomach. I ran my fingers through his hair.

"I should have seen this coming," he said.

"I hadn't realized you were a seer," I said mildly.

He snorted, but he didn't lift his head.

"I just don't understand how Regner got to our people. They're not children."

I scratched his scalp gently with my nails, and he arched his head like a cat. "He's wielding that grimoire in newer, even more terrifying ways. Hiding all those ships so he could sink half of Daharak's fleet... If he'd been able to do that even months ago, Daharak herself would be dead by now."

Demos lifted his head. His eyes were a little glazed, but they cleared as he watched me. "The more he uses the grimoire, the more he can do with it."

Slowly, he got to his feet. "That's why he wants to go to war now. He's the strongest he's ever been. And some part of him must know the dark god is coming for that grimoire. Regner needs to solidify his hold on this continent before that happens."

Despair gnawed at me. If Demos felt any hint of that emotion, it wasn't evident. His eyes were steady, focused.

"I won't let you die. You know that, don't you?"

I opened my mouth. Closed it. Opened it once more. "Demos…"

"I saw your face in that tent. When Stillcrest said we would die. And I want you to know, I will do whatever it takes to keep you alive, Asinia. You're going to live through this. I promise."

"Don't, Demos. Don't promise me that." I knew this man well enough to know he kept his word. Only the gods knew what or whom he would sacrifice to keep that promise.

He just gave me a sad smile.

"This isn't how I wanted us to do this," he murmured, pushing back a strand of hair that had broken free of my braid. "And I have only myself to blame for wasting so much time. I kept telling myself there would be more time later for me to become the man you deserved. I was sure that once we won this war, I could do this properly. I could court you."

He leaned even closer, until we were inches apart. His fingers gently traced my face, his gaze following each stroke, as if he was memorizing it. Green-gold eyes met mine, and my breath caught.

"I wasn't being completely honest when I told you I didn't know what I wanted. That I hadn't let myself think about what comes after this war. The truth is, I want to know you're safe. That you're happy and fulfilled. That you're creating beautiful clothes and living the life you always dreamed of in that village. And if I'm still breathing, I want to be part of that life."

My heart was pounding so hard, I could hear it in my ears. My vision swam. "You will be breathing. Promise me."

He grinned, looking suddenly younger. And I could see a hint of the man he might be one day when he didn't spend those days consumed by war and death. A man who smiled often, who used his strategic mind in ways that improved people's lives, instead of those that caused death. A man who came home each night and kissed me lavishly before dropping to the floor to play with our children.

I could see that life. It was so close, I could almost touch it. And yet, it also seemed like an impossible dream.

"I promise," he said. "I'll be there. If you'll have me." He cupped my cheek, his thumb gently brushing away a tear that had slipped free. "Now, promise me."

"I promise."

He moved his hand to the back of my head, and I sank into his kiss, breathing in the scent of him. Never could I have imagined that it would be Demos who would be the one person I needed. But looking back now...

From the moment we'd met, and he'd bullied and

cajoled me into eating, forcing me to survive each night in that cell, this had always been inevitable.

"Ahem." Someone coughed outside the tent. Clearly, Demos was needed.

I wanted to hold him to me, to demand that whoever was waiting leave us in peace.

But we were at war.

Demos pulled away with a long sigh. "Get some rest." He glanced around. "Stay here." *In my tent,* his eyes said when they met mine. *Where you belong.* "I'll see you soon."

PRISCA

Asinia and Demos had the amulet.

Over the past days, I'd repeated that thought over and over, until it seemed to echo inside my mind. Armies took time to move. And this feeling of helplessness, the urge to *do* something, was tearing me apart.

But we now had all three amulets and Tor. I had to believe it would be enough to kill Regner and end this war.

My horse shifted beneath me, likely sensing my anxiety. Next to me, Lorian glanced my way. Concern flickered in his gaze as he ran his eyes over my face.

I nodded at him, and he turned in his saddle, surveying the soldiers formed in their lines behind us, supply wagons bringing up the rear.

Thankfully, we'd been in the process of packing up the camp, ready to march south. Still, learning the truth of Regner's plans had filled us with a new urgency. I'd sent sixteen of our most powerful hybrids ahead in Regner's ship, hoping they would reach our people quickly enough to buy us time.

My hand found my hourglass. Time. It all came down to time.

For the past two days, we'd marched south from the Cursed City, stopping only to sleep huddled around campfires each night. In the glow of those fires, I'd listened to the hybrid soldiers talk of war. They'd spoken of great, long-dead heroes. They'd told stories about battles past, each retelling becoming more outlandish than the last. They'd laughed and boasted and gently mocked those who had never strode onto a battlefield.

My teeth had almost chattered in fear each time I'd thought about what was to come next. And I'd looked around at those soldiers—many of whom would be on the front lines—and wondered how they could speak so easily of the death and horror of war.

If not for their refusal to linger on the reality of what they were to face, these fathers and sisters and mothers and sons would be thinking of the people who might leave them, along with those they might leave behind. And so, it seemed as if they focused on the potential glory of battle instead.

When I mentioned this theory to Shara, a burly soldier with a long scar down the left side of her face, she nodded. "Bravery is a choice. However, you can't wait until the moment you need to be brave to reach for that bravery. Because if you haven't been purposefully tending to it, building it up, you may find that it is not there when you need it. You must stoke the fires of courage little by little, day by day, so they are burning bright long before you ever need them. And you fuel or douse those fires— fanning the flames or snuffing them out—with the words you say to yourself. And with the words you allow others to say about you in your presence."

Now, as my horse plodded along, I let myself listen to the words I had been saying to myself since I'd woken in that cabin after bringing Lorian back. The words I'd stuffed down as much as I could.

And my cheeks burned.

I was a cheat. A woman who had ignored the laws of both humans and the gods. Someone who had violated the most fundamental rules of her own power. I was arrogant and prideful—refusing to admit that my actions were in any way wrong. Because Lorian had lived, and that was all that mattered to me.

The happiness I felt was stolen. Lorian was being haunted by the dead because of me.

And...

I took a shaky breath. Gods, it hurt to examine these thoughts.

But I dug deeper.

That little voice in my head taunted me about how none of this had needed to happen at all. I'd been given a prophecy, which I had studied night and day. If I had just understood what was happening *three seconds earlier*, Lorian would never have been struck by his brother's power.

I'd failed. And then I'd covered up my own failure by cheating the gods.

And I would do it again.

"What is it, wildcat?" Lorian murmured.

"I'm just...thinking."

I could feel his concern, but I couldn't seem to look at him.

Not when I felt so unworthy.

Briefly closing my eyes, I poked at the place where my power should be.

Still nothing. And yet, somewhere along the way, my fury and frustration had turned to resignation. Depression. I'd accepted that my power was gone, thought only of how I would manage the loss of it.

And so, I glanced over my left shoulder, to where Zathrian was riding next to Kaliera, both of their hands manacled, the chain leading to Galon's saddle.

My cousin's eyes met mine, and he raised one brow.

"If you somehow lived through it, the fates would demand an equal sacrifice. The kind of sacrifice that would haunt you."

When my power hadn't returned, I'd assumed that was the sacrifice. And even as I'd hoped and wished for it to come back, to aid us in this war...Zathrian had been correct.

His voice played through my mind once more.

"I didn't say they can't hide magic. They can, after all, play with us in all kinds of diabolical ways."

I'd weighed my power against Lorian's life and considered them equal. I'd been more than willing to trade one for the other if it meant Lorian would live.

So, the gods had tricked me.

"That which can be hidden can also be found. Perhaps you didn't truly want to find it. Or perhaps you just didn't try hard enough."

Just as I had in that tent, I attempted to push Zathrian's words away.

But they continued to taunt me.

"You know what I think? I think you woke up without your power, and you subconsciously latched on to that as the punishment the gods gave you for turning back time those few seconds. Some part of you was relieved at the thought that the loss of your power was your punishment. Because it meant your punishment wouldn't involve losing anyone else you loved in this war."

If he was right…

My hands tightened on the reins, and my horse threw her head. I immediately loosened my grip, stroking her neck.

I didn't know if I could live with the thought that I'd crippled myself during this war.

Lorian said something in a low voice to Galon.

And then we were stopping. Our eyes met, and I realized he was standing next to my horse, holding out his hand.

I allowed him to help me down.

"A brief break," he said carefully. "For the soldiers to rest their feet."

I nodded. "I need a moment," I choked out.

Frustration flickered across his face. Lorian wasn't used to feeling helpless. And he wouldn't like the thought of me out of sight. Still, I knew he would allow it, if only because he could sense something was very wrong.

I took a short walk to a copse of trees nearby. When I was out of view, I took a deep breath.

Somehow, I'd rejected the very power that had allowed me to save Lorian's life, suddenly fearful that I would use it again in a way that would make Telean disgusted in me. A way that would put more people at risk. After Stillcrest's camp had been attacked, it was as if some part of me had decided it was my power that was at fault. Even though it was the choices I'd made with that power that had led to those consequences.

"You are my blood. And I expect better from my granddaughter than a queen who hands her power over to anyone."

My grandmother had warned me. As much as she could. And directly after that conversation, I'd handed my power—both my time magic and my autonomy—over to the gods.

I closed my eyes. And this time, I didn't merely prod at my power. I didn't pull at the threads that usually came so easily to me.

No, I clutched a metaphorical sword and slashed blindly at whatever was keeping me from feeling my own magic.

And suddenly, I *could* feel it. The barest whisper of my power, hidden but not stolen. A heady rush surged through my veins.

My power wasn't gone.

It wasn't gone. It was merely trapped behind a wall of stone and fae iron.

The gods had hidden it. But I'd found it. And I would

free it.

Some part of me still wished the gods truly had taken my power, even now. Because the thought of telling everyone I loved that I had done this to myself...

Nausea swept through my body, and I panted through it.

My power disappeared. As if it had never been there.

No. No, no, no!

I focused on the blade of my sword, sharpening it with every drop of willpower I had. Lengthening it with thoughts of the hybrids waiting for us. Strengthening it with the rage that burned within me. Drawing back my sword, I put everything into my next swing. The blade hit the stone and fae iron of the wall. And the wall began to crumble.

I heard a sob leave my throat, but I kept my eyes closed, even as I was suddenly encompassed in a deep, seething pool of disgust.

Zathrian was right. No one had done this to me. The gods hadn't taken my power. I hadn't burned it out.

No, I'd crippled *myself*. Which was much, much worse.

I'd made *myself* helpless. I'd made *myself* a victim.

And if I wasn't careful, I'd build that wall higher around my power, using my own self-loathing.

I could feel it now—like a thick, angry black cloud, settling over the stone and fae iron in front of me.

No matter how much I crumbled that wall, it rebuilt. Again and again and again.

My chest ached, and I took a deep, shaky breath, searching for a new approach.

Leaning against the tree, I let the horrible, poisonous feelings flood through my body. My stomach turned, my limbs tingled, and my throat clogged.

For once, I didn't push those feelings away. I didn't pretend the voice in my head didn't exist.

I felt all of the shame and disgust and fury and helplessness.

The world didn't end. The feelings didn't kill me. They came in waves, receding further each time.

And then...for a few seconds...I was at peace.

The feelings were still there, but muted somehow. I could think around them.

Allowing the feelings to swamp me if they wished— because I could handle them—I reached for my power.

And it leaped at me like a puppy who'd been left alone for days.

I snatched it to me, but I didn't need to. My power was strong and deep...so deep, it was as if it had just been waiting for me to acknowledge it once more.

Clutching the hourglass hanging around my neck, I took another deep breath, opening my eyes.

I'd never agreed to play by the gods' rules. I didn't care that they said what I had done with my power was forbidden.

All that mattered was what I could do with my own power. Whatever possibilities that power gave me were mine to exploit.

I was done feeling guilty for using what I'd been born to wield. If there was the slightest chance I could use it in the same way to save someone I loved—and not die—I would do it again.

Nausea roiled through me. I needed to talk to Lorian. I would have to tell him what I'd done. How much I'd almost cost us. For a long moment, I wrestled with the shame of it. I caught movement out of the corner of my eye.

"You can come," I croaked out.

Lorian was instantly in front of me.

"What is it?"

"I have my power back."

He nodded.

"You don't seem surprised. You knew it was there, didn't you?" For a moment, betrayal choked me. But it made sense. Galon and Marth must have known too. According to my cousin, the only reason I hadn't known the gods' limitations was because I'd grown up with humans.

"Your burnout was very real. But as it continued to go on, I knew the gods were playing some kind of trickery."

I took a very careful step back. Lorian looked as if I'd hit him.

"Why wouldn't you tell me this?"

"What do you think would have happened if I'd told you that you could access your power? That the gods were likely hiding it from you? I saw you with a headache every single day as you attempted to use it."

"I would have become consumed by it," I admitted. "I would have allowed myself to marinate in my own disgust. I would have second-guessed every single decision."

Lorian cupped my cheek. "Some part of me wondered if the gods truly had taken your power, wildcat. They're too interested in you. And if that had been the case, you needed to learn that you were just as deserving of your crown without it." He stared down at me, studying my face. A faint frown tightened his brow. "Even now, after all we've been through, some part of you thought I'd turn on you when you told me."

Denial rushed through me, and I clutched at his shirt. "No. I didn't think you would turn on me. But I was nervous. I would never want to disappoint you."

"I thought I'd made myself clear, wildcat. There is nothing you could do. Nothing you could tell me, no shame too great for you to share with me."

Winding my arms around his neck, I tugged at him. Lorian didn't hesitate, his lips caressing mine as his arms tightened around me.

"We need to get back," I murmured against his mouth.

Reluctantly, he led me back to my horse. Galon passed down the message that we were about to begin marching once more.

Just as the first drops of rain hit my face.

27

MADINIA

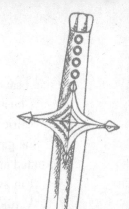

Rythos continued to attempt to make conversation. I ignored him, counting the time based on the meals we were given. Eventually, though, I began to lose track. All I knew was that we'd been here too long. Long enough that Prisca and the others could be on the front lines bleeding and dying, while we were trapped here slowly going insane.

A low, male grunt sounded. Rythos had wound his legs through the bars of our cage and was hanging upside down doing sit-ups. When the main cell door opened, he almost fell.

I smirked. Rythos untangled himself from the bars and leaned against them. His insistence on touching the bars made with fae iron was likely all part of some game he was playing with his brother. If it hurt him, it was impossible to tell from the predatory look in his eyes.

The woman who stepped into the corridor was taller than me by at least a footspan and looked like she spent her days on the battlefield, swinging her sword. She wore a dark-gray dress, and when she smiled at me, I saw Rythos in her smile.

"Cousin," she said, stepping up to the bars.

"Miric. This is Madinia."

She gave me a nod. But her smile disappeared, and she tutted at Rythos. "You really fucked up this time."

"I'm aware."

"Verdion and Brevan sent me in here to convince you to cooperate with them. Pretend I'm doing that, and tell me exactly what happened *and* what you were thinking."

Despite the situation, a tendril of amusement curled through me. Any woman who could order around one of the domineering fae was a force to be reckoned with.

Rythos told her everything. When he got to the part about Verdion agreeing to cooperate with Regner long before we knew war was even a possibility, Miric's eyes turned haunted.

"And your brother sees no problem with this?"

"My brother isn't king. Yet."

She waved her hand. "That doesn't mean he's without influence. Lorian and the others…they will be waiting for you."

"They will be waiting for *us*. For the fleet of Arslan ships that could determine whether any of us lives through this war."

She let out a shaky breath. Rythos leaned against the bars.

"Exactly how am I supposed to cooperate?"

"They want you to remove your magic from the council."

I jolted. "His magic is still working?"

"Yes. My cousin has become more powerful since he

has been gone." She cast him a fond look. "The council has continued to disregard Verdion and Brevan's orders, and they are readying the fleet for war."

My heart raced, and I turned to Rythos. "How much longer will that power last?"

"I don't know. I was hoping it would be long enough for my brother to have at least listened to what we have to say."

And then the true conversation began happening. Rythos and Miric began speaking using their hands. I'd seen this language before—one of the servant's children in Regner's palace had lost her hearing at a young age in an accident. But I'd never learned how to communicate with her.

Rythos glanced at me. "Madinia usually has a lot to say about such situations." He flicked his gaze to his hands and then to the door.

We were being listened to. And everything we said would be reported back to his brother and father.

I took the hint. And I paced the cell, letting loose with a tirade I'd been holding back for days. The conditions were unimaginable. I hadn't had *any* fresh air. My first introduction to the Arslan had proven they were an intolerant, dull, arrogant people who didn't deserve the beautiful island they lived on.

Miric laughed at that, losing her concentration. Rythos shot me a look.

So, I switched to more important topics. I told her—and whoever was listening—of everything I'd seen, living in Regner's castle. I told her what it had truly been like, growing up in his court as a hybrid. And I told her just how much he hated the fae—*all* of the fae.

Someone hit the door with a closed fist. I spoke faster. I would not be silenced. Rythos's and Miric's hands moved so quickly, they were almost a blur. I could see them cutting each other off, nodding, planning something.

And then the guard opened the door. Their hands froze, and Miric turned toward the guard.

"I suggest you think about what I said, Rythos," Miric said, following the Arslan guard toward the door.

"I will."

ASINIA

I woke up to an empty bed. The indent in the pillow next to me told me Demos had slept beside me all night. And I hadn't even noticed.

I scowled, rolling out of bed to dress. When I poked my head out of the tent, it was clear Demos had let me sleep late. Most of the tents around mine had already been packed away. Cursing, I pulled on my boots, grabbed my cloak and weapons, and apologized to the waiting soldier.

Demos was tacking my horse when I found him. His gaze caressed my face as I approached.

"Have you eaten?"

I shook my head. "I'll eat in a few hours."

He reached into his cloak pocket and pulled out a neatly wrapped package, handing it to me. My chest warmed.

I took half the bread and dried meat, giving him the rest back. He shook his head but took it.

"You didn't wake me last night," I murmured.

"You needed your sleep."

I swallowed. After everything Demos had said...was he backing away from me once more?

"Sin." He took my arm. "I wanted you to rest. Today will be a long day, and you looked so exhausted. Besides, I liked seeing you sleeping in my bed."

My cheeks heated, and he gave me a slow grin. "The next time I get you in my bed, you won't be sleeping for hours," he murmured, and my thighs tensed.

Shifting his hand to my boot, he helped me mount.

Vicer had sent a pigeon to let the hybrids know of our impending arrival, and Vicer's scouts had reported that Regner's soldiers would arrive by nightfall tomorrow.

We traveled quickly, and it felt more difficult to breathe as the ground sloped up into the foothills. I kept my cloak wrapped around my shoulders for most of the journey, although the sun seemed to spear through my clothes, and the breeze held a chill that danced across my skin. A few hours before twilight, we reached the camp where a group of hybrids waited for us several hundred footspans from the pass.

Tibris's face was the first I saw, Herne by his side. I jumped off my horse, stumbling a couple of steps as my legs protested walking after so many hours in the saddle.

He threw his arms around me. And I held him for a long moment. Demos stepped up next to us, and I hugged Herne as Demos and Tibris greeted each other.

Herne stiffened slightly and then relaxed into my hug.

"It's good to see you."

Demos nodded. "You didn't need to come to meet us."

"Yes, we did." Tibris shot Herne a look filled with pride and adoration. "Since our arrival, we've spent every minute setting up traps for any enemies who happened to approach." All joy drained from his face. "We didn't truly think we would need such traps. They were just a precaution."

"Now, they'll save lives," Vicer said, his horse trotting up behind us. Tibris grinned up at him.

"How did the hybrids know how to approach?" Demos asked.

"We've had sentries posted every day. They allow our people to pass and tell them how to stay safe."

Tibris gestured, and we followed him, Demos and I leading our horses.

Each of the waiting hybrids took a different route, our small army separating into groups that followed those hybrids. Demos didn't look pleased by the additional time it would take for us to reach the camp, but even he let out several low whistles as Tibris explained some of the traps we passed.

Many of them were hidden beneath layers of leaves and branches. The deep pits were lined with spikes or left empty to break the limbs of those unlucky enough to fall in. But there were also hundreds of smaller, shallower pits, carefully concealed and waiting for unsuspecting soldiers to break an ankle.

Demos's favorites were the swinging log traps, which were triggered by trip wires. Large logs would swing down from the trees and, according to Herne, the force was capable of knocking down multiple soldiers at once— and slowing the soldiers behind them.

Spiked barricades were planted at various points, particularly in narrow passages between trees. Hidden nets would ensnare the enemy, and Herne's people had even found a way to rig certain trees to fall when triggered.

Grim satisfaction flooded me when Tibris and Herne pointed out each trap. Each soldier who couldn't make it to the hybrids was a soldier who couldn't kill one of our people.

"Give us an update," Demos said.

Tibris glanced over his shoulder at him. "In good weather in daylight, it takes the average hybrid six to eight hours to traverse the pass. Obviously, it can take much longer if they're traveling with children. The moment we received Prisca's message, we sent as many hybrids as possible, but there are still hundreds of people currently moving through the mountains.

"We've sent messages to all our contacts, telling any hybrids who were planning to travel here to stay where they are. But those who were already traveling are still arriving. We just had a group show up this morning. This is the camp entrance," Tibris announced as we approached a small incline. I ducked my head, avoiding a low branch, and swept my gaze over the camp.

Nestled against the Minaret Mountains, this place had always been a temporary refuge. Now, it was evident many more hybrids had been here recently—and that many of those hybrids had fled. The tents were a patchwork of canvas and cloth, clustered together in groups. Most of those tents were empty, surrounded by an array of clothes, cooking supplies, and children's toys—left where they'd been dropped moments before the hybrids had taken the Asric Pass.

The air was heavy with the scent of pine and earth, which mingled with the smoky whispers of campfires. Several small streams surrounded the clearing, the bubbling melody a soothing counterpoint to the tension that hung in the air.

The hybrids who remained gave us wobbly smiles as we walked through the camp. The word had likely spread, and they knew what was coming.

They'd also been cooking for the soldiers while they waited. And standing by a huge black pot was Margie— the woman who had become almost like a mother to Vicer. Prisca would be relieved to know she was well.

As we watched, Margie ordered the soldiers into lines for dinner—a simple affair of hard bread, cold meat, and a stew that looked like it was more water than flavor. Still, the soldiers gratefully took their rations, nodding their thanks to the other hybrids who had prepared the meal for them.

Demos stood at the edge of the camp, watching as the soldiers did their best to prepare for the battle ahead without terrifying the women and children, the sick and the elderly. His expression was thoughtful, his mind clearly on strategy once more.

A group of children approached, their expressions a mixture of curiosity and awe. They moved with the carefree energy of the young, a stark contrast to the somber preparations happening around us.

"You're the prince," a little girl said, no more than seven winters. Her mop of curly hair framed her face like a lion's mane, her stance bold, chin lifted.

Behind her, a slightly older boy fidgeted with the hem of his shirt, his gaze darting between Demos and the ground.

Demos glanced over his shoulder, as if looking for someone else. Then he pointed at his chest. "Who, me?"

"Yes, you!" This girl was younger than the first, and she clutched a threadbare doll as she peered out from behind the bold girl's shoulder. Beside her, twin boys gripped each other's hands tightly, their excitement palpable as they watched wide-eyed.

"Are you sure?" Demos asked.

"Yes! My mama said."

"Well, in that case, I suppose I must be."

A feminine voice began calling out, and the children scampered away. Demos glanced at me. "Will you still want me when I'm a prince, Sin?"

He asked it casually, but I saw a flicker of vulnerability in his eyes. Amusement warred with a strange kind of tenderness inside me. It was a feeling I'd never felt before.

"You've always been a prince. Besides, my best friend became a queen and mated the *Bloodthirsty* Prince. That's far more impressive."

He laughed. "You better not let Prisca hear you call him that."

I knew what he was doing. Focusing on a future we might get to have. It helped.

Demos turned, surveying the camp once more. "We need to meet with the others."

I nodded, shifting back to reality as I followed him to where Tibris had set up his healer's tent.

Telean, Stillcrest, and Vicer were already waiting. All three of them looked as exhausted as I felt.

Herne and Tibris stepped into the tent, and Tibris gestured for Telean to sit on the bed. She must have been beyond tired because she actually took him up on the offer. I sat on the ground, and the others joined me.

"Regner's ships have been sighted moving south. He's not hiding them anymore. Likely, he's conserving magic. The sea serpents will prevent the ships from making it across the Sleeping Sea until Rothnic takes down our ward—which will signal to the serpents that they shouldn't attack. When the ward falls, Regner will attack from the north and east, blocking off the chance for our people to get to the tunnel."

A sick panic took up residence in my chest. My throat constricted, and I forced my expression to stay neutral, breathing through the worst of it.

"How does the tunnel work anyway?" Herne asked.

"When, when Prisca used it to visit the elders...one minute she was there, and the next she wasn't," I said. "Later, I asked her what happened, and she said she was just dropped into a long tunnel. I think perhaps the island can sense the hybrids—and their intentions."

Tibris nodded. "I've seen it myself. Once they get to the correct spot on the peninsula, they don't return."

"Our kingdom has magic of its own," Telean said. "And the elders will be in the tunnel, ensuring our people are safely brought to Lyrinore."

Demos got to his feet. "The first thing the Eprothans

will do is block off access to that spot. And when they do, we'll have hundreds—if not thousands—of hybrids to protect. Is there anywhere for them to hide?"

Tibris cleared his throat. "There are several caves on the other side of the mountains. We could transport the sick, young, and injured into those caves."

Stillcrest frowned. "They'll still be trapped until we can clear a way to the tunnel."

"But at least they won't be waiting within the pass," Demos said, walking back over to us. "The pass is too narrow for our soldiers to attempt to move around them, and if the Eprothans make it past our soldiers, it will be a slaughter within the pass."

"*When*," Stillcrest said. "You mean *when* the Eprothans make it past our soldiers."

I clenched my teeth so they wouldn't chatter.

Demos met her eyes. "Yes. When. We will hold the line here to give our people as much time as possible to get through the pass. When there is no other option, we will retreat." He glanced at Herne. "And your people will set as many traps as possible within the pass for the soldiers who follow. Traps that we can finish putting into place within seconds."

Herne's eyes lit up.

"Tomorrow, we send all remaining hybrids into the pass. Those who can't walk will be carried by our soldiers. The rest of us will spend our day preparing this camp for a siege."

"And then?" I asked.

"And then we hope reinforcements come. From somewhere."

28

PRISCA

The sudden storm had brought three days of pounding rain, the briny scent of the ocean overpowered by the unexpected, unyielding downpour.

To our right, the endless expanse of the sea stretched toward the horizon, its surface tumultuous under the gray sky as agitated, frothy waves crashed against the shore.

On our left, the foothills of the Normathe Mountains loomed as shadowy silhouettes, their verdant blanket of trees and shrubs obscured by rainfall. Occasionally, the land rose sharply, giving way to rocky outcrops that jutted out like the spines of an ancient beast. The rocky outcrops wept rivulets, and the path beneath our feet became a laborious slog through mud and puddles. The rhythmic march of our soldiers was replaced by splashes and curses as we all slipped and tripped.

The air was heavy with moisture, each breath I took laden with dampness that clung to my skin. The rain soaked through cloaks and uniforms, the chill seeping into our bones.

Would Daharak's fleet make it through this storm? Or would we be on our own when we finally reached the mouth of the Asric Pass?

As dusk melded into the darkness of night, we began the miserable task of setting up camp in the relentless downpour. The sodden ground became a sea of mud that threatened to suck down tents. Each peg hammered into the earth ended up swimming in a shallow puddle. Several soldiers gaped at the sight of me attempting to set up my own tent while Lorian met with Galon. When Marth took over, I didn't protest.

Two days later, the rain still showed no sign of abating. At night, it flooded tents, despite our best efforts to line them with cloaks and blankets. Galon and a group of twenty or so hybrids with power similar to his removed as much water as possible. But that water was quickly replaced as the deluge continued.

Visibility was reduced to mere shadows in the mist, the foothills half hidden in dense fog. Those with horses were forced to lead them through treacherous rivers of mud, which soon became torrents of water cascading into dangerous streams of fast-moving water and debris. Rockslides and mudslides were a constant threat, the rain loosening the earth and making our path perilous.

Galon and the others continued directing the water as much as possible. But they quickly burned through their power, deep lines of exhaustion on their faces.

Morale plummeted. Faces that just days ago had been lit with determination were now marked by misery. Even the simplest tasks became arduous—those with a connection to fire could light them for cooking, but the wood was soon soaked through, the unrelenting rain smothering any flames. Meals were eaten cold, while walking, unaccompanied by the usual banter.

Communication was reduced to hand signals and shouted commands. Lorian had broken the army into sections, giving each a trowth stone for communication. Those marching near the back bore the worst of the weather, the thousands of boots that came before them stirring the mud into deep, treacherous puddles.

This amount of rain, this close to the mountains, at this time of the year…

Every soldier marching with us was aware that it was unusual.

"What are they saying?" I asked Lorian as we led our horses through a particularly muddy section of path.

He was silent for a long moment. Because he wanted to protect me, I reminded myself. And yet, we didn't have the luxury of sparing anyone's feelings, especially my own.

"Lorian. I need to know."

"Galon's handling it, wildcat."

"I can tell you what they're saying," Kaliera said scornfully.

Turning, I glanced over my shoulder. She sat on her horse, which was currently being led by a soldier. Previs, I think his name was.

Lorian made a warning sound in his throat. Kaliera either didn't hear it or chose not to heed it.

"They're saying you're cursed. That the gods are punishing us for following you," she announced, her voice loud enough that it would have carried through the first few lines of soldiers behind us.

"You're not following," Marth said. *"You're* a

prisoner." He looked at me. "You sure you don't want me to kill her?"

Previs tensed. Ah. She had gotten to him. I should have expected that. Next to Marth, Galon's gaze lingered on the soldier. He'd noticed too.

"No," I said. "We promised Jamic we wouldn't." A reminder of the son she claimed to love so much. The son currently with Lorian's brother.

Yet Kaliera gave me a smug smile. Water dripped down her face. "Why exactly are we following you?" She glanced over her shoulder to where Zathrian was leading his own horse, the heavy manacles on his wrists clinking against the chain between them. "After all," Kaliera said, raising her voice until she was almost yelling, "you no longer even have access to your power."

Zathrian's eyes met mine. And he smiled.

The sight of it set my teeth on edge. Hot fury roared through me. Perhaps I'd only imagined that voice screaming at me not to kill him. Already, the decision was proving to be a mistake.

His smile disappeared.

We were traveling beneath a shallow outcrop in an effort to avoid the worst of the rain. And it allowed me to hear the whispers that broke out among the soldiers marching in the front lines. Those whispers turned to murmurs.

Lorian had moved a few footspans ahead, checking the path for any slips or blockages. But a moment later, he was suddenly next to me, his movement so fast, I jolted, startling my poor horse.

Galon soothed my horse, murmuring to her as Lorian

looked at Kaliera. I glanced over my shoulder and found the fae everyone had known as the Bloodthirsty Prince. His cheekbones looked sharper, his ears more pointed, and his eyes burned with barely restrained wrath.

Kaliera froze. Her skin slowly drained of color, and a fine tremble shuddered through her as she stared her death in the face.

Lorian's gaze turned from her, flickering warningly over the soldiers in the front lines.

They went silent.

But it was too late. I had no doubt Kaliera's words were making their way back through our army.

"Previs, switch with Reon," Galon ordered.

The soldier nodded immediately. But he gave Kaliera one last glance as he turned.

Galon's eyes lingered on him.

"We need to keep moving," I said. I should have accounted for Kaliera's poison. Should have ordered that only the most experienced, loyal soldiers were to interact with her.

Lorian leaned forward, ignoring the eyes on us as he placed a gentle kiss on my cheek. Shockingly, my eyes burned.

I was just tired. That's all it was.

But as we continued marching toward our friends and families, who even now might be dying beneath Regner's onslaught...

The insidious thought played over and over in my mind.

Perhaps the gods were punishing us.

Or perhaps they were punishing me for reclaiming

my power. And everyone else would suffer for it.

ASINIA

Tonight would be our last chance to sleep before we were fighting for our lives. The moment the sun went down, everyone but the posted sentries crawled into their tents, taking whatever rest they could find. I found myself pacing the camp, listening to one of the children cry as his mother soothed him.

I'd never thought much about being a mother myself. Now, with Demos, I could almost see that future—just in time for me to accept that chances were low I'd live long enough for it.

Irony.

"Asinia."

I turned to find Demos standing next to me. I hadn't seen him for a few hours as he met with Herne and Vicer. I'd turned my attention to helping Tibris prepare the remaining hybrids to travel tomorrow.

Now, Demos gave me a look so heated, I almost blushed. But it was tempered by a deep tenderness that made my heart stutter in my chest.

He held out his hand. "Will you come to my tent?"

I knew what he was asking. We'd been sharing a tent since we arrived, but by the time Demos had fallen into the blankets next to me, I'd rarely woken. When I had, he'd been instantly asleep.

I didn't hesitate, immediately taking his hand. "Yes."

The air was damp tonight, something that seemed unusual this close to the mountains, but Demos's tent was cozy, a single light orb dancing above our heads, and several blankets hung in strategic places to buffer against any cool winds.

Demos turned to me. Cupping his face, I stroked my thumb along one of the small scars on his cheek. He turned his face into my hand, nuzzling my palm.

"You're an incredible woman, Asinia. I knew it the moment I saw you struggling to survive in that cell. I knew it when you fought through the pain from your head wound to get to Prisca. And I knew it when you hauled me over your shoulder and carried my dead weight through the forest at night."

My skin turned clammy at the memory. I'd thought I would lose him. Even now, I sometimes jolted from nightmares where I *had* lost him.

"You're strong," he said, bringing my mind back to this moment. "You're loyal. You're so beautiful it sometimes hurts to look at you. When I saw Tor...it brought up a lot of memories. Memories of being helpless when I lost the people I loved. And I pushed you away. I'm sorry for that."

His eyes had darkened, but they remained serious as he watched me.

"I forgive you," I said. "But you need to forgive yourself."

He gave me a faint smile. "One day, perhaps."

Leaning down, he pressed a gentle kiss to my forehead, the tip of my nose, my lips. I opened for him, and he wrapped one arm around me, pulling me close, until I could feel the thick heat of him against me.

I tensed.

Demos immediately lifted his head.

"Problem?"

"I'm just…it's been a long time. And only once."

His smile was wreathed in lust, tempered by something softer.

"Then we get to take this slow. I get to…savor you."

Picking up my hand once more, he turned it over, pressing his lips to the sensitive skin along my inner wrist. Pure sensation danced along my arm, and he kissed his way up to my inner elbow.

My toes curled. And Demos took a step closer, guiding me back toward his bed.

Nerves fluttered in my stomach. I had wanted this for so long. Part of me was worried that we'd be interrupted again. But Demos was looking at me with eyes that seemed to see into my soul. And his mouth curved as if he'd found exactly what he was looking for.

My hands shook as I raised them to his tunic, attempting to push it over his head. Demos complied, revealing an expanse of smooth, golden skin gliding over rippling muscle.

His muscular body might have been intimidating if I hadn't seen how carefully he wielded that large form. He knew his strength and made allowances without apologizing for what the gods had given him.

And why would he apologize? With his shirt off, he looked like a god himself.

"Your eyes are looking a little glazed, Sin." His voice

dripped with humor. Humor and smug satisfaction. I met his eyes, cheeks heating, but his smile was almost...shy.

His hands weren't, though. They were already pulling my own tunic over my head, sliding teasingly across the flexible band covering my breasts. One day, I wanted to wear a pretty dress and lace for this man.

"What are you thinking?"

I told him, and his eyes heated. "Just the sight of you like this is almost bringing me to my knees. Have mercy before you make promises like that."

His arms flexed as he slid them to my ass, and my breath hitched when he lifted me, slowly lowering me down onto the bed.

"You belong here," he said. "I hope you know what you're signing up for, Sin, because I'm feeling possessive."

When he leaned close enough to touch, my hands found him again, stroking over his chest, his back. His eyelids drooped to half-mast.

"Good," I murmured. "Because I'm feeling possessive too."

Leaning down, he nipped my chin, the movement so unexpected, I laughed. My laugh turned to a hiss as he slid down my body, his teeth gently teasing as he stroked his tongue against places I hadn't known could be so sensitive.

I let out a gasping moan, and he went still.

"Make that sound again."

My cheeks blazed, and I clamped my mouth shut.

Demos gave me a slow, wicked grin. "I guess I'll just have to make you."

His mouth dropped, and this time, I barely breathed. A fine trembling began in my limbs, and Demos muttered a curse, green-gold eyes meeting mine. He slid his hands to the waistband of my leggings.

"Yes?"

Breathlessly, I nodded. His gaze never left my face as he rolled them down, helping me kick free of them. His eyes stayed on mine as his mouth lowered, pressing kisses across my hips, stomach, inner thighs.

Another moan-gasp, and I felt him smile against my skin.

And then I was bared for him, and he let out a rough sound of his own. His warm breath caressed my skin, and I shivered.

"Tell me you want this."

"You know I do." Sliding my hands into his dark hair, I smiled.

Without hesitation, Demos pushed my thighs apart and dropped his mouth to my core.

My cheeks flamed. "Oh!"

His eyes rolled up and looked at me. He didn't move. Until…

A long, wicked swipe of his tongue.

"Ohhh."

He chuckled against me, and that created a whole new sensation. A sensation that made me arch, gasping for him.

"You taste so good," he murmured. And then he was lapping at me, his tongue circling my clit. One finger pushed inside me, and I moaned. Another finger, and the world narrowed until all I could see, all I could feel, was *him.*

He varied the pressure, his pace. Sweat broke out over my skin. My nipples were so hard they ached.

"Demos."

It was as if his name was the key. Lowering his mouth to me once more, he didn't stop this time. Didn't stop until I was crying out his name again, my climax thundering through me, on and on.

When I came back to myself, he was standing in front of the bed, his pants gone. And he was looking at me like I was all he'd ever wanted.

His cock was long and thick. Intimidating, if I was being honest. But when I looked at it, my mouth watered.

Demos cursed as I rolled up, crawling toward him.

"Not tonight."

"I want to make you feel good."

"You do. Gods, you do. But I want you too much." The words were a stark admission. "And I need to be inside you."

He met me on the bed, his hand sliding into my hair and holding me in place for him as he took my mouth. My thighs clenched, and I slid my hand down, circling his cock.

"You're big."

"I'll fit."

My back hit the bed, and Demos pushed my thighs wide, settling himself in between them. "We go at your pace. You need to stop…"

"I won't."

He gave me a look. It was the same look he'd often given me in the training arena right before he'd muttered about stubborn women, and I choked on a laugh.

And then he was pushing inside me, and my nails were digging into his forearms.

He froze.

"I'm fine. I just…"

Leaning down, he nuzzled my neck. I could feel him trembling now, could feel his need. But he didn't move an inch. Except for the hand he was sliding down my belly.

When he found my sensitive clit, I gasped. The gasp turned into a moan, which Demos caught with his mouth. I angled my hips, needing him inside me.

"Shh, Sin. Slowly."

But I didn't need slow. His hand was featherlight against me, and he wouldn't *move*.

Wrapping my legs around his waist, I angled for him, and he thrust inside me.

He froze again.

"Don't stop," I snarled.

Lifting his head, he met my eyes. And he didn't stop.

Angling me so he caressed my clit each time he thrust, Demos finally took what he wanted.

Giving me what I *needed*.

I panted, and he found my mouth, stroking his tongue against mine, until the need to breathe was secondary to my need for him.

My entire body felt as if it was a burning flame. And Demos drove those flames higher as his thick cock plunged into me, slowly dragged out, and then drove in again. He hit a new angle each time, until he found a spot that made me tighten even further around him.

"There, huh?"

Leaning up on one arm, he cupped my cheek with the other, watching me until some part of me wanted to hide. But he wasn't analyzing each reaction from a place of cool distance. No, each time I moaned or gasped or tensed, his expression grew tighter, his eyes burned brighter. And my body came alive in a way it never had before, as if tiny sparks were darting along my every nerve.

"I want centuries with you." He pressed a kiss to my mouth, his thrusts increasing in speed. "Just like this."

He slid his hand to the back of my head, cradling it as his lips caressed mine.

"I love you."

The words were stark. Almost solemn.

My breath caught, and my release hit like a storm, my body shuddering as pleasure careened through me.

Cursing, Demos drove deeper, drawing out my climax, until he tensed and I felt warmth, felt him pulsing within me as his arms tightened around my body, holding me tight.

"I love you too," I gasped. He lifted his head. But now that the words were out, I couldn't believe I'd waited so long. "I love you too."

We dozed for a while, neither of us speaking about what would happen tomorrow. And then Demos shifted, pressing a kiss to my temple.

"Wait here," he murmured.

When he returned, I was almost asleep, my eyes heavy-lidded.

The cool night air swept into the tent as Demos stepped inside, and I shivered, sitting up.

For the first time since I'd known him, Demos looked almost...uncertain.

I dropped my gaze to the crossbow in his hand and shot up in bed. "What happened? Are we under attack?"

"No." Crossing the room, he held it out to me. "I had this commissioned for you before we left. I asked Tibris to bring it with him."

My hand shook as I took the crossbow. Crafted with meticulous attention to detail, it seamlessly blended both beauty and lethality.

The stock was carved from some kind of dark wood. Whatever it was, it felt sturdy yet surprisingly light in my hands. Its surface was so smooth, it felt almost like silk when I ran my hand across it, broken only by a delicate pattern engraved along the wood.

The limbs of the crossbow were flexible, but they'd been reinforced with something. I could feel the strength when I pressed on one of them. And the bowstring... it hummed softly when I plucked it, the sound almost familiar.

I brushed my fingers across the trigger mechanism. I could tell the release would be as smooth as butter.

"You'll need to—"

His words broke off as I looked up at him, my eyes filled with tears.

I'd never been given a gift like this before. A gift that was so...*me*. A gift that combined beauty with necessity and had been created to make my life easier.

"You like it," he smiled.

"It's incredible, Demos, truly."

He handed me a new quiver filled with sleek arrows. "To go with it."

I took them, placing them next to the bed. "You had this commissioned in Gromalia. Before we left the castle."

He nodded.

I watched him some more. I'd been so confused by him. So irritated. I'd understood he was hurting after seeing Tor, but I'd hated that he was pushing me away. It had felt like he'd only cared about me sometimes.

But even as we'd readied for war, he'd been thinking of me.

I glanced back down at the crossbow in my arms. He could have commissioned something plain. Sturdy. But he'd taken the time to ensure it was something I would find beautiful. My stomach tumbled, and the grin that broke out on my face was so wide, my cheeks ached.

"I love it."

"Good. I had a protection charm placed within it."

Of course he had.

Burying my hand in his shirt, I pulled him closer, showing my appreciation with a kiss. Our kiss deepened, and before I knew it, I was riding him with a crazed desperation.

We dozed for a few more hours, made love once more, and the next time I opened my eyes, the tent had lightened.

The air in my lungs froze, and I took several moments to come to terms with what that meant.

The sun was rising.

Demos stroked my back. "I'm not going to let anything happen to you."

I lifted my head, finding him looking down at me. Each time he told me that, I heard what he was saying. That he would prioritize my life over his own.

"Stop. I don't want to think like that. I don't want *you* to think like that."

He just watched me. My heart was pounding in my throat, and my entire body felt like it was suddenly too small. Demos was the kind of man who would sacrifice himself for the people he loved in the blink of an eye. He'd barely known Pris before he took an arrow for Tibris— all so she wouldn't have to face losing the brother she'd known for longer than him.

I sat up, rolling out of bed. I needed to move. Needed to do something about the unrestrained fury that burned through me at the thought of Demos not being here when all of this was over.

He was standing a moment later, my hand in his. "Sin."

"I want you to focus on staying alive," I said.

He pressed his lips to my cheek, my jaw, my neck. "Of course I will." His tone was slightly affronted. Teasing. "I'm looking forward to having you all to myself."

Demos stepped away to pull on his clothes. I did the same. And even with the undercurrents simmering in this tent with us…

Readying myself for the day with him felt natural. As if we had been doing it for years.

I pulled on my boots and picked up my crossbow, still admiring it. When I raised my head, I caught Demos's lips quirk, but he also looked…proud.

"You should go work with it," he said. "It's a new weapon. You need to get a feel for it."

"Do I have time?"

He strode toward me, and my skin tingled as he gave me one of his smirks. "I'll cover for you."

His mouth found mine, and the world disappeared for

just a few moments.

But boots had begun to march past our tent, and he sighed against my lips. "I'll see you soon."

When he left, I stared around the empty tent, the crossbow in my hand, and just soaked in everything that had happened.

We had a future. I knew we did. And I wouldn't let Regner take it from us.

Grabbing my new quiver, I strode out of the tent, making my way to the small training area one of Vicer's people directed me to.

The space was little more than a narrow clearing for swordplay, with a lone target set up for archers. It was quieter here, the tense voices of the camp little more than a murmur as I plucked my first arrow and loaded it.

The crossbow was surprisingly light, and yet its balance was perfect. It fit into my hands as if created specifically for them—as if Demos had somehow measured the width of my palms, the length of my fingers.

The bowstring was made of a material I didn't recognize. It was both supple and strong, pulling back smoothly with far less effort than I was accustomed to.

The sighting mechanism had been refined, making it easier to align my shots. I could already tell that it would improve my long-distance accuracy.

I released the bolt. The arrow cut through the air with minimal deviation, its flight almost impervious to the light breeze I'd almost compensated for.

I hadn't needed to compensate.

Thunk.

Holy gods. This crossbow was better than sex.

Well, better than sex with anyone but Demos.

I laughed to myself as I reached back into the quiver slung over my shoulder for my next arrow. I was completely, entirely swept up in the thought of spending the rest of my life with the autocratic, overprotective hybrid prince. My best friend's brother.

At least I knew Prisca would be delighted.

Thunk.

Each arrow flew true, the crossbow's superior construction minimizing the usual variables that affected my accuracy—even when I was allowing my power to trickle down from the deep lake within me. Its lighter weight meant my arms and shoulders wouldn't be as strained during battle, and the smoother mechanism would reduce the wear on my fingers.

The target blurred in front of me and my eyes stung. It still rocked me—that even when he'd been impossible to talk to, Demos had arranged for this weapon to be created just for me. It was a fae weapon—I could already tell. And to me, it was priceless.

Striding to the wood, I plucked the arrows free, marveling at them as I tucked them away. I'd already lingered too long, but it would be worth it later today, when I instinctively knew the capabilities of this crossbow.

Making my way back to everyone else, I took in the group of hybrids gathered at the edge of the camp. They huddled together, mothers carrying children in their arms, the elderly helped by those who were too young to fight. Tibris stood in front of them, speaking slowly and carefully, Herne by his side. Tibris must have said something amusing, because several people laughed, and some of the tension seemed to disappear.

And then Telean crossed the camp, her canvas bag slung over her shoulder. She was murmuring to a dark-haired woman with the bluest eyes I'd ever seen. Ameri. That was her name. We'd only met a couple of times before, but I'd never seen such an intense expression on her face.

With a nod, Telean said her goodbyes to Ameri, who hurried away. Telean went to Tibris first. His face grew grave, and he nodded at whatever she said. When he gestured at me, she turned.

I met her halfway.

"You'll keep Demos safe." It wasn't a question.

"Yes," I vowed. "I'll keep him safe."

"Telean." Demos's voice was thick with warning, but I heard the grief beneath it.

We both turned. He planted his hands on his hips, but Telean waved her hand through the air. "You'll keep each other safe," she amended. "Now come and give me a kiss."

A strange disquiet filled me as I watched him lean down and wrap her in his arms. A single tear rolled down her cheek, and she clutched him to her with everything she had.

Someone called out, and she untangled herself from him. "Kill Regner," she ordered.

"We will."

With a last glance at me, she turned and joined the group gathered at the edge of camp. Moments later, they began moving out of the camp toward the pass, a group of hybrid soldiers traveling with them.

Several voices were calling out to one another to

my right. As I watched, a large group of soldiers hauled a massive tree trunk out of the forest and into the clearing. They set it down with a thud, immediately jumping out of the way for the next tree. And the next.

I jumped into position to help them roll one of the larger trunks across the camp. That tree became the base for the wall on the other side.

We worked for hours. The tree trunks formed a crude but effective wall. The natural curve of the wood meant that the trees nestled somewhat awkwardly against each other, leaving gaps that were both a vulnerability and a vantage point. I began snapping off branches, weaving them into the gaps to create a dense mesh of wood and leaves.

While we worked, I was conscious of Demos sharpening weapons, pausing to give a thoughtful word to a group of soldiers, working with Herne to plan our defense.

And with every minute that passed, my hands shook and my mouth grew even drier, until I found myself continually gulping at my waterskin.

It was still hours before sunset when one of the scouts arrived, his breath coming in sharp pants, his eyes wide.

"They're almost here."

Another large group of hybrids had arrived not long ago. They'd taken one look at the barricade, and their eyes had filled with dread. Several families had entered the pass at a run.

They would not die today.

I said the words over and over.

The little girl who had waved to me over her mother's

shoulder, too young to understand the danger she was in. She would not die today.

The group of young boys, lips trembling, who'd offered to stay and fight—only for Demos to crouch down and tell them gently that he needed such brave soldiers to guard the others on the way through the pass.

They would not die today.

The camp mother who'd insisted on cooking one last meal for as many soldiers as she could, before Tibris made her leave—her eyes filled with tears as she'd watched those soldiers get into position.

She would not die today.

My head whirled, and I was suddenly in Demos's arms.

His mouth crashed down on mine, and I let out a choked sob, my hands clutching his shirt, pulling him close.

Someone called to him, and he pulled away, his gaze still on my face. My body ached at the loss of his warmth. "No stupid risks."

"From you either."

He nodded. His gaze swept over my face. And he tucked a strand of my hair behind one ear.

"Into position, Sin." Demos turned, striding toward our meager front lines.

Screams sounded. One of Regner's soldiers had encountered one of Herne's traps.

Terror punched into me.

They were here.

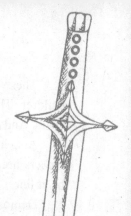

29

ASINIA

Most of Regner's foot soldiers had traveled through the Normathe Mountains.

But there were still at least ten thousand soldiers marching on our camp.

The traps Herne and Tibris had set slowed Regner's army down.

But most of the soldiers simply strode past those who had fallen, leaving them for their healers.

Our barricade gave us a scant amount of cover. We might not be sheltered in a keep or a castle, but we held the high ground, and the large boulders near the beginning of the pass gave our archers good spots to wait.

And wait, I did.

The moment the first Eprothan soldier's boot crossed the invisible line I'd delineated in my head, I nocked my first arrow and shot him through the throat.

My shot was smooth, fast, almost effortless. It felt wrong to admire my new crossbow while the soldier bled his life away beneath us.

But I still gave it one quick, appreciative stroke.

These men were coming here to kill women and children. The sick and the old. I hardened myself and shot again. And again.

Also hidden behind rocks and trees nearby, the other archers fired as well. Those we didn't hit made it to our front line.

Demos had divided our best shielders, putting some of them near the front lines and the remainder at the back, close to the entrance to the pass. If we fell—I refused to think the word *when*—those shielders would stand their ground, buying the hybrids within the pass as much time as they could.

Human soldiers with attack powers slammed those powers into our wards. From here, I could see four hybrids with defensive magic scattered throughout our front lines. One of them flinched, and a sea of fire suddenly swept toward our right flank, immediately doused by a hybrid who used some kind of water power.

The shielder rebuilt his ward, and all four of them held the line. I caught a glimpse of an Eprothan soldier screaming at their front lines—likely a general growing frustrated at the wasted power. I rolled my shoulders.

The closest soldiers were drained of magic and replaced twice before our shielders could no longer hold their wards. Demos roared an order, and they sprinted back toward us.

I shot faster than I'd ever shot before. Even as I chose each target, the sight of Demos and Tibris and Herne fighting together was imprinted on my mind. Stillcrest fought like a woman possessed just a few footspans away from them. Madinia had told us about her strange ideas about female and male roles in war—more common among humans. But clearly, she'd let those ideas go now.

When the archer next to me leaned too far to the right and was caught by an Eprothan bolt through the heart, there was no time to mourn. Leaning down, I picked up his quiver, slung it over my shoulder, and nocked my next arrow.

We began to take losses. One of the archers to my left screamed a name as a woman went down, his voice filled with horror and grief.

Blades clashed, magic attacks were rebuffed and then slipped through, killing any who were unable to be shielded.

But we had power of our own, and Demos unleashed the fae and hybrids. While I found myself longing for Madinia, Gwynara and the others were thinning Regner's front lines.

And still, the Eprothan soldiers kept coming.

I reached for another arrow, my eyes automatically scanning for the best target. A soldier had pinned his gaze on Stillcrest, as she took down one of the men near him. He fought his way toward her, a bear of a man, huge in his armor.

My arrow took him in the arm. He snapped the end off and kept moving. My head spun.

"Stillcrest," I screamed. "Demos!"

Neither of them could hear me over the sound of the battle.

I shot again, but the soldier darted to the right. Stillcrest's shoulders tensed, and I saw the moment she realized he'd targeted her.

She turned, swinging her sword.

He matched it with his own sword. My next arrow took him in the gap in his armor, right beneath his arm pit.

Stillcrest's sword broke beneath his. She ducked, backpedaling, but it was too late.

The Eprothan soldier shoved his sword between her ribs. My arrow hit him in the face, and he slumped.

I prepared to run. I could get Stillcrest to Tibris. I could—

Vicer was already dragging Stillcrest away as Demos and Herne stepped in to fill their places. Vicer had made it behind the front lines when he stopped, kneeling next to Stillcrest.

I couldn't hear what she said to him as the blood poured from her mouth.

But I read his lips as he took her hand. *"I forgive you."*

Her head fell back. She was gone.

My chest hollowed out. I hadn't liked the woman. But she'd deserved better than this. We all deserved to live long enough to rectify our mistakes.

Vicer bowed his head for a single moment. And then he was forced to roll free as an Eprothan soldier lunged toward him.

Demos's sword cut through the Eprothan's neck, and I sighted my next target.

The sun began to sink below the tree line. Our front line lost ground, until they were positioned behind the barricade.

They held the Eprothans back for hours. Until we could barely aim our arrows, most of the light gone. The lump in my throat was so large, it seemed to have spread down to my chest, the pain of it constant.

Someone was suddenly hauling me to my feet. My shot went wide, and I cursed. Demos's face appeared in front of mine.

"It's time," he said. "We have to fall back. Most of the hybrids should be through the pass now. Herne made sure Tibris left earlier. When you get to the end, ensure any who haven't made it to the tunnel are well hidden in the caves."

I nodded. Then I froze.

"When *I* get to the end?"

"In this light, with the higher ground, a few good soldiers can hold that entrance for hours."

Terror engulfed me, almost taking me to my knees. Clearly, Demos had designated himself as one of those good soldiers.

"I'm a good soldier," I croaked out.

Demos's smile was slow, wicked, and entirely inappropriate. "You *are* a good soldier," he purred.

I snarled at him. "I know what you're doing." Once again, he was attempting to distract me. But he couldn't distract me from the thought of him standing just a few footspans into the pass, with an entire regiment attacking him.

The corner of his mouth kicked up. "It was always going to happen this way, Sin."

I made a tiny, broken noise, and Demos pulled me into his arms. He didn't give me any false assurances, though. Instead, he practically dragged me toward the pass. Clearly, he'd given up cajoling me and was moving straight into pushy, domineering arrogance.

I wasn't surprised. This kind of behavior came much more naturally to him.

"You're going to do this, Asinia." His voice was grim. "You're going to live through this war. And if I'm not around, you're going to find a man who makes you happy. You're going to become a renowned seamstress and have children who look exactly like you, and you're going to live a long life filled with peace and happiness."

"You fucking bastard," I choked out. "How *dare* you?"

Demos waited for a group of other archers to sprint past, and then he continued yanking me after them.

"I can walk," I snarled.

He released me. "Good. Go."

I couldn't resist kicking Demos in the shin. His brows drew together, and he suddenly looked pained— as if my boot had been made of lead—but he pointed at the pass. My throat thickened until it felt as if I couldn't take a full breath. But Demos was standing defenseless, watching me, and the Eprothan soldiers were still coming.

Without another word, I went.

My rage lasted for approximately three minutes.

I knew Demos well enough to know he'd planned for that rage to last for the hours it would take me to traverse the pass. He'd imagined I'd burn through that rage all night, using it to drive me forward.

If I'd been Prisca or Madinia, perhaps it would have.

But I'd spent most of my childhood carefully sewing perfect stitches in the corner of our main room, while wealthier humans sneered at the home my mother had made. While they talked relentlessly of how the corrupt would die.

If I'd allowed myself to bask in my rage, it would have burned me alive long before Regner ever got the chance.

I'd gotten very good at tucking that rage away to examine later.

So, I would do that now. But oh, Demos was going to be very unhappy when we took that rage back out to look at together.

Taking a long, slow breath, I focused on why he wanted me gone—to save my life—and what I needed to do to save his.

He'd been right about one thing. The mouth of the pass was narrow enough that only four or five people could walk side by side. Here, the mountains were so close, it felt as if I could reach my arms out and touch both of them on either side.

As I hesitated, a group of soldiers ran past me. I recognized one of them as the archer who'd called out for the woman who had died on the front lines. His eyes were red, his face swollen. And yet he offered me a gentle smile.

"I know you're scared," he said. "But you have to move forward."

"That's very kind of you. But I'm not going forward. I'm going up."

It took him a single moment to understand what I was going to do. And then he nodded. "I'm coming with you."

I'd be a hypocrite if I attempted to stop him. And I

could use the help. "Fine. Help me find the best way up."

First, he stopped several more archers. "We need your arrows," he said.

One of them opened her mouth to protest. Then she realized what we were up to. With a shake of her head that made it clear she was marveling at our stupidity, she handed over half of the arrows in her quiver.

So did the other archers.

"May the gods be with you," they said. And then they were gone.

I stared at the man. He stared back.

"My name is Cryton," he said.

"Asinia."

He gestured at the rock to our right. "I think this is the best way. It's close enough to the entrance that we won't have to climb for long. See how it slopes down here?"

I did see. Already, I could hear swords clashing as our soldiers retreated toward us. We either had to move forward or go up. If we stayed here, we'd be in their way.

The Eprothans had brought light orbs with them. Without the glow from those orbs, we never could have made it up. I went first, my heart hammering in my chest as a pained scream sounded from just footspans away.

My breaths came in frantic, strained gasps.

"Fingers and toes," Cryton said from below me. "Just remember to dig in as hard as you can."

I nodded, although he likely couldn't see it in the dim light. But I ran my hand up, searching for each little hold, mound, crack. The rock cut into my hands, making my palms slippery, and I pressed my hands harder into the stone. My new crossbow thumped across my shoulders, threatening to throw me off-balance. But the feel of it made Demos's face flash before my eyes. The pride in his eyes when he'd realized how much I liked it. The fact that he'd found a gift so perfect for me.

I dug in deeper. When I dared to look up, pushing harder into the rock with my feet, I could see a tiny ledge, perhaps ten footspans above my head. Carved by the elements, it would provide just enough space for the two of us to position ourselves and enjoy an unobstructed view—as long as the ledge didn't crumble beneath us.

A few more footspans of inching up the rock until I could reach for it, stretching my left hand high. My hand slid, and the shift in balance jolted the rest of my body, turning my mouth watery with fear.

But my gaze caught on another hold just a little lower—not quite as easy to grasp, but it would work. Slowly, carefully, I focused on each finger and toe, pressing them into the rock.

My legs began to shake.

"You can do it," Cryton murmured. "Let's make them pay, Asinia."

I didn't have any rage or vengeance left in me at that moment. But what I did have was terror. Terror for Demos, who might be bleeding and dying even now.

Letting out a strangled sob, I threw my hand over the edge and onto the ridge. My arms ached, but I hauled myself up, shifting over for Cryton.

For a moment, we jostled for space as both of us reached for our crossbows and quivers. And then, I nocked my first arrow.

We had a perfect vantage point.

And below me, Demos fought for his life.

Three Eprothans had pinned him, the rock at his back. My entire body jolted, and Cryton placed his hand on my arm.

"It's not as bad as it looks," he whispered.

One of the soldiers stepped forward, and then paused, hesitating. Ah. They hadn't pinned *him*. He'd positioned himself strategically, the rock at his back. Each soldier needed room to attack, but with the three of them so close, Demos could easily notice any change in body language that warned of an impending attack. When the soldiers did make a move, they would get in one another's way.

They had no choice but to attack as one.

My first arrow hit the closest soldier in the side of his neck. Demos kicked him free, and I saw the moment he realized what I'd done.

He never looked up. But he killed the other two with fresh rage. And the next three Eprothans who attacked after that.

That was fine. My fury had returned too. Because this was where Demos had decided to die. He knew eventually his sword arm would tire and his movements would slow. He was simply trying to take as many Eprothans with him as he could.

Cryton and I fired arrow after arrow. The soldiers hadn't been expecting it, and several of them fell, making life difficult for those behind them, who were still attempting to get into the pass.

Cryton turned his attention to the Eprothans who still had some magic left, while I fired relentlessly at the closest soldiers.

They caught on to our position quickly, and their own archers began firing back. Both of us ducked our heads, and several arrows thunked into the rock behind us. My hands wanted to shake, but I clenched my teeth, forcing them to steady.

And then the Eprothans began screaming.

Not the soldiers closest to us.

But the Eprothans' rear guard.

They were under attack.

The first fragile thread of hope wound through me. Please. *Please.*

"Who is it?" Cryton muttered.

"I don't know." I peered into the distance, where fae orbs cast a dim light over the Eprothans' foot soldiers. "I think they're humans. They're not wearing uniforms or armor…"

The Eprothans began to scatter. Our soldiers sprinted into the pass, and Cryton and I kept firing, until most of the front lines decided not to follow them. One of their generals screamed at them to reform the lines, and Cryton's arrow went through his eye.

I winced.

That was enough to buy us some time. Whoever was attacking, it would allow Demos and the others to get through the pass.

"Let's go."

Strangely, wiggling down the side of the rock was easier than going up had been. A few footspans from the ground, I let go, expecting my feet to hit the path.

Instead, I landed in someone's arms.

Panic slammed into me, but it was Demos's mouth that caught mine in a brief, hot kiss.

"One of these days you're going to learn to follow my orders."

"Who is it? Who is attacking?"

He shook his head with a stunned laugh. "Caddaril the Cleaver and his criminals. He must have rounded up several thousand men. I'm betting most of them abandoned Regner's army or disappeared right around the time conscription was announced."

Demos nodded at Cryton, and together with the remainder of Demos's "good soldiers," we sprinted into the pass.

Herne had talked us through what to do with his traps, and together, we rolled a dark red rock into place, covered up several neatly dug holes, and laid the trip ropes.

And then we ran.

The pass narrowed, and we only had a single light orb between us. Gwynara had waited for us, and my chest lightened at the sight of her, alive. But she was clearly out of magic, and she simply gave us a relieved nod.

Our sprint became a jog, which became a slow trudge.

The hours passed mostly in exhausted silence. Demos kept hold of my hand, refusing to release it. "We lost over half the hybrids we arrived with," he told me at one point, his voice a low, lifeless murmur.

At least fifteen hundred hybrids hoping for a new life. For freedom.

Gone.

A voice came from someone's trowth stone. Demos

pulled it out of his pocket. Obviously, we were within distance, but from the monotonous sound of the voice calling to us, they'd been trying for some time.

"Here," Demos said.

The voice came alive. "Help. We need help. Regner's ships are moving into the Sleeping Sea to bring down the ward. And on land…the creatures…oh gods, no!"

The voice cut off.

The mountains around us seemed to cave in, and my mind turned blank.

Without a single word spoken, we began to run once more.

It felt as if it took years to get to the end of the pass. Even Gwynara began stumbling along with us, her natural fae grace no match for her exhaustion. The trail angled up, and then down. And then up once more.

Suddenly, the rock surrounding us seemed to fall away. And for a single moment, all I could see was a tapestry of stars above us. My legs trembled from our relentless pace, and after the silent oppressive confines of the pass, the frenetic energy of soldiers preparing once more for attack was jarring.

But beyond those soldiers, a few hundred footspans to our right, a dark, oily presence oozed across the ground.

I blinked, and the truth of what I was seeing settled on me like a boulder. Terrovians. Thousands of the four-legged fae creatures that Regner had twisted to obey his every whim.

"They've been there for some time," one of the soldiers said. "Waiting for a signal likely."

Demos nodded. "This is what Regner does. He targets

morale. So by the time the battle is upon his enemies, they barely have any strength and courage left to summon."

I swept my gaze over our soldiers. They were exhausted. It was clear with every long, slow blink. But they weren't out of courage. They had no dearth of bravery. Even now, knowing what was about to happen, they were forming their lines, ready to die to protect the hybrids hidden in the caves nearby.

Something in my chest wrenched. They might never get to see the world we were hoping to create.

But they believed in that world enough to sacrifice everything for others to experience it.

"Well," I said, licking my suddenly dry lips. "It's a good thing we killed the last of his skyrions."

A few people chuckled at that. Demos nudged me, and I realized he was guiding me to a sizable hill. It was almost a geographical anomaly, standing guard between the mountain pass and the sea. Covered in a patchwork of grasses and low shrubs, it offered the best possible view of the area. Natural rock formations and scattered trees provided some cover, and already, tents were being set up for generals and healers.

My thighs burned as I followed him up the craggy side of the hill.

"Something's happening!" a voice shouted.

Regner's fleet was positioned in the distance. Thousands of ships, small enough from here that they appeared as nonthreatening as dinghies.

But a solitary ship approached from the north, arrowing toward shore. It was also one of Regner's, but it was being followed by at least ten other ships—almost as if it were being chased.

A fight broke out between the ships. Even from here, I could see the spark of weapons as Regner's captains all turned on that single ship.

A strange disquiet slid between my ribs.

The ship blew apart. No one spoke. And I had the horrible feeling that whoever had been on that ship had come to help us.

One of Regner's ships moved too far south—crossing an invisible line. A long, scaled tail slipped from the water and smashed into the hull again and again and again. A savage vindication filled me as the ship began to sink.

As long as those wards stayed up, the serpents would see any ship in their waters as an attack.

More of Regner's ships lingered in the distance.

Demos stiffened. "They're trying to shift the wards. I can feel it."

I shuddered.

Almost immediately, one of the archers brought Demos a trowth stone. He eyed it. "Report."

"The scout who contacted you..." the voice said. "He got too close to one of the creatures. It...took him."

I glanced away. Beneath the soldiers' murmurings, I could hear the crash of the waves against the shore. And I watched as the first light of dawn crept over the horizon, painting the sky in strokes of soft pinks and oranges. The light illuminated Regner's ships in the north, unable to come closer until they brought down our kingdom's wards.

Turning my gaze back to the sunrise, I ignored the enemy ships silhouetted against the glowing backdrop of the sun. I ignored the staggering number of banners flying menacingly in the morning breeze. I ignored the growls of the terrovians and the way every hair on my body stood at attention.

For a brief moment, I watched the sun climb above the water. And it felt like a gift.

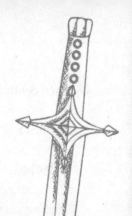

30

ASINIA

Our people died courageously. With weapons in their hands and fury in their eyes. With bared teeth and shields held high as they protected our most vulnerable.

But still, they died.

And died.

And died.

When Demos began steadily cursing, I knew Regner had managed to shift Lyrinore's wards. Our kingdom was defenseless.

And Regner's ships began to sail south without repercussions—just as the terrovians attacked. Our own wards were only useful for magical attacks, and so our warders were hidden away, where they might do some good when Regner's foot soldiers came for the hybrid children.

Cryton and I were perched on a rock about five footspans high. And together, we fired at the creatures again and again.

"They don't like the water," Cryton said suddenly, raising his head.

I watched. He was right. Any terrovians who came close to the seawater would instantly flee backward, far from their kin, as they continued to attack.

My heart pounded as I picked up the trowth stone Demos had left with us.

"Drive them toward the sea!" I yelled into it. "They hate the salt water."

Demos didn't reply. I searched for him, my gaze finding him fighting at the front, dispatching terrovians so fast, his sword was a blur. But he must have heard my voice coming from the trowth stone in his tunic, because he began roaring instructions. Slowly, our people began pushing the terrovians toward the shoreline. More and more of the creatures began to flee.

But it wasn't enough.

In the wide expanse of the sea, more of Regner's fleet had arrived. They knew we were here, and they knew we had the better location, even if we were horrifyingly outnumbered. When they attacked, they would march together, wiping us out with methodical precision.

"What the fuck is that?" Cryton yelled.

I whipped my head in the direction he was pointing. A few hundred footspans from us, where Prisca had dropped into the tunnel to our kingdom…

Vynthar sprinted toward us. And at least fifteen other Drakoryx loped out with him.

My heart tripped. I remembered Telean telling me there were so few Drakoryx left, to see even one was considered a special event.

Of course, if they didn't consider you worthy, they would also be the last sight you'd ever see.

The Drakoryx tore into the terrovians with a viciousness that made the fae creatures seem meek by comparison. The hybrids who'd never seen them were visibly shocked, but they immediately roared their approval.

I continued firing. But I was almost out of arrows.

Fog filled my head, a heavy weight pressing on the back of my neck.

Someone began cheering hoarsely. Others joined in.

I scrambled for a better view, almost falling off my rock.

My throat ached viciously. My lower lip trembled until I sank my teeth into it. But I couldn't hide the tears rolling down my cheeks in twin rivers.

In the distance, behind the terrovians, Prisca and Lorian rode toward us on horseback, Galon and Marth by their sides.

Rekja rode near Prisca and Lorian, Thora on one side, Tor on the other.

And behind them was an army.

The army that had somehow made it across the pass before Regner's foot soldiers. Fae, humans, and hybrids marching together for a better life.

And in the Sleeping Sea…Daharak Rostamir's fleet slammed into Regner's ships.

MADINIA

I'd lost track of time again.

When Miric left, Rythos had sat on my bed. Slowly,

in a whisper so faint I'd barely heard him, he'd relayed their conversation.

Miric would try to find a way to get us out of here. But it would take some time. Time that Rythos needed to use to distract his brother. To bargain with him.

While Rythos's cousin had warned that Brevan would be coming "soon," it was still hours before the Arslan prince strolled through the main cell door.

"You know what I want," he said, meeting Rythos's eyes.

"My power only allows the council to feel friendship, Brevan. If they've continued to work to prepare our fleet, perhaps it is because they truly feel it is necessary."

"Then remove your power and let us see what happens."

"I will."

Triumph flickered across Brevan's face, almost too quickly for me to catch it. But I had.

"Your father sent you down here?" I smirked at him. "Why doesn't he come down himself?"

Brevan ignored me. But several tiny lines appeared next to his eyes. Tension.

Rythos shot me a warning look before turning back to his brother.

"I will remove any remaining power from the council," Rythos conceded, and I considered finding the cheese knife once more. "But only if you will agree to listen to what I have to say."

Fury raged in his brother's eyes. "I know what you will say. You want our fleet for your own use. Even after leaving this island so many years ago, you believe you can now come back and take whatever you want."

Rythos stared at him. "That's what you think this is?"

Brevan's expression grew flat once more. But Rythos let out a disbelieving laugh. "This is no power struggle. This is about the future of this continent."

His brother paused. After a long moment, he waved his hand. "Then speak."

And so Rythos spoke. He told his brother about meeting Prisca and learning she was the hybrid heir. He told him of the grasp Regner had on his kingdom—but that it would never be enough. He told him of the invasion of Gromalia, and how Rekja had been forced to concede the kingdom's shining star to Regner's soldiers.

He told him of Prisca and Lorian and their mating and marriage.

He told him of the barrier, and how bringing it down had given thousands of humans back their power.

Brevan had a chair brought in at one point, and food was delivered for all of us. I'd expected him to lose interest by now, but he was clearly a man of his word, because he gestured at Rythos to continue.

Likely, Brevan was simply toying with him.

But Rythos told him of the spiders. He told him about Cavis and exactly what had happened to the man he'd considered a true brother. Brevan's eyes had flashed at that, and Rythos simply continued speaking. He told him of Cavis's sacrifice and warned him of just how many spiders Regner had in various courts.

Finally, Rythos fell silent, his voice hoarse.

But not before telling his brother one final thing.

"If you help us, I promise I will never return."

Brevan studied him. And I couldn't read his expression. "That would be too easy."

Confusion flickered across Rythos's face.

"You never *wish* to return," Brevan clarified. "For you to stay away and live a life of ease and little responsibility would be a reward. One you haven't earned."

"He has spent his life fighting for the future of all four kingdoms," I snarled. "What exactly have you done?"

Brevan ignored me, although those lines had appeared near his eyes once more.

His gaze was steady as he looked at Rythos. "When this war is won, you will not go to the hybrid kingdom with your friends. You will not live out your days in indulgent luxury. No, you will return here. And you will serve beneath me when I am crowned."

"You fucking bastard," I breathed.

Brevan glanced at me then. "I suggest you hold your tongue."

Rythos took a deep, shuddering breath. And I watched as he pictured his future—the life he *had* earned with each drop of blood spilled for the hybrids and fae. Grief hunched his shoulders and twisted his mouth. And Rythos let that future go.

"I agree," he said.

We'd spent so much time in such close quarters that even the way Rythos breathed currently irritated me. And yet my stomach churned at the bleak hopelessness in his eyes.

Brevan nodded. "In that case, I will order the council members here tomorrow."

Rythos jumped to his feet. "Tomorrow is too late.

Brevan, please—"

"It will have to do."

Getting to his feet, he turned and walked out of the corridor.

PRISCA

Regner wasn't here. But he was close.

I could practically feel him as our army marched toward the wide shoreline where his monsters had pinned our people. Out of the corner of my eye, I caught sight of Tor riding like he'd been born in the saddle, Rekja close to his side. The Gromalian prince had personally guarded him every moment since we'd left.

Wild green eyes met mine. And the steadiness in them calmed the worst of my fear. "Are you ready, wildcat?"

"Yes."

Lorian's power swept out of him, the fae fire incinerating at least ten thousand snarling creatures.

Pulling at the threads of my power, I froze time for the creatures that remained too close to our own people to risk using fae fire.

And I paused time for the fae fire too.

This would have been impossible just weeks ago when we brought down the barrier. Now, it was as if I had stepped into my power in a way I had never imagined I could.

Galon urged his horse forward, his water ready.

Marth already had a huge canvas sack of damask powder, and as we watched, he threw it into the air.

Right into the path of Galon's water. It soaked into Lorian's fae fire, ensuring that when time resumed, it wouldn't spread to the forest—and to our own people.

"Go!" Marth yelled.

Whoops and screams of frenzied delight rang out as our soldiers filed past, killing as many terrovians as they could while they were vulnerable.

Kaliera looked as if she'd tasted something terrible.

I gave her a wide smile. I hadn't wanted to waste one drop of my power proving myself. Because I'd needed it for this.

Zathrian snorted out a laugh. I ignored him, nudged my horse, and rode toward my brothers.

"Faster!" Marth roared.

Hooves and boots thumped against the hard sand, increasing the pace but remaining in sync.

I was attempting to make this look easy. Like it didn't cost me. But gods, it did. Stopping time for this many creatures, and holding it for this long...

And still...if I hadn't been unable to use my power for so many weeks, I wouldn't have had enough strength to hold time hostage for this long.

Our army was only halfway past their lines when I had to let the threads go. I couldn't risk burning out. Not before we killed Regner.

Steeling myself, I glanced over my shoulder.

One moment, the terrovians had been slaughtering our people.

And the next, thousands of our soldiers were fighting

in their place from the edge of the forest to the wide expanse of sand.

"Toward the sea!" someone roared from the hybrids waiting ahead of us. "Turn them toward the sea."

Lorian used his lightning now, sweeping a long, hair-raising blue bolt from the west side of the island near the forest, across the sand.

Terrovians touched by Lorian's power died instantly. Those that were forced back close to the seawater turned and sprinted away.

I blinked. Was that—

There.

Preventing the terrovians from fleeing toward our people...

A group of Drakoryx.

Vynthar leading them as he snarled threateningly, refusing to cede a single inch of ground. I swallowed a sob. My friend hadn't abandoned us. No, he'd gone to gather the remainder of his kind.

And by fighting with us here today, they were risking their extinction.

"They'll reform the lines when Regner's foot soldiers arrive," Lorian said. "But for now, we've achieved what we needed to."

Shouts and laughs, and joyous hollers broke out when we made it to the hybrids near the pass. We were directed toward a hill that seemed to be an extension of the mountains, and Demos wrapped his arms around me.

We'd made it in time. My heart soared, and for just a moment, I could forget everything else except for the fact that he was still alive.

"That was quite an entrance," he rumbled.

"I thought you'd appreciate it," I pulled away. "Tibris? Asinia? Vicer?"

"All alive."

My breath shuddered out of my lungs, my knees weakening. But despite the joy that had lightened his expression, his eyes were flat.

My smile faltered. "How many, Demos?"

"Two-thirds of the hybrids you sent with Vicer. They died protecting our most vulnerable."

Heat seared the backs of my eyes. "We sent sixteen hybrids ahead of us. Some of our most powerful people."

"They were in one of Regner's ships?"

"Yes."

"Something went wrong. We watched as Regner killed them."

I closed my eyes. Orivan had been convinced that the hybrids were some of the best shielders in our army. But Regner had prepared for them.

"Pris?" Demos's voice was soft.

I opened my eyes. This was not the time to fall apart. That would come later.

He pressed something cool into my hand and I glanced down. The amulet. My throat tightened. "Thank you."

"I couldn't have done it without Asinia." He glanced over my shoulder, and I pivoted.

Asinia, Tibris, and Vicer strode through the crowd, picking their way through tents and a few fires already burning. Behind them, I caught a glimpse of a man who must be Herne.

He walked with the stride of someone who was used to giving orders. Our eyes met, and he sliced a single glance at Tibris.

In that glance, I saw a kind of bemused affection. Like Herne wasn't sure exactly how he'd ended up here, but he'd stay as long as Tibris was by his side.

They reached me, and as I hugged Asinia and Tibris, the heavy stone I'd been carrying in my gut disappeared. Tibris stepped back. "Pris, this is Herne."

Herne gave me a steady look. And he bowed his head. "Majesty."

"Call me Prisca. Thank you for keeping my brother safe."

Humor flickered in Herne's eyes, and next to him, Tibris's posture visibly relaxed.

"You brought your rebels," I said.

"I did. You've given us all something to believe in."

"Your Majesty?" a gruff voice said. I turned.

"Dashiel?"

He grinned at me. I barely recognized him from his time in Regner's dungeon. I'd promised him vengeance for his brother's death. And now he was taking it. And next to him...

"Margie!" It had been too long since I'd seen the woman who considered Vicer her adopted son. She patted my back when I hugged her.

"It's good to see you. Let me know when you need something to eat."

Demos let out a low curse, and I turned. He was staring down at the ground below us, where a few of our soldiers had ordered Zathrian and Kaliera off their horses.

"You didn't kill Zathrian?"

I delicately cleared my throat. "I felt his arrest would have more impact."

Demos rolled his eyes.

I ignored that. "Where's Telean?"

"We evacuated her from the hybrid camp this morning. She should currently be safe in one of the caves—if she actually followed orders for once."

"She did not."

I grinned at my aunt's displeased tone, turning to find her standing next to Lorian. She'd planted her hands on her hips, and while exhaustion lined her face, her gaze softened as it met mine.

Demos just sighed. But his eyes lit up as he glanced behind me.

"Rostamir came through."

"She did. No sign of Conreth or Rythos?"

"No."

My stomach twisted. I turned my gaze to our soldiers, where our generals were forming their lines. Regner's ships were currently preoccupied with defending themselves from Daharak's fleet. But when we'd met up with Rekja, he'd told us the Eprothan soldiers were just a few hours behind them, making their way across the Normathe Mountains.

And their numbers...

Even without the terrovians Regner was guaranteed to send thundering back toward us, the Eprothans outnumbered us at least two to one.

But it wasn't just the numbers that we needed. Conreth wore one of the fae amulets. Which meant we couldn't kill Regner without him.

Blynth strode past, nodding at Demos, and I knew they would soon be discussing strategy. Apparently, when Rekja had learned of the Eprothans' true plans, he'd convinced the general to begin moving our army north.

While Blynth had met Rekja in his capital, they'd also shared a drink at our wedding. So he'd trusted the Gromalian prince enough to order our soldiers to march before receiving my message confirming the order.

Telean held up her hand. "Eye tonics," she said, handing out vials to each of us without fae senses. "They've been created to last for a few days."

My aunt was always thinking about these kinds of things. I took my vial as the others did the same and downed it, grimacing. Whatever had been added for longevity had given it a sour, spoiled aftertaste. "Thank you, Telean."

I glanced around. Lorian had moved away to speak to Rekja.

"If we only have hours, we need to make the most of it," Demos said, handing his empty vial back to Telean. "No one slept last night. I'm ordering our people to rest in shifts until our scouts report a sighting of Regner's foot soldiers. In the meantime, I've posted three of my most trusted guards on Tor. No one will get to him, Pris."

My breath shuddered out of me. I wouldn't be surprised if Regner knew Tor's power was our only hope.

"The hybrids who made it through the pass?" I asked.

"They're in the caves. I wanted to try to get them to the tunnel when we arrived, but…one of the terrovians killed a scout who got too close. There's no way they would have made it."

"The elders?"

"Nothing from them yet."

Bitterness flooded my mouth, but I swallowed it down. Demos was watching me closely. "I want to show you something," he said. "Follow me."

Lorian's gaze immediately found mine as he noted me leaving. He was at my side a moment later, and I held out the amulet.

His lips curved, and he handed it to Galon, who was the closest. Both amulets gleamed in the sunlight as Galon slipped it over his head.

"I'll be right back," I said.

Lorian didn't look happy, but he nodded at Demos.

The forest wasn't as lush along this part of the shore as it was just a little south, where I'd docked last time I'd been on this continent. Scraggly undergrowth caught at my boots as Demos led me away from the hill where we'd set up camp. But within a few minutes, I heard voices.

"There are hundreds of caves here," Demos said. "Some of them are more shallow shelters than anything else. Others are deep and wide enough to hold twenty or thirty hybrids."

In one of the caves, a child was chortling—one of those belly laughs that made anyone within earshot smile. The first cave was partly hidden by the trees and underbrush, situated on the higher ground, where the forest met the base of the mountain. The mouth of the cave was shielded by overhanging foliage, making it difficult to spot.

I peered inside. Several wide eyes met mine.

"It's the queen," a small boy hissed. "I met the prince too."

"Did not."

"Did too!"

Demos leaned over my shoulder.

"See! That's him!"

I hid my smile.

"Shh," a harried-looking woman shushed them. She bowed her head. "Your Majesty."

"Do you need anything?"

"The others have ensured we have enough food and blankets for a few days. Thank you." Her terror was evident in her wide eyes, the tremble of her lower lip. But she glanced at the children watching us closely and squared her shoulders, firming her mouth.

"If we get the chance to move you to the tunnel, can you all be ready?"

The woman gave me a nod, her gray eyes flashing in the dim light. "We'll move quickly."

"Stay safe."

"You too. May the gods bless you."

Demos jerked his head, and I followed him away from the cave. "Why did you want me to see them?" I asked.

"Because I saw your face when you learned how many people we'd lost. And we're going to lose thousands more, Pris. If Rythos and Conreth don't get here in time... we're all dead. All of us. There will be no one left to save."

I took a shaky breath. "And you wanted to remind me that the children were relying on us?"

"No." His mouth firmed. "I wanted to remind you

that we're fighting for more than just our lives. Every decision we make will come down to one question—will this ensure the children of Lyrinore have a future?"

I glanced at another cave, not as well hidden as the others but guarded by two hybrid soldiers who bowed their heads at us. "And that cave?"

Demos's mouth tightened. "Prisoners."

"What kinds of prisoners?" Had we taken some of Regner's soldiers?

"Spiders." Demos hesitated. "Finley is in there, Prisca."

I met his eyes. Demos had told me what Finley had done. How he'd used his replication magic for Regner. None of us could figure out the timeline of when it had occurred. But no one had kept a close eye on his comings and goings. Because no one had suspected him. And clearly, we had all come to the wrong conclusion about Regner's dark magic.

He no longer needed to twist our people's minds when they were children. He could now do it to anyone of any age.

"I want to see him."

Demos nodded, as if he'd expected that.

"He helped us in so many ways, Demos. He proved over and over he was on our side." I could hear myself. Could hear the denial in my voice. But…

"So did Cavis," Demos said, his voice gentle. "Regner getting to Finley doesn't make him evil, Pris. It just means we can't trust him until we find a way to reverse Regner's filthy magic. And we need to keep him where we can see him."

The cave was dim, lit only by a few light orbs. Finley was the closest prisoner to the cave entrance. The moment I saw him, leaning against the cave wall, his head on his knees, I had to suppress my instinct to instantly order for him to be unchained.

He'd only seen sixteen winters.

And then he lifted his head. Demos leaned down and swept a hunk of Finley's curly brown hair away. The web crawled across his temple, disappearing into his hairline and peeking out across the shell of his ear. And his eyes... Gone was the shy boy who'd replicated my dagger. Now, his eyes were dazed, confused, almost blank. Just as Cavis's had been.

My head spun, and I stumbled.

"Pris..." Demos caught my arm and yanked me from the cave.

"I'm sorry." Bile crawled up my throat, and I panted, clamping down on the urge to vomit.

"Don't be sorry," he said. "I should have thought... I'm the one who's sorry."

"How many more?"

"I don't know. There are another ten proven spiders in that cave, and a handful of others died while traveling with Vicer and the hybrids."

Kaliera and Zathrian walked toward us, surrounded by three guards. I'd managed to stifle my emotions when I interacted with them. But seeing them strolling toward us as if *they* were inconvenienced, watching my cousin, who was a traitor to our people by choice, directly after seeing Finley, whose will had been stolen from him...

Zathrian's gaze met mine and immediately flicked away.

"Demos," he said. "Put a sword in my hand."

Demos's expression was cold. "So you can use it to stab us in the back?"

"I'll keep the manacles on. Just let me fight for the hybrids. Please." Desperation and false sincerity glittered in his eyes. He was nothing but a honey-tongued liar.

"You've never fought for the hybrids a day in your life," Demos said. "Why would you start now?"

I must have made some kind of sound, because Demos met my eyes. "You cannot be serious."

Zathrian smiled. Because he thought I was soft. Weak.

I looked at him, and his smile disappeared. "He's an inconvenience," I said to Demos, my gaze still on our cousin. "A loose end. What kind of future does he have in our kingdom after everything he's done? And I don't want to begin my rule by killing a family member. He knows if he tries anything, Lorian will make his death last for *years*. Let him die fighting instead."

I'd shown him mercy. Dying with a sword in his hand was more than he deserved. Surely my grandmother couldn't expect more than this. Zathrian and I stared at each other for a long moment. Finally, he nodded, his expression tight.

"Fine," Demos growled. "*She* goes nowhere," he said to the guards on either side of Kaliera. She gave my brother that cold, haughty stare I'd seen often while in her castle.

"Watch her the way you'd watch a poisonous snake slithering toward one of your children," I said.

Kaliera looked at me now, and I could almost see her planning my death. I gave her a cool smile as Demos nodded at one of the guards, who unchained Zathrian, leaving the heavy manacles around his hands. They would stop him from interfering with my power, but he would indeed be able to swing a sword.

If he wanted to go down fighting while pretending that he truly did have our people's interests at heart...

Fine. We needed every soldier we could get at this point.

Zathrian was silent as he followed Demos and me out of the forest and onto the shore. Just a hundred footspans from here, the ground became hard sand. A few hundred footspans more, and it turned soft. That sand would leach our soldiers' energy with every step.

Marth took one look at Zathrian and shook his head at me.

I wrinkled my nose back at him, and he laughed.

Lorian appeared by my side. Leaning over, he whispered something in Zathrian's ear. My cousin's face drained of color, until he was almost gray. Lorian gave him a feral smile and slapped him on the back.

Demos gestured at one of the soldiers to give Zathrian a sword, and Lorian tensed, moving even closer to me.

A horn sounded.

Rough curses followed from everyone around me. I barely noticed. I was too busy watching the remainder of Regner's army appear in the north.

They came in an endless stream, like a dark river flowing down from the cold heart of the mountains, their black armor swallowing the light. As they filed onto the beach, it was as if they were crawling across the sand like lice, their armor a perfect match to the terrovians' dark, oily pelts.

But it was the noise that replaced my heartbeat, turning my knees weak. Their march was a constant, oppressive rumble. A reminder of just how heavily we would be outnumbered. From my vantage point, it was easy to see their formation cutting across the landscape, as the army fell into line after line.

My entire body went numb. But our soldiers watched me from all directions. I couldn't afford to show a hint of fear. Not a single drop of weakness. Forcing my trembling knees to straighten, I lifted my head, curling my lip at the sight of Regner's army.

Lorian stepped closer, the warmth of his body a silent comfort.

"They're still coming," I whispered, knowing he would hear.

"Yes."

Lorian had never once softened the truth to make it more palatable for me. He wasn't about to start now.

But he would be by my side until the end. Of that, I had no doubt.

His eyes met mine. "It's time."

A chill slid over me as I donned the armor Lorian had commissioned for me.

My palms turned slick with sweat. Nausea slithered through my gut as I swept my gaze over our people, standing in lines that seemed to stretch for thousands of footspans—until I imagined double those numbers marching toward us.

My gaze found Rekja's. The Gromalian king stared calmly back at me, refusing to give in to fear or hopelessness.

There was no separation between soldiers wearing Gromalian green stripes on their helmets and those who were not. Our people would fight side by side, and we would live or die by this decision.

Thousands of gazes still clung to my face. I could feel them. Could feel their hopes and fears.

Regner's foot soldiers continued to file onto the shore. But Regner hadn't been able to resist gilding their helmets. The sun glinted off the gold.

"That gold will make it easy to see who to kill," Orivan said, stepping up next to me. Both he and Blynth had considered attacking now, while Regner was still forming his lines. But Rekja and Demos had won that argument.

We needed every second we could find. Because all of us were still holding out hope that reinforcements would arrive.

"Tor?" I asked.

"Safe," Demos said. "He knows what to do. And he'll wait for our signal."

"Your Majesty!" someone yelled.

And that's when I saw it. Even with the charm Telean had given me, it was impossible to tell what was stumbling toward us.

Or who.

I frowned, squinting. It was a man. A man who staggered on the sand, almost falling.

My breath caught in my throat, and I broke into a run.

Lorian plucked me out of the air. "No, Prisca."

Vicer lunged forward, slamming into Demos, who blocked his way. Vicer let out a string of curses. "It's Natan, you cold bastard."

"Regner is waiting for you to go to him," Demos snarled. "His archers are poised. We wait until he's close enough that our wards can cover you."

I squinted into the distance. Natan shuffled along so slowly, it was clear he was critically wounded.

"Get Tibris," I choked out.

Movement behind me. Someone turned and ran.

"This was my call," Demos said softly. "I told him to slow them down. Natan knew exactly what he was doing, Prisca. He knew the risks."

I couldn't speak. Not without tears rolling down my cheeks. And I wouldn't allow our soldiers to see that. But gods, I wanted every single person in all four kingdoms to know that the reason Rekja's army made it before Regner's was because of the courageous man limping toward us.

He'd bought us much-needed time. And he'd paid for it.

Natan wore no shirt. Which made it easy to see the daggers that had been stabbed into his chest and stomach. Thin black lines curved out from those daggers, indicating poison. His feet were bloody, and his hands had been tied behind his back.

"Tibris is here," Demos whispered. "Just a few moments longer, Pris."

It felt as if it was years before Natan was within our

wards. The moment he made it, several of our soldiers leaped forward, catching him as he fell to his knees and slicing the rope from his wrists.

Regner's soldiers instantly slammed their power into those wards. But Tibris and Vicer had already shoved past Demos, crouching by Natan's side.

I followed them, dropping to the ground.

Natan's eyes met mine. He attempted to speak but couldn't.

"Water," Vicer demanded.

Someone handed him a waterskin. Natan managed a couple of sips.

"We need to remove the knives," Tibris said, holding his hands against Natan's chest. "But we need another healer to help. The poison…"

Natan caught his hand. "We both…know…not… living through…this."

"Yes, you are," I said, turning my head. "Healer!"

One of the fae healers rushed forward. When she saw Natan, she inhaled sharply.

Natan dropped his gaze to the daggers in his torso. "Worth it," he said.

"Natan…" My voice broke.

"Home," he whispered.

"Yes," Vicer said, taking his hand. Why wasn't he doing something? Why wasn't he—

"We'll bury you at home." Tibris's face was grief-stricken, his eyes hollow. Natan was his oldest friend. If there was anything to be done, he would be doing it.

No. *Please* no.

Natan smiled at Tibris and Vicer. He turned that

smile to me.

He was still smiling as he died.

My blood went cold. I got to my feet. "Stone," I said.

Demos must have known I wasn't asking for a trowth stone. Instead, he handed me a small red nerth stone, designed to make my voice carry across a large crowd.

"This is what Regner does," I said. My voice shook with rage, and I forced myself to firm it. "He creates loss and then basks in it. He creates lies and then enjoys the lack of trust. He creates hopelessness and benefits from the lives spent lost to it.

"But this is not what *we* do. We create joy. We create friendship. We create life and love and hope. And when we have to—when someone forces us to—we create *death*. Today, we will make Regner regret choosing to target our people. We will make him regret the grief and loss and hopelessness he has wielded for centuries. We will defend our kingdoms and refuse to yield to the madness of the Eprothan king."

Cheers sounded, our soldiers thrusting their swords into the air. There would be time for mourning later. For now, I couldn't afford to let Regner's evil chew at me. I handed the stone back to Demos. He said something into the stone, and our people began to march.

In front of us, Regner's soldiers were doing the same.

Most of his left flank was made up of terrovians. Lorian had killed many of his skyrions when they'd attacked Sorlithia, and Asinia and Demos had clearly taken care of the rest when they'd destroyed Regner's mine. Even as the thought pleased me, I found myself staring at the snarling, four-legged creatures slinking toward us.

I knew why Regner had placed them closest to the forest. To the mountains.

Because when he cut through our army, those creatures would be the best suited for hunting down anyone who thought to run. They'd sniff out hybrids in the caves, in the forest, or fleeing back through the pass.

"We need to kill the terrovians fast."

"We do," Demos said. He nodded at Vynthar and the other Drakoryx prowling toward the terrovians. "And we will."

Nearby, Lorian was speaking with Galon and Marth.

"For Cavis," he said.

"For Cavis." Marth's voice was hoarse.

"For Cavis," Galon agreed. "And for us." His gaze drifted over the soldiers before landing on Natan's body, Tibris and Vicer still at his side. "For all of us."

31

PRISCA

Soldiers marched toward their enemies, weapons in their hands, shields raised.

"Fire!" someone roared, and our archers let loose, the sky filling with black arrows. Some of those arrows belonged to Asinia, and I let myself take a single moment to beg the gods to keep her safe.

The arrows landed. Some of our wards buckled, and where they fell, our people died. But the same was true for Regner's army.

Demos had ordered any fae, human, or hybrid wielding enough long-distance power to aim for the terrovians first. Our wards would protect us from magic and would guard against fae-iron tipped arrows for some time, but only Regner's ward offered protection from physical attacks.

The two armies smashed into each other in a clash of steel and power and blood.

Both Demos and Lorian had told me to wait. To use my power sparingly. Strategically. I could have overruled them, but their logic was sound. So I was forced to watch as our people died violently, so close to their homeland.

Behind us, anyone who wasn't fighting

or caring for the wounded was building a large barricade out of wood from the forest. If we had to fall back, it would offer at least a little protection.

We'd sent our messages to Tymriel and the other elders. At some point during this battle, we would have to move the hybrids from the caves to the tunnels. Because it was only a matter of time before Regner learned they were there. And because if we lost this battle, there would be no one standing between the hybrids and the Eprothans.

"The older hybrids and fae talked of war as if it was something teeming with adventure. A saga brimming with heroism and thrill," a voice said behind me, interrupting my dark thoughts. I turned. Ameri stepped close, her gaze on the battle.

"They have to," I said. "Or no one who had lived through it would ever step onto a battlefield again."

She nodded, and when her gaze met mine, her eyes were wet. "Part of me wishes I'd trained like the soldiers. So I could make a difference."

"You've saved more lives during this war than almost anyone else."

Ameri's power wasn't made for the harsh daylight of battle. It was made for dark alleys and the shadowy silence of night. For quiet exchanges cloaked under the cover of darkness, where a single message could kill an enemy or a stealthy rescue could save a life. She might have been destined to be one of the unsung heroes of this war. Except I knew how she'd worked with Vicer in the city, smuggling out hybrids and feeding us information. If we lived through this, I would ensure everyone knew just how much she had contributed.

Her gaze lingered on one man near the front. And there was so much longing in her eyes, I found myself turning my head.

Ah.

The only way for Vicer to have used his power effectively would have been if we could have somehow snuck him into one of Regner's generals' tents. Since that was impossible, he fought sword-to-sword in the center lines, Dashiel at his side. I knew every soldier Dashiel felled was for his brother Thayer, who hadn't had a chance once his power erupted.

But Vicer fought for every hybrid and human. For the lives he couldn't save, and the ones he might save today.

"You should tell him how you feel."

"If we live through this, perhaps I will," Ameri said softly. She turned and walked away.

ASINIA

Arrow after arrow flew from my new crossbow. Next to me, Cryton nocked his own bolts just a hair slower. But what he lacked in speed, he made up for in distance, his muscular upper body giving him incredible power.

We aimed over our own lines, hitting as many of Regner's soldiers as we could while our more powerful hybrids continued to focus their own power on the terrovians.

Regner hadn't bothered shielding the humans on his front lines. They were the distraction. The bodies that would tire our own people just in time for his more experienced, powerful soldiers to take their places.

The humans on the front would be Eprotha's poorest. These were the villagers I'd grown up among. The people who'd lived without their own power for most of their lives. The fathers and sons who'd been conscripted and who'd had no choice but to fight for their king. Some of them wouldn't even have been able to read the conscription notice they'd been handed.

I choked out a sob, and my hand shook violently as I reached for my next arrow.

"I know," Cryton said grimly next to me. "I know, Asinia, but it's them or the children hidden in those caves. Let their faces blur and pretend they're just targets."

I tried. But I couldn't.

Still, I kept shooting until my arm ached, until my new crossbow felt as heavy as stone. And the most cowardly part of me was relieved when the armies clashed and we could no longer shoot from this position without risking our own people.

More of our archers were stationed in the mountains behind us, doing what little they could to slow down Regner's soldiers. I turned to Cryton. "You need to go join the others."

"Come with me."

"You know I can't."

His lips thinned. "Then may the gods watch over you."

I gave him a shaky smile. "I'll see you when this is over."

He turned and scrambled off the rock. I picked one final target, a human who was barreling toward one of our hybrids, a snarl on his face.

My bolt took him in the throat.

And then all I could see was the silver armor of our people as they closed ranks. As they marched and killed. In the distance, I caught sight of the occasional black helmet touched with gold, too close to our own people for me to aim.

But I could hear the harsh clash of swords, the thud of arrows meeting wooden shields and flesh, the hair-raising screams.

I could see the flash of magic, punctuated by the guttural cries of agony that followed.

I could smell the fear-sweat that hung on the air, mingling with the acrid bite of smoke from the Eprothans' fires in the distance.

But underlying those scents was the salty tang of the ocean breeze. The sweet, earthy fragrance of the forest at our backs. Occasionally, I could hear the crash of waves against the shore.

It seemed almost ludicrous that death would reign in this endless expanse of sky and sand and sea. Above our heads, gulls circled. Soon, they would be replaced by crows, feasting on corpses.

And in the vibrant, blue-green sea, the Eprothan ships that Daharak's fleet couldn't reach were anchoring in the shallows and sending skiffs of soldiers to paddle toward us, moving those soldiers up to the shore, where they joined Regner's camp behind their lines.

One of those ships drew close to the place where Rythos's childhood friend Fenreth had died so long ago when Prisca visited our kingdom. Soon, Regner's soldiers would attempt to come ashore and enter Lyrinore through that tunnel.

But that tunnel had its own magic, and I had a feeling that it would make those humans very, very sorry.

As I watched, one of Daharak's ships nimbly slid around one of Regner's, and the gold-clad ship was engulfed in fire and magic, smoke curling up to darken the cloudless sky.

Just as another of the Eprothan ships drew closer to the shore, lingering for far too long. As if it were taunting us.

And when the ship turned to display its mast, I could see why.

PRISCA

Lorian, Galon, and Marth raged across the battlefield. They were so deadly, I had to force myself to tear my eyes away, to focus on the rest of our army.

"Regner is too safe," Blynth murmured. "We have to infuriate him and then convince him he has nothing to lose by taunting us. We need a clear shot."

But we couldn't take that shot without the amulet Conreth wore around his neck.

Now, Blynth began cursing viciously. Dragging my

attention away from the battle, I followed his gaze.

An Eprothan ship was moving closer to shore. But unlike the others farther north of us, it didn't appear to be docking to add soldiers to Regner's lines.

No, this ship was tauntingly close for a whole different reason.

Tied to the mast of the ship hung the brutalized body of one of the sea serpents that had guarded our kingdom for so many years.

Just months ago, I'd stood entranced, watching one of these magnificent creatures glide through the water, surfacing only to showcase its huge wings. It had stared back at me with intelligent gold eyes that seemed to see deep into my soul.

My stomach lurched. My heart cracked. My entire body tightened, until all I could hear was the liquid churning in my ears.

Was this the same serpent? Or was it one of its family members? Perhaps a friend?

These majestic water beasts had prevented Regner from invading my kingdom for all these years. And now his people were enjoying their petty revenge.

My rage was endless, as if it might swallow me whole.

But rage required energy. Required hope. And I was gradually becoming drained of such things.

I should have understood what Regner was really doing. By the time we knew his plan, it was too late.

What would happen when Conreth arrived, only to find all of us already dead?

How would Rythos go on without his brothers, if he

was even still alive?

And Madinia... Regner and Rothnic would make her death horrifying if they found her after this.

"Your Majesty. Nelayra!"

Blynth again. I slowly turned my head, meeting his eyes.

The general flinched.

But he lifted his hand, pointing.

One of Regner's soldiers had been planted in the front lines. Only he was safely protected by a ward so thick, it shimmered in the sunlight. Surrounding him was a group of humans who were clearly meant to be little more than fodder.

The soldier wore a stripe of red beneath the gold on his helmet—clearly some designation Regner had created. He raised one gauntleted arm, and when he pointed, our soldiers *melted*.

Skin and bones liquefied, until where—until a moment ago—living, breathing people had been fighting for their lives, there was now nothing more than puddles of blood and *other things,* leaking beneath empty silver armor.

Behind me, I heard retching.

But I caught the moment Galon's head whipped to the right, toward the soldier.

Exactly where Demos was already aiming from the left, his sword carving a path through anyone who dared get in his way.

I'd wanted more than this for my brother. I think he'd wanted more than this for himself. And yet there was no question that a part of him came alive on the battlefield.

The most savage, vicious part.

Galon and Demos had never fought together. Oh, they might have sparred once or twice, but nothing that could explain the way Demos instinctively aimed for the humans between the soldier wielding death and Galon—still footspans away.

He took them down in two blows in such quick succession, it seemed almost as if they'd simply tripped and fallen. Just in time for Galon to slam his power into the remaining soldiers protecting their target. The ward glowed, fighting Galon's magic. But Demos had gotten close enough.

Just as that gauntleted arm came up once more.

I didn't hesitate. Yanking on my power, I froze time for the barest moment. Just long enough for Demos to slash out with his sword, removing the threat for good.

The soldier's head rolled free from his body. Galon and Demos both looked my way, wearing identical snarls.

Time resumed.

"You're fucking welcome," I muttered.

Behind me, Blynth made a choked noise. It sounded suspiciously like a laugh.

"Your Majesty!" The voice was panicked, and I whirled, sweeping my gaze toward the tents behind me, where a young soldier wiped blood from his face as he approached.

"Who?" I asked, dread pooling in my gut.

"Orivan."

"Take me to him."

The hybrid general had been dragged into Tibris's tent. And yet my brother wasn't working on him. Our eyes met, and Tibris shook his head.

"What happened?" I demanded.

The soldier had followed me inside the healer's tent. "He saw Yars go down. The general was friends with Yars's father. He trained that boy since the day he could hold a sword." He wiped a hand over his face and only succeeded in smearing more blood across his cheek. "I think maybe the general went a little crazed, Your Majesty. He leaped into the battle as if he were still a young man."

Tibris gestured him forward. "You need stitches for that cut."

Their voices faded to a murmur as I stared down at what was left of Orivan. The broadsword had almost cut him in half. He hadn't had a chance.

Turning, I walked out of the tent. And the slaughter continued.

32

PRISCA

When our soldiers had told stories of battle while we traveled here, I'd attempted to listen to what they didn't say.

I'd tried to pick apart their words, to prepare myself for just how horrifying this battle would be.

But nothing had prepared me for the smell of blood, heavy in the air. Nothing had prepared me for the brutal screams of the wounded and dying. And nothing had prepared me for this part—when I would be forced to do nothing but watch.

Despite our plan, soon, I would have no choice but to join the battle and use my power to buy my people as much time as I could. Enough time for them to run as fast and as far as possible.

I let my gaze drift to Lorian, my chest clenching.

His head suddenly whipped around. And he wasn't the only one. On the battlefield, Marth began roaring, his sword slashing so fast, it was a blur of blood and death.

Galon grinned, pointing behind me.

I whirled. Far in the distance—so far, I

had to squint despite the eye tonic I'd taken—marching in neat rows, silver armor gleaming in the sun…

Conreth's fae army. He'd marched his army through the northwestern fae lands and over the Minaret Mountains.

Our people fought with renewed vigor as that army marched toward us. A few footspans away, someone was sobbing, thanking the gods.

The color drained from Blynth's face, and the stern general suddenly looked as shaken as I'd ever seen him.

He'd accepted his death, I realized. He'd come to terms with it, and now Conreth was offering a tiny glimpse of hope.

The fae soldiers wasted no time. With no other choice, they marched straight into our lines, fighting shoulder to shoulder with our own soldiers as their power slammed into the Eprothans.

The moment Conreth was close enough, I threw my arms around him. The amulet he wore clinked against my armor.

Conreth stiffened, his surprise evident. But his hand came up to pet my shoulder. "My army is exhausted," he said. "An early snowfall hit, and we had to make camp for three days. Jamic helped there." He turned to glance at Jamic, who strode up to me with an easy confidence. Clearly, leaving him with Conreth had been the right choice.

"But we're here," Conreth said. His gaze slid over my shoulder, and I knew without looking that Lorian had left the battlefield to Conreth's fae.

They had a short, silent conversation.

"Good timing," Lorian said finally.

Conreth gave a sharp nod, something that might have been disappointment in his eyes.

A few of his people cut away from the rest of the army, making their way toward us. My heart thudded a joyful beat. "The wardens," I breathed.

"All but Verdion," Conreth confirmed. "I don't suppose you've heard—"

"No," Lorian bit out. "No word from Rythos."

Conreth's canted his head, and his eyes turned flat. He was watching someone closely.

Sylvielle.

The fae king's gaze flicked to Regner's army. But it wasn't the soldiers he was watching. No, his gaze lingered on the terrovians.

I turned to Lorian. But he was watching his brother. And from the look in his eyes, he'd come to some conclusion.

"Sylvielle," Lorian purred, and I almost shivered at the sharp edge in his voice, the cruel, cold smile he gave her.

She was wearing dark-green armor that looked like snake scales, her hair braided back into a crown that circled her head as she leaned on the wooden barricade. Our people were extending it as fast as they could. One of the hybrids gave her an impatient look as he attempted to hammer a piece of wood behind her.

Sylvielle's eyes lit up. "Yes?"

"Do me a favor and walk toward our archers."

She pouted. "Why?"

"Because I asked you to."

Anyone who truly knew Lorian would have heard the death that laced his tone. But Sylvielle clearly only heard the caress. She sent me one victorious look beneath her lashes and turned, walking toward them.

"What am I missing?" I demanded, my voice low.

"Shh," Lorian said. "Watch."

Sylvielle moved closer, every step sinuous, her body created to draw the male gaze. I ground my teeth, glancing at Lorian and Conreth. But they weren't watching her.

No, they were watching the terrovians once more.

And as soon as Sylvielle got within range, every terrovian on the battlefield seemed to go still.

Looking at her.

Turning back to us, Sylvielle swept her gaze over Conreth and Lorian, sending a poisonous smirk my way. When she found them looking beyond her, she glanced over her shoulder.

Her eyes were wide with horror when she turned back to us.

"Your Majesty," she mouthed, running toward us.

Conreth let out a growl like a wounded animal. Behind him, Romydan, Thorn, and Caliar echoed him.

A warden. One of their own. This was proof. Proof that she had given fae creatures to Regner. Proof that those creatures had a deep connection to her.

"Please!" she shrieked.

Conreth raised his hand. His power sliced into her, and she shattered into a million pieces.

Just like Lorian had.

The world dimmed around me. Lorian cursed, pulled me away, and wrapped his arms around my shaking body.

"I'm fine." My voice sounded very far away. But I didn't have time to fall apart. I wiggled and he released me.

He had to get back to the front. So did the wardens. I turned, finding Conreth watching me.

"I'm sorry," he said.

"Don't be. At least we know she can't do any more damage now."

"Prisca," Lorian said.

"Look," someone called. "Some of the terrovians are fleeing."

They were right. Hundreds of the creatures seemed to have responded to Sylvielle's death with blind terror. That terror was overriding whatever power Regner had used to make them obey his orders.

The sight helped me rebuild my walls.

"Go. Please. We'll talk about this after," I promised, my voice a low murmur.

Lorian pulled me close once more, pressed a gentle kiss to my lips, and strode away, his brother following in his footsteps.

THE QUEEN

The sounds of battle raged on and on and on.

After Zathrian convinced Prisca to put a sword in his hand—and I would never understand how he'd achieved *that*—I'd been left here alone, two guards posted outside my cave.

"I need to use the bathing room," I'd called at one point.

"Piss yourself," one of them had replied with a low laugh before they'd returned to ignoring me once more.

How had it come to this?

Even as I asked the question, I knew the answer.

Pelysian. The man I'd considered loyal for so many years. And his bitch mother.

Every step they'd allowed—no...*urged*—me to take had ensured I'd end up here as one of my enemy's prisoners.

For years, I'd believed in Pelysian's loyalty. Even as I saw the way he began looking at me. Even as I heard what he didn't say in the space between his words. Still, I'd been convinced that he would see I only wanted what was best for this continent and the people living on it.

"You!" one of the guards said.

Twin thuds. As if two bodies had hit the ground.

Jamic stepped into the cave. "Hello, Mother."

My eyes flooded with tears. "How did you know?"

"Pelysian told me you'd be here."

I was wrong, then. Wrong to question Pelysian's loyalty.

It wasn't too late. My son was here, freeing me. We would finally be together.

But Jamic was crouching next to me, and his eyes looked far too old for his face. Ancient in a way that made me shiver.

And when he spoke, it was clear he expected to be obeyed.

"Jamic..."

Shaking his head, he handed me the dagger. "You know what you need to do."

My hand trembled as he reached for it. And then he pulled it away several inches until our eyes met once more. "Don't make me regret this."

"You won't."

In the end, it would be Jamic and me ruling this continent.

And no one would ever dare to hurt us again.

PRISCA

Bodies lay scattered across the battlefield like fruit rotting in an orchard.

Our wounded were carried to safety whenever possible—taken to healers' tents, where I knew Tibris was saving as many lives as he was able. I'd heard from Asinia that Telean had planted herself in there with him and was helping however she could.

Lorian had sent Marth and Galon for me. And they'd wedged me between them as we fought our way toward the front lines. It was time to use my power.

Lorian had used much of his own power turning thousands of the terrovians to ash when we'd arrived. But he still struck again and again, his lightning targeting Regner's most powerful.

When he switched to using only his sword, I knew

Lorian was conserving the last of his power for Regner.

I could taste dirt and sweat and blood on my tongue, infiltrating each of my gasps for air amid the relentless onslaught.

Above our heads, the sun had almost disappeared, a heavy cloak of ash and smoke hanging low in the sky.

There was nothing left but the cacophony of steel clashing against steel, the sparks of magic slamming into wards, and the anguished cries of the fallen. Beneath my feet, the hardened sand had been churned until each step was a struggle. Exhaustion pressed down onto me, reflected in the faces of each and every soldier fighting on both sides.

Reaching for the threads of my own power, I panted, holding as tightly as I could. Our soldiers had gotten used to the way their enemies would go unnaturally still now, and they knew they had to kill as many of them as possible while I leashed time itself.

With each attack, our people rallied, cutting down those who would gladly kill us.

And as I let time resume, I saw death where there had previously been life. I heard screams as Eprothan soldiers fought next to their friends one moment, only to see them dead at their feet the next.

The battlefield became a bloodbath. A horror so great, part of me wondered what a life after this could possibly look like for me. I would see these men in my nightmares for the rest of my days.

But even with all the death we wielded, it wasn't enough. We were being forced back, our numbers simply too small against Regner's army.

"Now!" Lorian roared, and I clutched the hourglass around my neck. I no longer had to fight with the hourglass to drain my power slow and steady. It was as if discovering my power hidden within me had unlocked some new facet of control.

Demos was suddenly at my elbow as our soldiers surged forward. He pulled me back, nodding at Lorian, who yelled something to Marth and Galon. A moment later, Lorian was falling back with me while the others moved farther into a sea of blood, launching themselves toward the front lines.

Demos pulled me to where our archers had taken their stand. Asinia appeared exhausted as she shoved several arrows into her quiver. When I looked between our barricade and the battle raging to our north, it was evident just how much ground we had lost.

Hevdrin and Blynth approached. Both generals looked grim.

"We're too heavily outnumbered," Demos said. "We have to think smart. Have to take Regner by surprise in some way."

Hevdrin wiped at his sweaty face with the back of his arm. "What are you suggesting?"

"We put everything into our left flank. And we hit hard."

With the water to the west, Regner's soldiers would have nowhere to go—unlike the soldiers closest to the mountains, who could turn and flee.

"We take soldiers from the rear lines to funnel into the left flank," Demos continued. "Those on the front must stand their ground. And not cede an inch."

The blood drained from my face. I could see what Demos wanted to do, and it made perfect, logical sense. But it might also kill—

"What about Vicer and Herne and the others?" Asinia demanded, ripping the words from my mouth. "They're fighting right where you want to pull the most soldiers."

My stomach hollowed out. The man who had sacrificed so much for our people. And the man my brother loved.

Demos's jaw firmed. "We have to trust them to hold on for just a little longer. We have to thin Regner's army before we fall back ourselves. And the best way to do that is to break his lines and make his soldiers panic. Otherwise, Regner will stay protected. He won't appear until he thinks we're almost done. And if we don't break his lines, we'll truly be done soon."

Next to me, Lorian pulled out his waterskin, handing it to me. "Drink," he ordered.

"What do you think?" I asked him.

"I think it's the hardest call you'll have to make in your life, wildcat. But it's the kind of tactic that may just save us. We're losing. At this point, it's only a matter of time."

"We break their right flank, and it could give us a chance to get to Regner," I said.

But if this didn't work, anyone on our weakened right flank was dead.

No. I couldn't afford to think like that.

I turned my gaze to the sea, where Regner's ships bore down on Daharak's fleet with brutal ferocity. Daharak's pirates had defended our kingdom so far, but the enemy was relentless, the sheer numbers tipping the scale, exploiting gaps and weaknesses.

In the water, the sea serpents were now fighting back, slamming their tails into Regner's hulls. But each of the Eprothan ships proudly bore one of those dead serpents hanging from its mast.

"The ward falling took the serpents by surprise," Demos said, his voice heavy with grief.

"How many do you think are left?"

He swallowed. "The ones the humans managed to kill? They're the babies."

I closed my eyes against his words, but I was forced to open them once more as several people inhaled sharply.

Many of Daharak's ships were ablaze, the sea around them a graveyard of floating debris. And Regner's ships were arrowing away from us.

Toward our kingdom.

"The elders have prepared our people," Demos said, but his voice was grim. "The Eprothans won't find any hybrids near the coast. What they will find are vicious traps that will keep them busy until we finish this."

Firming my lips, I nodded. Demos turned back to the others.

"For this to work, we need to make sure we're ready. The trowth stones will help us communicate across the battlefield, but the noise and chaos on the front lines will still make it difficult."

Lorian gazed out at the battle, and his hand tightened on his sword. "Our army is highly disciplined and well-trained, but it will still take time to realign forces without confusion or breaking the formation."

"Terrain and visibility are good," Demos countered. "Our biggest issues are speed, timing, and the risk of exposure. If it's too slow or poorly timed, Regner's commanders will realize what we're doing, and they'll hit our right flank hard the moment they sense weakness." Demos's eyes met mine. "This is where you come in, Pris. How much power do you have left without burning out?"

My heart raced, and my skin suddenly felt too tight.

"If you can ensure our soldiers are ready to move, I'll buy them the time they need."

Lorian nodded. "The Bazinith," he said. "This is what they trained for. Get them to the front lines of the left flank to lead the charge with us. Now."

It took time to move soldiers from the right flank to the left. The word had to spread, and our people began to slowly move to the left. It was messy. It was disorganized. But soon, as I stood on the hill above the battle, Lorian once more fighting on the front lines, I could see the restructure taking place.

We'd needed a distraction to hide exactly what was happening. And Conreth gave it to us. He attacked with his wardens, crashing their power into Regner's left flank again and again.

This would drain most of what they had left. Already, one of the fae generals was screaming something at Conreth—likely begging him to retreat. And he was right. If the fae king went down...

But Conreth ignored him, his vicious, deadly power cutting through creatures with four legs and those with only two.

My eyes stung at the screams. But Demos was

suddenly standing next to me. "Ready, Pris?"

"Ready."

"Now!" He roared the word into his trowth stone, and I strained, tiny dots appearing in my vision as I clutched at my hourglass and willed my power to give me more. After using so much power, I was tiring, my hands shaking, my eyes blaring. My knees wobbled, and I gripped Demos's arm to steady myself.

The thread snapped.

I hadn't been able to hold time for long—perhaps a minute at most. Our soldiers were still moving from the center lines and the right flank. Conreth and the others were attacking with everything they had. Hopefully their distraction would help hide my own failure.

It wasn't enough. *I* wasn't enough.

"Nelayra."

I ground my teeth at the sound of Zathrian's voice. He was supposed to be on the front lines, a sword in his hand.

Demos slowly turned his head. "What is he doing here?"

"I brought him," Telean said.

I glanced over my shoulder. Demos kept his gaze on Zathrian, who stood next to Telean, his shoulders square, his head oddly canted, as if bracing for a blow.

Demos's eyes filled with cool disdain. "When we need someone to neutralize Prisca's power, we'll let you know." He turned back toward the battle. "Ready to go again?" he asked me.

"Yes."

"Neutralizing isn't all I can do," Zathrian said from

behind us. "Allow me to show you. Please."

Demos ignored him. But...Telean had asked. And she was giving me that calm, steady look that demanded I listen. "You will need your power to help strip Regner of his wards," she said. "If you use all of it now, we are doomed. You know I would not ask this of you if it was not necessary."

No, Telean would never expect me to work with the man who'd risked our kingdom unless she knew it could truly make a difference. My gaze dropped to his wrists, and I sighed. My aunt had already removed the manacles he'd been wearing.

"Fine."

Demos didn't argue. But he drew his dagger, his hand clenched around the hilt as if it was taking everything in him not to plunge it into our cousin's heart.

Zathrian merely nodded at Demos. "Ready."

Demos lifted the trowth store with his other hand. "Now."

I reached for the thread of my power, and a cool wind swept through me. The shock of it was almost enough to make me drop the thread of my power. But that cool wind seemed to make it *easier* to lift that thread somehow. I yanked my power to me and held it. And this time...it was lighter. It was as if the thread was balanced, and I merely had to hold it gently. My vision didn't blur. My knees didn't tremble. I could still feel the drain, but it was tempered this time, bolstered by the icy gust of Zathrian's power.

Demos must have felt me jolt, because he grabbed my arm. "Hold on," he urged.

And together with the cousin whose parents were responsible for the loss of my own, the cousin who had killed my husband and mate while challenging me for my throne...

We held time hostage and gave our people everything we had.

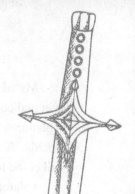

33

PRISCA

O n my right, Demos roared orders into the trowth stone, choosing the best possible moments for me to use my power. To my left, Zathrian poured everything he had into me, and I gladly took what he had to offer.

The three of us were the last of my grandmother's bloodline.

I hoped she was watching. And I hoped that even if we died today, some part of her would be proud.

Finally, just when I was convinced this had been the worst possible decision…A hint of movement in Regner's right flank.

Thanks to both Telean's eye tonic and the ground we had lost, I could see the panicked expressions of Regner's generals as their soldiers fell and died. As others turned to run.

And still, it wasn't enough. Regner was safe behind his soldiers.

For now.

The air was thick with the scent of iron and blood, the metallic tang sliding along my tongue and stinging my nostrils. Demos held up a hand. "Enough. Conserve what you have left."

My head spun dizzily. Next to me, Zathrian leaned over and panted, placing his hands on his thighs. "Kaliera is planning something," he said. "She has someone on the outside. A man named Pelysian. She feels confident he will come for her to free her. So she can kill you."

I stared at him. If he was telling me this now, it was because he'd been planning to join with her.

Demos cursed. "I'll have someone check her guards," he said.

I opened my mouth.

"Your Majesty!" Blynth strode up to us. His eyes were half wild. "We've heard from the elders. It's time."

I swallowed, my stomach fluttering. So much could go wrong...

"Pris!" Asinia screamed.

I whirled, scanning the distance. And a choked sob ripped its way free from my throat.

Hundreds of Arslan ships began to rise from deep beneath the water, directly behind Regner's fleet.

Rythos and Madinia had made it happen.

Regner's ships began to burst into flames. Except they weren't just burning. No, they were turning to ash.

Madinia was here.

And she was *furious*.

"Who is that?" Zathrian asked behind me.

I couldn't help but laugh, picturing Madinia's reaction when she learned who Zathrian was. "I suggest you make yourself scarce."

Asinia reached us, a wide grin on her face. And Demos scooped her up, his mouth crashing down on hers.

I gaped. That was new. Telean would be pleased.

She'd muttered about how the two of them were wasting time. I turned, searching for my aunt. But she'd disappeared. Likely, she couldn't stand to watch Regner's ships breaking through Daharak's lines, his soldiers prepared to slaughter our people in their own kingdom.

A strange kind of panic began to thump in my chest. She was likely fine. But...

"Has anyone seen Telean?"

Demos shrugged, unconcerned. I nudged him with my elbow. "When you see her, find a way to keep her with Tibris," I ordered. I hadn't had a chance to check in on him, but I had no doubt he would put her to good use and keep her safe.

"I'll keep an eye out for her," Asinia said.

Demos nodded, but his gaze was on a skiff that was moving toward the shallows.

Madinia stood by Rythos's side. Her remaining power was best spent here, where she could help us get to Regner, and Rythos had clearly determined the same.

Rythos's cousin stood behind them, and her ward held easily as they made their way toward us. By the time they'd landed on the beach, Regner's soldiers had given up their attempts to slice their power through that ward.

Finally, Madinia reached us. Surprisingly, she hugged each of us, something heavy in her cloak pocket thunking against my armor. Asinia's gaze dropped to it, and she opened her mouth, eyes sparking—

"We need you at the front," Demos told her. "Thanks to the hybrids, we've reclaimed the peninsula. And of course, thanks to the Arslan, Regner's ships won't be able to invade our kingdom. That means we have the tunnel, and it's time to get the hybrids out. Prisca, you stay here, ready to step in if the Eprothans realize what we're doing. But don't use your power unless there's absolutely no other option."

Madinia stripped out of her cloak, revealing armor of her own.

"I'll take that," Margie said, handing us each a waterskin as she took Madinia's cloak, throwing it into one of the tents behind the barricade.

Margie handed us each a piece of bread and an apple. She couldn't be on the battlefield, but she was determined to help in her own way.

The food and water did help.

Madinia's eyes met mine. "Get our people home."

"I will. Be careful."

With a nod, she was gone, striding toward the battlefield.

"Where's Jamic?" Demos raised his voice.

"Here." Jamic immediately appeared at his side. Compared to the rest of us, he seemed rested, and I could almost feel his power curling through the air like smoke.

"You need to be ready," I told him.

"I am ready," he said gravely. There was something strange about the look in his eyes.

Tor appeared by his side. "I'm ready too."

"We get this done, and then we strike," I said.

At this very moment, our people were filing out of the caves, gathering at the edge of the forest. At our signal, they would run for their lives.

I waited, my heart pounding erratically as I stared at the peninsula.

Movement.

Rivenlor appeared first, his head popping above the sand, as if he'd been buried beneath it. Tor was standing close enough to me that I felt him jolt as Rivenlor was followed by Sylphina, Gavros, Tymriel, and Ysara.

Grief clawed at my chest. But each of them had known the cost of such power. And they had been insistent.

As one, the elders turned to face Regner's army. They linked their hands, their lips moving as they channeled an ancient magic.

Demos's voice thundered from the forest behind us. "Go!"

The hybrids slipped out of the forest. A few of our soldiers carried children, holding them close as they sprinted across the sand. The elders had warned us that this kind of power wouldn't last. The power to hide this many hybrids from the Eprothans would take all they had to give.

Thousands of hybrids, tripping on the sand, making it to their feet, hauling children and the elderly, carrying the sick.

Tymriel dropped to his knees, before slumping to the ground. The others clutched his hands and kept chanting.

Gavros dropped next, followed by Ysara.

My heart leaped into my throat, and I prepared to freeze time. Some of the hybrids were only halfway to the tunnel.

Vicer appeared, carrying a child in each arm, his teeth bared in a feral snarl. Behind him, the hybrid soldiers we'd left to guard the caves were carrying others, all of them hurtling toward the elders.

Sylphina keeled over. But the elders still clasped hands, continuing to chant. Only Rivenlor remained standing, and even from here, I could see his body quaking.

I sucked in a deep breath. Using the last of my power here could leave us with no way to kill Regner. But I couldn't watch hundreds of hybrids lose their lives when the elders could no longer keep chanting.

A howl sounded, followed by several others.

Vynthar appeared, sprinting along with the hybrids. One after the other, more Drakoryx joined him.

What was he...

Rivenlor fell. Regner's soldiers began slamming their power into the ward that was protecting the hybrids as they ran toward the entrance to the tunnel—our people suddenly visible to the Eprothans once more. But our left flank held the line, giving everything they had for our most vulnerable.

And when the Eprothans power slipped through our wards, the Drakoryx leaped to shield the hybrids. Protecting them with their bodies.

I'd used my power against Vynthar once, and it hadn't impacted him at all.

Now, they shook off most attacks. But they'd been fighting for hours too.

And when one of the Drakoryx went down, it didn't get back up.

Neither did the next.

I raised my hands. Asinia caught them, slowly shaking her head. Tears streamed down her face.

One by one, the Drakoryx fell, until there were just

seven left.

The final hybrid—a woman who limped as she ran—was hauled into the tunnel.

The elders lay near the tunnel entrance, their hands still clasped, their bodies unmoving. The final sacrifice to bring our people home.

As one, Vicer, the remaining soldiers, and all of the remaining Drakoryx sprinted back toward the battle, aiming for those who would dare attempt to kill our most innocent.

"Your Majesty."

Blynth strode toward me, a trowth stone in his hand. "Something has happened," he said. "Regner's soldiers—especially his generals—they're clutching their stomachs and falling to their knees."

I stared at him.

"And immediately losing their heads," he clarified. "Our people are taking full advantage of the situation."

"Poison?"

"I don't know, but it seems likely. Perhaps your friend Natan was able to do more than we'd thought."

Sorrow threatened to drown me at the thought of Natan. "They're the safest behind Regner's wards," Blynth continued hurriedly. "With them dying, it's creating chaos behind their lines. This is it, Nelayra. This has to be the final push."

LORIAN

Prisca fought like a warrior.

If we lived through this, I would commission a portrait of her, teeth bared, eyes glowing gold as she killed savagely for her kingdom.

Nearby, Conreth's brutal power froze and shattered groups of soldiers each time. To our right, Conreth's wardens had broken through the front lines, fighting deep within Regner's ranked soldiers. Rekja used his own power to explode the towers the humans had built for their archers.

And that was *Brevan* fighting next to Rythos. I shook my head, dazed. If there was one sight I'd never expected to see, it was the Arslan brothers fighting together on the same side.

Someone had managed an insidious attack behind Regner's lines. Every few minutes, one of Regner's generals would stumble, eyes glassy. Occasionally, they would fall to the ground, already dead. Most of the time, our people would take advantage of their weakness.

I noted each death.

And each time, I found one thing in common.

Those generals were drinking from their waterskins before they died.

They had time to do so since most of them weren't fighting at the front.

Poison.

And that poison was turning the tide. Without the generals using their stolen power…without them roaring orders, the humans on the front lines—the ones who'd been forced to fight and die for the man who'd magically crippled them—began to turn and run.

Immediately, one of Regner's generals lashed out at them with a dark power of his own. Shadows that twisted across his own soldiers' skin, pouring down their throats to suffocate them.

Dead. He was dead.

Our eyes met, and the sadistic light left his gaze. Gradually, fear and realization replaced it.

I gave him a slow smile, not bothering to take my eyes off him as I lifted my sword to block the thrust of a knife from the right, kicking out and slamming my boot into the human's gut.

The general backed up, but there was nowhere for him to go. He looked over my shoulder. And he was smiling as I sliced my sword through his neck.

Dread sank into my bones.

"Lorian!"

That was *Cavis*'s voice.

I whirled, searching desperately for my wildcat.

Prisca was too fucking far away. I'd told her to stay close, but she'd darted several footspans to the right to pull a wounded hybrid to her feet. Swinging my sword, I cut my way back toward her, my instincts urging me faster and faster.

A dark storm of power slid through Galon's ward as if it were fog. He bolstered the ward, but it was too late. I knew it was too late.

"Prisca!" I roared. I slammed my boot into a human chest, elbowed another in the face, and sliced my sword through the neck of yet another as he lunged at me.

Prisca couldn't have heard me over the sound of the battle.

But she turned toward me, eyes wide with stark realization.

It was as if she was using her power to slow time as more dark power arrowed toward her.

A dull roar filled my head. My vision grayed.

Prisca whirled to meet the threat.

Conreth flew through the air. The dark power slammed into him as he tumbled into Prisca, both of them hitting the ground. Conreth didn't move. His skin slowly began turning gray.

Marth had him in his arms a moment later. He tore the amulet from Conreth's neck and threw it to me. I caught it, shoving it over my head to hang with my own.

Marth began to run. Rythos cut down a soldier who lunged toward Prisca. The moment she was safe, he sprinted after Marth. From the easy smiles that broke out among our enemies, Rythos was using his power to keep them both covered from attack.

Panic carved into my chest. Prisca sobbed through her teeth, scrambling to her feet as I fought my way back to her.

Conreth had looked dead.

I made it to Prisca, hauling her to my chest.

A human soldier launched himself at me and died instantly, my sword slashing out before I realized I'd moved. The next soldier died the same way. And the next.

A hole opened up around us.

Safe. Prisca was safe.

"Lorian!" Galon roared. He pointed to the right.

Caliar lashed out with his power, aiming for Regner's leadership in the rear guard. I had no doubt Regner himself was in one of the tents a hundred footspans away, carefully warded.

Regner's generals lifted something. I blinked, and Caliar was gone—nothing but a curl of smoke rising into the air where seconds ago, one of Conreth's most powerful people—a warden—had stood.

That *fucking* mirror.

Our own lines began foundering.

But now we knew where Regner's mirror was. Close enough for him to use it to ensure his personal ward remained impenetrable, while allowing his most important generals to protect themselves.

Shouts rang out, rising over the din of battle. And unlike when Conreth's army had arrived, these were not shouts of jubilation. No, they were shouts of dismay and horror and hopelessness.

Steeling myself, I squinted in the direction of pointed hands and turned heads. Even with my fae senses, it would have been difficult to see exactly who was approaching.

But I knew that deceptively slow, shambling walk.

The hags moved south, close to the sea. Unlike the terrovians, they had no problem with salt water. They moved casually, as if simply enjoying the weather.

Soon, they were in line with the main body of Regner's army.

Prisca wiggled free from me.

"Fuck," she said, her voice heavy with dread. She raised her hands, likely about to attempt to buy us just a little time. But I leaned close.

"Trust me, wildcat. This is the distraction we need to get behind the barricade. And Regner won't be able to help himself. He'll follow us." I raised my voice to a roar. "Those stone bitches betrayed us once again!"

The hags' presence seemed to revitalize Regner's flagging front lines. The Eprothans attacked with a new fury.

Prisca's eyes met mine.

"Fall back!" she screamed. Our soldiers cursed, and I caught betrayal on several faces nearby. Betrayal and terror.

Once the order was given, it happened quickly. Just as Regner's lines had broken, so did ours. And our soldiers ran for the barricade. We'd lost so much ground, they didn't have far to run. Many of them sprinted for the peninsula, aiming for the tunnel that might take them home.

That was what we wanted. Over half of Regner's remaining soldiers had fled. Most of our own soldiers had used all of their power and were fighting only with sword and shield.

We needed them gone. Needed nothing between us and Regner's rear guard.

"You fucking coward!" Zathrian roared at Prisca. And despite our plan, my hand itched with the urge to slice his throat.

Prisca held time for Regner's remaining men. And Galon, Demos, Madinia, Asinia…all of us screamed for our people to *run*.

Prisca bought us long enough for our warders to pour their remaining power into our shields as everyone sprinted across the battlefield.

"I won't follow a queen who calls a retreat at the exact wrong moment," a soldier spat.

Demos was striding toward me. He reached out with the flat of his hand, smacking the soldier in the back of head. "Go."

The soldier went.

I grabbed Prisca's hand, pulling her with me toward the barricade where the others were positioned. And we watched.

There he was. I could see the Eprothan king in the distance behind his lines, surrounded by his generals. And, of course, warded by that mirror.

He thought we were done. He wanted to watch Prisca die. Needed to see it happen himself.

And that would be his downfall.

"Lorian, look!"

I followed her gaze. In the water, the wreckage of Regner's fleet burned. Hopefully, Rostamir could get some of her pirates here in time to help fight.

I pressed a kiss to Prisca's cheek. "I'll be back."

She nodded absently, her brow furrowed.

Yanking Conreth's amulet from around my neck, I strode to where Brevan was watching Regner in the distance.

He fixed me with a long stare. "I hope you know what you're doing."

I didn't bother replying to that. But I held out my

hand, the blue jewel of the amulet winking in the sunlight.

His gaze dropped to it. And immediately flicked back up to mine. His eyes were wary.

"Take it."

Three amulets.

Three of our most powerful fae.

Conreth had fallen. I had no idea if he was still alive. Rythos and Marth were gone, likely by his side. Hopefully they would return in time, but...

But this choice felt *right*.

Brevan swallowed, his expression saying without words what the action meant.

I was trusting him to use the amulet to kill our greatest enemy.

If he wanted, he could turn on us. But he'd listened to Rythos. He'd brought his people here to defend the fae.

Brevan's eyes warmed. And he nodded at me, slipping the amulet over his head.

I nodded back, turning to find Prisca.

"That was a good thing you did."

I tensed, my eyes meeting Telean's.

She smiled at me. It was the same smile she always wore around me. Slightly perturbed, as if she still couldn't quite understand exactly how her niece had ended up with the Bloodthirsty Prince.

But I knew no one else could see her.

Sorrow struck, thick and deep.

As deep as the vicious wound through her neck.

I hoped her death had been quick.

"It was you. The poison. The generals."

"I spent every last coin I had on those ingredients,"

she smiled. "Ameri was born for such tasks. But I knew only one of us would get out. I bargained with the gods to keep Nelayra alive, and I was always going to die today. I'm glad I died doing something that made a difference. Tell her to check Tibris's healer's bag."

My chest clenched. This woman was braver than almost anyone on that battlefield. "Thank you. For keeping her alive."

She bowed her head. "Look after our people, Your Majesty."

My throat tightened. The title was more than an acknowledgment. From her, it was a priceless gift.

All I could do was nod. But Telean was already fading, her gaze on something beyond me. Beyond all of us. Her eyes lightened, her face turning radiant, and she suddenly looked like a young woman once more.

And then she was gone.

ASINIA

Our retreat may have been planned, but it was also very much necessary. The battle continued to rage, only now, Regner also had the hags—those huge, deadly creatures who lumbered toward us.

My blood turned thick and slow, my limbs suddenly heavy.

But Lorian was surveying those hags from where he stood in front of the barricade, Prisca's hand in his. And since I was watching him, I saw his mouth curve.

I pivoted back to the hags just in time to see them turn. Stone hands crashed into flesh and bone as they rampaged through Regner's right flank.

Human soldiers were fleeing by the thousands, giving us a straight path to the Eprothan king. Meanwhile, Daharak's pirates were pouring onto the beach, sprinting toward our own army.

This was it.

"Now!" Prisca yelled.

Tor stood near the wooden barrier, surrounded by Rekja, Herne, and Demos. His face was stark white, but he lifted his head, aiming his power straight at Regner's ward. The ward glowed white in response, and a tiny crack appeared.

Regner smiled. With a wave of his hand, his ward reformed and the crack disappeared.

Tor aimed again and again. Nausea rose, thick in my throat, as Regner countered each time.

We'd hoped to have a chance without attempting to break an artifact gifted from the gods.

Next to me, Prisca let out a string of curses, lifting a trowth stone close to her mouth. "Tell everyone who can be spared to use whatever magic they have left to hit any generals surrounding Regner. Get all three amulets ready to strike the mirror. Now."

Within moments, Lorian, Galon, and Brevan stood together, each of them wearing an amulet. As one, they aimed their power through Regner's remaining ranks, straight at the mirror.

Jamic added his power. And gods, what power he

had. His hair flew back from his face, and that power slammed into the mirror. Whatever training he'd done with Conreth…it all came down to this.

The mirror glowed. A tiny crack appeared in the glass.

I could see the despair on Prisca's face as she used the dregs of her own power. After the way she'd used it to buy our right flank the time we needed, I'd thought she would have nothing left.

Marth and Rythos had returned from getting Conreth away from the battlefield, and they swung their swords through anyone who attempted to attack, working their way toward her.

To our left, I caught sight of Daharak wielding a sword—at least one hundred pirates fighting with her.

But we would never be able to kill Regner while that mirror protected him. Within hours, any terrovians left would be feasting on us.

Unless I did something. Something so terrifying, it made a chill spread through my bones.

I began to quake. A wave of nausea pitched up my throat.

If I did this, there would be no time to come to terms with my decision.

But the screams of the dying were burrowing deep, through my ears and into my mind, where they echoed over and over.

Prisca was just footspans away now. My blood pounded in my ears, and it was as if the drumbeat of it snagged Prisca's attention.

Her eyes met mine.

"I know how to break the mirror," I screamed to her. "Tell them to wait just a few minutes. They'll know when they need to try again."

Prisca opened her mouth, and I shook my head.

"Don't ask how I can do it. We don't have time. You have to trust me."

Someone jostled me, and Marth was suddenly there, launching himself past us to address the threat.

Prisca stared at me. But she didn't hesitate. The words were easy to read on her lips.

"Do it."

Turning, I sprinted behind the barricade. Madinia sat on an overturned log, Tibris by her side. Blood dripped from the side of her neck as he worked to close the wound.

"I need to get back," she said.

"Not until I'm finished. Do I have to tell Prisca?"

Madinia was pale, her hands shaking as she took a couple of sips of water. But she still scowled.

"One minute," Madinia said.

"Three minutes." Tibris's tone was unrelenting. "If this was a hair deeper, we wouldn't be having this conversation."

Madinia's eyes met mine. "What are you doing here?"

I darted past her into the tent, rolling the orb from the pocket of her cloak. I'd instantly known what she'd been carrying with her when she hugged us. And it didn't surprise me at all that Daharak Rostamir didn't want the temptation of it near her.

I clutched the blue orb to me as I sprinted back toward the battle.

"Asinia!" Madinia was screaming, running alongside me now. Tibris would be furious with her.

I sliced a glance to my left, but Madinia wouldn't make it around the soldiers in front of us in time to stop me. All I had to offer her was a single shaky smile.

The weapon required someone pure of heart. I'd killed. Many times.

I wasn't making it through this alive.

I'd wanted to become infamous. To be a legend. To make a name for myself.

I'd wanted recognition. And if I did this, no one would ever know. It was bitterly ironic.

But *I'd* know. And thousands of people would live. That was a price I was willing to pay.

I'd promised Demos no stupid risks.

I'm sorry.

34

PRISCA

Asinia had asked us to wait, but we couldn't wait much longer. Lorian gave me a look as Regner's army continued to advance. Soon, we would—

Madinia grabbed my arm, and I jolted. The side of her neck and armor were covered in blood. "We have one chance!" she screamed, shaking me viciously enough that Lorian turned to give her a feral snarl.

"Asinia is going for the mirror," Madinia said, ignoring him. I pushed away the confusion and disbelief. Asinia had asked me to trust her. She must have some kind of plan.

"Anyone between Asinia and the mirror is dead. Get our people out. Now."

Lorian must have heard us, because he shouted the order at Marth, who carried it down the line.

This was it. Our one chance. We had to strike now.

I dug into the pouch around my waist for my trowth stone and handed it to her.

Madinia took it, turning away to repeat the order.

And Demos began roaring Asinia's name. Where was she? Where—

Sprinting from the right, her silver armor stark against all the black, Asinia ran toward Regner's front lines.

Demos was fighting his way toward her, brutally cutting down anyone who stepped into his path. Rythos and Marth jumped into place, guarding Tor.

Asinia hurtled down the edge of Regner's lines, barely avoiding the human soldiers fleeing into the mountains. One of them struck out at her, and she ducked, rolled, and came back up on her feet.

A path had cleared between Demos and Asinia. His eyes were wild. It seemed as if the stress of the war, the horror of this battle, had broken something in Asinia.

And my brother...his screams...the agony in his voice burrowed deep into my chest.

"Madinia—" My voice cracked.

"No, Prisca. You have to trust her."

And I knew. A hole opened up inside my chest as the realization slammed into me. Asinia was doing something she couldn't take back.

Memories flashed before my eyes.

The first time Asinia asked her mother if I could stay for dinner, because she knew we had little food left.

The mixture of hope and fury in Asinia's eyes when she realized I'd come for her in Regner's dungeon.

The strained tension between her and Demos, slowly transforming into something deep, something precious.

And the way she'd thinned her lips just weeks ago, referring to herself as a liability.

Telean's voice sounded in my head. *"She was my best friend. We were supposed to have centuries."*

No. *Please* no.

ASINIA

I approached from the east. The human soldiers fleeing into the mountains paid me little attention as I worked my way parallel to Regner's mirror.

The orb heated in my hand, as if it knew what I was about to do. And it truly hit me then. I was going to die. And I would also likely kill thousands of human soldiers—some of whom had been forced to fight this war. Perhaps that was the irony of using this weapon—and why no one without a pure heart could survive—because anyone who truly had a pure heart would never contemplate doing such a thing.

Somehow, using the weapon was all instinct. I knew what I had to do. And so I focused on Regner standing behind his lines, his expression a twisted mask of hate.

Blind terror rampaged through my body. I didn't want to die. The orb cooled slightly, and I forced myself to focus on the battle in front of me. And I pictured the world after Regner was dead.

A better world. A happy world. A world where our people could be free.

Perhaps…perhaps it didn't matter much after all if I wouldn't be here to see it—not if it meant my friends would live.

My fear disappeared. And it was as if I was standing above my body, watching my own actions.

Someone ran with me. One of Conreth's fae. He sliced his way through anyone who attempted to get close. And strangely, it was Lorian's words that circled through my mind as I sprinted toward Regner.

"I think that has to be the worst part about dying. Leaving the people you love and regretting."

My only regret was that I wouldn't get more time. But I could never regret losing my life to save theirs. And suddenly, the thought that I'd wanted glory or notoriety during this war... It was silly now. All I really wanted was to know they would all survive. I didn't need prestige.

And then I was turning, and the orb was heating once more—this time becoming so hot that it was as if it could sense my resolve.

I looked at the fae who'd guarded me this long.

"Run."

He didn't argue. He simply turned and sprinted away.

"I don't think it's the memories of your life that you see when you die. I think it's the people you'll miss the most. The people who made your life worth living. And sometimes, if you're lucky, you see the one person you would defy the fates and stay for—if you could."

Lorian was right. Because even though I was doing this for Pris and everyone else, it was Demos's face that flashed in front of my eyes and stayed as I clenched my teeth and forced my hands to hold tight as my palms began burning, until my eyes watered and my lungs ached with a suppressed sob.

And then I heard him. The roar Demos unleashed echoed across the battlefield. "Asinia!"

"It brought up a lot of memories." His voice played

through my mind. *"Memories of being helpless when I lost the people I loved."*

I hated myself for doing this to him again.

But he would live. And it was enough.

And then I was the one screaming as the burning in my palms spread throughout my entire body.

Every living creature between me and the mirror disintegrated.

My vision turned white.

MADINIA

A bright white light shone around Asinia, directed straight at the mirror.

Anyone who had power left to use joined her, along with Lorian, Brevan, and Galon, who channeled the power from their amulets. Jamic swayed on his feet, while Tor continued to slice at Regner, providing a distraction.

My vision speckled, my mind struggling to comprehend what I was seeing.

Anyone who had been standing between Asinia and the mirror was...

Gone.

Regner's soldiers ran for their lives.

Prisca was running too.

Lorian's expression was agonized as he watched her, but he couldn't stop. Couldn't remove his power from the mirror.

Prisca's face crumpled. And then she began screaming as if she were being gutted. Because her best friend—the friend she had sacrificed so much for...

Asinia slumped to the ground, her eyes open and empty, skin drained of color.

The mirror shattered.

Demos dropped to his knees at her side. "Sin." His voice broke, and he rocked her, a howl leaving his throat.

Prisca wouldn't stop screaming.

And then Tibris was there, tears rolling down his cheeks as he shook his head.

Grabbing Prisca's shoulders, I shook her. Just footspans from the mirror, Regner stood, face purple, his eyes filled with fury as he roared at one of his generals.

"Now, Prisca."

My voice was harsh, the words thick around the lump in my throat. Her bloodshot eyes found the wreckage of the mirror. And then they cut to me.

For the first time, I was truly afraid of the hybrid queen.

"You *knew*," she hissed.

"Asinia chose," I snapped. "And the longer you wait, the higher the chance that sacrifice is worth nothing. So, kill our enemy and end this war, Your Majesty."

The look she gave me was chilling. But the grief had left her face. In its place was a kind of remote coldness. An expression that made goose bumps rise on my skin.

Clutching her hourglass, she froze time for Regner and only Regner.

No one spoke as Prisca crossed the space between them. I barely breathed.

Her face was drawn and pale, tears still drying on her cheeks. But her eyes were filled with icy wrath.

She released her hold on time just as she pulled her sword.

Regner's eyes widened.

And Prisca buried that sword in his chest.

He choked, his expression uncomprehending. And slowly, his face began to change. His nose lengthened, his eyes turned a dusky blue, his cheeks slimmed. Those were the features he would have had if he hadn't killed and replaced the boys he'd pretended were his own.

My eyes found Jamic. He stared uncomprehendingly at Regner. As if his mind couldn't reconcile what he was seeing.

Regner dropped to the ground. Lifeless.

And just like that, the Eprothan king was dead.

Prisca turned and walked away, her eyes filled with anguish and despair.

Asinia still clutched the orb, even in death. Demos had curled up next to her, and he snarled at us as we approached.

When he looked at me, I shivered.

Daharak stepped up next to me. "I know when a man wants to kill someone, and I suggest you get on my ship sooner rather than later."

I nodded. "Glad you're alive."

"You too. Sorry about your friend."

This time, I didn't deny that Asinia had been a friend. A deep, dark hole was opening up inside my chest.

Prisca sat next to Asinia and took her hand. Her face was as lifeless as Regner's.

And then the orb began to glow once more.

"It's heating up!" Tibris said.

Lorian snatched Prisca and hauled her away, ignoring her struggles. Herne grabbed Tibris, who cursed at him but allowed him to pull him several feet from Asinia's body.

Demos didn't move. His sister screamed for him, and he still didn't move.

Daharak tensed. "Purehearted," she laughed, but it was bitter. "Perhaps the gods are the ones who decide such things."

What did she—

The light flared, until several people cried out. I slammed my eyes closed.

And when I opened them again, Demos was holding Asinia's body and rocking once more.

Only this time, she was holding him back. Her eyes slid open, and I caught sight of something *more* within them.

And then it was gone. "Please tell me Regner is dead," she said.

Prisca was immediately by her side. "You're in so much trouble."

She threw her arms around Asinia, and both of them burst into tears.

Daharak sucked a breath between her teeth, and I followed her gaze. She wasn't looking at Prisca and Asinia. No, she was staring down the beach at where Regner's generals were gathering near his body.

35

THE QUEEN

Regner was dead.

I'd seen that much from my hiding place in the forest. And still, it was difficult to believe. The hybrid queen had been too busy mourning her little friend to take the grimoire.

Zathrian should be killing her at this very moment.

My entire body trembled. I was so, so close to getting everything I'd ever wanted.

I could practically feel the grimoire calling to me from where it would be tucked inside Regner's cloak.

Tymedes had fallen to his knees close to the edge of the forest, disbelief stark on his face as he watched his soldiers turn and retreat.

Rothnic bled heavily from one arm, stumbling around as if he were drunk. Nearby, the remaining patriarchs stood in a circle. They would be planning their next moves. Debating who would take Regner's crown. And the moment they had the chance to kill my son, they would take it.

Unless I killed them first.

I mapped out my approach. Tymedes

had to die first. Otherwise, the moment he saw me—or Jamic—we were dead.

There was a chance the other patriarchs would fall in line the moment they realized I was back. And when I had the grimoire, they would be forced to bow to me.

Rothnic was too dangerous to let live. Already, he was stumbling closer to Regner's body.

He wasn't as wounded as he was pretending.

No, he knew about the grimoire. And he was about to take it.

I had to strike *now*.

Tymedes stiffened as I stepped up behind him, the blade my son had given me wedged against his throat.

"And so it ends like this," he said, his voice dead. "Killed by the hybrid heir."

"Not quite," I hissed.

He tensed, angling his head until his eyes met mine. And those eyes were wide. "You?" He let out a choked laugh. "Of course it would be you."

I'd thought slitting his throat would feel more satisfying. But as his lifeblood gushed over my hands, all I wanted was more.

He was choking on his own blood, and yet he still managed a laugh.

The sound sent a chill down my spine, and I whirled.

Jamic was just steps away, his eyes wide as he watched me slaughter Tymedes.

"You said you would run." His eyes... They were so wounded, it was as if he was that little boy once more.

"I know." My voice sounded thin and desperate even to me. "But I'm doing this for us."

"The bitch killed Tymedes!" Rothnic cried out, suddenly no longer dazed.

"Kill the boy. Now!"

A strange expression came over my son's face. An expression that looked almost like…resignation.

My gut tightened. Jamic hadn't expected to live through the war. All he'd wanted was for Regner's rule to end.

A man walked out from the forest, drawing my attention. Even the patriarchs went silent.

"Pelysian?"

Lightness swept through my body. This man was little more than his mother's puppet. But if he was here, it was because he had a plan. It wasn't over.

Rothnic laughed. "I've wanted to do this for years," he hissed. He lifted one hand.

My eyes met Pelysian's.

And realization swept through me.

He wasn't here to help me rule. He was here to watch me die.

"Jamic, run!" My voice was a desperate shriek. I just had to buy him a little time. Just enough time to disappear into the forest. Leaping toward him, I caught sight of wide green eyes already filling with tears.

He didn't need to cry. I would—

Pain. So much pain. Searing straight through my back and into my gut.

I'd expected magic to slam into me.

It was a bolt from a crossbow instead. And from the acid that swept through my body, that bolt was poisoned.

I hit the ground, agony blazing through every inch of

me. I screamed, writhing.

Someone laughed.

The laughter abruptly cut off, sending my heart plummeting down into my stomach.

Time had frozen. The hybrid heir had arrived.

My gaze found Jamic's. "Take...grimoire."

Pelysian stepped in front of me, breaking my line of sight.

"Help us," I mouthed.

He simply shook his head. "Nelia knew you needed to die here. She gave her life to ensure it would happen. To ensure you would help the others find the amulet and kill the king."

Nelia...

The pain was blinding now. A glimmer of pity flickered in Pelysian's eyes.

No. It...it wasn't fair. I'd just needed more *time*.

"Why?" I gasped out.

"You would never stop. You have been twisted by Regner's evil. And if you lived, you would have twisted your son. Our people would suffer for it. And I would never allow that to happen."

My eyes burned. My son had endured everything Regner had put him through and somehow remained *good*. But that goodness was a kind of weakness. And he would be preyed on.

"Protect him."

"I will." Pelysian's expression tightened. "If only you'd chosen differently. I had...hopes for you. For us." His expression hardened. "In times of war, sacrifices must be made. Goodbye, Your Majesty."

His gaze moved past me to Prisca. I was already gone to him. Already nothing more than a corpse. But sorrow glittered in his eyes when he looked at Jamic.

My son was suddenly stumbling toward me, his lost expression making him appear so young, my heart broke all over again.

PRISCA

My power slipped from my grasp. The patriarchs cursed, falling back.

And Galon…

Galon killed them all, his sword slicing them to pieces.

He moved so quickly, it took me a moment to understand what he had done.

My stomach swam. I was so, so tired of death. But they had already tried to kill Jamic, and he wasn't yet crowned.

The Eprothan heir sat by his mother's side, stroking Kaliera's hair back from her face.

It was a bad death. Long black tendrils had formed over her skin, poison ravaging her body. She shuddered in agony.

But she died looking at the only person she'd ever loved.

Perhaps such a death wasn't so bad after all.

The man beside him was staring at Daharak, who

582   Stacia Stark

gave him a narrow-eyed glare. "What are you doing here?"

"Mother sent me."

This was Pelysian. And he'd just calmly watched Kaliera die.

Daharak seemed to accept that, but her gaze darted between him and Kaliera's body.

Slowly, Jamic got to his feet. And he was looking at Madinia.

"My power was not returned to the fae when they used the amulets," Jamic said. "There is something... different about it."

Prickles slid across my skin. Next to me, Lorian stared at Jamic as if he was now a new threat.

But Jamic was still speaking.

"Do you remember that promise you made me? That you would do something for me?"

Madinia nodded. "I do."

Trepidation raked an ice-cold finger down my spine.

"Will you keep your promise?"

"Yes."

"Then you know what we need to do."

Jamic held out his hand. All of us stood and watched. Asinia, wrapped in Demos's arms, Tibris, his hand clutching Herne's. Marth, Galon, Rythos, Vicer, every general and several curious soldiers.

Madinia took Jamic's hand.

And he led her toward Regner's body.

I pulled at the threads of my power.

Nothing.

Whirling, I found Zathrian watching me. His eyes

flickered with sorrow.

"You fucking bastard."

Demos bared his teeth and launched himself at my cousin.

Zathrian ducked, rolling away.

"Just fucking wait," he snapped. And unlike on the battlefield, when he'd called me a fucking coward, there was no disdain or fury in his voice now. No, it was filled with baffled frustration.

"Leave him," I said.

Demos cursed, turning on me.

But his eyes went wide. Next to me, Lorian jolted forward, raising a hand of his own.

But Madinia had already picked up the grimoire. Jamic held one of her hands, and his skin glowed slightly. He was channeling power into her.

Oh gods.

"Don't open it!" Lorian roared.

She ignored him, flipping it open. Jamic used his other hand to balance the grimoire, and Madinia turned the pages quickly, as if searching for something. Her eyes...

"Her eyes are turning black," someone yelled. "She's lost. Kill her before she becomes a threat like Regner."

"No," I croaked. "No." My voice was louder this time as I studied Madinia's face. Yes, her eyes had darkened and her hands were shaking—as if the strain was tearing her apart. But there was no victorious flush to her skin. She wasn't celebrating the fact that she had the dark book. No, she looked as coldly irritated as ever, as if seconds away from snarling at all of us.

She was still *her*.

"Give her a moment," I said.

Demos growled. "You've always given her too much rope."

"No," I said as she lifted her head. "You've never given her enough."

MADINIA

Power surged through me in a rush, heady and addictive. My nerves tingled with a new awareness, as if coming to life.

A strange kind of warmth settled over my body. Inside me, something that had been sleeping…something I had never acknowledged… opened one eye.

There was no pain. My jaw no longer clenched while I ground my teeth against the ache of my wounds. My power came to me easily, urging me to burn and destroy.

I was power. I was might. I was *reborn*.

"Madinia!" Someone was screaming. I frowned, glancing down at the book in my hands. There was something I was supposed to do.

The power reached for me, seductive, curling around my skin and stroking. It was somehow…familiar.

It was the familiarity that sliced through the fog.

I understood now just why Regner had become who he had become. It wasn't an excuse—he'd chosen to embrace everything this grimoire offered.

But I wanted no part of it.

My power came to me easily, and I closed my eyes, visualizing it as an orb of fire. The grimoire's magic was seeping toward my mind, whispering of all the changes we could make. The *good* we could do together.

I poured my fire toward the black cloud of magic, and something dark roared back at me.

Moments. I'd have only moments.

Desperately, I continued flicking through the pages. I couldn't explain exactly how I knew, but I was certain the page I needed would—

There.

It seemed to glow, dragging my attention to it.

The words were foreign—a language my mouth had never been meant to speak—but they came to me easily.

For a single, terrifying moment, I wondered if the book had tricked me. But the dark, malevolent power seemed to howl its displeasure.

The words rolled off my tongue as if I had spoken them every day of my life.

Regner had used oceartus stones to steal, transport, and gift human power.

He'd used the curse of his webs to turn those who loved their family and friends into traitors.

I would undo what he had done. *This* would be my legacy before I left this continent.

I spoke the final word. The book thumped closed. For a moment, it seemed as if nothing had happened.

And then the screams sounded.

Horror sliced through me. But...

The screams were jubilant. Celebratory. Joyful.

Sparks began to rise from Regner's body. And from every general nearby.

In the distance, back toward our camp, human rebels were raising their weapons in the air. Many of them glowed with magic.

I'd done it. I'd taken the power from where it wasn't supposed to be and given it back to those it truly belonged to.

My knees buckled. Jamic hit the ground. And it was Demos who caught my arm. He nodded at me, his eyes filled with…respect.

Prisca limped over to me. And she was using that red stone once more as she spoke. "Let it be known across all four kingdoms. The human power was returned by Madinia Farrow."

I winced, and she laughed, the sound rolling across the shore.

36

PRISCA

The war was over. Regner was dead.

We shuffled back toward our camp, and I stared unseeingly at the remnants of the battlefield.

And the bodies.

For a long time, I simply stood, Lorian's arms around me as I trembled, grief and horror swamping me until it felt as if they might drag me under.

"We won," I mumbled against his shirt. "I should be happy."

He stroked my hair. "You will be. For now, feel however you need to, wildcat."

Slowly, I eased away from him. My face was wet, and I gazed down the beach to where the others were gathered.

"I need to see Telean. And Tibris."

Lorian flinched.

And my heart cleaved open.

His eyes met mine, and his face was all I could see.

"Which one?" The words were a hoarse rasp.

"Telean. I'm so sorry, Prisca. She was the reason Regner's generals were dying from poison. She snuck into their camp with Ameri."

"You saw her."

"Yes. She left something for you in Tibris's healer's bag."

My entire body had gone ice-cold. "Demos."

"I'll find him."

Pulling away from Lorian, I made my way up the hill.

"Prisca."

I wrapped my arms around Tibris and rocked. And then I pulled away.

"I need your healer's bag."

With a confused frown, he handed it over.

The parchment had been folded carefully and tucked into one of the leather pockets.

Grief sliced at me with poisonous claws, until it felt as if I was the one who was withering and dying. Lorian stepped inside the tent, Demos behind him.

My brother's face was white.

And as our eyes met, he seemed to realize it was true. Dropping to the healer's cot, he buried his head in his hands.

Tibris stared at us. And then he closed his eyes. "Telean."

My hand shook as I handed the letter to Lorian.

"Will you..."

"Anything, wildcat."

He sat beside me. And then he read.

Nelayra and Demos,

If you're reading this, then everything has gone according to my plan.

Getting to know you both was a gift I had never imagined I could have. And the close bond you have formed is everything your mother could have wanted.

Nelayra,

I wasn't lying on the day of your wedding. I could understand exactly why you chose to use your power in such a dangerous way. Why, in the heat of the moment, when you watched the love of your life die in front of you, you defied the laws of the gods—even knowing there would be repercussions. I was furious. But I don't blame you. As we discussed, I can see exactly why you made the choice you did.

A love like yours and Lorian's is rare. You have every right to cling to it with everything in you.

When you told me you saw your mother and grandmother that day—and what they said to you—my decision came to me instantly.

I am old. I am tired. I miss the people I love. Your mother was my best friend. Even after all these years, I find myself constantly searching for your mother's face in a crowd or reaching for parchment to write to her.

I know Yorin waits for me too. And when I get to see your mother and grandmother again, it will be with the knowledge that I was able to spare you just a little pain. Losing me will be difficult. But I had a long life, and— if everything happened the way I intended—I died while bringing our people home. I can think of no better way to spend my last moments.

I know you, Nelayra. And I know your mind will be lingering on the fact that I didn't get to see our kingdom rise. That after everything, I never got to step foot in Lyrinore. But I can assure you, I will be watching as you take your throne. And I count myself lucky that I was able to see you become the queen you were meant to be.

Tell Asinia I'm sorry. But she doesn't need me to teach her—she only thinks she does. I expect her to open her business within the year.

Demos,

I'm sure you feel tricked. I'm sure you are enraged by the fact that you unsuspectingly helped me that day when you found the sanctuary for me. Yes, I bargained with the gods. And no, I have no regrets.

The worst period of my life was knowing you were in that dungeon and I couldn't get to you. That you had to watch your friends—the people you considered family—slaughtered and never know why you were spared. Occasionally, I wondered if it might have been kinder to have let you go.

And then I met Nelayra.

You are the general our people have needed for so long. But I urge you to remember that you are more than just a general. When peace comes, you must embrace it. When love is within reach, you must grab it with both hands.

It is time to lay down your sword and live. You are more than just that sword. You are also a man. And Asinia won't wait forever.

I love both of you so much. I hate that I have to leave you. But it is right for the young to outlive the old.

Live a life you will be proud to tell all of us about when we see you again.

—Telean.

Sorrow swallowed me, and I fell down into its dark belly. I wanted to think of Telean in a better place. A place where her bones didn't ache and her joints weren't stiff each morning. A place where she was with my mother and grandmother—and finally, finally with the man she loved.

One day soon, I would be able to think of my aunt that way and smile. But now...

All I could think was that it was horrifyingly unfair and Telean should be here and she would never get to see our homeland and how dare she leave me and Demos when we had barely found her and gods, it hurt to *breathe*.

We'd never enjoyed peace with her. Never spent long hours sitting and talking together, all three of us, about subjects that weren't related to war and death.

And now we never would.

PRISCA

That night, I was crowned beneath the stars in a kingdom that wasn't my own. But the elders had left instructions. Apparently, they'd felt it necessary to ensure my role as queen was immediately formalized.

Even after all of our disagreements, I mourned the fact that they wouldn't get to see our people return home. And selfishly, I wished they would be around to help me form my court. To help our people settle into their kingdom.

Lorian would be crowned a week from now. The advisers felt that our people would enjoy an excuse to celebrate the end of the war and the start of a new life for all of us.

My grandmother had worn this crown. My mother would have worn it if Regner hadn't invaded. Several people had gasped at the sight of it, and I knew it was a glorious example of our kingdom's exquisite craftsmanship and rich history.

Set with jewels, the crown was cold and heavy. I much preferred the diadem Lorian had given me. But I understood the symbol for what it was. A promise that I understood the true weight of this crown. And that I would bear it for my people.

So, I bowed my head, repeated the vows that Blynth read, and promised to love and protect my kingdom.

And as soon as it was done, the crown was safely tucked away while we turned our attention to the dead and wounded.

Asinia's friend Cryton hadn't made it. I'd never met him, but she'd sat next to his body and wept, Demos by her side.

Tibris's magic was so drained, he could no longer heal even the tiniest cut. Herne had forced him to rest, and I'd carefully hidden a smile as my healer brother—who was so obsessed with taking care of others—was dragged into a tent, a sleep tonic poured down his throat.

"I suppose you're furious," Herne said when he stepped out of the tent.

"Furious? No. You just proved you're perfect for my brother. Welcome to the family."

He stared at me, clearly dazed, and I took pity on him. "You should rest too."

With a nod, he disappeared into his tent.

I turned to look for Lorian, nodding to Galon as he walked past. We'd only been separated for a few minutes, but after today, I wanted him by my side.

But...

Zathrian sat at the edge of camp, ignored by everyone. Our eyes met, and he got to his feet, walking toward me.

Galon changed his direction, stalking our way.

I sighed. "He's not going to hurt me."

"You're tired. We're all fucking tired," Galon muttered. "He should be chained up somewhere."

Zathrian ignored him, which was impressive given how much threat Galon exuded.

"Jorvik," Zathrian said to me. "He's dead, isn't he?"

I glanced at Galon. "Go away."

He narrowed his eyes, clearly having some internal

deliberation. With a low oath, he turned and moved back toward one of the fires.

I turned my attention back to Zathrian. "Yes," I said. "Daharak told me the ship was struck by one of Regner's and didn't have a chance."

Grief darkened his eyes. Clearly, Jorvik had been important to him in some way. "I'm sorry."

"It was his idea to get that close to you." Zathrian's voice was low. "I told him it was stupid, but he thought it might rattle you enough to make you make a mistake. Instead, it just made you more determined. Didn't it?"

"Yes."

We were quiet for a moment, and the sounds of the waves in the distance made my eyes heavy-lidded.

"I've been wondering something," I murmured.

"So have I. I'll answer your question, if you answer mine."

"Deal."

"Eadric," I said. "When he tortured us, it seemed… personal. Like he hated me."

"He did. His father was in love with your mother. When she met your father, it was clear she was never going to be able to love Eadric's father. Of course, Eadric was born years later, but his father's bitterness remained. He became friends with my father."

I could imagine both boys learning to hate my family as they grew up. It didn't excuse anything they had done, but…it still hurt to imagine the people they might have been without that hate.

"Thank you for telling me."

Zathrian just nodded. And his gaze slid in the

direction of the water, as if he couldn't quite bear to look at me when he asked his question.

"I heard you saw our grandmother when you turned back time."

There was nothing malicious in his question. No, he just sounded...tired.

"I did."

He kept his gaze fixed on the darkness, his voice carefully neutral. "Do you... Do you think perhaps one day she could be proud of me? Even after everything I've done?"

My eyes burned. "I heard her voice that day when we fought in your arena. She was screaming, completely enraged. She didn't want you dead. Likely because she knew you would use your power to help us. She could see good in you, Zathrian. I don't know if that means anything to you..."

He still didn't look at me. But the corner of his mouth tipped up. "It means enough," he said.

An inconvenience, I'd called him. A loose end. I'd said he had no future in our kingdom, and I'd seen how my words had cut at him even as he tried to hide it.

"There's a place for you in Lyrinore. If you want it."

Zathrian sliced a glare in my direction. After a long moment, his eyes widened. "You're serious, aren't you?"

"Why wouldn't I be?"

"Because I killed your mate. Your husband. Because Eadric killed your friend. Because I would have happily killed you. Because I'm a threat to your throne."

A deadly snarl cut through the night. Zathrian flinched.

I just sighed. "Lorian—"

"Tell her again about how you're a threat," he crooned, leaning over my shoulder.

I glanced toward the fire. Galon stared stubbornly back at me.

Sighing again, I turned back to the posturing males. I elbowed Lorian in the gut, and my cousin gaped at the action.

"You said you *would* have happily killed me," I said to Zathrian. "Do you still feel the same?"

"No. You don't have to believe me. But no."

"Then the offer stands. But there would be rules in place." This was, after all, the same man who had killed an innocent man simply for watching him under our orders. The same man who would have murdered everyone I loved. One day, I might be able to forgive. But I would never forget.

"A blood vow," I said.

Lorian radiated approval.

Zathrian just stared at me, as if he still couldn't understand.

"Let me know your decision before we leave tomorrow," I said. Taking Lorian by the hand, I pulled him away.

"That crown looked good on you, by the way, wildcat," Lorian murmured in my ear. Ah. A change of subject so I would overlook his unhinged behavior.

Fine.

"You've got a matching one waiting in the capital," I said. "So don't feel too smug."

He looked pained by that, but he kissed my cheek.

"Rythos wants to talk to you. And then you should get some sleep."

The Arslan had wasted no time taking their dead and returning home. Madinia had told us about how she and Rythos had been caught attempting to escape with Miric—and the fleet. For reasons they still couldn't understand, Brevan had defied his father and chosen to fight with us.

"But if he attempts to make Rythos fulfill that bargain, I'll castrate him," Madinia had muttered.

Rythos was waiting near the water, his hands in his pockets. He offered me a faint smile when I approached, but his expression was tight.

"Brevan...he'd decided I was to return to the island in exchange for the Arslan ships, but for some reason, he changed his mind."

"That was the bargain Madinia was talking about."

He nodded. "I can never return to Quorith. I don't want to. But...there's something I have to tell you."

I waited, and he sighed. "I did what I'd sworn I would never do. I used my power on my father's council."

It was clear from the expression on his face that he didn't need soft assurances.

"Would you ever use that power on my council?"

He reared back. "Of course not. If you believe I would—"

"I don't. But I need you to believe it too. Without the Arslan, there's a good chance we would have lost this war." I gestured out across the sea toward the hybrid kingdom. "Regner would have invaded once more, and this time, he would have killed any hybrids who remained. Your power is both beautiful and terrible. I'm sorry you had to use it. But I'm not sorry you did."

He let out a shaky breath. After a long moment, he attempted a smile. "I think I traumatized Madinia."

I laughed. "A little fear is probably good for her."

"She wielded that grimoire and gave humans their power back," Rythos said.

"That's not all she did," a hoarse voice said.

I turned, my eyes meeting dark brown. Finley.

The web had disappeared from his face. His eyes were slightly shadowed but alert.

It was bittersweet. I could see that in the way Rythos stared at the empty place on Finley's temple where the web had been. If Cavis had lived…

He would be free now. His life would be his own.

"All of them?" Rythos asked.

Finley nodded. "All of the spiders I've seen. Your brother let us go," he told me. "But I want to apologize."

He'd been a quiet boy when I'd last seen him. Now, he seemed like he'd aged a decade overnight.

"I don't want your apology."

He flinched and I sighed. "Because there's nothing to apologize for. Now, we have to find a way to move on. To make the best of the lives that were spared." I clasped the hourglass hanging around my neck. "And to cherish every moment."

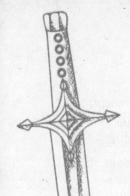

37

LORIAN

I stared down at Conreth in the healer's bed. Ten days was a long time for the fae to fight for their lives. Especially when that person was their king.

And yet, the only reason my brother had survived was likely because of his own personal ward and the amulet he'd worn around his neck. I'd insisted on bringing him here, to Lyrinore, where I could be sure no one would make an attempt on his life while he was vulnerable.

His skin had always been pale, but now, it seemed as if all life had been drained from him. He was so still, so silent, he appeared almost dead.

An invisible hand must have clamped around my throat. Because I was suddenly finding it difficult to breathe.

"Why, Conreth?"

He was the fae king. He had no heir. He knew exactly how important it was that he stay alive. Hence his reliance on Renit. And yet, he had saved Prisca's life.

And nearly died himself.

"Because before I was the fae king and you were the Bloodthirsty Prince, we were brothers." Conreth's eyes opened, hazy with pain. "Since you're fretting at my bedside, I assume Regner is dead?"

My throat tightened. "I'm not fretting," I muttered. "That power would have killed Prisca."

I half expected him to defend his actions with the fact that we'd needed her time magic to kill Regner. I braced myself for those words.

"I would never have allowed your mate to die. Not if I could stop it."

I angled my head, raised one brow, and stared at him.

Conreth let out a choked laugh and winced, holding a hand to his chest.

"I'll summon a healer."

"No, Lorian, wait." He attempted to sit up, grimaced, and relaxed once more, sweat beading on his brow. "This war has been the worst thing either of us has lived through—since our parents died," he said. "And yet, I can't find it in me to regret it. Some part of me is almost thankful for it. Not because of the death or despair, but because I was finally forced to see you. To see us. Watching the way you are with Galon and the role he plays in your life—the role that should have been mine— it made me realize all we have lost."

"Conreth—"

He held up his hand. "I'm truly sorry, Lorian."

"You've already apologized."

"Not properly. I'm sorry I became so consumed with what it meant to wear the crown, and I forgot about what it meant to be your brother."

I hadn't wanted to do this. Hadn't wanted to have this conversation. Hadn't even thought I would need it.

And yet... The man in that bed wasn't a ruthless king. He was the man who'd saved Prisca's life. The same man who'd brought me into his chambers and read to me to keep my nightmares at bay all those years ago.

"I forgive you," I said roughly.

Ice-blue eyes studied my face, as if searching for the lie in my words. But I did forgive him. I'd forgiven him the moment he'd saved the love of my life, prepared to lose his own.

"Emara is here," I said, and his eyes lit up. "She stepped away when I forced her to get some fresh air. She'll be very unimpressed that you woke to the sound of my voice and not her own."

Another choked laugh. "Go find my wife."

Emara was too frantic to be unimpressed. She rushed past me, darting into the room, and as the door slid closed, I heard her burst into tears.

He'd gone to war without her, leaving her to run their kingdom. And then he'd almost died.

I shook my head. Emara was going to make him very, very sorry.

Now, where was my wildcat?

The castle had been kept in relatively good condition, with a full wing for healers to use their power for anyone in the city who needed it.

While the elders had ensured basic upkeep was completed, the castle was several centuries out of date, with much of the furniture and drapery needing to be replaced.

When the hybrids learned their queen was settling here, they'd swept through the castle like a storm, and groups of them were gathered at various points, frowning at cracked walls and discussing planned improvements.

I'd taken to sneaking around. Otherwise, I was surrounded, drawn into discussions about the differences between two shapes of tile, the benefits of cream curtains versus white.

Already, our lives were becoming ordinary. With normal problems. Well, as normal as our problems could be, considering we still had to form our court and oversee the settlement of thousands of hybrids to this kingdom.

But…the thought of those kinds of problems… I reveled in it.

Still, I waited until the group of hybrids turned the corner before making my way into our rooms. Daselis and Erea bustled out, nodding to me. While Prisca had offered them almost any position they could have wanted, they'd insisted on working with her right here.

And there was Prisca, standing on the balcony, staring out at our kingdom.

She glanced over her shoulder at me and smirked as I closed the door and crossed the room. "Did you decide between cobalt blue and cerulean paint?"

Wrapping my arms around her, I nuzzled her cheek. "Why is it that these women think I am the one who should be asked these questions?"

Prisca's entire body shook. And a strange snorting sound left her throat.

"What did you do?" I nipped her ear and turned her in my arms.

"I may or may not have told everyone you truly enjoy making such important decisions."

"You. Did. What?"

She grinned, and she was so fucking beautiful, my breath caught in my throat.

"The people who've stayed in this kingdom haven't interacted much with the fae. And you're...you. I wanted people to see that you could be patient and interested. That you're not that scary after all."

She peered up at me through her lashes, her fingers playing with one of the buttons on my shirt.

I suddenly saw a lot of decisions about furniture in my future.

"Fine. But you owe me."

Her eyes heated, but dark circles lingered beneath them. Prisca was still grieving the people we'd lost. Each night before bed, she read her letter from Telean.

"I was just thinking..." she said.

I nipped her ear. "Always dangerous."

"About the hags. What did you give them to turn on Regner?"

"The Cursed City."

"I don't understand."

"The curse will be dropped now that the war is over and your people are free. If Jamic wanted, he could rebuild it. I told them I wouldn't let a single building stand in the territory they've claimed."

"And what did Jamic say?"

"He pinched the bridge of his nose and said, 'Fine, I have plenty of other things to figure out.' We may need to visit him sometime soon."

Jamic was newly crowned, already working to remove the rot from Eprotha and ensure the human soldiers who had rampaged across cities—harming innocent people—never had the opportunity to do such a thing again.

"We will."

Her mouth had turned down, and I didn't like it.

"I'm taking my payment now," I said.

"Is that so?"

Taking her hand, I led her into the bathroom.

"What are you—"

"You're taking a bath, wildcat. You need to relax. These are my terms."

"Bossy," she muttered, but she didn't protest as I helped her strip out of her gown. "Will you join me?"

I hardened instantly. "No."

She frowned over her shoulder at me, and I tapped her on her lush, round ass.

"In."

Her expression turned wicked, and I nearly bent her over the tub.

Then she paused, cupping my face. "I love you."

"I love you too, wildcat. Now get in the tub."

She grinned at me. My mouth watered as she climbed into the water, and I hissed out a breath when she leaned back, the water caressing her flushed skin, steam rising to bring a sheen to her cheeks.

Her grin turned into a smirk. "So scowly," she murmured.

I turned, stalking from the bathing room. Spotting a gauzy robe lying on the bed, I delivered it to her, keeping my eyes averted as if I were a boy of sixteen winters.

Prisca's low laugh followed me out the door.

Stepping into the hall, I found a maid who brought

what I needed. Busying myself with lighting candles and warming the fragrant oil with my power, I carefully ignored the sounds of water splashing from the bathing room.

And then Prisca opened the door.

She wore the robe. It clung to her curves, displaying more than it hid, and my mouth watered as my gaze dropped to her hard nipples.

"Yesterday, when you took a nap, I missed you," I admitted. "We were separated for an hour at most, and I found myself glancing around the room as if looking for you."

Her mouth curved, her eyes shone gold, and I crossed the room, pressing my lips gently to her forehead.

"It seems as if we might have a problem," she said. "Because when I woke up, I was instantly irritated that you weren't there."

I leaned back far enough to meet her gaze. "This is embarrassing."

"Humiliating," she agreed. "Let's never tell anyone."

"Deal."

She gave a low laugh, and I took her mouth, swallowing her moan. She splayed her hand against my chest then curled it into my shirt, pulling me closer.

My hands had already found the tie to her robe, and it fluttered to the floor, displaying Prisca's warm, smooth skin. I teased her bottom lip with my teeth, gently nibbling, then backed her toward the bed.

My blood was hot, pounding through my ears. But I had plans. And she wouldn't wrest control from me yet.

She was pushing my shirt up in an attempt to strip

me out of it, and I yanked it over my head, enjoying her low sound of contentment. She reached for my pants, and I spun her until she faced the bed.

"What are you doing?"

"Lie on your stomach, wildcat."

She glanced over her shoulder at me. When I raised one eyebrow, she bent over, keeping her movements achingly slow as she crawled onto the bed.

I snarled. "Little tease."

She let out a low, taunting laugh, and I took a moment to soak in the sight of her. A moment to memorize the curve of her ass, the sharp blades of her shoulders, the smooth line of her back.

A moment to revel in the fact that she was mine.

"Are you going to stare at me all night?" Her tone turned sulky. But she wiggled on the bed, clearly wanting to feel my hands on her.

I poured warm oil into my palm, stroking it along Prisca's shoulders. She let out a gasp that turned into a strangled moan as I found a particularly tight spot between her left shoulder and her neck.

"Gods…"

I smiled, digging my thumb a little deeper, watching her response carefully to gauge the right pressure. I'd craved this for some time—the chance to tease out some of the tension that she carried each day. The opportunity to stroke her soft skin, to turn her limp and relaxed.

When I'd cajoled the knots from her shoulders and neck, I moved down, using long, sweeping strokes along her spine, feeling the muscles twinge and jump when I found the places that caused her pain. I frowned.

"You should have told me you were sore."

"Mmmmfff."

I smiled, moving to her lower back, the base of her spine, the top of her ass. She shivered, and I teased her, my hands running lightly over her delicate skin, until she shifted impatiently.

"Something you want, wildcat?"

She growled.

I moved back up to her shoulders, then focused on her arms. She let out a displeased sound, but I was far more displeased when I found the stiffness and swelling in her sword arm.

"A healer could have taken care of this," I grumbled.

"I don't need a healer. I have you."

I found a few places in her arm that made her tense, and I soothed her, working out the worst of the knots. But I would be dragging her to that healer at the first opportunity.

Her left arm wasn't as bad. By the time I caressed each of her fingers, she was shifting restlessly.

So I moved down to her thighs, using those same long, sweeping strokes. She'd gone limp once more, and she let out a sound that was almost a purr when I reached her first calf.

By the time I'd massaged her other leg, working my way down to her toes, her skin gleamed with oil, and she breathed deeply. The tiny line of tension between her brows had disappeared.

A savage pride roared through me.

She opened her eyes.

"Thank you."

I almost laughed. "You don't thank me for that, wildcat. I'm the one who should be thanking you."

One side of her mouth kicked up. "In that case, you're welcome."

Leaning over, I gently bit her ass. She gasped, wiggled, and I slipped a hand beneath her to find her slick.

She pushed up onto her knees, and I placed one hand on her back, keeping her face pressed to the pillow.

"Stay right there."

Dipping my hands in the oil, I cupped her breasts, caressing and squeezing and flicking her nipples until she moaned. I slipped one hand lower, and she spread her legs wide, arching her back.

"You're ready for me, aren't you, wildcat? You're always ready for me."

"Always," she mumbled, pushing her ass back toward me as I stroked her. "Please, Lorian. I need you inside me. Now."

I caressed her some more, keeping my touch light, ensuring she stayed balanced on the edge. I wanted to continue teasing her, but stroking every inch of her skin had made me almost insane with lust.

I didn't bother removing my pants, simply lowered them, a growl leaving my throat as Prisca shoved her ass against my cock.

"Don't make me wait." Her voice was high, thready. This was usually when I enjoyed teasing her the most.

Not today.

Flipping her, I rolled her on top of me, until she was staring down at me, her hair tumbling over her shoulders, her eyes wide. But she didn't hesitate. Her hands found my cock, and I clamped down on my self-control as she lifted, then slowly lowered herself down.

We both groaned.

Her tight, wet heat, the sight of her, skin slick and glowing in the candlelight, eyes so gold, head tipped back as she ground down onto me.

She squeezed my cock like a vise, and my hands gripped her hips. Even when she was on top, I couldn't help but take control, lifting her until I was plunging in and out of her.

She began trembling, her pale pink nipples tight and straining. Lifting my head, I guided her close, latching my mouth around one of those nipples, my mind going blank as she squeezed me even tighter.

"Lorian..."

I thrust up into her, and she let out one of those tiny gasps that made me fucking wild.

Her gasp turned into a long, filthy moan, and I almost came.

Grinding my teeth, I angled her until I knew I was hitting that perfect spot inside her. Prisca went wild, arching her back, snapping her hips as she chased her pleasure.

That was my favorite sight.

"It will be this way for the rest of our lives," I vowed. "You and me, like this, forever. I'll never let you go, wildcat."

Her eyes opened to slits, burning with passion.

"You're mine. And I'm yours. Until the end of time."

She nodded, breathless now. Her entire body trembled, and it took everything I had to hold back.

Sliding one hand down her body, I found her clit. She rode me like she had been born for this. My hand stroked faster, and her mouth dropped open in a soundless scream.

"Come for me, wildcat."

She contracted tightly around me as her eyes rolled back, her entire body stiffening. I guided her hips down, up, down, and came so hard I saw stars.

Prisca slumped down, lying on my chest as both of us gasped for breath. I gently stroked her back, enjoying the feel of her limp and sated as she lay on me.

We dozed for a while, until Prisca lifted her head, blinking. When she began untangling herself from me, I tightened my hands.

"And just where do you think you're going?"

She raised one brow. "I have things to do."

So did I. And I very much resented everything that was preventing us from spending the next several days just like this.

Prisca sat up, swinging her legs off the bed. "I should probably get dressed."

With that, she scooted her perfect ass off the bed. Her hips rolled as she walked toward the closet, and I was standing next to her before I realized I'd moved.

"Lorian," she said warningly, but her nose wrinkled as she grinned.

"Fine," I muttered. "I need to go talk to Rythos anyway."

"I'll see you tonight."

This time, I gave my opinion as I strolled through the castle. Not once, but twice. And I even smiled.

Prisca was right. I could see the change—the way

people relaxed when they spoke to me. Only days ago, I'd been crowned the hybrid king, and I wanted the people here to know I wasn't just someone who would fight for them on the battlefield. I was someone they could bring their petitions and grievances to. Someone who wanted them to have long, full lives.

I might never have anticipated I'd be king of any kingdom, but this was the life we had fought so hard for.

When I finally made my way out of the castle, I swept my gaze over the grounds. They'd been kept tidy, although Demos had decided a large section of the gardens would be turned into a training arena.

Already, a sanctuary had been built. I hadn't liked the idea, but it looked nothing like the mockery of religion Regner had created. It was merely a quiet place for any who needed it. And Regner's High Priestess had settled here.

As much as Jamic liked Mona, he hadn't felt that he could guarantee her safety in his kingdom just yet.

And Mona was a solitary creature who mostly wanted to wander the gardens.

Occasionally, she appeared to be staring into the distance, lost in memories. The kinds of memories that drained the life from her skin.

When that happened, Prisca or Asinia would usually take her by the hand and lead her back to her rooms. Most recently, though, it had been Rythos, of all people, who had linked his arm with hers and walked her out of the gardens.

Unsurprisingly to anyone who knew my wildcat, Zathrian was working in the castle.

I'd overseen his blood vow. Zathrian would never betray her. Because even if he one day became tempted to harm her, he now couldn't.

Vynthar appeared from between two trees. He stared at me but didn't speak. We were currently "feuding," as Prisca liked to call it. The creature had decided his proper place was napping in her bed.

And I was feeling more than a little territorial.

I showed him my teeth. He snarled back. Both of us turned and went our separate ways.

I found Rythos and Marth sitting by the small pond behind the castle, Piperia leaning against Marth's shoulder as Sybella watched from a few feet away.

Occasionally, after one of these afternoons with Piperia, Marth would disappear for a while. But most of the time, he would tuck Piperia under his arm and haul her to the stables or into one of the sitting rooms to play with her dolls.

I'd approached quietly enough that they hadn't sensed me yet. And warmth spread through my chest as Marth threw a stone, skipping it across the water. Piperia was still too young for skipping, but she threw a pebble of her own, clapping her hands and stamping her feet as it splashed.

I sensed movement out of the corner of my eye.

And there he was.

Watching with misty eyes, a half-smile curving his mouth.

Sybella glanced around, and I wondered if some part of her knew he was there. And if she would feel the loss of him when he was truly gone.

Because this was it. I could tell from the joy on Cavis's face as Rythos tickled Piperia, throwing a ridiculously oversized rock just to make her squeal.

I took a single step closer to Cavis, and his eyes met mine—dreamy once more. "Look after them."

Lifting his hand in a final wave, he turned, his steps measured as he faded out of sight.

ASINIA

I'd imagined that as soon as the war was over, our lives would be perfect.

No one had warned me that the aftermath would be mired in grief and loss, interspersed with flashes of joy and gratitude that made me want to fall to my knees and weep.

I still woke up in the middle of the night, shaking from nightmares that were too real. So real that Demos occasionally took me outside, so I could feel the wind on my face and remember we had lived through it.

At least, some of us had.

I wasn't the only one finding it difficult. All of us were coping in our own ways. Vicer had moved in to a small apartment near the dock, needing to spend time alone. I knew he was still processing Stillcrest's death. Still blaming himself for the attack on the hybrid village.

Prisca rarely slept. I knew Lorian was concerned. But she smiled more than I'd ever seen, and she was already settling into her role as queen.

Demos mourned Telean deeply. For the first few days after we'd arrived, even hearing his aunt's name had made him stiffen and walk out of whatever room he'd been sitting in.

And then there were the hybrids who had been born in Gromalia or Eprotha. This kingdom might be their heritage, but it was still new. Thankfully, those who had managed to survive Regner's first invasion knew just how lucky they had been. And the hybrids here had welcomed all our people, ensuring they had everything they needed to start new lives.

But all of us were getting through it together. Just days ago, we'd traveled to the wreckage of our village. The place where this had all begun. Tibris, Demos, Prisca, Vicer, Lorian, and I had been joined by Lina, who finally mourned her grandparents.

And there, we had buried both Natan and Thol. I hadn't known at the time, but Lorian had used a spark of his power to protect Thol's body from predators and decomposition. The man known across this continent for his cruelty had given Thol dignity in death and allowed us to say goodbye to him on a clear summer's day beneath a forest canopy.

Prisca had sat outside the abandoned, derelict husk that had once been her home. She'd found a scrap of material from a dress. A dress often worn by the woman she'd once called Mama. And there, on that broken wooden step, she'd sobbed in Lorian's arms.

I'd once believed there was nothing heroic about war. Now, I knew it brought out the best and worst in everyone. When I thought about heroes, I thought about Natan and the precious hours he'd given us. I thought about Conreth, saving Prisca's life. I thought about Telean, fighting in the only way that made sense to her.

I thought about our people risking everything to keep the hybrids hidden in those caves alive.

"Sin."

Demos's voice was soft. Gentle. I'd gone away again. When all I really wanted was to be here.

Standing in the marketplace in Celestara—the capital of Lyrinore. Surrounded by hybrids who went quietly about their day. Some of them jumped at the occasional loud noise. Others looked at the world through haunted eyes. But a group of children was running beneath a huge fountain, their shrieking laughs echoing across the square.

Demos linked his fingers with mine, and I met his eyes. "I'm sorry."

He kissed my temple. A silent support.

Tor had left this morning, returning to his family in Gromalia. He was planning to bring his wife and children back with him and had asked Demos to meet them. It wasn't much, but it was a start.

In the days following the battle, we'd barely spoken. His gaze had been shuttered when he looked at me, as if by using the orb, I'd broken everything we could have been.

Until one night, he'd come to me. And oh, how he'd raged.

He'd told me exactly what it had done to him to see me lying there. To know that I'd chosen to die to save everyone else. He'd told me that nothing he'd endured up to that point had hurt him as much as the sight of me gone from this world. He'd told me that some part of him had hated me for that. And that it would take time for him to forgive me, even knowing that he would have done the exact same thing in my place.

So, I'd listened. And when he'd curled up next to me, I'd tentatively put my arms around him. Until he'd wept. The next morning, we'd taken one of Daharak's ships out to the middle of the sleeping sea, and I'd dropped the orb down into the depths of the ocean, where it could never be used again.

We all had scars. Demos's would take time to fade too. Until then, I could wait for his forgiveness.

"I've got something to show you," he rumbled.

When he looked at me like that, my chest lightened until it felt like I might fly away. Yesterday, I'd explored what felt like every inch of this city with Prisca, until our feet had ached and Prisca's voice had grown hoarse from the many conversations she'd had with any who were brave enough to approach her. Lorian had insisted on sending Galon to trail after us—a threat to anyone who came too close.

But today was for Demos and me. A slow wander, soaking up the scents and sounds of the city.

"What is it?"

He popped me on the nose with his finger. "A surprise."

Was he...nervous?

Several hybrids waved at Demos, and he nodded at them as he led me down cobbled streets, where I couldn't help but stare at winged creatures—no larger than my thumb—their silver bodies glittering in the sunlight as they darted through the air.

And then Demos stopped.

I glanced around. We stood in a quiet side street, close

enough to the city market to attract those who were done with their errands from the day, but away from the worst of the hustle and bustle. To my left, a bookstore called to me, and I made a note of the location. To my right, a small bakery was operating, and as a patron opened the door, the scent of freshly baked bread made my mouth water.

Nestled between the bookstore and the bakery stood an unassuming building. The paint, once vibrant, had faded to a gentle blue hue, and the wooden door bore the scratches and chips that came with age. Large windows were dulled by dust, but the sun was valiantly attempting to fill the space within.

Demos stepped forward, pulled a key from his pocket, and unlocked the door with a soft click.

"What are you doing?"

He just tugged on my hand, guiding me inside. The interior was spacious and bare, with scuffed wooden floors and high ceilings.

His expression held a strange mixture of hope and anticipation. "I thought this could be the start of something new for you. For us. A place where you could start that business you've always dreamed of."

For me?

"There is no pressure tied to this, Sin. No time limit. There was some money tucked away for us—an inheritance created for Prisca and me and kept safe. I bought the building, but your name is on the deed. Use it to sell your creations. Use it just to have somewhere to sew or weave or whatever you want. Hell, set it on fire if you want to," he snarled when I didn't reply.

I burst into tears.

His arms instantly surrounded me. "I'm sorry. It's too much. You don't want it. You wanted to do this alone."

"Stop talking," I wailed.

He shut his mouth, but I could practically feel the misery radiating off him.

Pulling myself together, I lifted my head. "Demos... this is the most incredible thing anyone has ever done for me. I want to strangle you for spending so much money, but I also want to snatch that key before you change your mind."

A slow grin broke out on his face, and he tucked the key in the pocket of my dress. "Yours, Asinia. No matter what. Even if someday you choose to leave me. If you decide you want someone else."

All the air seemed to disappear from the room. I frowned at him. "Why would I *ever* do that?"

"I'm not going to hold you to the things you said the night before you thought you were going to die."

I narrowed my eyes at him. "That's big of you."

His jaw clenched. "I'm trying to be reasonable about this."

Drilling my finger into his chest, I glowered at him. "I don't need you to be reasonable. I love you, you idiot. Nothing has changed for me. If it's changed for you..."

Taking my hand, he pressed a gentle kiss to my finger. Nothing had changed for him.

He wanted to help me make my dreams come true.

"So," I said, rolling up my sleeves as I turned to survey the space around us, the door leading to what was likely a back room. "You want to explore?"

Epilogue

PRISCA

Tibris let out a vibrant laugh that rolled toward us. He stood at the end of the dock, Herne's hand clasped in his. As I watched, my brother leaned up, pressing his lips to Herne's.

Later today, Tibris was planning to propose. He'd been inspired by my wedding. And he wanted to share his love for Herne with the world. Margie had already developed a fondness for both of them and would no doubt insist on helping with the food.

I was so excited for him, I was afraid to talk to Herne in case I let something slip.

"You can't ignore what's happening, wildcat." Lorian's voice was low, amused.

Sighing, I turned my attention to the reason we were here.

Next to me, Madinia chuckled. I ignored her for another few moments, and her chuckle became a full-fledged laugh.

Daharak stood at the bow of her ship, casting a wary glance at two sea serpents who were dancing among the waves. Her brother Pelysian stood at her side. Together with their mother—the seer I'd met that day in Kaliera's rooms—he had worked in the background to shape the future of this continent.

I'd known this day would come. The war was won. Our people were safe. Even Regner's spiders were free of his web.

And yet...

I heaved a sigh, finally looking at Madinia. As usual, she wore the leather leggings she preferred, although I was pleased to see she was wearing the new boots I'd gifted her for this journey. Her cloak fluttered in the wind, and she pulled it around her.

"Stay," I said, my voice tight. "Stay with us, Madinia. We need you."

For the first time, Madinia smiled at me without restraint. Her smile was broad, beautiful...almost blinding. Her belongings were already on that ship, and despite my plea, I knew she would never stay.

"I need to go, Prisca. I have an itch in my feet and a craving within me to see other lands. I once thought this part of the world was nothing but death and horror. You've taught me that it's much, much more than that. But there are other places too."

My eyes burned, but I understood it. There was something wild about Madinia. Something that had been carefully leashed all these years. But she'd gnawed away at that leash little by little, until it had finally snapped.

And now she was free.

"I'll return," she said. Hesitantly, she took my hand. "I *will* come back one day."

"Promise." My voice was thick.

"I promise."

"Don't wait too long."

She smiled again. And then she turned and walked toward Daharak's ship.

My gaze caught on a man who'd appeared farther down the dock. He stood so still, it was as if he was a statue, his hands planted on his hips, body language intent. Something about the way he stared at Madinia made my skin prickle.

Madinia's cloak fluttered in the wind, revealing the grimoire tucked within her inside pocket.

The man went unnaturally still. And then he was striding toward her.

Daharak strode halfway down the gangplank, a smirk on her face. She said something that made Madinia laugh, and the man hesitated for the barest moment.

Madinia stepped onto the gangplank, and the man began to sprint.

Realization slammed into me. I knew that man. I'd been imprisoned with him once, in Regner's cells.

Calysian.

He was going to catch Madinia. And something told me that if that happened, it would be very, very bad.

I stopped time with a thought. But only for him.

Daharak waved to me. Madinia turned, raising her own hand, and I forced myself to wave back, as if they weren't taking the tiniest piece of my heart with them.

"They'll be back," Lorian murmured in my ear, his arms coming around me.

"I know. In the meantime, I have someone to question."

I wiggled in his arms, turning to survey Calysian.

My heart stopped.

He was gone.

Pelysian's mother Ravynia stood nearby, her gaze on the ship. For some reason none of us could understand, she'd chosen to make our kingdom her home. Perhaps it was because she was less likely to be bothered here. I'd certainly had enough of seers and their prophecies to last a lifetime.

"That girl is going to regret ever leaving this place," she said.

My heart resumed beating, and I glowered at her. "Madinia is going to have a long life filled with happiness and adventure."

She just frowned at me. "She goes, traumatized by life and armed with one of the dark god's grimoires. You have loosed a woman who has the potential to become a monster."

Lorian's grip tightened on me. "Mind your words, woman."

"Have you *seen* her become a monster?" I asked.

The seer shook her head slowly. "Her future is currently closed to me."

I blew out a breath, and Ravynia tutted. "This is not a good thing, girl."

"Madinia's life is her own," I said. "All of our lives are our own."

She tutted again, turning away. But I was already gazing up at the man who'd changed everything for me.

"My life is yours," he reminded me. "Every life."

I smile at him. "Every life."

LORIAN

Dear L,

Thank you for your recent update. I enjoy hearing how you're settling in as king, although some part of me is still shocked at how easily you made the transition from "mercenary" to monarch.

You'll be pleased to know I took your advice. While Father liked to think that allowing the wardens the power of self-determination would prevent the need for a stronger hand, he was wrong (and even admitting such a thing is uncomfortable). When we needed our territories to unite and address the threat Regner presented, they chose to play opportunistic power games, costing us precious time.

They have now learned that what can be given, can also be taken away.

In happier news, Emara tells me the first fae-hybrid-human school will be ready to open in the spring. I admit, I was doubtful when she introduced the idea to me. But she—with enthusiastic support from your own queen—was not to be deterred. Just days ago, she convinced me to visit, and I must admit, picturing young students so eager to put the horrors of war behind them and focus on the future...it gave me hope.

And as we've both learned, hope is worth more than gold after war.

I hope Prisca is well. Pass on my love. You can tell her that, yes, I'll discuss the trade agreements she won't stop messaging me about.

We'll visit after the school opens in spring.

C

Dear C,

This won't be a long letter. Prisca is insisting we go to Asinia's new store. She hasn't named it yet, but she's already managed to convince all of us to donate our time to stripping the walls, clearing the dust, and setting up shelves.

I know my wildcat, and she'll want to visit your school as well. I'll talk to her today about a visit.

But that's enough pleasantries. Have you been taking the tonic the healer gave you? Have your lungs healed? What does your healer say about the fatigue?

L

Dear L,

Emara is pregnant. Truthfully, I had begun to think such a thing might not ever happen. Some part of me believed that dying without an heir in place might be my punishment for defying the gods' wishes and forsaking my mate. But Emara is the woman I love, the woman I have always loved. And our love has created twins. (I can picture you laughing as you read this letter.)

While we both hope for healthy children, Emara wishes for a boy and a girl. Me? I am hoping for two boys. Brothers who will love each other and grow together and live their lives as best friends.

And no matter which twin comes first—and becomes my heir—I promise to teach them to remain openhearted and warm, and not to see threats where there are none. I vow that my second-born will not be responsible for your duties as the Bloodthirsty Prince. And should I die, not only will they have each other, but they will also have you and Prisca.

The most thankful father-to-be.

C

PS: Lungs are fine. Healer has given me the all clear. Now I know why your mate calls you a mother hen.

Dear C,

Prisca sits next to me, her face wet with tears, a wide smile on her face. She asked that I send both of you her love and says we will visit at the time most convenient to you.

Piperia just toddled into our room, escaping her mother once again. She is currently gnawing on one of the tables with her few teeth as if she is a wolf cub in disguise.

The thought of my formal, restrained brother dealing with two of these tiny creatures at once... Well, I must admit, I laughed and laughed. Congratulations, brother. You have truly been blessed, and I cannot wait to meet them. Kiss your beautiful wife for me.

The proudest uncle in all four kingdoms.

L

THE END